D1293345

FIREFIGHT

BRANDON SANDERSON

Copyright © Dragonsteel Entertainment, LLC 2015

The right of Brandon Sanderson to be identified as the author
of this work has been asserted by him in accordance with
the Copyright, Designs and Patents Act 1988.

First published in Great Britain in 2015
by Gollancz
An imprint of the Orion Publishing Group
Carmelite House, 50 Victoria Embankment
London EC4Y 0DZ
An Hachette UK Company

This edition published in Great Britain in 2015
by Gollancz

1 3 5 7 9 10 8 6 4 2

A CIP catalogue record for this book
is available from the British Library

ISBN 978 0 575 10449 5

Printed in Great Britain by Clays Ltd, St Ives plc

The Orion Publishing Group's policy is to use papers that
are natural, renewable and recyclable products and made
from wood grown in sustainable forests. The logging and
manufacturing processes are expected to conform to the
environmental regulations of the country of origin.

www.brandonsanderson.com
www.orionbooks.co.uk
www.gollancz.co.uk

For Nathan Goodrich,
  A dear friend who was patient enough
    To read my books when they were bad.

Prologue

I watched Calamity rise.

I was six years old then, as I stood in the night on the balcony of our apartment. I can still remember how the old air conditioner rattled in the window next to me, covering the sound of Father's crying. The overworked machine hung out over a plummet of many stories, dripping water like perspiration from the forehead of a suicidal jumper. The machine was broken; it blew air but didn't make anything cold. My mother had frequently turned it off.

After her passing, my father left it on; he said that he felt cooler with it running.

I lowered my popsicle and squinted at that strange red light, which rose like a new star above the horizon. Only no star had ever been that bright or that *red*. Crimson. It looked like a bullet wound in the dome of heaven itself.

On that night, Calamity had blanketed the entire city in a strange warm glow. I stood there—popsicle melting, sticky liquid dripping down around my fingers—as I watched the entire ascent.

Then the screaming had started.

PART ONE

1

"DAVID?" The voice came from my earpiece.

I shook out of my reverie. I'd been staring at Calamity again, but nearly thirteen years had passed since Calamity's rise. I wasn't a kid at home with my father any longer; I wasn't even an orphan working the munitions factory in the understreets.

I was a Reckoner.

"Here," I answered, shouldering my rifle and crossing the rooftop. It was night, and I swore I could see a red cast to everything from Calamity's light, though it had never again appeared as bright as it had that first evening.

Downtown Newcago spread out before me, its surfaces reflecting starlight. Everything was steel here. Like a cyborg from the future with the skin ripped off. Only, you know, not murderous. Or, well, alive at all.

Man, I thought. *I really do suck at metaphors.*

Steelheart was dead now, and we had reclaimed Newcago's upper streets—including many amenities the elite had once reserved for themselves. I could take a shower every day in my own bathroom. I almost didn't know what to do with such luxury. Other than, you know, not stink.

Newcago, at long last, was free.

It was my job to make sure it stayed that way.

"I don't see anything," I whispered, kneeling beside the edge of the rooftop. I wore an earpiece that connected wirelessly to my mobile. A small camera on the earpiece allowed Tia to watch what I was seeing, and the earpiece was sensitive enough to pick up what I said, even when I spoke very softly.

"Keep watching," Tia said over the line. "Cody reports that Prof and the mark went your direction."

"It's quiet here," I whispered. "Are you sure—"

The rooftop exploded just beside me. I yelped, rolling backward as the entire building shook, the blast spraying bits of broken metal across me. *Calamity!* Those shots packed a *punch*.

"Sparks!" Cody yelled over the line. "She got around me, lad. Coming up on your north side—"

His voice was drowned out as another glowing energy pulse shot up from the ground below and ripped the side off the rooftop near where I hid.

"Run!" Tia yelled.

Like I needed to be told. I got moving. To my right, a figure materialized out of light. Dressed in a black jumpsuit and sneakers, Sourcefield wore a full mask—like a ninja might wear—and a long black cape. Some Epics bought into the whole "inhuman powers" thing more than others. Honestly, she looked ridiculous—even if she did glow faintly blue and crackle with energy spreading across her body.

If she touched something, she could transform into energy

6

and travel through it. It wasn't true teleportation, but close enough—and the more conductive the substance, the farther she could travel, so a city made of steel was kind of like paradise for her. It was surprising it had taken her so long to get here.

As if teleportation weren't enough, her electrical abilities also made her impervious to most weapons. The light shows she gave off were famous; I'd never seen her in person before, but I'd always wanted to see her work.

Just not from so close up.

"Scramble the plan!" Tia ordered. "Prof? Jon! Report in! Abraham?"

I listened with only half an ear as a globe of crackling electricity whizzed by me. I skidded to a stop and dashed the other way as a second globe passed right through where I'd been standing. That one hit the rooftop, causing another explosion and making me stumble. Shards of metal pelted my back as I scrambled to the side of the building.

Then I leaped off.

I didn't fall far before hitting the balcony of a penthouse apartment. Heart pounding, I darted inside. A plastic cooler waited on the other side by the door. I threw open the lid and fished around, trying to remain calm.

Sourcefield had come to Newcago earlier in the week. She'd started killing immediately—random people, no perceivable purpose behind it. Just like Steelheart had done in his early days. Then she'd started calling out for the citizens to turn in the Reckoners, so she could bring us to justice.

A twisted brand of Epic justice. They killed whomever they wanted, but to strike back was an offense so great they could barely conceive it. Well, she'd see soon enough. So far, our plan to bring her down wasn't going terribly well, but we were the Reckoners. We prepared for the unexpected.

From the cooler, I pulled out a water balloon.

This, I thought, *had better work.*

Tia and I had debated for days on Sourcefield's weakness. Every Epic had at least one, and often they were random. You had to research an Epic's history, the things they avoided, to try to figure out what substance or situation might negate their powers.

This balloon contained our best guess as to Sourcefield's weakness. I turned, hefting the balloon in one hand, rifle in the other, watching the doorway and waiting for her to come after me.

"David?" Tia asked over the earpiece.

"Yeah?" I whispered, anxious, balloon ready to throw.

"Why are you watching the balcony?"

Why was I . . .

Oh, right. Sourcefield could travel through walls.

Feeling like an idiot, I jumped backward just as Sourcefield came down through the ceiling, electricity buzzing all around her. She hit the floor on one knee, hand out, a ball of electricity growing there, casting frantic shadows across the room.

Feeling nothing but a spike of adrenaline, I hurled the balloon. It hit Sourcefield right in the chest, and her energy blast fizzled into nothing. Red liquid from the balloon splashed on the walls and floor around her. Too thin to be blood, it was an old powdered fruit drink you mixed with water and sugar. I remembered it from childhood.

And it was her weakness.

Heart thumping, I unslung my rifle. Sourcefield stared at her dripping torso as if in shock, though the black mask she wore kept me from seeing her expression. Lines of electricity still worked across her body like tiny glowing worms.

I leveled the rifle and pulled the trigger. The *crack* of gunfire indoors all but deafened me, but I delivered a bullet directly toward Sourcefield's face.

That bullet exploded as it passed through her energy field. Even soaked with the Kool-Aid, her protections worked.

She looked at me, her electricity flaring to life—growing more violent, more dangerous, lighting the room like a calzone stuffed with dynamite.

Uh-oh . . .

2

I scrambled into the hall as the doorway exploded behind me. The blast threw me face-first into the wall, and I heard a *crunch*.

On one hand, I was relieved. The crunching sound meant that Prof was still alive—his Epic abilities granted me a protective field. On the other hand, an evil, angry killing machine was chasing me.

I pushed myself back from the wall and dashed down the metal hallway, which was lit by the mobile I wore strapped to my arm. *Zip line,* I thought, frantic. *Which way? Right, I think.*

"I found Prof," Abraham's voice said in my ear. "He's encased in some kind of energy bubble. He looks frustrated."

"Throw Kool-Aid on it," I said, panting, dodging down a

side hall as electric blasts ripped apart the hallway behind me. Sparks. She was furious.

"I'm aborting the mission," Tia said. "Cody, swing down and pick up David."

"Roger," Cody said. A faint thumping sounded over his communication line—the sound of copter rotors.

"Tia, no!" I said, entering a room. I threw my rifle over my shoulder and grabbed a backpack full of water balloons.

"The plan is falling apart," Tia said. "Prof is supposed to be point, David, not you. Besides, you just proved that the balloons don't work."

I pulled out a balloon and turned, then waited a heartbeat until electricity formed on one of the walls, announcing Sourcefield. She appeared a second later, and I hurled my balloon at her. She cursed and jumped to the side, and red splashed along the wall.

I turned and ran, shoving my way through a door into a bedroom, making for the balcony. "She's afraid of the Kool-Aid, Tia," I said. "My first balloon negated an energy blast. We have the weakness right."

"She still stopped your bullet."

True. I jumped out onto the balcony, looking up for the zip line.

It wasn't there.

Tia cursed in my ear. "That's what you were running for? The zip line's two apartments over, you slontze."

Sparks. In my defense, hallways and rooms all look very similar when everything's made of steel.

The thumping copter was near now; Cody had almost arrived. Gritting my teeth, I leaped up onto the rail, then threw myself toward the next balcony over. I caught it by its railing, my rifle swinging over one shoulder, backpack on the other, and hauled myself up.

"David . . . ," Tia said.

"Primary trap point is still functioning?" I asked, climbing over a few lawn chairs that had been frozen in steel. I reached the other side of the balcony and jumped up onto the railing. "I'll take your silence as a yes," I said, and leaped across.

I hit hard, slamming into the steel railing of the next balcony over. I grabbed one of the bars and looked down—I was dangling twelve stories in the air. I shoved down my anxiety and, with effort, hauled myself up.

Behind me, Sourcefield peeked out onto the balcony I'd left. I had her scared. Which was good, but also bad. I needed her to be reckless for the next part of our plan. That meant provoking her, unfortunately.

I swung up onto the balcony, fished out a Kool-Aid balloon, and lobbed it in her direction. Then, without looking to see if the balloon hit, I jumped onto the railing and grabbed the zip line handle, then kicked off.

The balcony exploded.

Fortunately, the zip line was affixed to the roof, not the balcony itself, and the cable remained firm. Bits of molten metal zipped through the dark air around me as I dropped along the line, picking up speed. Turns out those things are a lot faster than they look. Skyscrapers passed me on either side in a blur. I felt like I was *really* falling.

I managed a shout—half panicked, half ecstatic—before everything lurched around me and I crashed into the ground, rolling on the street.

"Whoa," I said, pushing myself up off the ground. The city spun like a lopsided top. My shoulder hurt, and although I'd heard a crunch as I hit, it hadn't been loud. The protective field that Prof had granted me was running out. They could only take so much punishment before he had to renew them.

"David?" Tia said. "Sparks. Sourcefield cut the zip line with one of her shots. That's why you fell at the end."

"Balloon worked," a new voice said over the line. Prof. He had a strong voice, rough but solid. "I'm out. Couldn't report earlier; the energy bubble interfered with the signal."

"Jon," Tia said to him, "you weren't supposed to fight her."

"It happened," Prof snapped. "David, you alive?"

"Kind of," I said, stumbling to my feet and picking up the backpack, which had slipped off as I rolled. Red juice drink streamed from the bottom. "Not sure about my balloons, though. Looks like there might be a few casualties."

Prof grunted. "Can you do this, David?"

"Yes," I said firmly.

"Then run for the primary trap point."

"Jon," Tia said. "If you're out—"

"Sourcefield ignored me," Prof said. "It's just like before, with Mitosis. They don't want to fight *me*; they want *you*. We have to bring her down before she gets to the team. You remember the path, David?"

"Of course," I said, searching for my rifle.

It lay broken nearby, cracked in half in the middle of the forestock. Sparks. Looked like I'd messed up the trigger guard too. I wouldn't be firing that anytime soon. I checked my thigh holster and the handgun there. It seemed good. Well, as good as a handgun can be. I hate the things.

"Flashes in the windows of that apartment complex, moving down," Cody said from the copter. "She's teleporting along the outer wall, heading toward the ground. Chasing you, David."

"I don't like this," Tia noted. "I think we should abort."

"David thinks he can do this," Prof said. "And I trust him."

Despite the danger of the moment, I smiled. I hadn't

realized until joining the Reckoners just how lonely my life had been. Now, to hear words like those . . .

Well, it felt good. Really good.

"I'm bait," I said over the line, positioning myself to wait for Sourcefield and searching in my backpack for unbroken balloons. I had two left. "Tia, get our troops into position."

"Roger," she said reluctantly.

I moved down the street. Lanterns hung from the old, useless street lamps nearby, giving me light. By it, I caught sight of some faces peeking through windows. The windows had no glass, just old-fashioned wooden shutters we'd cut and placed there.

In assassinating Steelheart, the Reckoners had basically declared all-out war on the Epics. Some people had fled Newcago, fearing retribution—but most people had stayed here, and many others had come. During the months since Steelheart's fall, we'd almost doubled the population of Newcago.

I nodded to the people watching. I wouldn't shoo them back to safety. We, the Reckoners, were their champions—but someday, these people would have to stand on their own against the Epics. I wanted them to watch.

"Cody, do you have a visual?" I asked into my mobile.

"No," Cody said. "She should be coming any moment. . . ." The dark shadow of his copter passed overhead. Enforcement—Steelheart's police force—was ours now. I still wasn't sure how I felt about it. Enforcement had done its best to kill me on several occasions. You didn't just get over something like that.

In fact, they *had* killed Megan. She'd recovered. Mostly. I felt at the gun in my holster. It had been one of hers.

"I'm getting into position with the troops," Abraham said.

"David? Any sign of Sourcefield?" Tia asked.

"No," I said, looking down the deserted street. Empty of

people, lit by a few lonely lanterns, the city almost felt like it had back in Steelheart's days. Desolate and dark. Where was Sourcefield?

She can teleport through walls, I thought. *What would I do in her case?* We had the tensors, which let us tunnel through basically anything we wanted. What would I do now if I had those?

The answer to that was obvious. I'd go down.

She was underneath me.

∃

"SHE'S gone into the understreets!" I said, pulling out one of my two remaining water balloons. "She's going to come up nearby, try to surprise me."

Even as I said it, lightning moved across the street, and a glowing figure materialized up through the ground.

I hurled my Kool-Aid balloon, then ran.

I heard it burst, then heard Sourcefield swear. For a moment, no energy blasts tried to fry me, so I assumed that I'd hit her.

"I'm going to destroy you, little man!" Sourcefield yelled after me. "I'll rip you apart like a piece of tissue paper in a hurricane!"

"Wow," I said, reaching an intersection and taking cover by an old mailbox.

"What?" Tia asked.

"That was a really good metaphor."

I glanced back at Sourcefield. She strode down the street, alight with electricity. Lines of it flew from her to the ground, to nearby poles, and to the walls of the buildings as she approached. Such *power*. Was this what Edmund—the kindly Epic who powered Newcago for us—would be like if he weren't constantly gifting his abilities away?

"I refuse to believe," the woman shouted, "that you killed Steelheart!"

Mitosis said the same thing, I thought. He'd been another Epic who had come to Newcago recently. They couldn't accept that one of their most powerful—an Epic that even others like Sourcefield had feared—had been killed by common men.

She looked magnificent, all in black with a fluttering cape, electricity leaping from her in sparks and flashes. Unfortunately, I didn't need her magnificent. I needed her *angry*. Some members of Enforcement crept out of a building nearby, carrying assault rifles on their backs and Kool-Aid balloons in their hands. I motioned them toward an alley. They nodded and pulled back to wait.

It was time for me to taunt an Epic.

"I didn't kill only Steelheart!" I shouted at her. "I've killed dozens of Epics. I'll kill you too!"

An energy blast hit my mailbox. I dove for cover behind a building, and another blast hit the ground only inches from where I crouched. As I brushed the ground with my arm, a *shock* ran up it, jolting me. I cursed, putting my back to the wall, and shook my hand. Then I peeked around the side of the building. Sourcefield was running for me.

Great! Also, *terrifying*.

I sprinted for a doorway across the street. Sourcefield tore around the corner just as I entered the building.

Inside, a path had been cleared through what had once been some kind of car showroom. I ran straight across it, and Sourcefield followed, teleporting past the front wall at speed.

I dashed through room after room, following the pattern we'd set out earlier.

Right, duck into that room.

Left down a hallway.

Right again.

We'd used another of Prof's powers—the one he disguised as technology called the tensors—to drill doorways. Sourcefield followed on my tail, passing through walls in flashes of light. I never stayed in her sight long enough for her to get off a good shot. This was perfect. She . . .

. . . she slowed down.

I stopped beside the door out the back of the building. Sourcefield had stopped following. She stood at the end of a long hallway leading to my door, electricity zipping from her to the steel walls.

"Tia, you see this?" I whispered.

"Yeah. Looks like something spooked her."

I took a deep breath. It was far less than ideal, but . . . "Abraham," I whispered, "bring the troops in. Full-out attack."

"Agreed," Prof said.

The Enforcement troops who had been lying in wait stormed in the front of the car dealership. Others came down the steps from above; I heard their tromping footfalls. Sourcefield glanced back as a pair of soldiers entered the hallway in full gear, with helms and futuristic armor. The fact that they lobbed bright orange water balloons slightly spoiled the coolness of the effect.

Sourcefield laid a hand on the wall beside her, then transformed into electricity and melded into the steel, disappearing. The balloons broke uselessly on the floor of the corridor.

Sourcefield emerged back into the hallway and released bursts of energy down the corridor. I squeezed my eyes shut as the shots blasted the two soldiers, but I heard their cries.

"This is the best the infamous Reckoners can do?" Sourcefield shouted as more soldiers came in, throwing water balloons from all directions. I forced myself to watch, pulling out my handgun, as Sourcefield dropped through the floor.

She came up behind a group of soldiers in the middle of the corridor. The men screamed as the electricity took them. I gritted my teeth. If they lived, Prof would be able to heal them under the guise of using "Reckoner technology."

"The balloons aren't working," Tia said.

"They are," I hissed, watching as one hit Sourcefield. Her powers wavered. I took a shot, as did three Enforcement gunmen who had set up opposite me on the far end of the corridor.

All four bullets hit; all four were caught in her energy field and destroyed. The balloons were working, just not well enough.

"All units on the southern side of the corridor," Abraham's voice said, "pull back. Immediately."

I ducked out the door as a sudden barrage of bullets shook the building. Abraham, who had set up behind the Enforcement sharpshooters at the far end of the corridor, was unloading with his XM380 gravatonic minigun.

I grabbed my mobile and patched into Abraham's video feed. I could see it from his perspective, gun flashing in the dark, bullet after bullet ricocheting down the steel corridor, throwing sparks. Any that reached Sourcefield *still* got trapped or deflected by her electric field. A group of men and women behind Abraham lobbed balloon after balloon. Above, soldiers pulled back a trapdoor in the ceiling and dumped a bucket of Kool-Aid.

Sourcefield jumped away, dodging it. Step by step, she retreated from that splashing liquid. She *was* afraid of the stuff, but it wasn't working completely. An Epic's weakness was supposed to negate their powers totally, and this wasn't doing so.

I was pretty sure I knew why.

Sourcefield unleashed a barrage of energy blasts toward Abraham and the others. Abraham cursed and went down, but his protective field—gifted to him by Prof under the guise of a jacket with a technological forcefield—protected him and sheltered the people behind him. I heard groans through the feed, though I couldn't see anything. I flipped it off.

"You are *nothing*!" Sourcefield shouted.

I strapped the mobile to my arm and stepped back into the hallway in time to see her send a wave of electricity up through the ceiling toward those above. Screams.

I hefted my last water balloon, then threw it. It exploded across her back.

Sourcefield spun on me. Sparks! A High Epic in her glory, energy flaring . . . Was it any wonder that these things presumed to rule?

I spat at her feet, then turned and ran out the back door.

She shouted after me, following.

"Upper units, Haven Street," Tia said in my ear, "get ready to lob."

People appeared on the roof of the building I'd just left, and they hurled water balloons down as Sourcefield broke out after me. She ignored them, following me. If anything, the falling balloons just made her madder.

When they splashed near her, however, she stopped shouting.

Right, I thought, sweating, slamming my way into the

building across the street. It was a small apartment complex. I ran through the entryway and into the first apartment.

Sourcefield followed in a storm of energy and anger. She didn't stop for walls; she passed through them in flashes of light.

Just a little farther! I urged silently as I shut a door. This complex was populated, and we'd replaced many of the frozen steel doors with wooden ones that worked.

Sourcefield came through the wall as I leaped over a steel couch and entered the next room—which was pitch-black inside. I slammed the door.

The light of Sourcefield entering blinded me. Her aura hit, and suddenly that little shock I'd taken earlier seemed miniscule. Electricity shot through me, causing my muscles to go weak and spasm. I reached to press the large button on the wall, but my arms weren't working right.

I slammed my face into it instead.

I collapsed, succumbing to the shock of her energy. Above, the ceiling of the small darkened room—which had once been a bathroom—opened up, dumping several hundred gallons of Kool-Aid down on us. Above that, showerheads turned on, spraying red liquid.

Sourcefield's energy dampened dramatically. Electricity ran up her arms in little ribbons, but kept shorting out. She reached for the door, but it had locked after me. Cursing, she held up a fist, trying to summon the energy to teleport, but the constant rain of liquid disrupted her powers.

I struggled to my knees.

She turned on me and growled, then seized me by the shoulders.

I reached up, grabbing her mask by the front, then yanking it off like a ski mask. It had a plastic piece on the front that obviously fit over the nose and mouth. A filter of some sort?

Beneath the mask she was a middle-aged woman with curly brown hair. The liquid continued to rain down, and it ran in streams along her cheeks, across her lips. Getting into her mouth.

Her light went out completely.

I groaned, climbing to my feet as Sourcefield shouted in panic, scrambling at the door, rattling it, trying to get it open. I tapped my mobile, bathing the room in a soft white light.

"I'm sorry," I said, raising Megan's handgun to her head.

Sourcefield looked to me, eyes widening.

I squeezed the trigger. This time, the bullet didn't bounce off. She fell to the ground, and a deeper red liquid began to pool around her, mixing with what was raining down. I lowered the gun.

My name is David Charleston.

I kill people with super powers.

4

I unlocked the door and pushed out of the bathroom, dripping wet with imitation fruit juice. A group of soldiers stood in the room, weapons out. They lowered them as they saw me. I gestured over my shoulder, and Roy—captain of the Enforcement team—sent two officers to check the body.

I was drained and shaky, and it took me two tries to get Megan's gun holstered. I didn't say anything as several soldiers saluted me on my way out. They regarded me with a mixture of awe and reverence, and one whispered, "Steelslayer." In less than a year with the Reckoners, I'd personally killed almost a dozen Epics.

What would these men say if they knew that I owed most of my reputation to the powers of another Epic? The forcefield that cushioned me from harm and the healing that brought me back from near death . . . these were both part of Prof's power portfolio, things that he disguised as technology. He was what we called a gifter, an Epic who could lend his extraordinary talents to others. For some reason, that let him remain un-corrupted by them—others could use his powers for him, but using them himself threatened to destroy him.

Only a handful of people knew the truth about Prof. Those ranks didn't include the common people of Newcago—outside the building, a large group of them had gathered. Like the soldiers, they watched me with reverence and excitement. To them I was a celebrity.

I ducked my head and pushed through them, uncomfort-able. The Reckoners had always been a shadowy group, and I hadn't joined up for the notoriety. Unfortunately, we needed to be seen so that the people of the city would know that someone was fighting back—and hopefully that would inspire them to fight back as well. It was a hard line to walk; I cer-tainly didn't want to be worshipped.

Beyond the gawkers, I spotted a familiar figure. Dark-skinned and well-muscled, Abraham wore a black and grey military uniform—camouflage for a city made of steel. The clothing was ripped and scuffed; I knew enough to recognize that the protective field Prof had given him had been stretched to its limits. Abraham gave me a thumbs-up, then nodded toward a building nearby.

I headed that direction while, behind me, Roy and his team carried out the dead Epic to show off the body. It was im-portant that the people see Epics as mortal, but I didn't glory in the death. Not as I might once have.

She looked so terrified at the end, I thought. *She could have been Megan, or Prof, or Edmund . . . just a normal person caught up in all of this. Driven to do terrible things by powers she didn't ask for.*

Knowing that the powers *literally* corrupted the Epics changed my perspective on all of this. A lot.

I entered the building and climbed the steps, eventually entering a room on the second floor, lit by a single light in the corner. As I'd anticipated, I found Prof here, watching out the window with crossed arms. He wore a thin black lab coat that draped down to his calves, a pair of goggles tucked into the pocket. Cody waited on the other side of the dark room, a lanky silhouette wearing a flannel shirt with the arms cut off, sniper rifle slung over his shoulder.

Prof, aka Jonathan Phaedrus, founder of the Reckoners. We fought Epics. We killed them. And yet we were led by one. When I'd first found out, that had been difficult to reconcile. I'd grown up practically worshipping the Reckoners, all the while loathing the Epics. Discovering that Prof was both . . . it had been like discovering that Santa Claus was secretly a Nazi.

I'd gotten over it. Once upon a time, my father's idea that good Epics would come had been laughable to me. Now, after meeting not one but three good Epics . . . well, the world was a different place. Or I guess it was the same place—I just saw it a little more accurately.

I stepped up beside Prof at the window. Tall, with salt-and-pepper hair, he had square features. He looked so *solid* standing there, arms clasped behind his back. Something stable, immobile, like this city's buildings themselves. As I joined him, he raised his hand, gripping my shoulder, then nodded to me. A nod of respect, and of approval.

"Nice work," he said.

I grinned.

"You look like hell, though," he noted.

"I doubt hell has this much Kool-Aid," I replied.

He grunted, looking back out the window. More people had gathered, some raising cheers at the victory. "I never realized," Prof said softly, "how paternal I would grow for these people. Staying in one place, protecting the city. It's been very good for me to remember why we do this. Thank you for encouraging us. You've done something great here."

"But . . . ?" I asked, recognizing the catch in Prof's tone.

"But now we have to make good on what we've promised these people. Safety. A good life." He turned to me. "First Mitosis, then Instabam, now Sourcefield. There's a pattern to their attacks, and I feel that someone is trying to get my attention. Someone who knows about what I am, and who is sending Epics to target my team instead of me."

"Who?" Who could possibly know what Prof was? Even most members of the Reckoners didn't know about him. Just the team here in Newcago was in on his secret.

"I have suspicions," Prof said. "But this isn't the time to talk about it."

I nodded, knowing that pushing him on the topic wouldn't get me any further at the moment. Instead I looked down at the crowd, and the dead Epic. "Sourcefield trapped you, Prof. How did it happen?"

He shook his head. "She caught me straight-out with that electricity-bubble thing. Did you know she could make one of those?"

I shook my head. I'd had no idea.

Prof grunted. "To get free, I'd have needed to use my powers."

"Oh," I said. "Well . . . maybe you *should* use them. Maybe we could practice, and see if there's a way you can be an Epic without . . . you know. I mean, you can gift them without the corruption happening, so maybe there's some secret to using them yourself. Megan—"

"Megan is not your friend, son," Prof said, interrupting quietly but firmly. "She's one of them. She always has been."

"But—"

"No." Prof squeezed my shoulder. "You *have* to understand this, David. When an Epic lets their powers corrupt them, they choose to become the enemy. That's how we have to think of it. Any other way leads to madness."

"But you used your powers," I said, "to save me. To fight Steelheart."

"And both times, it almost destroyed me. I have to be firm with myself, be more careful. I can't let the exceptions become the reality."

I swallowed and nodded.

"I know that to you this has always been about revenge," Prof said. "That's a strong motivation, and I'm glad you've channeled it, son. But I don't kill them for vengeance, not anymore. This thing we do . . . for me, it's like putting down a rabid dog. It's a mercy."

The way he said it made me feel sick. Not because I didn't believe him or disliked what he said—sparks, his motives were probably more altruistic than mine. It was just that I knew he was thinking about Megan. He felt betrayed by her, and honestly, he probably had every right to feel that way.

But Megan *wasn't* a traitor. I didn't know what she was, though I intended to find out.

Down below, a car pulled up to the crowd. Prof glanced at it. "Go deal with them," he said. "I'll meet you back at the hideout."

I turned as the mayor climbed out of the car, along with a few members of the city council.

Great, I thought.

Honestly, I'd rather have faced another Epic.

5

I left the building as soldiers cleared a path for Mayor Briggs. She wore a white pantsuit and a matching fedora, similar to the other members of the city council. Unique clothing, well styled. That contrasted with the everyday people, who wore . . . well, basically anything.

During the early days in Newcago, clothing had been shockingly hard to come by. Everything that hadn't been on a person's back had been transformed to steel during the Great Transfersion. Over the years, however, Steelheart's foraging crews had scoured the suburbs, emptying warehouses, old malls, and abandoned houses. These days we had enough to wear—but it was a strange mix of different styles.

The upper class, though, wanted to stand out. They avoided

practical clothing like jeans, which lasted surprisingly long with a few patches here and there. During Steelheart's reign they'd had their clothing made, and had chosen archaic designs. Things from a classier time, or so they said. It wasn't the sort of clothing you could merely find lying about.

We'd decided that I would be our liaison with Briggs and the rest. I was the only Newcago native in the Reckoners, and we wanted to limit access to Prof. The Reckoners did not rule Newcago—we protected it. It was a division we all thought was important.

I stepped up through the crowd, ignoring those who whispered my name. The attention was embarrassing, honestly. All of these people worshipped me, but they barely remembered men like my father who had died fighting the Epics.

"Looks like your handiwork, Charleston," Mayor Briggs said, nudging the corpse on the ground with her foot. "Steelslayer puts another notch in his rifle."

"My rifle's broken," I said. Too harshly. The mayor was an important woman, and had done wonders helping to organize the city. It was just that she was one of *them*—Steelheart's upper class. I'd expected them all to end up out on their ears, but somehow—through a series of political maneuvers I couldn't follow—Briggs had ended up in charge of the city instead of being exiled.

"I'm sure we can get you a new gun." She looked me over, not smiling. She liked to convey a "no-nonsense" attitude. To me, it seemed more like a "no-personality" attitude.

"Walk with me a pace, David," Briggs said, turning to stroll away. "You don't mind, do you?"

I did mind, but I figured this was one of those questions you weren't supposed to answer. I wasn't *completely* sure, though. I wasn't a nerd, mind you, but I'd spent a lot of my youth studying Epics, so I'd had limited experience with social interaction. I mixed with ordinary people about the same way that a bucket of paint mixed with a bag of gerbils.

"Your leader," Briggs said as we walked off a little ways from the crowd. "I haven't seen him in a while."

"Prof is busy."

"I imagine that is so. And I must say, we truly appreciate the protection you and yours offer this city." She looked over her shoulder at the corpse, then cocked an eyebrow. "However, I can't say that I understand your entire game plan."

"Mayor?" I asked.

"Your leader allowed the wheels of politics to put me in charge of Newcago, but I know next to nothing of the Reckoners' goals for this city—indeed this country. It would be nice to know what you are planning."

"That's easy," I said. "Kill Epics."

"And if a band of Epics joins together and comes to attack the city at once?"

Yeah. That would be a problem.

"Sourcefield," she said, "terrorized us for five days while you furiously planned. Five days is a long time for a city to be under the thumb of another tyrant. If five or six powerful Epics got together and came with the intent to exterminate, I fail to see how you'd protect us. Certainly you might end up picking them off one at a time, but Newcago would turn into a wasteland before you were done."

Briggs stopped walking and turned to me, now that the others couldn't hear. She looked me in the eyes, and I saw something in her expression. Was that . . . fear?

"So I ask," she said softly, "what is your plan? After years of hiding and only attacking Epics of middling importance, the Reckoners revealed themselves and brought down *Steel-*

heart himself. That means you have a greater goal, right? You've started a war. You know a secret to winning it, don't you?"

"I . . ." What could I say? This woman, who had weathered the reign of one of the most powerful Epics in the world—and who had seized control following his fall—looked to me with a plea on her lips and terror in her eyes.

"Yes," I said. "We have a plan."

"And . . . ?"

"And we might have found a way to stop them all, Mayor," I said. "Any Epic."

"How?"

I smiled in what I hoped was a confident way. "Reckoner secret, Mayor. Trust me, though. We know what we're doing. We'd never start a war we expected to lose."

She nodded, looking placated. She went back into business-like mode, and now that she had my ear she had a dozen things she wanted me to ask Prof about—most of which seemed attempts on her part to position him and the Reckoners politically. Her influence among the elite of Newcago would grow a great deal if she could parade Prof around as a friend. That was part of why we kept our distance.

I listened, but was distracted by what I'd told her. *Did* the Reckoners have a plan? Not really.

But *I* did.

We eventually returned to where Sourcefield's body lay. More people had gathered, including some members of the city's fledgling press, who took pictures. They got a few shots of me, unfortunately.

I passed through the crowd and knelt beside the corpse. She'd been a rabid dog, as Prof had put it. Killing her *had* been a mercy.

She came for us, I thought. *And this is the third one who avoided engaging Prof.* Mitosis had come to the city while Prof had been away. Instabam had tried to lose Prof in the chase, gunning for Abraham. Now Sourcefield had captured Prof, then left him behind to chase me.

Prof was right. Something was going on.

"David?" Roy asked. He knelt, wearing his black and grey Enforcement armor.

"Yeah."

Roy held out something in a black-gloved hand. Flower petals in a vibrant rainbow of hues—each petal bleeding between three or four colors, like mixed paint.

"These were in her pocket," Roy said. "We didn't find anything else on her."

I waved Abraham over, then showed him the petals.

"Those are from Babilar," he said. "What used to be known as New York City."

"That's where Mitosis had been working before he came here," I said softly. "Coincidence?"

"Hardly," Abraham said. "I think we need to go show these to Prof."

6

WE still kept a secret base hidden within the bowels of New-cago. Though I visited an apartment up above to shower each day, I slept down here, as did the others. Prof didn't want people to know where to find us. Considering that the latest Epics to visit had all specifically tried to kill us, it seemed a good decision.

Abraham and I hiked in through a long hidden passage that was cut directly into the metallic ground. The tunnel's sides bore the distinctive smooth look created by tensors. When one of us held Prof's disintegration powers, we could reduce sections of solid metal, rock, or wood to dust. This gave the tunnel a sculpted feel, as if the steel were mud that we'd hollowed out with our hands.

Cody guarded the way into the hideout. We always set a

watch after an operation. Prof kept expecting one of the Epics who showed up to be a decoy—someone for us to kill while a more powerful Epic watched and tried to discover how to follow us.

It was all too possible.

What will *we do if a group of Epics decides to bring down the city?* I thought, shivering as Abraham and I entered the hideout.

Lit by yellow lightbulbs screwed directly into the walls, the hideout was a medium-sized complex of steel rooms. Tia sat at a desk at the far side; red-haired and middle-aged, she wore spectacles, a white blouse, and jeans. Her desk was a lavish wooden one that she'd set up a few weeks back. It had seemed a strange sign to me, a symbol of permanence.

Abraham walked up to her and dropped the flower petals onto her desk. Tia raised an eyebrow at them. "Where?" she asked.

"Sourcefield's pocket," I said.

Tia gathered up the petals.

"That's the third Epic in a row who's come here and tried to destroy us," I said. "And each had a connection to Babylon Restored. Tia, what's going on?"

"I'm not sure," she said.

"Prof seems to know," I said. "He said as much to me earlier, but he wouldn't give me an explanation."

"Then I'll let him tell you when he's ready," she said. "For now, there's a file here on the table for you. The thing you asked about."

She was trying to distract me. I dropped my backpack—the pieces of my rifle stuck out the top—and crossed my arms, but found myself glancing toward the table, which held a folder with my name written on the top.

Tia slipped away, entering Prof's room and leaving Abraham and me alone in the main chamber. He settled down in a seat at the workbench, placing his gun on it with a thump. The gravatonics glowed green at the bottom, but one of them appeared to have cracked. Abraham took some tools off the wall and began to work on disassembling the gun.

"What aren't they telling us?" I asked, taking the file off Tia's desk.

"Many things," Abraham said. His light French accent made him sound thoughtful. "It is the proper way. If one of us gets taken, we cannot reveal what we know."

I grunted, leaning back against the steel wall beside Abraham. "Babilar . . . Babylon Restored. Have you been there?"

"No."

"Even before?" I asked, flipping through the pages Tia had left me. "When it was called Manhattan?"

"I never visited," Abraham said. "Sorry."

I glanced at Tia's desk. A stack of folders there looked familiar. My old Epic files, the ones I'd made for every Epic I knew about. I leaned over, opening a folder.

Regalia, the first file read. *Formerly Abigail Reed.* The Epic who currently ruled Babilar. I slipped out a photo of an older, distinguished-looking African American woman. She looked familiar. Hadn't she been a judge, long ago? Yes . . . and after that, she'd starred in her own reality television show. *Judge Regalia.* I flipped through the pages, refreshing my memory.

"David . . . ," Abraham warned as I flipped a page.

"They're *my* notes," I said.

"On Tia's desk." He continued to work on his gun without looking at me.

I sighed, closing the folder. Instead I began reading the file that Tia had left for me. There was only one page inside; it was addressed to Tia from one of her contacts, a lorist—Reckoner talk for a person who studied Epics.

It is often hard to delve into who Epics were before their transformations, particularly the early ones, the file said. *Steelheart is an excellent example of this. Not only did we lose much of what was once recorded on the internet, but he actively worked to suppress anyone who knew him before Calamity. Now that we know his weakness—thanks to your young friend—we can surmise that he wanted to remove anyone who knew him before, in case they did not fear him.*

Still, I have been able to recover some little information. Named Paul Jackson, Steelheart was a track star in his local high school. He was also reputed to be a bully of some stature, to the point that—despite his winning record—he was not offered any major scholarships. There were incidents. I can't find the specifics, but I think he might have left some fellow teammates with broken bones.

After high school, he got a job working as a night watchman at a factory. He spent his days posting on various conspiracy theory forums, speculating about the impending fall of the country. I don't think this was precognitive—he was just one of a large group of eccentrics who were dissatisfied with the way the United States was run. He frequently said he didn't believe that the common people were capable of voting in their best interests.

That's about it. I will admit, however, that I'm curious why you want to know the past of a dead Epic. What is it that you're researching, Tia?

Underneath, scrawled in Tia's handwriting, were the words, *Yes, David, I'm also curious what it is you're digging to find. Come talk to me.*

I lowered the paper, then walked over toward Prof's room. We didn't use doors in the hideout, just sheets of cloth. I could hear voices inside.

"David . . . ," Abraham said.

"In these notes, she told me to come talk to her."

"I doubt she meant right away."

I hesitated by the doorway.

". . . these flowers are an *obvious* sign that Abigail is involved," Tia was saying inside, speaking in a low voice. I could barely hear.

"That's probable," Prof replied. "But the petals themselves are very obvious. It makes me wonder—either a rival Epic is trying to turn our attention toward her, or . . ."

"Or what?"

"Or she herself is trying to taunt us into coming. I can't help but see this as a gauntlet thrown down, Tia. Abigail wants me to come face her—and she's going to keep sending people to try to kill my team until I go. It's the only reason I can think of that she'd *specifically* recruit Firefight."

Firefight.

Megan.

I pushed into the room, ignoring Abraham's sigh of resignation. "Megan?" I demanded. "What about Megan?"

Tia and Prof stood face to face, and both turned on me like I was a piece of snot on the windshield following a sneeze. I lifted my chin and stared back at them. I was a full member of this team; I could be part of . . .

Sparks. Those two really knew how to *stare*. I found myself sweating. "Megan," I repeated. "You've, uh, found her?"

"She murdered a member of a Reckoner team in Babilar," Prof said.

The words took me like a punch to the gut. "It wasn't her," I decided. "Whatever you think happened, you don't have all the facts. Megan isn't like that."

"Her name is Firefight. The person you call Megan was just a lie she created to fool us."

"No," I said. "That *was* the real her. I saw it in her; I *know* her. Prof, she—"

"David," Prof snapped, exasperated. "She is one of *them*."

"So are you!" I shouted at him. "You think we can just keep doing this, like we've been doing? What happens when an Epic like Backbreaker or Obliteration comes to town? Someone who can simply vaporize the entire city to get at us?"

"That's why we never went this far!" Prof shouted back at me. "That's why we kept the Reckoners secret, silent, and never attacked Epics who were too powerful! If this city is destroyed, it will be *your fault*, David Charleston. Tens of thousands of deaths will be on *your* head!"

I stepped back, shocked, suddenly aware of what I was doing. Was I really arguing with Jon Phaedrus, head of the Reckoners? High Epic? The air seemed to *warp* around him as he shouted at me.

"Jon," Tia said, crossing her arms. "That was unfair. You agreed to attack Steelheart. We're all culpable here."

He looked to her, and some of the anger left his eyes. He grunted. "We need a way out of this, Tia. If we're going to fight this war, we'll need weapons against them."

"Other Epics," I said, finding my voice.

Prof glared at me.

"He might be right," Tia said.

Prof turned that glare on her instead.

"What we've accomplished," Tia said, "we've done because of your powers. Yes, David brought down Steelheart, but he'd never have survived long enough to do so without your shielding. It might be time to start asking ourselves new questions."

"Megan spent all of those months with us," I said, "and never turned against us. I saw her use her powers, and yes she got a little cranky afterward, but she was still good, Prof. And during the fight with Steelheart, when she saw me, she came back to herself."

Prof shook his head. "She didn't use her powers against us because she was a spy for Steelheart and didn't wish to reveal herself," he said. "I'll admit, that may have led her to be more reasonable—more herself—during her time with us. But she no longer has a reason to avoid using her abilities; the powers will have consumed her, David."

"But—"

"David," Prof said, "she *killed* a Reckoner."

"It was witnessed?"

Prof hesitated. "I don't have all the details yet. I know there is a recording at least, taken when she was fighting one of our people. And then he was found dead."

"It wasn't her," I said, then made a quick decision. "I'm going to go to Babilar and find her."

"Like hell you are," Prof said.

"What else will we do?" I asked, turning to leave. "This is the only plan we have."

"This isn't a plan," Prof said. "It's hormones."

I stopped at the doorway, blushing, then glanced back.

Prof picked at the flower petals that Tia had dumped on the dresser. He looked at her, still standing with her arms crossed. She shrugged.

"*I* am going to Babylon Restored," Prof finally said. "I have business there with an old friend. *You* may accompany me, David. But not because I want you to recruit Megan."

"Why, then?" I demanded.

"Because you're one of the most capable point men I have, and I'm going to need you. The best thing we can do to protect Newcago right now is keep the Epics from fixating upon it. We've overthrown one emperor, and in so doing made a statement: that the day of Epic tyrants is over, and that no Epic—no matter how powerful—is safe from us. We need to make good on that promise. We need to *scare* them, David.

Instead of a single free city, we need to present to them an entire continent in rebellion."

"So we bring down the tyrants of other cities," I said, nodding. "And we start with this Regalia."

"If we can," Prof said. "Steelheart was probably the strongest Epic alive, but I promise you that Regalia is the most wily—and that makes her just as dangerous, if not more so."

"She's sending Epics here," I pointed out, "to try to kill the Reckoners. She's scared of you."

"Possibly," Prof said. "Either way, in sending Mitosis and the others here, Regalia declared war. You and I are going to kill her for that—just like we did with Steelheart. Just like you did with Sourcefield today. Just like we'll do to any Epic who stands against us."

He met my eyes.

"Megan's not like the others," I said. "You'll see."

"Perhaps," Prof said. "But if I'm right, son, I want you there so that you can pull the trigger. Because if someone is going to have to put her down, it should be a friend."

"A mercy," I said, my mouth going dry.

He nodded. "Pack your things. We leave later tonight."

7

LEAVE. Newcago.

I'd never . . . I mean . . .

Leave.

I'd just said I intended to go. That had been in the heat of the moment. As Tia and Prof pushed out of the room, I stood there in the doorway, coming to a realization of what I'd just done.

I'd never left the city. I'd never *thought* of leaving the city. Inside the city there had been Epics, but outside the city there was chaos.

Newcago was all I'd ever known. And now I was leaving it.

To find Megan, I thought, forcing down my anxiety and

following Prof and Tia into the main room. *It will only be for a little while.*

Tia walked to her desk and began gathering her notes—apparently, if Prof was going to Babilar, she'd be going too. Prof started giving orders to Cody and Abraham. He wanted them to stay in Newcago to watch the city.

"Yeah," I said. "Gather my things. Leave the city. Of course. That's exactly what I'd been intending to do. Sounds like fun."

Nobody paid attention. So, blushing, I went to pack my bag. I didn't have much. My notebooks, which Tia had copied for redundancy. Two changes of clothing. My jacket. My gun—

My gun. I set my backpack on the floor and pulled out the broken rifle, then walked over to Abraham, offering it up like a wounded child before a surgeon.

He inspected it, then looked up at me. "I'll get you one of my spares."

"But—"

He rested a hand on my shoulder. "It is an old weapon, and it served you well. But don't you think you should upgrade, David?"

I looked down at the broken gun. The P31 was a great rifle, based off the old M14, one of the best rifles ever made. Those were solid weapons, designed before things got all modern, fancy, and sterile. We'd made P31s at Steelheart's munitions factory back when I was a kid; they were sturdy and dependable.

But Steelheart hadn't equipped his own soldiers with these; the P31 had been for selling to others. Steelheart hadn't wanted to give modern equipment to potential enemies.

"Yeah," I said. "All right." I set the rifle down. I mean, it's not like I was *attached* to it. It was just a tool. Really.

Abraham squeezed my shoulder in sympathy, then led

me to the equipment room, where he began hunting through boxes. "You'll want something mid-range. A 5.56 all right?"

"I suppose."

"AR-15?"

"Ugh. AR-15? I'd rather not have my gun break down on me every second week." Besides, every wannabe and their dog had an M16 or M4 variant these days.

"G7."

"Not accurate enough."

"FAL?"

"A 7.62? Maybe," I said. "Though I hate the triggers."

"As picky as a woman with her shoes," Abraham grumbled.

"Hey," I said. "That's insulting." I knew plenty of women who were pickier with their guns than they were with their shoes.

Abraham fished in a chest and came up with a rifle. "Here. What about this?"

"A Gottschalk?" I said skeptically.

"Sure. It's very modern."

"It's German."

"Germans make very good weapons," Abraham said. "This has everything you'll need. Automatic, burst, or semiauto settings, remote fire, electron-compressed retractable scope, huge magazines, the ability to fire flash-shots and modern bullets. Very accurate, good sights, solid trigger without too much or too little give."

I took the rifle hesitantly. It was just so . . . black.

I liked guns with some wood on them, a gun that felt natural. Like you could take it hunting, rather than only kill people with it. This rifle was all plastic and black metal. It was like the weapons Enforcement carried.

Abraham slapped me on the shoulder as if the decision had

been made and walked out to talk to Prof. I held the rifle up by its barrel. Everything Abraham said about it was right. I knew my guns, and the Gottschalk was a fine weapon.

"You," I said to it, "are on probation. You'd better impress me."

Great. Now I was talking to guns. I sighed and slung it over my shoulder, then pocketed a few magazines.

I stepped out of the equipment room, looking over my small pack of possessions. It hadn't taken long at all to put together my entire life.

"Devin's team from St. Louis is already on its way," Prof was saying to Abraham and Cody. "They'll help you hold Newcago. Don't let anyone know I'm gone, and don't engage any Epics until the new team arrives. Keep in touch with Tia, and let her know *everything* that happens here."

Abraham and Cody nodded. They were used to teams splitting up and moving around. I still didn't know how many people were in the Reckoners altogether. The members sometimes talked as if this were the only team, but I knew that was an affectation to throw off anyone who might be spying on the group.

Abraham clasped hands with me, then pulled something from his pocket and held it up. A small silver chain with a pendant in the shape of a stylized *S* hanging on the end. It was the mark of the Faithful, the religion to which Abraham belonged.

"Abraham . . . ," I said.

"I know you don't believe," he said. "But you are living the prophecy right now, David. It's as your father said. The heroes will come. In a way, they *have*."

I glanced to the side, where Prof set down a duffel bag for Cody to carry. I closed my fist around Abraham's pendant and nodded. He and his kind believed that the evil Epics were a test from God, and that good Epics would come if mankind endured.

It was naive. Yes, I was starting to think about how good Epics—like Prof—might help us, but I didn't buy into all of the religious mumbo jumbo. Still, Abraham was a friend, and the gift was sincere.

"Thanks," I said.

"Stand," Abraham said. "This is the true test of a man. He who will stand when others grow complacent."

Abraham picked up Tia's pack. She and Prof hadn't taken much longer to get ready than I had. As a Reckoner, you learned to live light. We'd already changed hideouts four times while I'd been with them.

Before we left, I ducked into Edmund's room to say good-bye. He was sitting and reading a novel by lamplight, an old science fiction book with yellowed pages. He was the strangest Epic I could imagine. Soft-spoken, slender, aging . . . He had a genuine smile on his lips as he rose.

"Yes?" he asked.

"I'm leaving for a while," I said.

"Oh!" He hadn't been listening. Edmund spent most days in this little room, reading. He seemed to take his subservient postion for granted, but he also seemed to enjoy his life as it was. He was a gifter, like Prof—in Edmund's case, he granted his powers to men and women in Enforcement who used them to charge the power cells that ran the city.

"Edmund?" I asked as he clasped hands with me. "Do you know what your weakness is?"

He shrugged. "I've told you before that I don't seem to have one."

And we suspected he was lying. Prof hadn't pushed the issue; Edmund complied with us in every other way.

"Edmund, it might be important," I said softly. "For

stopping the Epics. All of them." There were so few Epics people had actually had a *conversation* with, particularly about their powers.

"Sorry," Edmund said. "I thought I knew it for a while—but I was wrong. Now I'm as baffled as anyone."

"Well, what did you *think* it was?"

"Being near a dog," he said. "But it really doesn't affect me like I thought it did."

I frowned, making a mental note to tell Prof about this. It was more than we'd gotten from him before. "Thanks anyway," I said. "And thanks for what you do for Newcago."

Edmund walked back to his chair, picking up his book. "Some other Epic will always control me, whether it be Steelheart or Limelight. It doesn't really matter. I don't care to be in charge anyway." He sat down and continued reading.

I sighed and made my way back out into the main room. There, Prof slung a pack onto his shoulder, and I joined him as the last one out, entering the catacombs under Newcago.

We made little conversation as we hiked a half hour or so to one of the hidden garages near a road leading up out of the understreets and into the city. There, Abraham and Cody packed our gear into a jeep for us. I'd been hoping we'd take one of the copters, but that was apparently too showy.

"Watch out for púcas as you travel, lad," Cody said, shaking my hand. "Could be imitating anything out there."

"Once again," Tia said as she settled into the seat in front of me, "those are from *Irish* mythology, you nitwit."

Cody just winked at me and tossed me his camouflage baseball cap. "Y'all stay safe." He gave us a thumbs-up, then he and Abraham retreated back into the understreets.

So it was that—a short time later—I found myself sitting in the back of the jeep, wind blowing my hair, holding a new gun and watching my home for all nineteen years of my life retreat behind me. The dark skyline was something I'd rarely seen. Even before Calamity I'd almost always been among, or beneath, the city's buildings.

Who was I, if I wasn't in Newcago? It was similar to the hollowness I felt inside some nights when I wondered what I was supposed to do with my life now that *he* was gone. Now that I'd won, and my father was avenged.

The answer was beginning to settle on me like a dinosaur upon its nest. My life wasn't just about one city, or one Epic, anymore. It was about a war. It was about finding a way to stop the Epics.

Permanently.

PART TWO

PART TWO

8

PAPERS flapped in my hands as we sped down the highway. We'd hit a relatively unbroken patch of asphalt, though we still thumped across a rough section of road now and then. I hadn't imagined that a roadway like this could decay so quickly. Less than thirteen years had passed since Calamity, but already the highway was torn up with potholes and plants peeking up out of cracks like zombie fingers out of graves.

Many cities we passed were decayed, windows shattered, buildings crumbling. I spotted some cities that were in better repair, lit by bonfires in the distance, but these seemed more like little bunkers, surrounded by walls with fields outside— fiefdoms ruled by one Epic or another.

We traveled at night, and though I saw the occasional fire, I didn't spot a single glimmer of electric lights. Newcago really *was* an anomaly. Not only had the steel preserved the tall sky-scrapers and elegant skyline, but Steelheart's reign had also maintained basic services.

Prof drove with goggles on, the jeep's headlights replaced with UV floodlights that would be invisible to anyone without the proper headgear. I sat in the jeep's back seat and spent my time reading through the notes and essays Tia had given me. I held the sheets inside a small box in my lap that had a flash-light inside of it, and this mostly masked the light.

The car slowed, then thumped up and down as Prof care-fully navigated a bad patch of rubbled asphalt. Cars lay like the husks of enormous beetles along the sides of the road; they'd first been drained of their gasoline, then gutted for parts. Our vehicle, fortunately, had been converted to run on one of Ed-mund's power cells.

As we drove slowly over the rubble, I heard something out in the night, like a snapping branch. The jeep's back seat wasn't enormous, but it didn't have a roof, so I could easily set my box aside and maneuver my new rifle. I raised it to my shoulder and tapped a button that folded out the automatic scope. It worked very well, I was forced to admit, switching to night vision on its own and letting me zoom in on the source of the noise.

Through the holosights I picked out a few scavengers in ragged clothing squatting behind one of the broken cars in the darkness. They seemed like wild people, with long beards and sloppily stitched clothing. I watched them with the safety off, looking for weapons, until another head bobbed up. A little girl, maybe five years old. One of the men hushed her, pushing her down, then continued watching our jeep until we crossed the patch of broken street and sped up, leaving them behind.

I lowered the gun. "It really is bad out here."

"Anytime a town starts to band together," Tia said from the front passenger seat, "an Epic decides to either rule the place or lay waste to it."

"It's worse," Prof said softly, "when one of their own develops powers."

New Epics were rare, but they did happen. In a city like Newcago, we'd get maybe a single new one every four or five years. But they were dangerous, as an Epic who first manifested powers almost always went a little mad in the beginning, using their abilities wildly, destroying. Steelheart had quickly rounded up such individuals and subjugated them. Out here, there would be nobody to stop their initial rampage.

I settled back, disturbed, but eventually returned to my reading. This was our third night on the road. When dawn had broken after the first night, Prof had driven us into a hidden safe house. Apparently, the Reckoners had many of them along major roadways. Usually they were hollows sheared into rock with tensors, then secured with hidden doors.

I hadn't pushed Prof too much about the tensors. Even with me, he talked about them as if they were technology— and not secretly just a cover for his powers. He only allowed the Reckoners in his personal team to use them, which made sense. Most Epic powers had a distinct range. From what I'd been able to determine, you had to be within a dozen miles or so of Prof for the gifted tensors or energy shields to work.

What made it even more confusing was that the Reckoners *did* have technology that emulated Epic powers. Such as the gauss gun I'd used in fighting Steelheart, and the dowser, which was a device they used to test if someone was an Epic or not. I'd been suspicious that these things had also secretly been from Prof's powers, but he'd promised me they weren't. It *was* possible to kill an Epic, then use something about their

DNA to reverse engineer machines that mimicked their powers. That's what made Prof's deception so believable. Why assume that your team leader is an Epic when there's a perfectly good technological explanation for the things the team can do?

I flipped through to the back of the stapled series of notes that Tia had given me. There, I found the profile for Sourcefield, which we'd gathered soon after she'd come to Newcago. *Emiline Bask*, it read. *Former hotel desk clerk. Fan of Asian pulp cinema. Gained Epic powers two years after Calamity.*

I scanned through her history. She'd spent some time in Detroit, Madison, and Little Blackstone. She'd allied with Static and his band of Epics for a few years, then she'd vanished for a while before turning up in Newcago to kill the lot of us. This was interesting, but it wasn't what I was looking for. I wanted to know her pre-Epic history, in particular her personality before she became one of them. Had she been a troublemaker, like Steelheart?

For that, I only had a few paragraphs. She'd been raised by an aunt after her mother committed suicide, but the pages said nothing about her personality. There was a note at the end. *Mother's trauma related to grandparents, obviously.*

I leaned forward as the jeep picked up a little speed. "Tia?"

"Hmm?" she asked, looking up from her datapad, which she hid in a box like mine to shield the light.

"What does this mean—it references Sourcefield's mother's trauma being related somehow to her grandparents?"

"Not sure," she said. "What I gave you was part of a larger file that Jori had compiled; he sent us only the relevant information."

My own files didn't have much on Sourcefield. I looked at that paragraph again, lit inside my shoebox. "Would you mind asking him for the rest of the information?"

"What is it about dead Epics that fascinates you so?" Tia asked.

Prof kept his eyes forward, but he seemed to perk up.

"You remember Mitosis?" I asked. "That Epic who tried to take Newcago a few months back?"

"Of course."

"His weakness was rock music," I said. "Specifically his own music." He'd been a minor rock star before gaining his Epic powers.

"So?"

"So . . . it's a mighty coincidence, isn't it? That his own music should negate his powers? Tia, what if there's a pattern to the weaknesses? One we haven't cracked yet?"

"Someone would have spotted it," Prof said.

"Would they?" I asked. "Early on, nobody even *knew* about the weaknesses. The Epics weren't quick to tell people about them. Besides, there was mass chaos."

"Unlike now?" Tia asked.

"Now . . . there's institutionalized chaos," I said. "Look, how long ago did the Reckoners start working? How long ago did the lorists start gathering data on weaknesses? It's only been a few years, right? And by then, it was just common knowledge that Epic weaknesses are bizarre and random. Only, what if they're not?"

Tia tapped her datapad. "Worth looking into, I suppose. I'll get you more about Sourcefield's past."

I nodded, gazing between them, eastward along the road. I couldn't see much in the darkness, though a haze on the horizon took me by surprise. Was that light?

"Dawn already?" I asked, checking my mobile.

"No," Prof said. "It's the city."

Babylon Restored. "So soon?"

"David, we've been traveling for over two days," Tia said.

"Yeah, but Babilar is on the other side of the country! I figured . . . I don't know, like it would take at least a week. Or two."

Prof snorted. "When the roads were good, you could make this drive in one day, easy."

I settled back in my seat, bracing myself against the bumps as Prof sped up. He obviously wanted to reach the city well before daybreak. We passed a growing number of suburbs, but even still, things out here were just so . . . *empty*. I'd imagined buildings everywhere, maybe farms squeezed between them. The truth was that the landscape outside Newcago just seemed to be filled with . . . well, a lot of nothing at all.

The world was both a larger place and a smaller place than I'd imagined.

"Prof, how do you know Regalia?" I blurted out.

Tia glanced at me. Prof kept driving.

"What do you remember about Regalia, David?" Tia asked, perhaps to break the silence. "From your notes."

"I've been scanning," I said, getting excited. "She's one of the most powerful Epics around, and one of the most mysterious. Water manipulation, remote projection, hints of at least one other major power."

Tia snorted.

"What?" I asked.

"Your tone," she said. "You sound like a fan talking about his favorite movie."

I blushed.

"I thought you hated the Epics," Tia said.

"I do." Well, you know, all except for the one I'd kind of fallen for. And Prof. And I guess Edmund. "It's complicated. I hated Steelheart. *Really* hated Steelheart—and all of them because of it, I guess. But I've also spent my life studying them, learning about them. . . ."

"You can't immerse yourself in something," Prof said softly, "without coming to respect it."

"Yeah," I agreed.

When I'd been a kid, I was enthralled by sharks. I'd read every book I could find about them, including the most gruesome accounts of shark-related deaths. I'd loved reading about them precisely because they were so dangerous, so deadly, so weird. Epics were the same way, only so much more. Creatures like Regalia—mysterious, dynamic, powerful—were *fascinating*.

"You didn't answer my question," I noted, "about how you know Regalia."

"No," Prof said. "I didn't."

I knew better than to prod further. We soon reached the ruins of a larger city, but we didn't seem to have reached Babilar yet—at least, we hadn't reached the haze of light. This place was pitch-black, no fires, let alone any electricity. What I'd spotted earlier was beyond it, out a distance—and even that wasn't really "lights." More a faint glow in the air, like might be caused by a lot of lit areas, though I couldn't make out any distinct lights. We were still too far, and the buildings blocked my view.

I took out my rifle and watched the passing landscape through the night-vision scope. Most everything was rusted and crumbling here—though this city was bigger than the others we'd passed on our way. It also looked wrong to me for some reason. So grey, so decayed. So . . . fake?

Because it looks like the movies, I realized, thinking back to the films I'd watched with the other kids at the Factory. We'd all lived in Newcago, a city of pure steel. Faded signs, brick walls, woodpiles—these were things from another world. The only place I'd seen them before was in the films.

This was what the rest of the world thought was normal. How bizarre.

We drove through this dead city for a long while, still on the expressway, but going at a slow speed. I assumed that Prof didn't want to make any noise. Eventually he pulled onto an off-ramp and drove down into the dark city itself.

"Is this Babilar?" I asked softly.

"No," Prof said. "This is . . . was . . . New Jersey. Fort Lee, specifically."

I found myself on edge. Anything could be watching from among those broken husks of buildings. This place was abandoned, an enormous grave for the time that had come before Calamity.

"So empty," I whispered as Prof drove us down a street.

"A lot of people died fighting the Epics," Tia whispered back. "And a lot more died once the Epics started fighting back in earnest. But the most died in the chaos that followed, when civilization just . . . surrendered."

"A lot of people avoid the cities," Prof said. "Hard to grow anything here, and they attract the worst kind of scavengers. However, the land isn't as empty as you think." He rolled us around a corner. I didn't miss that Tia had a handgun out in her lap, though I'd never seen her fire a weapon before. "Besides," Prof added, "most everyone in this area has made their way to the island by now."

"Life's better there?" I asked.

"Depends." He stopped the jeep in the middle of a darkened road, then turned back toward me. "How well do you trust the Epics?"

It seemed a loaded question, considering the source. He climbed out of the jeep, boots scraping on asphalt. Tia got out the other side, and they started walking toward a looming building.

"What's this?" I asked them, standing up in the back of the jeep. "Where's the road into Babilar?"

"Can't drive into Babilar," Prof said, stopping by the door of the building.

"Too noticeable?" I asked, hopping down and joining them.

"Well, there's that," Prof said. "But mostly it's because the city doesn't have any streets. Come on. It's time to meet your new team."

He pushed open the door.

9

I followed Prof and Tia into the building. It looked like an old mechanic's garage, with large bay doors on the front. And it smelled . . . too clean. Not musty, like the forgotten chambers of Newcago's understreets. It was pitch-black, though, and creepy. I couldn't make out much besides some large dark shapes that might have been vehicles.

I unslung my rifle, feeling the hair on the back of my neck rising. What if this was some kind of trap? Had Prof prepared for that? I—

Lights came on in a sudden flare. Blinded, I cursed and jumped to the side, slamming my back against something large. I raised my rifle.

"Oops!" a feminine voice said. "Oh, sorry, sorry, sorry! Too bright."

Prof grunted nearby. Rifle stock firmly against my shoulder, I blinked until I could make out that we were in some kind of workshop. We were surrounded by tool-covered benches and a few half-disassembled cars, including one jeep just like our own.

The door clicked closed behind me, and I pointed my rifle that direction. A tall Hispanic woman in her early thirties had shut the door. She had angular features and dark hair with one lock in the front dyed purple. She wore a red shirt and a blazer, with a black necktie.

"Mizzy," the woman snapped, "the point of dimming the lights until they were in was to *avoid* alerting the entire neighborhood that this building has power. That doesn't work if you turn the lights back on while the door is still *wide open.*"

"Sorry!" called the voice from before, the sound echoing in the large room.

The Hispanic woman glanced at me. "Put that gun down before you hurt someone, kid." She strode past me and gave Prof a sloppy salute.

He extended a hand. "Val."

"Jon," Val said, taking his hand. "I was surprised to get your message. I didn't expect you back so soon."

"Considering what happened," Prof said, "I figured you'd be planning to do something brash."

"Here to stop me, sir?" Val asked, voice cold.

"Sparks no," Prof said. "I'm here to help."

Val's expression cracked, a hint of a smile tugging at her lips. She nodded to me. "That's Steelslayer?"

"Yes," Prof said as I finally stepped out of my cover.

"Excellent reflexes," Val said, looking me up and down. "Terrible fashion sense. Mizzy, where the hell are you?"

"Sorry!" that voice from before came again, followed by clanks. "Coming!"

I stepped up beside Tia as I spotted a young black woman climbing down from a catwalk above, a sniper rifle slung over her shoulder. She hit the ground and jogged toward us, a bounce in her step. She wore jeans and a short jacket, with a tight white shirt underneath. She had her hair braided in cornrows on the top, and it exploded into a frizzy puff behind her head.

Tia and Prof looked at Val; Tia cocked an eyebrow.

"Mizzy is quite capable," Val said. "She's just a little . . ."

As Mizzy scuttled toward us, she tried to duck under the front of a half-assembled jeep that was up on risers. However, the rifle over her shoulder stuck up too high, and it clanged against the front of the jeep, pushing her backward. She gasped, grabbing the jeep as if to steady it—though it hadn't budged. Then she patted it as if in apology.

She was maybe seventeen years old or so, and had a cute face with round features and creamy brown skin. *She smiles too wide to be a refugee,* I thought as she ran over and saluted Prof. *Where has she been living that hasn't beaten that bubbly nature out of her?* I wondered.

"Where's Exel?" Tia asked.

"Watching the boat," Val said.

Prof nodded, then pointed at Val. "David, meet Valentine, leader of this cell of the Reckoners. She and hers have been living in Babylon Restored for the last two years, doing reconnaissance on Regalia. You obey orders from her as if they came from me. Understand?"

"Got it. Val, are you point?"

Val's expression darkened. "Operations," she said, giving no indication why my words had bothered her. "Though if Tia is going to be joining this crew . . ."

"I am," Tia said.

"Then," Val said, "she'll probably run operations. I'd

rather be in the field anyway. But I don't run point. I do heavy weapons and vehicle support."

Prof nodded, gesturing toward Mizzy. "And this is Missouri Williams, I assume?"

"Excited to meet you, sir!" Mizzy said. She seemed the type to be excited about pretty much everything. "I'm the team's new sniper. Before, I did repairs and equipment, and I have experience with demolitions. I'm training to run point, sir!"

"Like hell you are," Val said. "She's good with a rifle, Prof. Sam had kind of taken her under his wing. . . ."

Probably the person they lost recently, I thought, reading Prof's stiff expression, Tia's look of sorrow. Sam. I guessed he'd been their point man, the one who shouldered the most danger—interacting with Epics and drawing them into the traps.

It was the job I did in our team. The job Megan had done before she left. I didn't know Sam, but it was hard not to feel a surge of empathy for the fallen man. He'd died fighting back.

But Megan had *not* been responsible, no matter what Prof claimed.

"Glad to have you, Mizzy," Prof said, voice even. I sensed a healthy dose of skepticism in that tone, but that was only because I knew him pretty well. "Go pull our jeep into the garage. David, go with her, scope out just in case."

I raised an eyebrow at him. He returned a flat gaze. *Yes,* the gaze said, *I'm getting rid of you for a few minutes. Deal with it.*

I sighed but followed Mizzy out the side door, turning off the lights on the way. That left the others in the dark, in order to make the opening and closing doors less noticeable.

I got out my new rifle, extending the night-vision scope, and walked with Mizzy toward the jeep. Behind us, one of the garage doors opened, making almost no noise at all. Inside, by the faint starlight, I saw Prof, Tia, and Val in hushed conversation.

"Sparks," Mizzy said softly, "he's *intimidating*."

"Who?" I asked. "Prof?"

"Yeaaah," she said, reaching the jeep. "Wow. Phaedrus himself. I didn't make *too* much a fool of myself, did I?"

"Um. No?" No more a fool than I had made of myself on several occasions after first meeting Jon. I understood how intimidating he could be.

"Good." She stared at Prof in the darkness, and frowned. Then she turned to me and stuck out a hand. "I'm Mizzy."

"They *just* introduced us."

"I know," she said, "but *I* didn't get to introduce *myself*. You're David Charleston, that guy who killed Steelheart."

"I am," I said, taking her hand hesitantly. This girl was a little weird.

She shook my hand, then pulled in closer to me. "You," she said softly, "are *awesome*. Sparks. Two heroes in one day. I will have to write *this* in my *journal*." She swung into the jeep and started it up. I did a sweep of the area with my rifle, looking to see if we'd been noticed. I didn't see anything, so I backed into the garage, following the jeep Mizzy drove.

I tried not to pay too much attention to the fact that Prof had asked her, and not me, to pull the jeep in. I could totally park a jeep without crashing. Sparks, I didn't even crash going around corners anymore. Most of the time.

Mizzy lowered the garage door and locked up the place. Prof, Tia, and Val ended their clandestine conversation, then Val led us through the back of the shop, down into a tunnel under the streets. I expected to keep walking for a while, but we didn't—only a few minutes later she led us up again, through a trapdoor to the outside.

Here, water lapped against a dock, and a wide river led out of the city into a dark bay. Colorful lights shone distantly on the other side. Hundreds upon hundreds of them. I'd looked at maps before coming, and could guess where we were. This was the Hudson River, and that was old Manhattan over there—Babylon Restored. They had electricity, it seemed, and that was the source of the distant haze of illumination I'd seen earlier. But why were the lights so colorful? And oddly dim?

I squinted, trying to make out details, but the lights were just clusters of specks to me. I followed the team along the docks, and my attention was quickly drawn by the water. Despite living in Newcago, I'd never actually been near a large body of water before. Steelheart had turned enough of Lake Michigan to steel that I'd never been to the coast. Something about those dark depths made me strangely uncomfortable.

Ahead of us at the end of the dock, a flashlight flicked on, illuminating a medium-sized motorboat with an enormous man seated at the back, wearing about five shirts' worth of red flannel. Bearded and curly haired, he waved at us with a smile.

Sparks, this man was large. It was like one lumberjack had eaten another lumberjack, and their powers had combined to form one *really* fat lumberjack. He stood up in the boat as Val hopped on. He shook hands with Prof and Tia, then smiled at me.

"Exel," the man said softly, introducing himself. He paused briefly between the syllables, as if he were saying it "X.L." I wondered which position in the team he'd fulfill. "You're Steelslayer?"

"Yeah," I said, shaking his hand. The darkness, hopefully, covered my embarrassment. First Val, then this guy, referring to me that way. "But you don't really need to call me that."

"It's an honor," Exel said to me, stepping back.

They expected me to climb onto the boat. That shouldn't be a problem, right? I realized I was sweating, but I forced myself to step onto the unsteady vehicle. It rocked a lot more than I'd have wanted—and then rocked even *more* as Mizzy climbed on. Were we really going to cross this enormous river in something so small? I sat down, discomforted. That was a *lot* of water.

"Is this it, sir?" Exel asked once we were all on.

"This is everyone," Prof said, settling himself by the prow of the boat. "Let's move."

Val took the seat at the back next to the small outboard motor. She started it with a soft sputtering sound, and we pulled away from the dock onto the choppy black water.

I held on to the rail tightly, watching the water. All of that blackness beneath us. Who knew what was down there? The waves weren't huge, but they did rock us. Again, I wondered if we shouldn't have something larger. I scooted closer to the middle of the vessel.

"So," Val said as she steered us along. "Have you prepped the new guy?"

"No," Prof said.

"Now might be a good time, considering . . . ," Val said, nodding toward the distant lights.

Prof turned toward me, his form mostly hidden in shadows. The wind ruffled his dark lab coat. I hadn't completely gotten over the awe I'd felt upon first meeting him. Yes, we were close now, but occasionally it still struck me—this was *Jonathan Phaedrus,* founder of the Reckoners. A man I'd practically worshipped for most of my life.

"The one who rules this city," he said to me, "is a hydromancer."

I nodded eagerly. "Rega—" I began.

"Don't say her name," Prof interrupted. "What do you know of her abilities?"

"Well," I said, "supposedly she can send out a projection of herself, so when you see her, it might just be her duplicate. She also has the portfolio of a standard water Epic. She can raise and lower water, control it with her mind, that sort of thing."

"She can also see out of any open surface of water," Prof said. "And can hear anything spoken near the water. Do you have any idea of the ramifications of that?"

I glanced at the open water around us. "Right," I said, shivering.

"At any time," Exel said from nearby, "she could be watching us. We have to work under that assumption . . . and that fear."

"How are you still alive?" I asked. "If she can see so widely . . ."

"She's *not* omniscient," Prof said to me, speaking firmly. "She can only see one place at a time, and it's not particularly easy for her. She looks into a dish of water she's holding, and can use it to see out of any surface of water that touches air."

"Like a witch," I said. "From the stories."

"Sure, like that," Exel said, chuckling. "I doubt she has a cauldron though."

"Anyway," Prof said, "her powers are extensive—but they don't make it easy for her to scan and find things randomly. Something has to draw her attention."

"It's why we avoid saying her name," Val added from the back of the boat. "Unless we're whispering over the mobile network."

Prof tapped his earpiece. I turned on my mobile, with voice amplification, and wirelessly connected it to my earpiece.

"Like this," Prof whispered, but it came into my ear loud enough to be heard.

I nodded.

"Right now," he continued, "we are in her power. We float across the open sea. If she knew we were here, she could summon tendrils of water and drag this ship into the depths. In this city, like most others, the Reckoners can exist because we are careful, quiet, and hidden. Don't let the way we've been acting in Newcago make you sloppy here. Understood?"

"Yeah," I said, whispering like he did, trusting that the sensors on my earpiece would pick up my voice and transmit it. "Good thing we'll be out of open water soon, eh?"

Prof turned toward the city and fell silent. We passed something nearby in the water, a large, towering length of steel. I frowned. What was that, and why had it been built into the middle of the river like this? There was another in the distance.

The tops of a suspension bridge's towers, I realized, spotting wires trailing down into the water. The entire bridge had been sunk.

Or . . . the water had risen.

"Sparks," I whispered. "We're never going to get off the open water, are we? She's sunk the city."

"Yes," Prof said.

I was stunned. I'd heard that Regalia had raised the water level around Manhattan, but this was far beyond what I'd taken that to mean. That bridge had probably once loomed a hundred feet or more above the river; now it was *beneath* the surface, only its support towers visible.

I turned and looked at the water we'd crossed. Now I could see a subtle slope to the water. The water bulged here, and we had to move *up* at an incline to approach Babilar, as if we were climbing a hill of water. How bizarre. As we drew closer to the city itself, I saw that the entire city was indeed sunken. Sky-scrapers rose like stone sentries from the waters, the streets having become waterways.

As I took in the strange sight, I realized something even odder. The glowing lights I'd seen on our approach didn't come out of the windows of the skyscrapers; they came from *the walls* of the skyscrapers. Light shone in patches, bright and fluorescent, like the illumination from an emergency glow-stick.

Glowing paint? That was what it seemed to be. I held to the side of the boat, frowning. This was *not* what I had expected. "Where are they getting their electricity?" I asked over the line.

"They aren't," Val said in my ear, whispering but fully audible to me. "There's no electricity in the city other than in our own hidden base."

"But the lights! How do they work?"

Suddenly the sides of our boat began to glow. I jumped, looking down. The glow came on like a dimmed light that slowly gained strength. Blue . . . *paint*. The side of the boat had been spraypainted. That was what was on the buildings too. Spraypaint . . . graffiti. In all its various colors, the graffiti was glowing vibrantly, like colored moss.

"How do the lights work?" Val said. "I wish I knew." She slowed the boat, and we sailed between two large buildings. Their tops glowed and, squinting, I made out spraypainted boards rimming the roofs. They shone with vibrant reds, oranges, greens.

"Welcome to Babylon Restored, David," Prof said from the prow. "The world's greatest enigma."

10

VAL cut the motor and handed oars to me, Mizzy, and Exel, keeping one for herself. The four of us took up rowing duty. We floated out from between the two taller buildings and approached a series of much lower structures, their tops only a few feet above the water.

They might have once been small apartment buildings, now submerged except for the uppermost floor or so of each. People lived on the roofs, mostly in tents—vibrant, colorful tents that glowed from the spraypaint casually marking them with symbols and designs. Some of the paintings were beautiful while others displayed no skill whatsoever. I even saw some glows beneath the water—graffiti that had been flooded over. So old spraypaint glowed as well as newer paintings like the ones atop the skyscrapers.

The city was so *alive*. Lines strung between poles hung with drying clothing. Children sat on the sides of the lowest buildings, kicking their legs in the water, watching us pass. A man rowed a small barge past us—it looked like it was constructed out of a bunch of wooden doors lashed together. Each had been spraypainted with circles of different colors.

After the lonely, empty trip here, I was shocked by the sudden sense of overwhelming activity. So many people. Thousands of them in little villages on the roofs of sunken buildings. As we moved farther into the city, I realized that these tents and buildings weren't just shanties or temporary places for transients. It was all too neat, and many of the rooftops had nice, well-made rope bridges strung between them. I was willing to bet that many of these people had been here for years.

"Should we be in the open like this?" I asked, uncomfortable.

"Babilar is a busy city," Prof said, "particularly at night, when the lights come on. We'd be a lot more conspicuous if we tried to sneak in. Right now we're just another ship."

"Can't use the motor, though," Exel noted. "Not a lot of people have working motors in the city."

I nodded, watching some youths paddle past in a glowing canoe. "They look so . . ."

"Destitute?" Mizzy asked.

"Normal," I said. "Everyone's just living their lives."

In Newcago, you'd never been able to simply *live*. You worked long hours at factories producing weapons for Steelheart to sell. When you were off work you kept your head down, always watching for Enforcement. You jumped when you heard a loud noise, because it could be one of any number of Epics looking for entertainment.

These people laughed, they played in the water, they . . .

lounged. In fact, very few people seemed to be doing anything productive. Perhaps it was the late hour. That was another oddity. It was the middle of the night, but even children were up and about.

We rowed past a larger building, which rose some three stories above the water. Through the broken glass windows I saw what appeared to be *plants*. Growing inside the building.

Fruit glowing a soft yellow-green studded the plants, and their leaves had the same painted look as the petals we'd found on Sourcefield. "What in Calamity is going *on* in this city?" I whispered.

"We have no idea," Val said. "I've been embedded here for over two years—I arrived about six months after Regalia stopped her tyranny and decided to clean the place up." As she'd indicated earlier, Val didn't seem to mind saying Regalia's name, so long as it was whispered to the rest of us via our earpieces.

"I feel like I know less than when I first came," Val continued. "Yes, plants grow inside the buildings, and seem to need no cultivation, no sunlamps, no human attention at all. The trees produce flowers, fruits, and vegetables in plenty, enough that nobody here wants for food—so long as one of the gang cartels hasn't monopolized everything."

"Regalia stopped that," Mizzy whispered over the line, dipping her oar into the water. "Things were pretty bad for us here before she came."

"For 'us'?" I asked.

"I'm from Manhattan," Mizzy said, "born and raised. I don't remember a whole lot of the early days, but I do remember Calamity. The glows came immediately afterward; anything spraypainted—old or new—started glowing. Only spraypaint works though. The plants started growing at the same time—they just grew in the streets back then—and nobody has a good explanation, except to credit Dawnslight."

"An Epic?" I asked.

"Maybe?" Mizzy said, shrugging. "Some think so. Dawnslight is what they call the person, force, Epic, or whatever who causes all of this. Except the waters, of course. Those came after, when Regalia arrived. Sweeping into the streets, flooding buildings. We lost a lot of people back then."

"She killed thousands," Prof continued, voice low. "Then she let the gangs rule for years. It was only recently that she decided to rescue the city. Even now she controls the gangs, though they don't terrorize. They watch."

"Yeah," Val said, looking at a group of people dancing atop a building. Drums banged to a pleasant rhythm. "It's creepy."

"Creepy?" Exel asked. "That an Epic wants to do something good for a change? I think what's happening here is *wonderful*." He waved affably to some of the people we passed.

They know him, I realized, studying the people who waved back at him. I assumed they didn't know what he really was, that his being "embedded" here had led to creating some sort of false identity and mingling with the people.

"No, Exel," Prof said over the line, his voice a harsh whisper. "Regalia is planning something. Her supposed benevolence worries me, particularly since she's been sending Epics to try to eliminate my team in Newcago. Don't forget that she also employs the . . . person who killed Sam."

Val, Exel, and Mizzy looked to him.

"So is that why you're here?" Val asked softly. "Are we finally going to bring Regalia down?"

I looked to Prof. He knew Regalia. Personally. I was increasingly certain of it. They'd been friends, perhaps, long ago. I wished I could get more out of him, but this was how

Prof was. Years of secrecy, of running the Reckoners, had taught him to be circumspect.

"Yes," he whispered. "We're here to bring her down. And every Epic allied with her." He looked straight at me, as if daring me to say something about Megan.

I didn't. I needed to know more first.

"Are you sure about this, Prof?" Exel asked. "Maybe Regalia really *has* decided to care for these people. She's been shipping in liquor, distributing it freely. She doesn't let any gangs prevent people from harvesting fruit. Maybe it's an actual attempt to create a utopia. Maybe an Epic has decided to change and be *kind* for once."

Something exploded on a nearby rooftop.

A blossom of fire lit the air, bringing with it screams of terror and pain. People splashed into the waters around us and another explosion followed.

Prof looked at Exel, then shook his head. I stood up, ignoring the exchange. I was so jarred by the explosions that I barely paid attention to how the boat rocked as I stood.

I listened to the distant moans of pain, and looked sharply at the team. "What is it?"

Exel, Val, Mizzy . . . all looked equally surprised. Whatever this was, it wasn't normal for the city.

"We should go help," I said.

"This isn't Newcago," Tia said. "Didn't you listen to Jon? We need to remain hidden."

Behind us, another explosion sounded, closer. I could feel the blast wave of this one, or I thought I could. I hardened my expression, then stepped to the side of the boat. I wasn't going to just sit here while people died.

I stopped, though, taking in the water that separated me from the nearest building.

"Tia, David is right," Prof finally said over our lines. "We can't let this continue, whatever it is, without seeing if we can help. We'll investigate, but carefully. Val, do people go about armed in the city?"

"It's not unheard of," Val replied.

"Then we can carry. But don't do anything unless I say. Sit down, David. We need you on your oar."

Reluctantly, I sat down and helped paddle us toward the nearest building. Above us people rushed across bridges, fleeing the explosions, crowding one another in their haste. The rooftop we reached was low enough—less than a single story showing above the water—and as soon as we arrived I was able to hop up, grab the edge, and tow myself over.

Here I could see the scene better. I was on the roof of a large apartment building that had a sister building on the other side. They were shaped the same with only a small gap of water between them. The other rooftop was where the explosions had happened; it was littered with half-burned tents. The living knelt beside charred loved ones. Others groaned in pain, covered in burns. I felt sick.

Prof heaved himself up beside me, then hissed in anger. "Three explosions," he said softly. "What's going on?"

"We have to help," I said, anxious.

Prof knelt silently for a moment.

"Prof . . ."

"Tia, Exel," he whispered into the line, "prepare to help the wounded. Take the boat over. Val, David, and I will cross this rooftop and give you cover support from here. Something about this doesn't look right to me—too much burning, not enough debris. This wasn't caused by a bomb."

I nodded. Val climbed up too, then the three of us ran across the rooftop toward the burning one. Tia and the other two maneuvered the boat through the water alongside us.

Prof stopped Val and me beside the rope bridge leading to

the next building. People pushed past us, faces ashen, cloth-ing singed. Prof seized the arm of one who didn't look too wounded. "What was it?" he asked softly.

The man shook his head and broke away. Prof pointed for me to provide fire support, and I knelt down beside a brick chimney, rifle out, covering Tia and Exel as they moved the boat up beside the burning building, then climbed out and onto it, carrying a pack that I assumed had a first-aid kit in it.

I sat, watching as Exel began to bandage the wounded. Tia took out something else, the small device we called the harmsway—the fake box with wires sticking out of it that we claimed healed people. Prof really did the work; he must have gifted some of his ability to Tia before joining me on the rooftop.

Tia would have to use it sparingly, only to bring the worst of the wounded from the brink of death. Miraculous healing would draw too much attention to us. Sparks. We might draw too much attention anyway. We were obviously organized, armed, and skilled. If we weren't careful, this might very well undermine Exel's and Val's cover stories.

"What about me?" Mizzy asked over the line. The young woman still waited in the boat, which rocked in the dark water near the side of the burning building. "Prof, sir?"

"Watch the boat," he said over the line.

"I . . ." Mizzy looked deflated. "Yes sir."

I focused on my duty, watching for threats to Tia and Exel on the burning rooftop, but my heart wrenched for the girl. I knew what it was like to feel Prof's skepticism. He could be a hard man. Harder lately. Poor kid.

You're treating her that way too, I realized. *She's probably not even a year younger than you are.* It wasn't fair to think of her as a kid. She was a woman. A pretty one at that.

Focus.

"Ah, here you are, Jonathan. Very prompt of you."

The voice, spoken in a businesslike tone, made me jump almost to the stars. I spun on the source of the sound, leveling my rifle.

An older black woman stood beside Prof. Wrinkled skin, white hair in a bun. Scarf at the neck, fashionable—yet somewhat grandmotherly—white jacket over a blouse and slacks.

Regalia, empress of Manhattan. Standing *right there*.

I planted a bullet in the side of her head.

11

MY shot didn't do much. Well, it made Regalia's head explode, so there was that—but it exploded into a burst of water. Immediately after, more water bulged up out of the neck in a giant bubble and formed into her head again. Color flooded it, and soon she looked exactly as she had a moment before.

Regalia's self-projections were apparently tied to her water manipulation powers. I hadn't realized that, but it made sense.

In order to kill her, we'd have to find her real body, wherever it was. Fortunately, most Epics who created projections had to be in a trance of some sort to do it, which would mean that somewhere she was vulnerable.

Regalia's avatar glanced at me, then turned back to Prof. This was one of the most powerful Epics who had ever lived.

Sparks. Hands sweating, heart thumping, I kept my gun on her—for all the good it would do.

"Abigail," Prof said to her, his voice soft.

"Jonathan," Regalia replied.

"What have you done here?" Prof nodded toward the destruction and the injured.

"I needed to draw you out *some* way, dear man." She spoke with elevated diction, like someone from the old movies. "I figured that a rogue Epic would focus your attention."

"And if I hadn't yet arrived in the city?" Prof demanded.

"Then knowledge of the destruction here would pull you faster," Regalia said. "But I was fairly certain you'd be arriving tonight. It was *obvious* that you'd be coming for me, after my last little . . . calling card arrived in Chicago. I counted the days, and here you are. You are nothing if not predictable, Jonathan."

Another blast of fire lit the night nearby, coming from a different rooftop. I spun, cursing, and pointed my weapon in that direction.

"Oh dear," Regalia said in an emotionless voice. "I guess he *is* going further than my instructions advised."

"He?" Prof said, voice tense.

"Obliteration."

I nearly dropped my gun. "You brought *Obliteration* here? Calamity! What is wrong with you?"

Obliteration was a monster—more a force of nature than a man. He'd left Houston in rubble, murdering Epics and regular people alike. Albuquerque after that. Then San Diego.

Now he was here.

"Abigail . . . ," Prof said, sounding pained.

"You had better stop him," Regalia said. "He's out of control. Oh my. What have I done. How terrible."

The color vanished from her avatar, and it fell, splashing down into water once again. I looked through my scope, surveying the destruction. Some people swam away from the burning rooftops, while others screamed and crowded across bridges. Another flare of light drew my attention, and I caught sight of a figure in black moving among the flames.

"He's there, Prof," I said. "Sparks. She wasn't lying. It's *him*."

Prof cursed. "You've studied the Epics. What's his weakness?"

Obliteration's weakness? I searched frantically, trying to remember what I knew of this man. "I . . . Obliteration . . ." I took a deep breath. "High Epic. He's protected by a danger sense tied to his teleportation powers—if anything is going to harm him, he teleports immediately. It's a reflexive power, though he can also use it at will, making him very hard to pin down. This isn't just a minor wall-traveling power like Sourcefield, Prof. This is full-blown instantaneous transportation."

"His *weakness*," Prof prodded as another flare blasted in the night.

"His true weakness is unknown."

"Damn."

"But," I added, "he's nearsighted. That's not related to his powers, but we might be able to exploit it. Also, when he's in danger, his teleportation kicks in and sends him away. That protects him, but it also might be something we can use, particularly since I think his teleportation powers have a cooldown of some sort."

Prof nodded. "Good job." He tapped his mobile. "Tia?"

"Here."

"Abigail just appeared to me," Prof said. "She's brought Obliteration to the city. He's causing the destruction."

Tia's response was a series of curses over the line.

I glanced at Prof, looking up from the scope of my gun. Though the sky was dark, all of this spraypaint—glowing around me on the bricks, wooden bridges, and tents—lit Prof's face. Were we going to move against Obliteration, or fade away? This was obviously some kind of trap—at the very least, Regalia would be watching to see how we handled ourselves.

The smart thing to do was to run. It's certainly what the Reckoners would have done a year ago, before Steelheart. Prof looked at me, and I could read the conflict in his expression. Could we really leave people to die?

"We're already exposed," I said softly to Prof. "She knows we're here. What would running accomplish?"

He hesitated, then nodded and spoke into the line. "We don't have time for the wounded right now. We have an Epic to bring down. Everyone meet in the center of the first burning rooftop."

A flurry of confirmations crackled over our line. Val and Prof started across the swinging rope bridge toward Tia and Exel, and I followed, nervous as I stepped on the bridge. The planks had been spraypainted alternating neon colors. That only helped highlight the darkness of the water staring up at me from below. As we walked, I took my mobile and zipped it into the shoulder pocket of my jacket—that pocket was supposed to be waterproof. Not that I'd tested it beyond the normal Newcago rains.

The water below reflected the neon lights, and I found myself gripping the rope side of the bridge tightly. Should I mention to Prof that I couldn't swim? I swallowed. Why had my mouth gone so dry?

We reached the other side, and I calmed myself by force. The air here smelled strongly of smoke. We jogged across the rooftop and met up with the others, who had been joined by Mizzy. A nearby tent had been *melted* to the ground; it outlined the bones of those who had been trapped inside, their flesh vaporized in a flash of destruction. I felt nauseous.

"Jon . . . ," Tia said. "I'm worried. We don't have enough of a handle on the city or the situation to take on an Epic like Obliteration. We don't even know his weakness."

"David says he's nearsighted," Prof said, crouching down.

"Well, David is usually right about such things. But I don't think that's enough to—"

Another flare of light. I looked up, as did Prof. Obliteration had moved, probably by teleporting, and was now two rooftops away from us.

Screams sounded from that direction.

"Plan?" I asked urgently.

"Flash and bump," Prof said. It was the name of a maneuver where one team drew the target's attention while the other team surrounded them. He reached out, taking me by the shoulder.

His hand felt warm, and now that I knew what to look for, I felt a slight tingling. He'd just gifted me some shielding power and some ability to vaporize solid objects. "Tensors won't be of much use here," he told me, "as there isn't much tunneling that we'll need to do. But keep them handy, just in case."

I glanced at Exel and Val. They didn't know Prof was an Epic; apparently I'd be expected to keep up his ruse in front of them. "Right," I said, feeling a whole lot safer now that I had some of Prof's shielding on me.

Prof pointed toward a bridge linking this rooftop to the next one. "Cross that bridge, then make your way over toward Obliteration. Figure out a way to distract him and keep his attention. Val, you and I will use the boat—motor on, no use trying to hide from Regalia now—to come up behind Oblitera-tion. We can plan more as we go."

"Right," I said. I glanced at Mizzy. "But I should take Mizzy to cover me. Obliteration might come for Tia, and you'll want someone with more experience covering her."

Mizzy glanced at me. She deserved a shot at being in on the action—I knew exactly how it felt to be left behind during times like this.

"Good point," Prof said, jogging off toward the boat. Val ran behind him. "Exel, you're guarding Tia. David, Mizzy, get moving!"

"Going," I said, sprinting toward another rope bridge leading to Obliteration's latest explosions.

Mizzy ran behind me. "Thanks," she said, sniper rifle over her shoulder. "If I'd gotten stuck on guard duty again, I think I'd have puked."

"You might want to wait to thank me," I said, leaping onto the rickety bridge, "until *after* we survive what comes next."

12

I shoved past fleeing people on the narrow rope bridge, rifle held high over my head. This time I kept my eyes *pointedly* off the water below.

The bridge sloped gently upward, and when I climbed off it I found myself atop a large roof crowded with tents. People huddled inside their makeshift homes or at the periphery of the rooftop. Others fled through waterways below us or across bridges onto other buildings.

Mizzy and I ran across the rooftop. The ground had been spraypainted with a sequence of yellow and green lines that glowed with a phantom light, outlining pathways. Near the middle of the roof we passed a group of people who, strangely, weren't hiding or fleeing.

They were praying.

"Trust Dawnslight!" shouted a woman in their center. "Bringer of life and peace, source of sustenance. Trust in the One Who Dreams!"

Mizzy stopped, staring at them. I cursed and yanked her along after me. Obliteration stood on the next rooftop over.

I could see him easily now, striding among the flames, trench coat flapping behind him. He had a narrow face with long, straight black hair, spectacles, and a goatee. He was the exact sort of person I'd learned to avoid in Newcago, the sort of person who didn't look dangerous until you saw his eyes and realized that something vital was missing in there.

Even for an Epic, this man was a monster. Though he'd originally ruled a city like many top-tier Epics, he'd eventually decided to *destroy* his city completely. Every single person in Houston. He was an indiscriminant killer. I was beginning to think some Epics might be redeemable, but this man . . . not a chance.

"Take up position over on that ledge," I said to Mizzy. "Be ready for instructions. You do demolitions for the team?"

"Sure do."

"You have anything on you?"

"Nothing big," she said. "A few brick-oven-blenders."

"A few . . . What?"

"Oh! Sorry. My own name for—"

"Whatever," I said. "Get them out and be ready." I lowered my rifle and sighted on Obliteration.

He turned to glance at me.

I shot.

He teleported in a burst of light—as if he'd become ceramic and then exploded, shards of his figure spraying outward like a broken vase and scattering along the ground.

Preemptive teleportation. Worked just like I'd read.

Mizzy ran the direction I'd pointed. I knelt, rifle to

shoulder, and waited. The rooftop where Obliteration had stood continued to burn. His primary power was heat manipulation. He could drain anything—people included—of heat with a touch, then expel it either in an aura or by touching something else and transferring it.

He'd melted Houston. Literally. He'd spent weeks sitting in the center of town bare-chested like some ancient god, drawing heat out of the air, basking in the sunlight. He'd stored heat up, then released it all at once. I'd seen photos, read the descriptions. Asphalt turned to soup. Buildings burst into flames. Stones melted to magma.

Tens of thousands dead in moments.

Well, from what I remembered of my notes, I should have a little time before he could reappear. He could only use his teleportation powers every few minutes, and—

Obliteration appeared beside me.

I felt the heat before I spotted him, and I spun that direction. Sweat prickled on my brow, like I'd stepped up to a trash can fire on a cold night.

I shot him again.

I heard half a curse from his lips as he again exploded into shards of light. The heat vanished.

"Be careful, David," Tia said in my ear. "If he gathers heat and pops up right next to you, that aura could overcome your Reckoner shield and fry you before you get a chance to shoot."

I nodded, scrambling away from where I'd been before, rifle still to my shoulder and sights lined up. "Tia," I whispered over the line, "do you have access to my notes?"

"I've pulled those up, along with notes from the other lorists."

"Aren't his teleportation powers supposed to have a recharge time?"

"Yes," she said. "At least two minutes before—"

Obliteration popped into existence again, and this time I caught him coming, like light coalescing. I had a bullet heading that way before he'd even completely formed.

Again the teleportation saved him, but I'd known it would. I was just a diversion. In truth, I had no *idea* how we were going to kill him, but at least I could inconvenience him and prevent him from killing innocents.

"My notes are wrong," I said, sweat trickling down the sides of my face. "There's barely a few seconds' delay between his teleports." Sparks. What else had I gotten wrong?

"Jon," Tia said over the line. "We're going to need a plan. Fast."

"I'm thinking of one," Prof answered in a staccato voice, "but we need more information." Across on the other rooftop, where Obliteration had been attacking before teleporting to me, Prof climbed up and took cover behind some rubble. "David, when he ports, does he automatically take everything touching him, or does he have to specifically choose to bring things like his clothing?"

"Not sure," I said. "Information on Obliteration is scant. He—"

I stopped as he appeared beside me, reaching his hand out to touch me. I jumped, swinging around, feeling a wave of heat wash across me.

A gunshot fired, and Obliteration ported just before he touched me. As before, he left a glowing outline hanging for just a second behind him. The figure exploded into fragments that bounced off me, then vaporized to nothing.

As the flash of light faded from my eyes, I saw Prof on the other rooftop lowering his rifle. "Stay alert, son," Prof said over the line, voice tense. "Mizzy, get some explosives ready. David, is there anything else—anything at all—you can remember about him or his powers?"

I shook myself. Prof's energy shield had probably saved me from Obliteration's heat. He'd just saved my life twice over, then. "No," I said, feeling useless. "Sorry."

We waited, but Obliteration didn't reappear. Instead I heard screams in the distance. Prof cursed over the line and gestured for me to follow the sounds, and I did, heart thumping—yet it was accompanied by the strange calm that comes with being in the middle of an operation.

I passed abandoned tents on one side, people swimming in the waters nearby on the other side. Following the screams led me to a taller building. Thick with vegetation glowing inside the broken windows, the building rose some ten stories or more above the surface of the water. Light flashed inside one of those upper stories, and I saw Obliteration pass in front of an opening. I sighted on him with my rifle and saw that he was smiling, as if in challenge. I fired, but he'd already stepped out of sight deeper into the building.

People continued to scream from inside. Obliteration knew he didn't have to come to us; we'd go to him.

"I'm going in," I said, jogging toward a rope bridge that ran to the taller building.

"Be careful," Prof said. I could see him moving onto his own bridge, heading the same way. "Mizzy, can you cook up a mother switch on something dangerous?"

"Uh . . . I think so. . . ."

Mother switch, short for "mother and child." A bomb that would stay dormant as long as it was receiving a regular radio signal. When the signal stopped, the bomb went off. Kind of like an electronic dead-man's switch.

"Clever," I whispered, crossing the rickety bridge in the night, dark water beneath me. "Stick the bomb to him, make him port with it. Blow him up wherever he goes."

"Yeah," Prof said. "Assuming that works. He takes his

clothing, so he can obviously teleport objects he's carrying. But is it automatic, or can he consciously choose?"

"I'm not convinced we can even stick something to him," Tia said. "His danger sense might trigger a teleportation if you even reach for him."

It was a good point.

"You have a better plan?" Prof asked.

"No," Tia said. "Mizzy, make it happen."

"Got it."

"Work on an extraction plan, Tia," Prof said. "Just in case."

I gritted my teeth, still on the bridge. Sparks. It was impossible to ignore that water down there. I moved more quickly, eager to reach the building, where at least the sea would be out of sight. The bridge didn't lead to the rooftop, but to an old broken window on the story where I'd seen Obliteration.

I reached the window and crouched down before going in, careful of the profile I'd present. Just inside, glowing fruit bobbed from branches and flowers drooped, the petals colored like swirled paint. It was a full-on *jungle* in there; the gloom of shadowed branches and phantom fruit cast an eerie light. Discomforting, like finding a three-week-old sandwich behind your bed, when you swore you'd finished the darn thing.

I checked over my shoulder. Mizzy had moved into position at the other side of the bridge to give me fire support, but her head was down over her pack as she got the explosives ready.

I turned back and, rifle at my shoulder, stepped through the window and checked to each side with a quick motion, looking through my scope. Vines hung from the ceiling and ferns sprouted up from the floor, displacing the carpeting of what had once been a nice office building. Desks—barely visible through it all—had become flowerbeds. Computer monitors were overgrown with moss. The air was thick with humidity, like the understreets after rain. Those glowing fruits were barely enough to illuminate the place, so I moved through a world of rustling shadows as I poked forward, making my way toward where I'd last heard screams—though those had stopped now.

I soon emerged into a small clearing with burned tents and a few smoking corpses. Obliteration was nowhere in sight. *He chose this place intentionally,* I thought, scanning the room with my rifle against my cheek. *We won't be able to back each other up in here, and we'll give our locations away by all the sound we'll make.*

Sparks. I hadn't expected Obliteration to be this clever. I preferred the image of him that I had in my head, that of the raging, mindless monster.

"Prof?" I whispered.

"I'm in," he said over the line. "Where are you?"

"Near where he attacked," I said, steeling myself against the sight of the corpses. "He's not here anymore."

"Come my way," Prof said. "We'll move in together. It would be too easy to take us if we're separated."

"Right." I moved back to the outer wall and edged along toward where Prof's bridge would intersect the building. I tried to move quietly, but growing up in a city made of steel doesn't exactly prepare you for things like leaves and twigs. Nature kept crunching or squishing unexpectedly under my feet.

A crack sounded just behind me. I spun on it, heart thumping, and caught sight of fronds rustling. Something had been back there. Obliteration?

He'd have killed you immediately, I thought. So what had it been? A bird? No, too large. Maybe one of the Babilarans who lived in this jungle?

What a *creepy* place. I resumed my progress, trying to look in every direction at once, moving steadily right up until the moment I heard Prof curse over the line.

Gunfire followed.

I ran then. It was probably a stupid move—I should have found cover. Prof knew my direction, and would avoid firing that way, but all kinds of crazy ricochets could happen in an enclosed space like this.

I charged anyway, bursting out into another clearing to find Prof kneeling beside the wall, bleeding from one shoulder. Dust rained down—the ceiling bulged with vines breaking through the plaster—where a stray bullet had hit. Nearby, shards of light evaporated on the ground, vanishing. Obliteration had teleported away just before I arrived.

I put my back to Prof, looking out into the dark jungle. "He has a gun?" I asked.

"No," Prof said. "A sword. The slontze is carrying around a bloody *sword*."

I covered us while Prof tied on a bandage. He could use his Epic powers to heal himself, but every use of his powers would push him toward darkness. In the past he had offset that by using only a smidge of power to heal from wounds, accelerating the process but not bringing him too much darkness. He could handle a little bit at a time.

"Guys," Val's voice cut in, "I'm setting up infrared surveillance of the building. I should have intel for you soon."

"You all right, Jon?" Tia asked.

"Yeah," he whispered. "Fighting in this place is crazy. We're likely to shoot one another in here. Mizzy, how's that bomb?"

"Ready, sir."

Prof stood and steadied his rifle against his good shoulder, the one Obliteration hadn't stabbed with his sword. Prof didn't often carry a gun. In fact, he didn't often go on point. I now knew that being in the field risked forcing him to use his powers to save himself.

"David," he said to me, "go fetch the bomb."

"I don't want to leave you in he—"

"Regalia says that you actually killed Steelheart."

We both froze. The voice had come from the darkness of the forest. A wind blew through one of the windows, rustling leaves.

"That is well," the voice continued. "Someday, I presume, I would have needed to fight him myself. You have removed that obstacle from my path. For that, I bless you."

Prof gestured curtly to the side with two fingers. I nodded, moving that direction. We needed to be close enough to cover one another, but far enough apart that Obliteration couldn't pop in near the two of us and potentially fry us both with one burst. I didn't know how long Prof's shields would hold up against Obliteration's heat, and I wasn't exactly eager to find out firsthand.

"I have told Regalia," Obliteration continued, "that I will kill her someday too. She doesn't seem to mind."

Where *was* that voice coming from? I thought I saw a shadow move near a tree that bulged with glowing fruit.

"Guys," Val said into our ears, "he's there, right in front of David. I can pick out his heat signature."

Obliteration stepped out of the shadows. He touched a tree and it frosted over, the leaves shriveling. The entire thing died in an eyeblink as Obliteration absorbed its heat.

This time, I didn't shoot him. I took a chance and shot at the ceiling.

Dust rained down.

Prof fired also. *He* shot at the ground near Obliteration's feet.

The Epic looked at us, dumbfounded, then thrust out his hand, palm first.

A shot through the window whizzed over my shoulder and took Obliteration in the forehead—or the glowing outline of his forehead, as he vanished. I glanced back through the window. Mizzy waved distantly from her position on a nearby rooftop, holding her sniper rifle.

"What was that about?" Prof demanded. "Missing like that."

"Dust from the ceiling," I said. "It fell all over him, covering his shoulders. Tia, if you run my video feed, you might be able to tell if the dust ported with him when he vanished. That will answer your bomb question, Prof—whether he teleports with objects automatically, or if he has to choose."

He grunted. "Clever."

"And your shots at his feet?" I asked.

"Wanted to see if his danger sense triggered when he *thought* he was in danger, or if it triggered when he was *actually* in danger. He didn't port when I wasn't trying to hit him."

I grinned across the room at Prof.

"Yes," he said, "we're very similar. Go get Mizzy's bomb, you slontze."

"Yes sir." I scanned the room one more time, then ducked out the window, with Prof covering me. We'd moved away from the bridges, however, which put me on a wide ledge suspended ten or so feet above the water.

I looked down at those dark waters, stomach lurching, then forced myself to edge along until I got to a bridge. The nearby rooftops had become a ghost town. The people had all fled, leaving only smoldering tents and glowing paint.

I reached the bridge and crossed quickly, taking cover beside Mizzy. She handed me a glove, which I put on. That was followed by an innocent-looking package, square, roughly the size of a fist.

"Don't drop it," Mizzy said.

"Right." Dropping explosives: bad.

"Not for the reason you think," Mizzy said. "It's coated with adhesive. The glove is no-stick, but anything else that touches the bomb will stick to it—including our bad guy."

"Sounds viable."

"I've got the mother signal; don't get more than three or four rooftops from me."

"Right."

"Good luck. Don't blow yourself up."

"Like I'd blow myself up. Again."

She looked up at me. "Again?"

"Long story." I shot her a grin. "Cover me as I head back."

"Wait a second," she said, pointing. "I've got a better vantage from the next building over."

I nodded and she started scuttling that way across a *very* precarious rope bridge. I turned back toward the building where Prof was, the one with the jungle inside. Using my scope and its night vision—which was kind of hard to do one-handed—I scanned the area.

There was no sign of him or of Obliteration. Hopefully Prof wasn't hurt.

He's practically immortal, I reminded myself. *It's not him that you have to worry about.*

I looked back over my shoulder and saw Mizzy reach the other end of her bridge—and then I heard screaming. From the building where Mizzy had just arrived.

"David," Mizzy's voice said in my earpiece. "There's something going on here. I'll be right back." She disappeared from view.

"Wait, Mizzy—" I said. I stood up.

And found Obliteration standing beside me.

13

I raised my rifle one-handed, but Obliteration slapped it aside and grabbed me by the throat. He lifted me off the ground by my neck.

Sparks! He had enhanced strength. None of my profiles mentioned that either. I was so panicked I didn't even feel pain—just terror.

Despite that, I managed to reach out and slap Mizzy's bomb onto Obliteration's chest. He didn't vanish. He just looked down as if curious.

I struggled in his grasp, growing more frantic as he choked me. I pried at his fingers in a fruitless attempt at escape as Obliteration casually kicked my gun away across the rooftop, then pulled my earpiece out of my ear and dropped it. He felt at my jacket pockets until he found the mobile there, then squeezed it between two fingers.

I heard it crack inside my pocket. I thrashed and writhed more frantically, gasping for air. Where was Mizzy? She was supposed to be watching my back. Sparks! Prof would still be inside the jungle, hunting Obliteration, Val supporting him. If I couldn't reach Tia on the mobile . . .

I had to save myself. *Make him vanish,* I thought. *The bomb will go off.* I punched at his head.

He ignored my weak battering. "So you're the one," he said, thoughtful. "She spoke of you. Did you really kill him? A youth, not yet a man?"

He let go of me. I dropped to my knees on the rooftop, my neck burning as I inhaled a ragged gasp of air.

Obliteration squatted down beside me.

Plaster dust on his shoulders, a piece of me thought. *When he ports, he takes things that are touching him along.* That spoke well for the bomb.

"Well?" he asked. "Answer me, little one."

"Yes," I gasped. "I killed him. I'll kill you too."

Obliteration smiled. "Behold also the ships," he whispered, "which though they be so great, yet are they turned about with a very small helm. . . . Do not sorrow for this end of days, little one. Make your peace with your maker. Today, you embrace the light."

He took hold of the shirt under his trench coat, then ripped it off—bomb included—and tossed it away. Strangely, underneath he had a bandage wrapped around his chest, as if he had recently survived some severe wound.

I didn't have time to think about that. Sparks! My hand darted toward Megan's gun, but Obliteration grabbed me by the arm and hoisted me into the air.

The world spun around me, yet I was lucid enough to notice when he held me out over the waters. I looked down at them, then struggled more frantically.

"You fear the depths, do you?" Obliteration asked. "The home of leviathan himself? Well, each man must face his fears, killer of gods. I would not send you to the undiscovered country unprepared. Thank you for slaying Steelheart. Surely your reward will be great."

Then he dropped me.

I hit the black waters with a splash.

I thrashed in that cool darkness, weak from near strangulation, not knowing which way was up. Fortunately, I managed to cling to consciousness and surface in a sputtering mess. I grabbed hold of the building's brickwork, then—breath coming in desperate wheezes—I began to climb toward the roof, which was about half a story up.

Exhausted, water streaming from my clothing, I flung an arm over the edge of the rooftop. Blessedly, Obliteration had moved on. I lifted a leg over the side, hauling myself up. Why would he drop me, then—

A flash of light beside me. Obliteration. He knelt down, something metal in his hands. A manacle? With a chain attached to it?

A ball and chain, like from the old days—the type prisoners would wear. Sparks! What kind of person had one of those handy, ready to go grab? He clasped it onto my ankle.

"You have a shield to protect you from my heat," Obliteration said. "So you are prepared for that. But not for this, I suspect."

He kicked the iron ball over the side of the roof.

I grunted as the ball fell, the weight wrenching my leg in its socket, threatening to tow me off the rooftop. I clung to the stonework ledge. How to escape? No rifle, no bomb. I had Megan's pistol in my thigh holster, but if I let go of the rooftop to grab it, that iron ball would pull me into the water. I panicked, grunting, fingers slipping on the stonework of the roof.

Obliteration bent down, close to my face. "And I saw an angel coming down out of heaven," he whispered, "having the key to the Abyss and holding in his hand a great chain. . . ."

At that he brought his hands up and shoved my shoulders, prying me off the rooftop. My fingernails tore and my skin scraped on the bricks as I fell. I splashed down again, this time with a great weight towing on my leg—like the dark waters were actively seeking to engulf me.

I flailed as I sank, searching for anything to stop my descent, and caught hold of a submerged window ledge.

Darkness all around me.

I clung to it as a flash of light shone above. Obliteration leaving? The surface seemed so far away, though it couldn't have been more than five feet.

Darkness. Darkness all around!

I hung on, but my arms were weak and my chest bursting for breath. My vision darkened. Terrified, I felt like the waters were crushing me.

That awful deep blackness.

I couldn't breathe. . . . I was going to . . .

No!

I summoned a burst of strength and thrust my hand upward to grab a brick ledge higher on the side of the building. I heaved myself toward the surface, but in the darkness of night I didn't even know how far away from the air I was. The weight beneath me was too strong. The blackness encircled me.

My fingers slipped.

Something splashed into the water beside me. I felt something brush me—fingers on my leg.

The weight vanished.

I didn't spare time to think. I pulled myself upward along

the submerged building with the last of my strength and burst into the open air, gasping. For a long moment I clung to the side of the building, breathing deeply, shaking, unable to think or really do anything but revel in oxygen.

Finally, I pulled myself up the five feet or so onto the rooftop. I got a leg over the side and rolled onto the stonework, lying on my back, utterly spent. I was too weak to so much as stand, let alone fetch my gun, so it was a good thing Obliteration didn't return.

I lay there for some time. I'm not sure how long. Eventually something scraped on the rooftop nearby. Footsteps?

"David? Oh, sparks!"

I opened my eyes and found Tia kneeling over me. Exel stood back a few feet, looking about anxiously, assault rifle in his hands.

"What happened?" Tia asked.

"Obliteration," I said, coughing. With her help, I sat up. "Dumped me in the water with a chain on my leg. I . . ." I trailed off, staring at my leg. "Who saved me?"

"Saved you?"

I looked at the still waters. Nobody had surfaced after me, had they? "Was it Mizzy?"

"Mizzy is with us," Tia said, helping me to my feet. "I don't know what you're talking about. You can brief us later."

"What happened to Obliteration?" I asked.

"Gone, for now," Tia said.

"How?"

"Jon . . ." She trailed off, meeting my gaze. She didn't say it, but I read the meaning.

Prof had used his powers.

Tia nodded toward the boat, which rocked in the water nearby. Mizzy and Val sat in it, but there was no sign of Prof.

"Just a sec." I fetched my gun, still dizzy from my ordeal.

Near it I found Mizzy's discarded explosives, which were still attached to the front of the T-shirt that Obliteration had been wearing. It wouldn't explode unless it got too far from the radio signal. I rolled the bomb in the remains of the shirt and made my way over to the small boat. Exel offered me a hand, helping me down into the craft.

I settled next to Mizzy, who glanced at me and then immediately looked down. It was hard to tell with her darker skin, but I thought she was blushing in embarrassment. Why hadn't she watched my back like she'd said she would?

Val started the small motor. It seemed she didn't care about drawing attention any longer. Regalia had located us, appeared to us. Hiding was pointless.

So much for keeping quiet, I thought.

As we motored away from the scene of the fight, I noticed people beginning to peek out of hiding places. Wide-eyed, they emerged to broken tents and smoldering rooftops. This was only one small section of the city, and the destruction wasn't wholesale—but I still felt we'd failed. Yes, we'd driven off Obliteration, but only temporarily, and we'd managed it only by falling back on Prof's abilities.

What I couldn't figure out was, how had he done it? How could forcefields or disintegrating metal stave off Obliteration?

Judging by the slumped postures the others wore, they felt the same way I did—that we'd failed tonight. We motored past the broken rooftops in silence. I found myself watching the people who'd gathered. Most seemed to ignore us—in the chaos, they had probably taken cover and missed a lot of the details. You learned to keep your head down when Epics were near. To them, we'd hopefully appear to be just another group of refugees.

I did catch some of them watching us go, though. An older woman, who held a child to her chest, nodding with what seemed to be respect. A youth who peeked over the edge of a rooftop near a burned bridge, wary, as if he expected Obliteration to appear at any moment to destroy us for daring to stand up to him. A young woman wearing a red jacket with the hood up, watching from among a small crowd, her clothing wet . . .

Wet clothing. I focused immediately, and caught a glimpse of her face beneath the hood as she looked at me.

Megan.

She held my gaze for just a moment. It was Megan . . . *Firefight*. A second later, she turned and vanished into the group of townspeople, lost in the night.

So you are *here*, I thought, remembering the splash, the feel of someone's hands on my leg in the moments before I was freed.

"Thank you," I whispered.

"What was that?" Tia asked.

"Nothing," I said, settling back in the boat and smiling, despite my exhaustion.

14

WE continued on through the darkness, moving into a section of the city that was obviously less inhabited. Buildings still sprouted from the waters like tiny islands, fruit glowing on their upper floors, but the spraypaint colors were faded or nonexistent and no bridges linked the structures. They were probably too far apart out here.

The area grew darker as we left the parts of the city with the bright spraypaint. Sailing across those waters in the blackness of night, only the moon to give us light, was thoroughly unsettling. Fortunately, Val and Exel turned on their mobiles, and together the glow created a bright enough light to give us some illumination.

"So, Missouri," Val said from the back of the boat. "Would

you mind explaining why you let David be attacked—and nearly killed—alone, without any backup?"

Mizzy stared at the boat's floor. The motor puttered quietly behind us. "I . . . ," she finally said. "There was a fire inside the building I was on. I heard people screaming. I tried to help. . . ."

"You should know better than that," Val said. "You keep telling me you want to learn to take point—then you do something like this."

"Sorry," the young woman said, sounding miserable.

"Did you save them?" I asked.

Mizzy looked up at me.

"The people in the building," I added. Sparks, my neck was sore. I tried not to show the pain, or my exhaustion, as Mizzy regarded me.

"Yeah," Mizzy said. "They didn't need much saving, though. All I did was unlock a door. They'd gone inside to hide, and the fires had burned down to their floor."

"Nice," I said.

Tia glanced at me. "She shouldn't have abandoned her post."

"I'm not saying she should have, Tia," I replied, meeting her gaze. "But let's be honest. I'm not certain *I* could have let a bunch of people burn to death." I glanced at Mizzy. "It was probably the wrong thing to do, but I'll bet those people are glad you did it anyway. And I managed to squeak by, so it all turned out all right. Nice work." I held out my fist for a bump.

She returned the bump hesitantly, smiling.

Tia sighed. "It is our burden to sometimes make difficult choices. Risking the plan to save one life may cause the deaths of hundreds. Remember that, both of you."

"Sure," I said. "But shouldn't we be talking about what

just happened? Two of the most powerful and most arrogant Epics in the world are working together. How in Calamity's name did Regalia manage to recruit *Obliteration* of all people?"

"It was easy," Regalia said. "I offered to let him destroy my city."

I jumped, scrambling away from the Epic, who was forming out of water beside the boat. The liquid melded into her shape, taking on her coloring, and she settled with one foot up on the rim of the boat, hands folded in her lap, the other foot still merging with the surface beside the boat.

She had an elegant, matronly look about her—like a kindly grandmother who had dressed up to visit the big city. A city she was apparently planning to destroy. She looked us over, and though I clutched my rifle, I didn't shoot. She was a projection, a creation of water. The real Regalia could have been anywhere.

No, I thought. *Not anywhere.* Projection powers like hers usually had very limited ranges.

Regalia inspected us, her lips downturned. She seemed confused by something.

"What are you up to, Abigail?" Tia demanded.

So you know her too, I thought, glancing at Tia.

"I just told you," Regalia said. "I'm going to destroy the city."

"Why?"

"Because, dear. It's what we *do*." Regalia shook her head. "I'm sorry. I can no longer help myself."

"Oh please," Tia said. "You expect me to believe that you, of all Epics, are out of control? What is your *real* motive? Why have you drawn us here?"

"I said—"

"No games, Abigail," Tia snapped. "I don't have the patience for it tonight. If you're going to spin lies, just leave right now and spare me the headache."

Regalia bowed her head quietly for a moment, then she slowly stood up, moving deliberately, carefully. She perched on the rim of the small boat, and I saw a hint of translucence to her—the water that made up her likeness showing through.

The sea around our boat began to churn and bubble.

"What," Regalia said softly, "do you take me for?"

Tentacles made of water broke the surface around us. Exel cursed, and I spun, flipping my rifle to fully automatic and unloading a spray of bullets into the nearest tendril. It splashed water, but didn't stop moving.

The tentacles of water moved in around us, like the fingers of some enormous beast from below. One seized me by the neck, and another snaked forward and wrapped my wrist in a cold, incongruously solid grip.

The others shouted and scrambled as each of us was snatched in turn. Exel unloaded his handgun at Regalia before being picked up and lifted, like a bearded balloon, in a ropy length of water.

"You think me some minor Epic to be trifled with?" Regalia asked softly. "You mistake me for someone of whom you can make demands?"

I thrashed in my bonds as the entire *boat* was lifted by the tentacles, and the outboard motor's pitch rose to a whine and was then silenced as some kind of kill switch engaged. Spouts of water curled up around us, forming bars, cutting us off from the sky.

"I could snap your necks like twigs," Regalia said. "I could tow this boat down into the deepest depths and imprison it there, so that even your corpses never again see the light. This city belongs to me. The lives of those here are *mine to claim*."

I twisted to look at her. My earlier assessment—that she seemed grandmotherly—now felt laughable. Lengths of water wrapped around her as she loomed over us, her eyes wide, lips curled into a sneer. Her arms were out before her, clawlike hands controlling the water like some crazed puppet master. This was not some kindly matron; this was a High Epic in all her glory.

I didn't doubt for a moment that she could do exactly as she said she could. Heart beating quickly, I glanced at Tia.

Who was perfectly calm.

It was easy to dismiss Tia as one of the less dangerous Reckoners. At that moment, however, she didn't show a hint of fear, despite being wrapped in Regalia's tendril of water. Tia met the High Epic's gaze while gripping something in her hand; it looked like a water bottle with something white inside.

"You think I'm afraid of your little tricks?" Regalia demanded.

"No," Tia said. "But I'm pretty sure you're afraid of Jonathan."

The two stared one another down for a moment. Then suddenly the water tendrils fell, dropping us to the boat, which splashed down into the water. I hit hard, grunting, as water soaked me.

Regalia sighed softly, lowering her arms. "Tell Jonathan that I tire of men and their meaningless lives. I have listened to Obliteration, and I agree with him. I will destroy everyone in Babylon Restored. I do not know . . . how long I can hold back. That is all."

Abruptly she vanished, her figure becoming water that collapsed back to the ocean surface. I found myself huddled between Val and Exel, heart thumping. The sea stilled around our ship.

Tia wiped water from her eyes. "Val, get us to the base. Now."

Valentine scrambled to the back of the boat and started up the motor.

"What's the point of hiding?" I asked softly as we began moving again. "She can look anywhere, be anywhere."

"Regalia is *not* omniscient," Tia said. She seemed as intent on pointing that fact out as Prof had been earlier. "Did you see how confused she was when she appeared here? She thought Jon would be with us, and was surprised that he wasn't."

"Yeah," Exel said, extending his hand and helping me right myself. His bulk took up about three seats' worth of space just in front of me. "We've been able to hide from her for almost two years . . . at least we think."

"Tia," Val said warningly, "things just changed in the city. She saw us. From now on, everything will be different. I'm not certain I trust anything in Babilar anymore."

Exel nodded, looking worried, and I remembered what he'd said earlier. *At any time, she could be watching us. We have to work under that assumption . . . and that fear.* Well, we knew she was watching now.

"She is *not* omniscient," Tia repeated. "She can't see inside buildings, for example, unless there is a pool of water inside for her to peer out of."

"But if we enter a building and don't come out," I said, "that'll be a dead giveaway to her that our base is inside."

The others said nothing. I sighed, settling back. The confrontation with Regalia had obviously left them disturbed. Well, I could understand that. Why did their silence have to extend to me, though?

Val guided the boat toward a building that was missing a large section of outer wall. The structure was one of the enormous office buildings that were common here in Babilar, and so a gap wide enough to drive a bus through made up only a fraction of its wall space. Val guided our boat right in, and Exel took out a long hook and used it to unlatch something on the side of the wall. A large set of black drapes fell over the hole and blocked out the world.

Val and Exel clicked their mobiles on, lighting the half-sunken chamber with a pale white glow. Val guided the boat to the side of the room, near a set of stairs, and I moved to disembark and climb them—eager to be off the boat. Tia took me by the arm, however, and shook her head.

Instead she got out that water bottle she'd held earlier, the one with something white inside. She shook it, then upended it into the water. The others dug similar bottles out of a trunk in the bottom of the boat, then dumped theirs out as well. Mizzy dumped an entire cooler of the stuff into the water.

"Soap?" I asked when I saw the suds.

"Dish soap," Val confirmed. "Changes the surface tension of the water, makes it almost impossible for *her* to control it."

"Also warps her view out," Exel said.

"That's awesome," I said. "Her weakness?"

"Not so far as we know," Mizzy said eagerly. "Just an effect on her powers. It's more like how dumping a lot of water on a fire Epic might make their abilities sputter. But it's reeeaaal useful."

"Useful, but perhaps meaningless," Val said, shaking out the last of her bottle of soap. "In the past we've used this as a precaution only. Tia, she's *seen* us. I'm sure she identified every one of us."

"We'll deal with it," Tia said.

"But—"

"Lights out," Tia said.

Val, Mizzy, and Exel shared a look. Then they clicked off their mobiles, plunging the place into darkness. This seemed another good precaution—if Regalia could look into the room, all she'd see was blackness.

Our boat rocked, and I grabbed Mizzy by the arm, worried. Something seemed to be happening in the room. Water streaming from somewhere? Sparks! Was the building sinking? Worse, had Regalia found us?

It stopped, yet the stillness was, for a second, even more unsettling. Heart thumping, I imagined I was back in that water with the chain on my leg. Sinking toward the depths.

Mizzy pulled on my arm. She was stepping out of the boat, but in the wrong direction. *Into* the water. But—

I heard her foot hit something solid. What? I allowed myself to be led out of the boat, and I stepped on something metal and slick. Had I gotten turned around? No, we were walking on something that had risen out of the water in the room here. A platform?

As we reached a hatch, and I felt my way to a ladder downward, it suddenly struck me. Not a platform.

A submarine.

15

I hesitated, standing in the darkness, holding the ladder leading down into the sub I couldn't yet see.

I hadn't realized that this whole "water" thing was going to be an issue for me. I mean . . . half the world is water, right? And we're all half water to boot. So stepping into the sub should have felt like a sheep falling into a big pile of cotton.

Only it didn't. It felt like a sheep falling into a pile of nails. Wet nails. On the bottom of the ocean.

I wasn't about to let the other Reckoners see me sweat, though. Even if they couldn't see me in the darkness. Hear me sweat? Ew. Anyway, I swallowed and climbed down into the submarine by touch. Exel's heavy footfalls followed last. Something thumped above us, and I assumed he was twisting the hatch closed, sealing it.

It was as black as charcoal at midnight inside. Or, well, as black as a grape at midnight—or pretty much anything at midnight. I felt my way to a seat as the machine started to putter, then sank down quietly.

"Here," Mizzy said, forcing something into my hand. A towel. "Wipe up any water you might have tracked in."

Glad to have something to do, I wiped my seat down, then the floor, which was carpeted. Another towel followed, and I dried myself as best I could. Obviously, hiding from Regalia required making certain that no open surfaces of water were around.

"Okay?" Mizzy asked a few minutes later.

"We're good," Val replied.

Mizzy turned on her mobile, bathing us in light, letting me see the chamber around us. It was lined on both sides with plush orange and blue vinyl benches under windows that had been covered with heavy black cloth. I realized that, unlike what I'd expected, this wasn't a military submarine. It was some kind of sightseeing vehicle, like one that might take people on tours around a reef. The carpet on the floor had obviously been installed later to help keep pools of liquid from forming.

Exel sat at the ready, watching for any puddles we'd missed in the darkness. "Regalia supposedly needs two inches or so to look through," he said to me, "but we prefer not to take chances."

"Does it matter?" I asked. "Can't she just look under the waves and find us?"

"No," Tia said. She'd settled into the last seat in the sub, near what appeared to be a restroom hung with a sign reading, MIZZY'S EXPLOSIVE BUNKER. ENTER AT PEACE. EXIT IN PIECES. The latch was broken, and the door kept swinging open and closed.

"Imagine you're contacting me via your mobile," Tia continued. "My face appears on your screen, and yours appears on mine. Could you instead, if you wanted to, turn your perspective around and look *inside* my mobile?"

"Of course not."

"Why not?"

"Because it doesn't work that way," I said. "The screen faces outward."

"That's how her abilities work," Tia said. "A surface of water exposed to the air is like a screen for her, and she can look out of it. She can't just look the other direction. Under the surface, we're invisible to her."

"We're still in her power," Val pointed out from the driver's seat up ahead. "She raised water to flood all of Manhattan—reaching down to rip apart this submarine would be nothing to her. In the past, we counted on her not knowing we were down here."

"She could have killed us in the boat above," Tia said. "She let us go instead, which means that for now she doesn't want us dead. Now that we're under the surface, she won't know where to look for us. We're free, for the moment."

Everyone seemed to accept this. At the very least, there wasn't much point in arguing. As we sailed—or whatever you did in a submarine—onward, I relocated to a seat just beside Tia.

"You know a lot about her powers," I said softly.

"I'll give you a briefing later," she said.

"Will that briefing include *how* you know all of this?"

"I'll let Jon decide what needs to be shared," she answered, then rose and moved to the front of the vehicle to speak quietly with Val.

I sat back and tried not to think about the fact that we

were underwater. We probably couldn't go very deep—this was a recreational craft—but that didn't bring me much comfort. What happened if something went wrong? If this sub started leaking? If it just stopped moving and sank down to sit on the bottom of the ocean floor here, with us all trapped inside . . .

I shifted uncomfortably, and my pocket crinkled. I grimaced, reaching in and pulling out my mobile. What was left of it at least.

"Wow," Exel said, settling down next to me. "How'd you do *that*?"

"Angered an Epic," I said.

"Give it to Mizzy," he said, nodding toward the girl. "She'll either fix it or get you a new one. Be warned, though: whatever she gives you might come with some . . . modifications."

I raised an eyebrow.

"All *good* and *very useful* additions," Mizzy said. She'd taken the bomb from me and was disarming it in her seat.

"So," I said, turning to Exel, "Mizzy is repairs and equipment—"

"And point," she said.

"—and other things," I continued. "Val is operations and support. I've been trying to place your job in the team. You're not point. What do you do?"

Exel put his feet up on the seat across from him, leaning with his back to the covered window. "Mostly I do the stuff that Val doesn't want to do—such as talking to people."

"I talk to people," Val snapped from the driver's seat ahead.

"You yell at them, dear," Exel said.

"It's a form of talking. Besides, I don't *only* yell."

"Yes, you occasionally grumble." Exel smiled at me. "We've

been a deeply embedded team, Steelslayer. That means lots of observation and interaction with the people in the city."

I nodded. The large man had a disarming way about him, with those rosy cheeks and that thick brown beard. Cheerful, friendly.

"I'll also bury your corpse," he noted to me.

Ooookaaaay . . .

"You'll look good in the coffin," he said. "Nice skeletal structure, lean body. A bit of cotton under the eyelids, some embalming fluid in the veins, and poof—you'll be done. Too bad your skin is so pale, though. You'll show bruises really easily. Nothing a little makeup can't solve, eh?"

"Exel?" Val called from the front.

"Yes, Val?"

"Stop being creepy."

"It's not creepy," he said. "Everyone dies, Val. Ignoring the fact won't make it not true!"

I took the opportunity to scoot a little farther away from Exel. This put me near Mizzy, who was packing away her bomb. "Don't mind him," she said to me as Val and Exel continued to chat. "He was a mortician, back before."

I nodded, but didn't prod. In the Reckoners, the less we knew about one another's family members and the like, the less we could betray if an Epic decided to torture us.

"Thanks for standing up for me," Mizzy said softly. "In front of Tia."

"She's intense sometimes," I said. "Both her and Prof. But they're good people. She can complain all she likes, but in your place I doubt that either of them would have let those people die. You did the right thing."

"Even if it put you in danger?"

"I got out of it, didn't I?"

114

Mizzy glanced at my throat. I felt at it, reminded of the soreness. It hurt when I breathed.

"Yeaaah," she said. "You're just being nice, but I appreciate that. I didn't expect you to be nice."

"Me?" I said.

"Sure!" She seemed to be recovering some of her natural perkiness. "Steelslayer, the guy who talked Phaedrus into hitting Steelheart. I expected you to be all intimidating and brooding and *'They killed my father'* and intense and everything."

"How much do you know about me?" I asked, surprised.

"More than I probably should. We're supposed to be secretive and all that, but I can't help asking questions, you know? And . . . well . . . I might have listened in when Sam told Val about what you guys were planning in Newcago. . . ."

She gave me a kind of apologetic grimace and shrugged.

"Well, trust me," I said. "I'm more intense than I look. I'm intense like a lion is orange."

"So, like . . . medium intense? Since a lion is kind of a tannish color?"

"No, they're orange." I frowned. "Aren't they? I've never actually seen one."

"I think tigers are the orange ones," Mizzy said. "But they're still only half orange, since they have black stripes. Maybe you should be intense like an *orange* is orange."

"Too obvious," I said. "I'm intense like a lion is tannish." Did that work? Didn't exactly slip off the tongue.

Mizzy cocked her head, looking at me. "You're kinda weird."

"No, look, it's just because the metaphor didn't work. I've got it. I'm intense like—"

"No, it's okay," Mizzy said, smiling. "I like it."

"Yeah," Exel said, laughing. "I'll remember that orange thing for your eulogy."

Great. A few hours into the new team, and I'd convinced them that Steelslayer was adorably strange. I settled back into my seat with a sigh.

We traveled for a while, an hour or more. Long enough that I wasn't certain we were still in Babilar. Eventually the sub slowed. A moment later the entire thing lurched, and some kind of clamps locked on from the outside.

Wherever we were going, we had arrived. Exel got to his feet and dug out some towels. He nodded to Val, who climbed up the ladder.

"Kill the lights," she said.

We obligingly put out the lights, and I heard Val undo the hatch up above. Water streamed down, but from the sound of it, Exel quickly mopped it up.

"Out we go," Mizzy whispered to me. I felt my way to the ladder, letting the others each go up before me. I heard them chatting above, so I knew that when Tia came to the ladder, she was last.

"Prof?" I asked her softly.

"The others don't know exactly what happened," she whispered. "I told them that Prof led Obliteration off, but that he was all right and would catch up to us."

"And what really happened?"

She didn't reply in the darkness.

"Tia," I said, "I'm the only other one here who knows about him. You might as well use me as a resource. I can help."

"He doesn't need either of our help right now," she said. "He just needs time."

"What did he do?"

She sighed softly. "He deliberately let himself get hit with a burst of fire, something no ordinary person could have sur-

116

vived. While Obliteration was standing over him gloating, Jon healed himself, leaped up, and snatched off the man's glasses. The tip about Obliteration being nearsighted? Turns out it was a good one."

"Nice," I said.

"Jon said that scared the wits out of the creature," Tia whispered. "Obliteration ported away and didn't return. Jon's safe; everything is okay. So you can stop worrying."

I let her pass. Everything wasn't okay. If Prof was staying away, it was because he was afraid of how he'd act around us. I reluctantly shouldered my pack and gun, then climbed up into a pitch-black room.

"You out, David?" Val's voice sounded in the darkness.

"Yeah," I said.

"Over here."

I followed the sound of her voice. She took me by the arm and steered me through a doorway with some black cloth on it. She followed, then closed a door behind us before opening one in front, letting in light so I could finally see the bolt-hole the Reckoners were using as a base here in Babilar.

Turns out it wasn't a hole at all.

It was a mansion.

16

LUSH red carpets. Dark hardwood. Lounge chairs. A bar with crystal that reflected the light of Val's mobile. Open space. A lot of open space.

My jaw hit the floor. Well, the door, technically. I smacked it as I stepped into the room and turned, trying to stare in all directions at once. The place looked like a king's palace. No . . . no, it looked like an *Epic's* palace.

"How . . ." I stepped into the center of the room. "Are we still underwater?"

"Mostly," Val said. "We're in some rich dude's underground bunker on Long Island. Howard Righton. Built the thing with its own airtight filtration system in case of nuclear fallout." She slung her pack onto the bar. "Unfortunately for him, he anticipated the wrong kind of apocalypse. An Epic knocked his plane out of the sky as he and his family were flying home from Europe."

I looked back toward the short hallway leading to the submarine room. Exel closed its door, locking the hallway in darkness. I had a vague impression that we'd risen up through the floor of the room, which probably had some kind of docking mechanism. But how had the submarine docked *under* a bunker in the ground?

"Storage basement," Exel explained as he waddled past. "Righton's bunker had a big chamber for food storage cut out underneath it. That's flooded now, and we broke open one side, forming a kind of cave we can drive the sub into. Prof cut into it through the floor and installed the docking seal a few years back."

"Jon likes to have safe places in every city he might visit," Tia said, settling on one of the plush couches with her mobile. It would work down here—they worked in the steel catacombs of Newcago, so I was pretty sure they'd work anywhere.

Honestly, I was feeling a little naked without mine. I'd saved for years working in the Factory to buy it. Now that my rifle was gone and the mobile destroyed, I found I didn't really have much from that time of my life.

"So now what?" I asked.

"Now we wait for Jon to finish his reconnaissance," Tia said, "and then we send for someone to pick him up. Missouri, why don't you show David to his quarters." *Which should keep him out of my hair for now,* her tone implied.

I shouldered my pack as Mizzy nodded and bobbed off down a corridor with a flashlight. It suddenly hit me just how tired I was. Even though we'd spent the trip here driving at night, I hadn't completely switched my days and nights. For the last few months it had been a novel thing for me to live in the light, and I'd enjoyed it.

Well, it seemed darkness would become the norm again. I followed Mizzy out of the main sitting room down a corridor lined with artistic photos of colored water being flung into the air. I figured it was supposed to look modern and chic. All it did was remind me that we were on the bottom of the ocean.

"I can't believe how nice this is," I said, peering into a library lined with books, more than I'd ever seen in my life. Small, emergency-style lights glowed on the walls in most of the rooms, so it appeared we had power.

"Yeaaah," Mizzy said. "People out on Long Island had it nice, didn't they? Beaches, big houses. We'd visit when I was a little girl, and I'd play in the sand and think about what it must be like to live in one of those mansions." She trailed her fingers along the wall as she walked. "I took the sub past my old apartment once. That was a hoot."

"Was it tough to see now?"

"Nah. I barely remember the days before Calamity. For most of my life I lived in the Painted Village."

"The what?"

"Neighborhood downtown," she said. "Good place. Not too many gangs. Usually had food."

I followed Mizzy farther down the corridor, and she pointed toward a door in the hallway. "Bathroom. Go in the first door and *always* close it. Then go through the other door. There is no light; you'll have to move by touch. There are facilities and a sink. That's the only running water in the place. Never bring anything out; not even a cup to drink from."

"Regalia?"

Mizzy nodded. "We're outside her range, but even if she almost never moves, we figure it's best to be safe. If she finds this place, after all, we're dead."

I wasn't certain. As Tia had pointed out, Regalia could

have killed us up above, but she hadn't. She seemed to be holding back the darkness, like Prof. "The gangs," I said, joining Mizzy as we kept walking. "Regalia got rid of those?"

"Yeah," Mizzy said. "The only gang left is Newton's, and even she's been pretty relaxed lately, for an Epic."

"So Regalia is good for the city."

"Well, other than flooding it," Mizzy said, "killing tens of thousands in the process. But I suppose by comparison to how terrible she used to be, she's not as bad now. Kind of like the dog chewing on your ankle is pleasant compared to the one that used to be chewing on your head."

"Nice metaphor," I noted.

"Though shockingly bereft of lions," Mizzy said, stepping into another larger room. How big *was* this place? The room we entered was circular and had a piano on one side— I'd never seen one of those except in movies—and some fancy dining tables on the other side. The ceiling was painted black, and . . .

No. That wasn't black. That was water.

I gasped, cringing down as I realized that the ceiling was pure glass, and looked up through the dark waters. Some fish swam by in a little school, and I *swore* I could see something large cruising past. A shadow.

"This guy built a bomb shelter," I said, "with a *skylight*?"

"Six-inch acrylic," Mizzy answered, shading her flashlight, "with a retractable steel plate. And before you ask, no, Regalia can't see through it. First off, as I've pointed out, we're far enough from the city that we should be outside her range. Secondly, she needs a water surface open to the air." She hesitated. "That said, I wish we could get the thing closed. Blasted plate is jammed open up there."

We passed quickly through that awful room and entered

another nice, windowless corridor. A little ways down it, Mizzy pushed open a door and gestured inside toward a large bedroom.

"Do I share with Exel?" I asked, peeking in.

"Share?" Mizzy asked. "This place has *twelve* bedrooms. You can have two, if you want."

I hesitated, regarding the dark wood shelves, the furry red carpet, the bed as large as a really, really big piece of toast. In Newcago having a tiny, single-room flat all to myself had cost most of my life savings. This bedroom was easily four times that size.

I walked in and set my pack down. It looked tiny in the spacious room.

"Flashlight on the counter there," Mizzy said, shining her mobile toward it. "We just got a new shipment of energy cells from your friend in Newcago."

I walked over and prodded at the bed. "People sleep on things this fluffy?"

"Well, there's also the *floor,* if you're so inclined. The light switches don't work, but some of the outlets do—try them to plug in your mobile, and you should be able to find one with juice."

I held up the shattered mobile.

"Oh," she said. "Right. I'll fix up something new for you tomorrow."

I poked at the blankets again. My eyelids drooped like angry drunk men stumbling down a street, looking for an alleyway in which to vomit. I needed sleep. But there were so many things I didn't know.

"Prof had you guys observing here," I said to Mizzy, sitting down on the bed. "For quite a while, right?"

"Yup," Mizzy said, leaning against the doorway.

"Did he say why?"

"I always figured he wanted every bit of information he could get on Regalia," Mizzy said. "For when we decided to hit her."

"Doubtful. Before Steelheart, Prof never hit Epics this important. Besides, Reckoners almost never do long-term observation. They're usually in and out of a city in under two months, leaving a few bodies behind."

"And you know that much about how the other Reckoner cells operate?" She said it laughing, as if that were silly.

"Yeah," I said, truthful. "Pretty much."

"Is that so?"

"I . . . kind of get a little obsessive about things." But *not* in a nerdy way. No matter what Megan says. "I'll tell you about it another time. I think I'm going to turn in."

"Sleep well, then," Mizzy said. She turned and trailed away, her light going with her.

Prof knew, I thought, climbing into the bed. *He didn't hit Regalia because he knew she was trying to be better. He has to wonder . . . if there's a way to make all of this work. To get around the powers ruining the people who use them.*

I yawned, figuring I should probably change out of my clothing. . . .

But sleep took me first.

PART THREE

PART THREE

17

I awoke to darkness.

Groaning, I stirred in the overstuffed bed. It was like swimming through whipped cream. I finally managed to reach the side of the bed and sit up, running a hand through my hair. By reflex I reached for my mobile, feeling around on the bedside stand until I remembered it was broken and I'd given it to Mizzy.

I felt lost for a moment. What time was it? How long had I slept? Living in the understreets, I'd often had to rely on my mobile to tell time. Daylight had been a thing of memories, like grass-filled parks and my mother's voice.

I stumbled out of the bed, kicking aside my jacket—which I'd taken off during the night sometime—and felt my way to the door. The hall outside was lit from one direction, and soft voices echoed distantly. Yawning, I made my way toward the light, eventually approaching the atrium—the place with the piano and the glass ceiling. It glowed with a soft blue illumination coming from above.

Filtered sunlight showed that we were about fifty feet deep. The water was murkier than I'd anticipated—not a crystalline blue, but a darker, more opaque color. Anything could be hiding in that.

I could hear the voices better now. Prof and Tia. I crossed the atrium, pointedly not looking up anymore, and found the two of them in the library.

"She sounded like she was genuinely conflicted, Jon," Tia said as I approached. "She obviously wanted you in Babilar, so you're right on that point. But she could have killed us, yet she didn't. I think she does want you to stop her."

I didn't want to eavesdrop so I peeked into the room. Prof stood by the wall of books, one arm resting on a shelf, and Tia sat at a desk, a notebook computer open beside her and surrounded by books. She held a kind of pouch drink with a straw coming out of it—a way to drink without risking a surface that Regalia could peer through, I realized. Knowing Tia, the pouch was filled with cola.

Prof nodded toward me, so I wandered in. "I think Tia's right," I said. "Regalia is fighting the use of her powers and resisting their corruption."

"Abigail is wily," Prof said. "If you assume you know her motives, you're probably wrong." He tapped his finger on the shelf. "Call Exel back in from his reconnaissance, Tia, and set up the meeting room. It's time for us to discuss a plan."

She nodded, then closed her notebook and slipped out of the room.

"A plan," I said, stepping up to Prof. "You mean for killing Regalia."

He nodded.

"After all this time watching, you're just going to up and murder her?"

"How many people died yesterday when Obliteration attacked, David? Did you hear the count?"

I shook my head.

"Eighty," Prof said. "Eighty people burned to death in a matter of minutes. Because Regalia unleashed that *monster* on the city."

"But she's resisting," I said. "She's fighting off whatever darkness it is that—"

"She's not," Prof snapped, walking past me. "You're mistaken. Go get ready for the meeting."

"But—"

"David," Prof said from the doorway, "ten months ago you came to us with a plea and an argument. You convinced me that Steelheart needed to be brought down. I listened to you, and now I want you to listen to me. Regalia has gone too far. It's time to stop her."

"You were friends, weren't you?" I said.

He turned away from me.

"Don't you think," I said, "it's at least worth *considering* whether we can save her or not?"

"This is about Megan, isn't it?"

"What? No—"

"Don't lie to me, son," Prof interrupted. "In regard to Epics, you're as bloodthirsty as men come. I've seen it in you; it's something we share."

He walked back into the room, stepping up to me. Man, Prof could *loom* when he wanted to. Like a gravestone about to topple on a sprouting flower. He stood like that for a moment, then sighed and reached up, placing his hand on my shoulder.

"You're right, David," Prof said softly. "We were friends.

But do you really think I should stay my hand just because I happen to like Abigail? You think our previous familiarity condones her murders?"

"I . . . No. But if she's under the sway of her powers, this might not be her fault."

"It doesn't work that way, son. Abigail made her choice. She could have stayed clean. She didn't." He met my eyes, and I saw real emotion in there. Not anger. His expression was too soft, his grimace too pained. That was sorrow.

He let go of my shoulder and turned to leave. "Perhaps she really is resisting her powers, as you say. If that's the case, then I suspect that deep down the reason she lured me here is because she's *looking* for someone who can kill her. Someone who can save her from herself. She sent for me so that I could stop her from killing people, and that's what I'm going to do. She won't be the first friend I've had to put down."

Before I could say anything to that, he walked out of the room and I could hear him moving down the hallway. I leaned back against the wall, feeling drained. Conversations with Prof always had a distinct intensity to them.

Eventually I went looking for a way to take a shower. It turned out I had to do it in the darkness, and with cold water. Both were fine. Back in my Factory days, I'd been allowed just one shower every three days. I appreciated anything more than that.

A half hour later, I stepped into the meeting room, a chamber a few doors down from my bedroom. One entire wall was glass and looked out into the water of the sound. Delightful. And everyone sat facing it too. It wasn't that I was frightened; I just didn't like being reminded that we were submerged under all that water. One little leak and we'd all end up drowning in here.

Exel sat in a comfortable-looking easy chair with his

feet up. Mizzy was fiddling with her phone, and Val stood by the doorway, arms crossed. The Hispanic woman looked like she had no intention to sit down and relax. She took life seriously—something I appreciated. We shared a nod as I walked in and settled myself in a chair next to Mizzy.

"How's the city up there?" I asked Exel.

"Lots of funerals," he said. "Attended a really nice one over near the central expanse. Flowers on the water, a beautiful eulogy. Terrible embalming, though I suppose you can't blame them, considering the lack of resources."

"You did reconnaissance at a *funeral*?" I asked.

"Sure," he said. "People like to chat at funerals. It's an emotional time. I caught some of Newton's flunkies watching from a distance."

Mizzy looked up from her mobile. "What did they do?"

"They just watched," Exel said, shaking his head. "Can't figure that group out, honestly. We may need to infiltrate them at some point. . . ."

"I doubt her gangs are recruiting fat dudes in their forties, Exel," Val said from the doorway.

"I'd just pretend to be a chef," Exel said. "Every organization needs both good chefs and good morticians. The two great constants of life. Food and death."

Tia and Prof entered a short time later, Prof carrying an easel under one arm. Tia took a seat in the room's remaining chair while Prof set up the easel and paper just in front of the aquariumlike window. How wonderful. I was going to have to stare at that water the entire time.

"Imager isn't set up yet," Prof said. "So we'll do this the old-fashioned way. Mizzy, you're low man on the team roster. You get scribe duties."

She hopped up from her chair and actually seemed excited by the prospect. She took a marker and wrote *Reckoner Super*

Plan for Killing Regalia at the top of the sheet. Each *i* was dotted with a heart.

Prof watched this with a flat expression, then soldiered onward. "In killing Steelheart, the Reckoners made a promise, one we need to keep. Powerful Epics aren't beyond our reach. Regalia has proven her disrespect for human life, and we are the only law capable of bringing her to justice. It's time to eradicate her."

"I'm worried about this," Exel said, shaking his head. "Regalia has been running a solid PR campaign lately. People in the city don't love her, but they don't hate her either. Are you certain this is what we should be doing, Prof?"

"She spent the last five months sending assassins to try to kill my team in Newcago," Prof said, voice cold. "Sam is dead by her order as well. It's personal, Exel. Good PR or not, she's murdering people right and left in this city. We bring her down. It's not negotiable."

He looked at me when he said it.

Mizzy wrote *Really important, and we totally need to do it* on the paper, with three big arrows pointing at the heading above. Then, after a moment, she added *Boy, it's <u>on</u> now* in smaller letters beside that one.

"All right," Val said from beside the doorway. "So we'll need to find her weakness, which is something we've never been able to do. I doubt soap is going to be enough."

Prof looked to Tia.

"Abigail isn't a High Epic," Tia said.

"What?" Exel said. "Of course she is. I've never met an Epic as powerful as Regalia. She raised the water level of the *entire city* to flood it. She moved millions of tons of water, and holds it all here!"

"I didn't say she wasn't powerful," Tia said. "Only that

132

she isn't a High Epic—which is defined as an Epic whose powers prevent them from being killed in conventional ways."

Mizzy wrote *Regalia totally needs to get with the business* on her sheet.

"What about Regalia's prognosticative abilities?" I asked Tia.

"Overblown," Tia said. "She's barely class F, despite what she'd have people believe. She can rarely interpret what she sees, and it certainly can't elevate her to High Epic status by virtue of its protective nature."

"I've theorized about that in my notes," I said, nodding. "You're sure it's true?"

"Very."

Exel raised his hand. "Um, I'm lost. Anyone else lost? Cuz I'm lost."

Mizzy wrote *Exel needs to pay better attention to his job* on the board.

"Regalia," I explained to him, "has no form of protective powers, not directly. *That's* what makes someone a High Epic. Steelheart's skin was impenetrable; the Clapper warped air around him so anything stabbing or hitting him was teleported to his other side; Firefight reincarnates when killed. Regalia has none of that."

"Abigail is powerful," Prof agreed, "but actually quite fragile. If we can find her, we can kill her."

It was true, and I realized I'd been thinking about Regalia like I had Steelheart. That was wrong. Killing him had been all about his weakness. The "weakness" that would stop Regalia's powers wasn't nearly as important as finding out where she was hiding her physical form.

"This, then," Tia said, taking a sip of her cola, "should probably be the core of our plan. We need to locate Regalia.

I've told you that the functional range on her abilities is just under five miles. We should be able to use that knowledge to pinpoint where she's hiding."

Mizzy obligingly wrote on the board, *Step One: find Regalia, then totally explode her. Lots and lots.*

"I've always wondered," Val said, regarding Tia, "how do you know so much about her powers? From the lorists?"

"Yes," Tia answered, completely straight-faced. Sparks. Tia was a *good* liar.

"You're sure," I said, "that there isn't more?"

Prof glared at me and I stared right back at him. I wasn't going to outright say things he'd told me in confidence, but this hiding things from the team made me uncomfortable. The rest of the team should at least know that Prof and Regalia had a history together.

"Well," Tia said, reluctantly. "You should all probably know that Jon and I knew Regalia during the years just after she became an Epic. This was before the Reckoners."

"What?" Val said, stalking forward. "You didn't tell me?"

"It wasn't relevant," Tia replied.

"Not relevant?" Val demanded. "Sam is *dead,* Tia!"

"We've passed on to you things we've thought you could use against her."

"But—" Val began.

"Stand down, Valentine," Prof said. "We have kept secrets from you. We will continue to do so if we think it's for the best."

Val fumed but crossed her arms, now standing beside my chair. She didn't say anything, though Mizzy wrote on the board, *Step Two: put Val on decaf.* I wasn't certain what that meant.

Val took a deep breath, but she finally sat down.

Mizzy kept writing. *Step Three: Mizzy gets a cookie*.

"Can I have a cookie too?" Exel asked.

"No," Prof snapped. "This meeting is going nowhere. Mizzy, write down . . ." He trailed off, looking at her sheet for the first time since we'd started, and realizing she'd already filled the entire thing up with her comments.

Mizzy blushed.

"Why don't you sit down?" Prof said to her. "We probably don't need that anyway."

Mizzy scurried to a seat, head down.

"Our plan," Prof said, "needs to be about locating Regalia's base of operations, then sneaking in to kill her, preferably when she's asleep and can't fight back."

My stomach lurched at that. Shooting someone in the head while they're sleeping? Didn't seem very heroic. But I didn't say anything, and neither did anyone else. At our core we were assassins, and that was that. Was killing them in their sleep really any different from luring them into a trap and killing them there?

"Suggestions?" Prof said.

"You sure that finding her base will work?" I asked. "Steelheart moved around a lot, sleeping in different places each night. I know a lot of Epics who maintain many different residences precisely to stop something like this from happening."

"Regalia isn't Steelheart," Prof said. "She isn't anywhere near as paranoid as he was—and she *likes* her comforts. She'll have picked one place and bunkered down in it, and I doubt she moves from it often."

"She's getting old," Tia agreed. "When we knew her before, she could spend days at a time in the same chair, receiving visitors. I agree with Jon's interpretation. Abigail would rather have one base, protected very well, than a dozen lesser hideouts. She'll definitely have a backup, but won't use it unless she knows her primary base is compromised."

"I've considered this before," Exel said, thoughtful. "A five-mile radius means she could be almost anywhere in Babilar and still have influence here. Her base could be over in old New Jersey, even."

"Yes," Tia said, "but each time she appears, she narrows that down for us. Since she can only make projections five miles away from wherever her base is, each time she does appear, we learn more about where she might be."

I nodded slowly. "Like a catapult that shoots enormous grapes."

Everyone looked at me.

"No, listen," I said. "If you had a grape catapult, and it was good at lobbing grapes, but sometimes lobbed them different distances, you could leave it firing over a long period of time. And maybe put it on some sort of spinner. Then, when you came back, even if someone had stolen the catapult you'd be able to tell where it was located—by the pattern of grapes it launched. It's the same here. Only Regalia's projections are the grapes, and her base is the catapult!"

"That . . . almost makes sense," Exel said.

"Can I be the one firing the catapult?" Mizzy asked. "Sounds like fun."

"Colorful description notwithstanding," Tia said, "this will work if we can get enough data points. And we won't need nearly as many of . . . uh . . . the grapes David mentions. Here's what we do: We pick predetermined locations and set up situations we're sure will provoke Regalia to appear via one of her projections. If she does appear in that location, we get a data point. If she doesn't, that might be outside her range. Do this enough times, and I'm sure I'll be able to pinpoint her location."

I nodded, understanding. "We need to go make some noise in the city, and see if we can make Regalia come out and interact with us."

"Exactly," Tia said.

"What about the range on her other powers?" I asked. "If she's raised the water around the city, can't we use the limit of those abilities to pinpoint her?"

Tia looked toward Prof.

"Her water manipulation powers come in two flavors," he said. "The little tendrils, like you've seen, and the large-scale 'shoving' of massive amounts of liquid. The small tendrils can only go out as far as she can see, so yes, spotting her using those will work for our plan. Her large-scale powers don't tell us much—they're more like the movement of tides. She can raise up water in a vast area, and can do it on a massive scale. This ability takes less precision—and she can do it from a lot farther away. So there's no telling from the shape of water in Babilar where exactly she might be hiding."

"That said," Tia added, "we're fairly certain Abigail doesn't know we discovered the range limit on her small-scale powers, so we have an edge. We *can* use them to find her. The trick is going to be coming up with ways to draw her attention—events so compelling that she'll either come confront us, or we'll be reasonably certain from her absence that she wasn't able to."

"Surefire ways to draw her attention?" I said.

"Yes," Tia replied. "Preferably done in a way that doesn't make it obvious we're trying to get her attention."

"Well, that's easy," I said. "We hit Epics."

The others looked toward me.

"Look, we're going to have to kill Obliteration eventually anyway," I said. "Regalia's using him as some kind of gun to our heads, a threat to the entire city. If we remove him, we remove one of her primary tools—and so a hit on him is really likely to draw her out to try to stop us. If we succeed, we've hindered Regalia, stopped the killing, *and* gained a point of data that we can use to further pinpoint her base. Plus, we avoid looking suspicious, since we're doing what the Reckoners always do."

"He has a point, Jon," Tia said.

"Perhaps," Prof said. "But we don't know where Obliteration will strike—we'll have to be reactive, which makes it difficult to lay a trap for him. It also makes it harder to pick a location that would give us information about Regalia, if she appears."

"We could try Newton instead," Exel offered. "She and her flunkies tend to do patrols around the city, and those are reasonably predictable. Newton's kind of become Regalia's right-hand woman. If she's put in danger, Regalia will show up for certain."

"Except," Val said, "Newton really isn't a threat these days. Her gangs are in check—they might bully a little, but they haven't been killing people. I agree with Steelslayer; Obliteration is a *serious* issue. I don't want to see Babilar go the way of Houston."

Prof considered for a moment, turning to look out through the shimmering blue water. "Val, does your team have operational plans for bringing down Newton?"

"Yes, but . . ."

"But?"

"That plan depended on having Sam and the spyril."

"The spyril?" I asked.

"Broken now," Val said. "Useless."

From her tone, I sensed it was a touchy subject.

"Work with Tia and David," Prof said to her. "Revise your plans and present me with several scenarios for bringing down

Newton, then devise another set for bringing down Obliteration. We'll move forward with David's plan, and use hits on those two to draw Regalia out. Also give me a list of places where your team has *confirmed* seeing Regalia's projections."

"Sure," Val said. "But there aren't many of that last one. We've only seen her once or twice, other than what she did last night."

"Even two points will give us a baseline to work from in locating her," Tia said. "Exel, do some reconnaissance in the city and gather every rumor about Regalia appearing or using her powers in an obvious way. Some might not be reliable, but we might be able to use it to build a map to work from."

"I was going to see some people in two days who might know something about this," Exel said. "We can start there."

"Very well," Prof said. "Get on it. Team dismissed. All but *you*." He pointed right at me.

Tia remained in her seat as the others left, and I found myself sweating. I shoved that down and forced myself to stand up and walk to Prof, who sat beside the big window filled with endless blue water.

"You need to take care, son," Prof said quietly. "You know things others don't. That is a trust I've given you."

"I—"

"And don't think I didn't notice you trying to deflect the conversation today away from killing Regalia and toward killing Obliteration."

"Do you deny it's better to hit him first?"

"No. I didn't contradict you because you're right. It makes sense to hit Obliteration—and perhaps Newton—first to remove some of Regalia's resources and help box her in. But I remind you not to forget that she is our primary target."

"Yes sir," I said.

"Dismissed."

I walked from the room, annoyed that I was singled out so specifically for that treatment. I made my way down the hall, and for some reason I couldn't help thinking of Sourcefield. Not the powerful Epic, but the regular person deprived of her powers, looking at me with dawning horror and utter confusion.

I'd never had a problem killing Epics. I still wouldn't have a problem doing it, when the time came. That didn't prevent me from imagining Megan's face instead of Sourcefield's as I pulled the trigger.

Once, I'd absolutely hated Epics. I realized I couldn't feel that way any longer. Not now that I'd known Prof, Megan, and Edmund. Perhaps that was why I rebelled against killing Regalia. It seemed to me she was trying to fight her Epic nature. And maybe that meant we could save her.

All of these questions led me toward dangerous speculation. What would happen if we captured an Epic here, like we'd done with Edmund back in Newcago? What if we tied up someone like Newton or Obliteration, then used their weakness to perpetually negate their powers? How long without using their abilities would it take for them to start acting like a regular person?

If Newton or Obliteration weren't under the influence of their powers, would they help us like Edmund had? And would that not, in turn, prove that we could do the same for Regalia herself? And after her, Megan?

As I reached my room, I found myself mulling over the idea, liking it more and more.

18

EVENING was just arriving as Mizzy, Exel, and I climbed from the sub into the dark, water-filled building. We moved by touch to the Reckoners' little boat. Once settled, Mizzy clicked a button on her mobile, and the sub silently slipped back into the depths.

I wasn't certain how effective this was at hiding from Regalia. Hopefully our precautions would at least keep her from finding the exact location of our base, even if she figured out about the sub itself. We took oars, turned on the lights of our mobiles, and set out down a flooded street.

It was evening—two days since the meeting where we'd settled on a plan for killing Regalia—and by the time we reached populated rooftops the sun had begun to set. We climbed out of the boat, and Exel tossed a water bottle to an old man who was watching over several boats tied here. Pure water was somewhat difficult to come by in the city; it needed to be fetched from streams across in Jersey. A bottle of it wasn't worth much, but enough to act as a basic kind of currency for small services.

The others set out across the rooftop, but I lingered, watching the sun set. I'd spent most of my life trapped in the gloom of Steelheart's reign. Why did the people of Babilar only come out at night? These people could know the light intimately, but they instead *opted* for the darkness. Didn't they know how lucky they were?

The sun sank down like a giant golden pat of butter melting onto the corn of New Jersey. Or . . . wait. That abandoned city was kind of more like spinach than corn. So the sun sank down into the spinach of Jersey.

And Babilar came alive.

Graffiti lit with vibrant, electric colors. A mosaic, unnoticed in the sunlight, burst outward at my feet: a depiction of the moon with someone's name signed in big, fat white letters at the bottom. I had to admit there was something organically magnificent about it. There hadn't been graffiti in Newcago, where it had been a sign of rebellion—and rebellion had been punishable by death. Of course in Newcago, picking your nose could have been construed as a sign of rebellion too.

I hurried off after Mizzy and Exel, feeling naked without my rifle—though I carried Megan's handgun in my pocket and wore my Reckoner shield, which really just meant Prof had gifted me with some of his forcefield energy. I wasn't sure why Mizzy and Exel had asked for me to join this reconnaissance mission. I didn't mind—anything to get out into the open air—but wouldn't Val have been better suited to meeting with informants and interpreting their intel?

We walked for a short while, crossing bridges and passing

groups of people who carried baskets of glowing fruit. They nodded affably to us, which was creepy. Weren't people supposed to walk with their eyes down, worried that anyone they passed might be an Epic?

I knew there was something profoundly wrong with those thoughts inside my head. I'd spent months in Newcago after Steelheart's fall trying to help build a city where people *wouldn't* be afraid all the time. Now I worried when these people acted open and friendly?

I couldn't help how I felt, though, and my instinct was that something was wrong with people around here. We crossed a low rooftop, passing Babilarans who lounged with their feet in the water. Others idled, lying on their backs, eating glowing fruit as if they didn't have a care in the world. Hadn't these people heard what Obliteration had done uptown just the other day?

I glanced down as we crossed onto another rope bridge, unnerved as a group of youths swam beneath us, laughing. The people of this city didn't need to display the beaten-down attitudes that had been common in Newcago, but a healthy dose of paranoia never hurt anyone. Right?

Mizzy noticed me looking at the splashing swimmers. "What?" she asked.

"They seem so . . ."

"Carefree?" she asked.

"Idiotic."

Mizzy grinned. "Babilar does tend to inspire a relaxed attitude."

"It's the way of life," Exel agreed from just ahead, where he led us toward the informants. "More specifically, it's the religion—if you want to call it that—of Dawnslight."

"Dawnslight," I said. "That's an Epic, right?"

"Maybe," Exel said with a shrug. "Everyone attributes the

food and the light to 'Dawnslight.' There's considerable dis-agreement over who, or what, that is."

"An Epic, obviously," I said, glancing toward a nearby building lit with glowing fruit inside the broken windows. I had nothing in my notes about such an Epic, however. It was disconcerting to know that I'd somehow missed such a power-ful one.

"Well, either way," Exel continued, "a lot of people here have learned to just let go. What good does it do to stress all the time about the Epics? You can't do anything about them. A lot of people figure it's just better to enjoy their lives and accept that the Epics might kill them tomorrow."

"That's stupid," I said.

Exel looked back, raising an eyebrow.

"If you accept the Epics," I said, "they've won. That's what went wrong; that's why nobody fights back."

"Sure, I guess. But there's no harm in relaxing a little, you know?"

"There's *all kinds* of harm in it. Relaxed people don't get anything done."

Exel shrugged. Sparks! He almost talked like he believed all that nonsense. I let the matter drop, though my unease didn't lessen. It wasn't just the people we passed, with their friendly smiles. It was about being so exposed, so in the open. With all these rooftops and broken windows around, a sniper could take me down with ease. I'd be glad when we reached the informants. Those types liked closed doors and hidden rooms.

"So," I said to Mizzy as we turned at another roof and stepped onto another bridge. Children sat along one side, kicking in unison and giggling as they made the bridge swing slowly side to side. "Val mentioned something at our meeting the other day. The . . . spyril?"

"It was Sam's," Mizzy said softly. "Special equipment we bought from the Knighthawk Foundry."

"It was a weapon, then?"

"Well, kind of," Mizzy said. "It was Epic-derived, built to mimic their powers. The spyril manipulated water; Sam would shoot it out beneath him, boosting him into the air, letting him move around the city easily."

"A water jet pack . . . ?"

"Yeah, kind of like that."

"A water *jet pack*. And nobody's using it right now?" I was stunned. "So . . . you know . . . I could maybe . . ."

"It's broken," Mizzy said before I could finish. "When we recovered Sam—" She had to stop for a moment. "Anyway, when we got him back, the spyril was missing its motivator."

"Which is . . . ?"

She looked at me as we walked on the bridge; she seemed dumbfounded. "The motivator? You know? It makes technology based on Epic powers work."

I shrugged. Technology based off Epics was new to me since I'd joined the Reckoners. Despite things like my shield and the harmsway—which were fake—we *did* have technology that didn't come from Prof's powers. Supposedly these had originally been crafted using genetic material taken from the corpses of Epics. When we killed them we would often harvest cells and use it as high-level currency for trading with arms dealers.

"So stick another motivator thingy in," I said.

"It doesn't work that way," Mizzy said, laughing. "You really don't know any of this?"

"Mizzy," Exel said from the bridge ahead of us, "David is a point man. He spends his time shooting Epics, not fixing things in the shop. Which is why we have people like you."

"Riiiight," Mizzy said, rolling her eyes at him. "Thank

you. Great lecture. Thumbs-up. David, motivators come from research into Epics, and each one is coded to the individual device." She sounded excited as she talked—this was obviously something she'd read a lot about. "We've asked Knighthawk for a replacement, but it could take quite a bit of time."

"Fine," I said. "As long as when we do fix the thing, *I* get to try it first."

Exel laughed. "Are you sure you want to do that, David? Using the spyril would involve lots of swimming."

"I can swim."

He looked back at me and raised an eyebrow. "Care to discuss the way you regarded the water on our trip into the city? You looked like you thought it would bite you."

"I think guns are dangerous too," I said, "but I'm carrying one right now."

"If you say so," he said, turning back around and leading the way onward.

I followed, sullen. How had he figured out about me and water? Was it that obvious to everyone? *I* hadn't even known about it until I'd gotten to this flooded city.

I remembered that sinking feeling . . . the water closing around me . . . the darkness and the sheer panic of water flooding inside my nose and mouth. And . . .

I shivered. Besides, didn't sharks live in water like this? Why weren't those swimmers afraid?

They're crazy people, I reminded myself. *They aren't afraid of Epics either.* Well, I wasn't about to get eaten by a shark, but I did need to learn to swim. I'd have to do something about the sharks. Spikes on my feet, maybe?

We eventually stopped at the lower end of a bridge that stretched high into the sky toward a glowing rooftop above. "We're here," Exel noted, then started the steep climb.

I followed, curious. Were we going to find the informants

hiding inside the jungles of that building, perhaps? As we climbed upward, I picked out an odd sound coming from above. Was that music?

Indeed it was. It enveloped me as we drew closer—the sound of drums and fiddles. Neon forms moved this way and that wearing spraypainted clothing, and beneath the music came the sounds of people talking.

I stopped on the bridge, causing Mizzy to pause just ahead of me.

"What is that?" I asked.

"A party," she said.

"And our informants are there?"

"Informants? What are you talking about?"

"The people Exel is coming to meet. To purchase information."

"Purchase . . . David—Exel, you, and I are going to mingle and chat with people at the party to see what we can find out."

Oh.

"Are you all right?" she asked.

"Yeah, sure, of course I am." I continued forward, pushing past her up the bridge toward the roof.

A party. What was *I* going to do at a party?

I had a feeling I'd have been much better off in the water with the sharks.

19

I stood at the edge of the expansive rooftop, concentrating on breathing in and out, wrestling with a mild panic as Mizzy and Exel entered the party.

People wearing glowing, painted clothing moved about in a frenetic mix; some danced while others feasted on the variety of fruits that had been heaped upon tables along the perimeter. Music crashed across us all—overwhelming sounds of drums and fiddles.

It felt like a riot. A rhythmic, and well-catered, riot. And most of the people here were my age.

I'd known other teenagers, of course. There had been many at the Factory in Newcago where I'd worked and lived since I was nine. But the Factory hadn't thrown parties, unless you counted the movie nights where we'd watched old films, and I hadn't interacted much with the others. My free time had been dedicated to my notes on Epics and my plans to bring down Steelheart. I hadn't been a nerd, mind you. I'd just been the type of guy who spent a lot of time by himself, focused entirely on a single consuming interest.

"Come on!" Mizzy said, appearing from the party like a seed spat from the mouth of a glowing jack-o'-lantern. She grabbed my hand and towed me into the chaos.

The tempest of light and sound enveloped me. Weren't parties about talking to people? I could barely hear myself in the middle of this thing, with all of the noise and the music. I followed Mizzy as she brought me to one of the food tables, which was surrounded by a small group of Babilarans in painted clothing.

I found my hand in my jacket pocket, gripping Megan's handgun. Being in this press of bodies was even worse than being exposed. With so many people around, I couldn't keep an eye on them all to watch for guns or knives.

Mizzy positioned me in front of the table, butting into a conversation among a group of older teenagers. "This," she declared, raising her hands to the side to present me like a new washer and dryer, "is my friend David Charleston. He's from out of town."

"Really!" said one of the people at the table, a tall guy with blue hair. "I'd never have been able to tell that from his boring clothing and goofy face."

I hated him immediately.

Mizzy punched the guy in the shoulder, grinning. "This is Calaka," she said to me, then pointed at the other three at the table—girl, boy, girl—in turn. "Infinity, Marco, and Lulu." She practically had to shout to make herself heard over the noise.

"So where *are* you from, new guy?" Calaka asked, taking

a drink of glowing fruit juice. That did *not* look safe. "Some-place small, I'd guess, considering your wide eyes and over-whelmed expression."

"Yeah," I said. "Small."

"Your clothes *are* dull," said one of the girls, Infinity. Blonde and perky, she grabbed a can of something from under the table and shook it. Spraypaint. "Here, we can fix that."

I jumped back and threw my left hand out while firming my other hand's grip on the gun in my pocket. Everyone else in this crazy city could go around glowing as much as they wanted, but I wasn't *about* to make myself an easier target in the night.

The four flinched away from me, eyes widening. Mizzy took me by the arm. "It's okay, David. They're friends. Relax."

There was that word again. *Relax.*

"I just don't want any spraypaint on me," I said, trying to settle myself.

"Your friend is weird, Mizzy," Marco noted. He was a short guy with light brown hair so curly it looked like he'd stapled moss to his head. He leaned on the table in an easy-going posture, turning his cup with two fingers.

"I like him," Lulu said, eyeing me. "Quiet type. Tall, deep, sultry."

Deep?

Wait . . . sultry?

I focused on her. Curvaceous, dark skin, lustrous black hair that caught the light. Going to parties was partially about meeting girls, right? If I made a good impression, I might be able to ask her for information about Dawnslight or Regalia.

"Sooooo," Mizzy said, slumping against the table and stealing Marco's drink. "Anyone seen Steve around?"

"I don't think he's here," Calaka said. "At least, I haven't heard the sounds of anyone being slapped nearby."

"I think he was there," Infinity said, her tone becoming mellow. "The other day. Uptown."

"Bad business, that," Marco said.

The others nodded.

"Well," Calaka said. "Suppose we'd better raise a cup for old Steve, then. Creep though he was, if the Epics finally got 'im, he deserves a proper sendoff."

Marco reached to take his drink back, but Mizzy ducked to the side, clinking it against Calaka's and then drinking. Infinity and Lulu raised their cups as well.

They bowed their heads while Marco grabbed some glowing grapes off a plate on the food table and wandered back. I bowed my head as well. I didn't know this Steve guy, but he'd fallen to an Epic. That made him kindred, to an extent.

Marco began tossing the grapes to various members of the group. I caught one. Grapes, the nonglowing kind, had been a rare treat back in Newcago. We hadn't starved at the Factory, but much of the food had been stuff that stored well. Fruit was for the rich.

I popped it in my mouth. It tasted *fantastic*.

"Good music tonight," Marco noted, eating a grape.

"Edso's been getting better," Infinity agreed, grinning. "I think the heckling made a difference."

"Wait," I interrupted. "Aren't you worried about Obliteration? After what he did to your friend? You're just going to drink and move on?"

"What should we do?" Marco said. "Gotta keep living."

"Epics might come," Calaka agreed. "Could take you today, could take you tomorrow. But so might a heart attack. No reason not to party today, while you can."

"There were some shots fired at that one last night," Mizzy said, speaking carefully. "Some people fighting back."

"Idiots," Calaka said. "Making things worse."

"Yeah," Infinity said. "Half the dead would still be alive if we just let the Epics do what they want. They always get bored and move on eventually."

The others nodded, Marco cursing under his breath about the "sparking Reckoners."

I blinked. Was this some kind of bad joke? But no, there was no mirth here—though I did notice Mizzy relaxing visibly. It appeared that although we'd fought back, she hadn't been recognized. I wasn't surprised; in the chaos of Obliteration's destruction, news of what exactly had happened—and who had been involved—hadn't likely been reliable in the city.

The group moved on to a further discussion of the music, and I just stood there feeling awkward and depressed. No wonder the Epics were winning, with attitudes like this.

At least they're enjoying themselves, a piece of my mind noted. *Maybe there's nothing they can do. Why judge them so harshly?*

It just felt that with some of us trying so hard, everyone should at least acknowledge the work we were putting in. We fought for the freedom of people like these. We were their heroes.

Weren't we?

As the conversation progressed, Lulu sidled up to me, a cup of glowing blue juice in her hand. "This is boring," she said, stretching up and leaning in close to speak into my ear. "Let's dance, handsome."

Handsome?

I hadn't even managed a reply before Lulu was giving her cup to Marco and towing me away from the table. Mizzy gave me a little wave, but otherwise completely abandoned me as I was pulled through the crowd. To the dancing.

I guess that's what you'd call it. It looked like everyone

had insects in their shirts and were trying really hard to get them out. I'd seen dancing in movies, and it had seemed a lot more . . . coordinated than this.

Lulu dragged me into the center of it all, and I wasn't about to admit I'd never danced before. So I started moving, trying my best to blend in by imitating what everyone else was doing. Though I felt like a cupcake on a steak plate, the other dancers were so absorbed in what they were doing, maybe they wouldn't notice me.

"Hey!" Lulu shouted. "You're good!"

I was?

She was better, always moving, seeming to anticipate the music and flowing with it. In the middle of a move, she threw herself my direction, wrapping her arms around me and pulling herself in close. It was unexpected, but not unpleasant.

Was I supposed to move with her, somehow? Having her that close was rather distracting. She barely knew me. *Is she an assassin, maybe?* a piece of me wondered.

No. She was just a normal person. And she seemed to like me, which was baffling. My only real experience with girls had been with Megan; how was I supposed to react to a girl who *didn't* immediately seem like she wanted to shoot me?

A little part of me figured I should ask about Dawnslight and Regalia—but that would be too obvious, right? I decided it was best to act natural for now, then try to get her to open up to me later.

So I just danced. Lulu had called me the quiet type. I could manage that, right? We continued for a while—long enough for sweat to start dripping down my brow as I tried to figure out the right way to dance. There didn't seem to be any form to it; Lulu alternated between gyrating around and pressing against me very close so we could move together. Several songs came and went, each different yet somehow the same.

Everyone else seemed to be having a great deal of fun. For me, it was stressful. I wanted to do it right and not give away that I'd never done this before. Lulu *was* attractive: warm face, great hair, curvaceous in all the right places. She wasn't Megan, not by a long shot, but she was here. And close. Should I talk to her? Tell her she was pretty?

I opened my mouth to say something, but the comment died on my lips. I found, in that moment, that I *really* didn't want to talk to another girl. It was stupid—Megan was an Epic. The entire time she'd been with the Reckoners, she'd probably been acting. Stringing us all along. I didn't even really know her.

But there was still a chance she'd been genuine, right?

I doubted Lulu carried grenades in her bra, ample though it was. She wouldn't know guns like Megan had. Lulu wasn't tough enough to bring down Epics, and that smile of hers was way too inviting. Megan had been tough to crack, tough to make smile. That, in turn, made it all worthwhile when she *did* smile.

Stop it, I thought at myself. *Prof is right. You need to get Megan out of your head. Enjoy what you have right now.*

A guy nearby suddenly grabbed Lulu by the arm and whipped her in his direction. She laughed as the crowd churned to the demanding music. Just like that, she was gone.

I stopped in place. Searching through the throng of half-glowing figures, I finally found Lulu again. She was dancing with someone else. Sparks. Did she expect me to follow? Was this a test of some sort? Or was it a rejection? Why didn't school at the Factory involve important lessons, like how to deal with a party?

As I stood there, feeling stupid to be alone amid the dancing, I spotted something else. A face I thought I recognized. An Asian woman, punk clothing, like from the old days. And . . .

It was Newton. Leader of the gangs of Babilar. Epic. She stood to the side of the dance floor, next to a table heaped with fruit that lit her face.

Oh, thank you, I thought, feeling an overwhelming sense of relief. Dancing was stressful—but murderous demigods, those I could deal with.

Hand in my pocket on the gun, I moved through the crowd to get a better look.

20

I quickly dredged from my memory everything I knew about Newton. *Force redirection,* I thought. *That's her main power.* Slap Newton, and none of the energy would transfer to her—it would all reflect back at you. She could also move inhumanly fast. I'd had some things in my notes about her background and family, but I couldn't remember them. I briefly considered calling Tia, but with the music blaring I wasn't sure if she'd be able to hear me—or me her.

Newton began walking around the perimeter of the dancing area, moving with an unhurried gait. No super speed for the moment. I kept pace, pushing through the press of bodies and reaching a place where the crowd was less dense.

Newton walked like someone who knew she had the biggest gun in the room—confident, unconcerned. She didn't

wear a single bit of spraypaint on her otherwise garish clothing: leather jacket, enormous cross-shaped earrings, piercings
in her nose and lip. Short purple hair. She looked like she was
about eighteen, but I thought I remembered something about
her age being deceptive.

She could kill everyone at this party, I thought with a chill.
*No consequences. Nobody would even question her. She's an
Epic. It's her right.*

What was she doing here? Why was she just walking and
watching? Of course, I didn't *mind* that she wasn't engaging
in wholesale slaughter—but she had to have some kind of
agenda. I pulled out my new mobile, the one Mizzy had given
me. I thought she'd said . . .

Yes, she'd loaded it with photos of all known members of
Newton's gang. A few of those were minor Epics, and I wanted
to be prepared. I shuffled through the photos quickly while
keeping one eye on Newton. Was any of the rest of her team
here?

I didn't spot any of them. Did that make her more or less
likely to be up to something? I moved to get closer, but a hand
caught me by the shoulder.

"David?" Mizzy asked. "Sparks, what are you doing?"

I lowered my mobile and turned, twisting Mizzy away
in case Newton glanced in our direction. "Epic," I said. "Just
ahead."

"Yeah, that's Newton," Mizzy said. "Why are you following her? Do you have a death wish?"

"Why's she here?" I asked, leaning down to hear Mizzy.

"It's a party."

"I know it is. But why is *she* here?"

"Uhhhh. For the party."

I paused. Epics went to *parties*?

I knew, logically, that sometimes Epics interacted with

157

their lessers. In Newcago, Steelheart's favored had served, worked for, and even—in the case of the attractive ones—dated Epics. I just hadn't expected someone like Newton to be . . . hanging out. Epics were monsters. Killing machines.

No, I thought, watching Newton as she moved to the drink counter—where she was immediately served. *Creatures like Obliteration are killing machines. Other Epics are different.* Steelheart had wanted a city to rule, with subjects to worship him. Nightwielder had gone to meet with arms dealers, bringing assistants with him. Many Epics behaved like ordinary people, save for their absolute lack of morals.

Those types killed not because they enjoyed it, but because they got annoyed. Or, like Deathpoint—the Epic who had attacked the bank the day my father died—they killed because they figured it was just plain easier than the alternatives.

Newton got her drink, then leaned back against the bar, watching the crowd. Her gaze passed by Mizzy and me, not lingering. Either Regalia hadn't described us to Newton, or she didn't care that the Reckoners were at the party.

The Babilarans made way for her and averted their eyes when she looked in their direction. They didn't bow or give any obvious signs of subservience, but they clearly knew who she was. This was a lion among the gazelles; the lion just wasn't hungry right now.

"Come on," Mizzy said, steering me back toward the dancing.

"What do you know about her?" I asked. "Her background, I mean. Who she was before Calamity." Fortunately, the current song was a little less overbearing than the previous ones, with a slower beat and not as much noise.

"Yunmi Park," Mizzy said. "That's her real name. Long

ago, before all this happened, she was your run-of-the-mill black sheep. A juvenile delinquent born to successful parents who didn't know what to do about her."

"So she was evil even then?" I asked.

Mizzy started dancing—not as frantically or as, um, *invitingly* as Lulu had. Just some simple motions. The dancing was probably a good idea, as we didn't want to stand out. I followed suit.

"Yeaaaah," Mizzy said. "*Definitely* evil. She'd committed murder, so when Calamity arrived, she was already in juvie. Then *bam*. Super powers. Must have sucked to be the guards at that detention center that day, I tell you. But why does it matter what she was like?"

"I want to know what percentage of Epics were evil before they got their powers," I said. "I'm also trying to tie their weaknesses to events in their past."

"Hasn't anyone tried that before?"

"A lot of people have," I said. "But most of them didn't have the level of research I've been able to gather, or the access to Epics that being in the Reckoners has given me. The connection, if there is one, isn't obvious—but I think it's there. I just have to find the right slant on it. . . ."

We danced for a few minutes. I could handle this dance. Less flailing was involved.

"What was it like?" Mizzy asked. "Killing Steelheart."

"Well, we set up in Soldier Field," I said. "We hadn't quite figured out his weakness yet, but we had to try anyway. So we made a perimeter, and—"

"No," Mizzy said. "What did it *feel* like to kill him? You know, inside of you. What was it like?"

"Is this pertinent to our current job somehow?" I asked, frowning.

Mizzy blushed and turned away. "Whoops. Personal information. Gotcha."

I hadn't intended to embarrass her; I'd just assumed I was missing something. I'd been too focused on the job at hand rather than on things like small talk and interpersonal interaction.

"It was awesome," I said softly.

Mizzy glanced back at me.

"I'd always heard that revenge doesn't pay off," I continued. "That when you finally got what you'd been hunting, you'd find the experience unsatisfying and depressing. That's a sparking load of *stupidity*. Killing that monster felt *great*, Mizzy. I avenged my father and liberated Newcago. I've never felt so good."

Mizzy nodded.

Now, what I didn't say was that killing Steelheart *had* left me wondering what to do next. The sudden and abrupt removal of my all-consuming goal . . . well, it was like I was a donut, and somebody had sucked all the jelly out of me. But I could stuff new jelly in there. It would just get my hands a little sticky in the process.

I'd moved on to killing other Epics, like Mitosis and Sourcefield. Which had its own problems. I'd interacted with Epics, even fallen for one. I couldn't see them uniformly as monsters any longer.

That look in Sourcefield's eyes as I shot her still haunted me. She'd looked so normal, so frightened.

"You take this all really seriously, don't you?" Mizzy asked.

"Don't we all?"

"Yeaaaah, you're a little different." She smiled. "I like it, though. You're what a Reckoner should be."

Unlike me, that line seemed to imply.

"I'm glad you have a life, Mizzy," I said. I gestured toward the party. "I'm glad you have friends. You don't want to be like me. Parties, real life . . . these are *why* we're fighting, in a way. To bring that world back."

"Even though Babilar is fake, like you think?" Mizzy said. "That this city, and everything in it, is a front for some plan Regalia is concocting?"

"Even then," I said.

Mizzy smiled, still shifting back and forth to the beat. She *was* cute. Not like Lulu at all, who was demandingly attractive. Mizzy was just . . . nice to be around. Earnest, amusing. *Real*.

I'd stayed away from people like her my entire life. I hadn't wanted attachments, or so I'd told myself. Really, I'd been so focused that I'd kind of weirded everyone out. But Mizzy . . . she considered me a hero.

I could grow to enjoy this sort of thing. I wasn't interested in Mizzy—not *that* way, and particularly not with Megan on my mind—but friendship with some people my age was something I did find myself longing to have.

Mizzy seemed distracted by something. Perhaps she was thinking along similar lines. Or—

"I need to be more like you," she said. "I'm too trusting."

"I like you how you are."

"No," Mizzy said. "The person I am hasn't ever even killed an Epic. This time it's going to be different. I'm going to do what you did. I'm going to find that monster."

"That monster?" I said.

"Firefight," Mizzy said. "The one who killed Sam."

Oh.

Megan was far from a monster, but I couldn't explain that to Mizzy, not until I had proof of some sort.

For now, I changed the topic. "So, what did you find out

from your friends? We're here for intel, right? Any clues that could lead us to . . . what we're looking for?" I didn't want to say it out loud, even though with the music—and with no water exposed to the air directly nearby—it was unlikely Regalia would be spying on us.

"I'm still looking, but I did find one interesting tidbit. Looks like Regalia has been bringing in scientists."

"Scientists?" I frowned.

"Yeah," Mizzy said. "Smart types of all kinds, apparently. Marco heard that a surgeon from Great Falls—one of Revocation's personal staff—relocated here. It's odd, as we don't have a lot of trained professionals in town. Babilar tends to attract people who like free food and fatalism, not scholars."

Huh. "See if any other professionals have come to town lately. Accountants. Military experts."

"Why?"

"Just a hunch," I said.

"Right. I'll get back to gathering intel." Mizzy hesitated. "Everything really *is* all about work for you, isn't it?"

Not by a mile. But I nodded anyway.

"I *am* going to find the Epic who murdered Sam," Mizzy said. "Then I'm going to kill her."

Sparks. I needed to clear Megan's name, and quickly. Mizzy nodded to herself, looking resolute as she stepped out of the dancing area.

I went and checked on Newton as surreptitiously as I could. The Epic still lounged by the bar, sipping her drink, standing out like a punk guitarist in a mariachi band. Farther down the improvised bar—it was mostly made of old wooden boxes—Exel chatted with a group of women. They laughed at something he said, and the whole crowd of them looked sincerely interested in him.

Sparks. Exel was a *ladies' man*? And at least *he* was sticking to the plan. I toyed with the idea of looking for Lulu so I could ask her if she'd ever seen Regalia. Instead I found myself walking to the bridge at the edge of the building, then out into the night, wanting to be alone with my thoughts for a while.

21

BABILAR was starting to grow on me.

True, all the color was garish, but I couldn't help but admire it just a little, particularly in contrast to the desolation between here and Newcago. Every glowing line coloring the walls and roofs here was a mark of humanity. A mixture of primitive cave paintings and modern technology, sprayed out of a can and humming with life all around me.

I walked down a bridge—different from the one we'd come in on. It led me to a quiet rooftop, with only a few deserted-looking tents and shanties. People preferred the roofs closer to the water level, it seemed. This one was a little too high.

I wasn't certain why more people didn't live inside the buildings. Wouldn't that be safer? Of course, the insides of the buildings were jungles—humid, shadowy, and obviously un-natural. Perhaps the rooftops were just something the people could claim.

I strolled for a time. Maybe I should have been worried about the danger, but sparks, Regalia had held us all in her grip—then let us go. This wasn't like Newcago, where Steelheart would have killed us in an eyeblink if he'd been able to find us. This was complicated. This was Epics and people living in a bizarre ecosystem, where the humans accepted that they might die at any moment—but still threw parties. Parties the Epics *themselves* might decide to visit.

Newcago had made far more sense. Steelheart at the top, lesser Epics beneath him, the favored serving them. The rest of us hiding in the corners. What sense did this city make?

Regalia has leashed the city's gangs, I thought. *And she's somehow been gaining the loyalty of powerful Epics. She lets the common people have all the food they want, and has now attracted at least one highly trained specialist.*

That all spoke of someone who was planning to do what Steelheart had in creating a powerful city-state. Regalia made the place inviting to bring people in from outside, then she gained the loyalty of several Epics to use in building an aristocracy. But if that was the case, why unleash Obliteration? Why would she build a city like this—imposing law, working for peace—only to destroy it? It made no sense.

Footsteps.

Growing up in the understreets of Newcago taught you a few things. The first was to jump the moment you thought someone was sneaking up on you. If you were lucky, it was just a mugger. If you were unlucky, you were dead.

I backed up against the side of a wooden shanty, crouching down and staying out of sight. Blue paint glowed out from behind me. *Idiot,* I thought. *This isn't Newcago. It's normal for people to wander around here.* There was probably no need to have hidden so quickly. I peeked up.

And found Newton crossing the rooftop at a prowl. She passed by in near silence, her figure dark against the spray-painted ground. She didn't seem to have spotted me.

I ducked back down, sweating. Where was she going? I hesitated briefly, considering my options, and then peeked out to watch her cross the roof.

Then I followed her.

This is stupid, a part of me thought. I had no preparation, no plan to negate her powers. She was a High Epic—her powers actively protected her from harm. If my surveillance went poorly, I wouldn't be able to simply shoot her, as my bullets would bounce back at me.

But she was involved with Regalia directly. Whatever was really going on in this city, Newton would be part of it, and watching her might give me important information. I moved in a crouch, taking cover behind old shanties as I tailed her. When I had to cross out into the open I did so quickly, and only once Newton had gotten far enough ahead. The buildings in this stretch were all about the same height and had been built very close together; you didn't even need bridges to cross from one to the other, though ramps did connect some where the height difference was larger than a few feet.

I kept pace with her, and in so doing passed a few people lounging against the side of the otherwise-deserted building. Their clothing glowed with green paint, and they gave me a strange look before glancing toward Newton.

Then they scrambled to hide. Sparks. I was glad they had some sense to them, but I didn't want their sudden motion to startle her. I hid beside a fallen wall.

Newton turned toward a long rope bridge. Sparks, that

would be difficult to cross inconspicuously. How would I follow? Instead of crossing the bridge, however, Newton hopped off the side of the building. I frowned, then took a deep breath and snuck up to the edge of the roof. A small balcony rested below, with an open doorway leading into the building itself.

Right. Inside the building. Where my visibility would be limited, and I might stumble into a trap. Of course. I swung over the side and carefully climbed down to the balcony, then peeked in through the doorway.

The glowing fruit here had been harvested recently, probably for the party several rooftops over. That left the place dark, only a few phantom pieces of immature fruit giving light. It smelled of humidity—of that strange scent of plants and earth that was so different from the pristine steel of Newcago.

A rustling sound in the distance indicated the direction that Newton had gone. I climbed in through the broken doorway and followed cautiously. This had been a bedroom, judging by the bed overgrown with vines spilling onto the floor. I glanced out the door and found a narrow hallway. No—not a bedroom . . . a hotel room.

The confines were cramped—these rooms hadn't been large in the first place, and a hallway lined with trees didn't help. How *did* these plants live in here? I snuck forward, crawling over piled-up roots, when a dangling half-grown fruit tapped the side of my head.

Then it started blinking.

I stopped immediately, turning my head and staring at the strange fruit. Looked like a pear, and it was blinking off and on like a neon sign from one of the old movies. What . . . ?

"They were at the party," a female voice said.

Sparks! It came from a room just ahead of me. I'd almost crept right past, oblivious of the open doorway. I ignored the fruit, sneaking up and listening. "Three of them. Steelslayer left early. I followed, but lost him."

Was that Newton talking?

"You *lost* him?" That deep voice was familiar. Obliteration. "I thought you didn't do that."

"I don't." Frustration in her tone. "It's like he vanished."

Sparks. I felt a chill run up my arms and wash across my body. Newton had been *following* me?

Quite aware that I was exhibiting a special brand of crazy, I peeked into the room. The foliage had been cleared away inside, the plants chopped down, opening up the small hotel room, making its bed and desk usable. One of the windows even still had intact glass, though the other was open to the air.

It was dark inside, but some spraypaint around the window gave just enough light for me to see Obliteration. He stood in his long black trench coat with hands clasped behind his back, looking out the window toward a city full of neon paint and partying people. Newton lounged beside the wall, spinning a katana in one hand.

What was it with people in this city and swords?

"You should not have allowed that one to slip away from you," Obliteration said.

"Because you did such a good job of killing him?" Newton snapped. "Against orders, I might add."

"I follow the orders of no man, mortal or Epic," Obliteration said softly. "I am the cleansing fire."

"Yeah. Whatever, creepshow."

Obliteration raised an arm to the side in an almost absent motion, holding a long-barreled handgun. Of *course* he'd have a .357. I plugged my ears right as he pulled the trigger.

The bullet deflected. I could actually see it happen, which I hadn't expected. A little flash of light from Newton, and a drawer in the desk near Obliteration exploded, wood chips scattering. The punk woman stood up straight, looking annoyed as Obliteration fired five more shots at her. Each one bounced off harmlessly.

I watched with fascination, my rational fear evaporating. What an incredible power. Hawkham in Boston had used force redirection, but bullets that bounced off him had usually ripped apart in midair. Here, the bullets *actually* changed direction, shooting backward away from her. How did they not collapse in the sudden change of trajectory?

They didn't fly well, as far as I could tell from what I was seeing. Bullets weren't meant to fly backward.

Obliteration lowered the gun.

"What is *wrong* with you?" Newton demanded.

"To whom shall I speak, and give warning, that they may hear?" Obliteration said, passionless. "Behold, their ear is uncircumcised, and they cannot hearken."

"You're crazy."

"And you are very good with a sword," Obliteration said softly. "I admire your skill."

I frowned. What? Newton seemed to consider the remark odd as well, as she hesitated, lowering the katana and staring at him.

"Are you done shooting at me?" Newton finally said, sounding disturbed. Glad to hear I wasn't the only one who found Obliteration supremely unnerving. "Because I want to get back. I'm hungry, and the food at that party was pathetic. Nothing but homegrown fruit."

Obliteration didn't glance at her. He whispered something, and I struggled to hear. I leaned forward.

"Corrupt," Obliteration whispered. "All men are corrupt. The seed of the Epic is inside each one. And so, all must die. Mortal and immortal. All are—"

I slipped.

Though I caught myself quickly, my booted foot scraped across some bark. Obliteration spun, and Newton stood up straight, raising the katana in a firm grip.

Obliteration looked right at me.

But he didn't seem to see me.

He frowned, looking past where I crouched, then shook his head. He strode over to Newton and took her by one arm. Then both teleported, a crash of light leaving behind glowing figures that crumbled away into nothing.

I righted myself, sweat streaming down the sides of my face, heart thumping.

I'd somehow managed to shake Newton without even realizing I was being followed. I didn't accept that my quick duck out of the way had been enough, not if she'd been actively tailing me. Now this.

"All right, Megan," I said. "I know you're there."

Silence.

"I have your gun," I said, taking out the handgun. "Really nice weapon. P226, custom rubber grip, finger grooves, worn down a little on the sides. Looks like you took a lot of time fitting this to your hand."

Silence.

I walked to the window and held the gun out of it. "Probably sinks really well too. It would be a shame if—"

"If you drop that, you idiot," Megan's voice said from the hallway outside, "I'll rip your face off."

22

MEGAN! Sparks, it was good to hear her voice. The last time I'd heard it, she'd pulled a gun on me.

Megan stepped from the shadows of the hallway. She looked wonderful.

The first time I'd seen her—way back when I'd been trying to join the Reckoners—she'd been wearing a sleek red dress, her golden hair tumbling down around her shoulders. Her narrow features had been accented by blush and eye shadow, tied with a bow of bright red lipstick on her lips. Now she wore a sturdy army-style jacket and jeans, her hair pulled back in a utilitarian ponytail. And she was way more beautiful. This was the real Megan, with one holster under her arm and another on her hip.

Seeing her brought back memories. Of a chase through

Newcago, of gunfire and exploding copters. Of a desperate flight, carrying her wounded in my arms, followed by an impossible rescue.

She'd died anyway. But not, I'd discovered, for good. I couldn't help grinning at the sight of her. Megan, in turn, raised a nine-millimeter square at my chest.

Well, that was familiar, at least.

"You spotted that I was interfering," Megan said. "Which means I've grown predictable. Either that or you know too much. You've always known too much."

I looked down at the gun. You never get used to having one pointed at you. In fact, the more you know about guns, the more disconcerting it is to face one down. You know exactly what they can do to people—and you know that a professional like Megan does not point a weapon at someone without being prepared to shoot.

"Um . . . it's good to see you too?" I said, pulling my arm—with Megan's gun in it—carefully out of the window, then dropped the gun to the floor in a nonthreatening way and kicked it gently in her direction. "I'm unarmed. You can lower the gun, Megan. I just want to talk."

"I should shoot you," Megan said. Keeping her gun trained on me, she stooped to retrieve the other one from the floor with her left hand, then slipped it into a pocket.

"What sense would that make?" I asked. "After you saved me from drowning the other day, and then saved me again tonight when Newton was tailing me? Thanks for both, by the way."

"Newton and Obliteration think you're dangerous," Megan said.

"And . . . you disagree?"

"Oh, you're dangerous. Just not in the way that they—or you—think. You're dangerous because you make people believe you, David. You make them listen to your crazy ideas. Unfortunately, the world *can't* be what you want it to be. You're not going to overthrow the Epics."

"We overthrew Steelheart."

"With the help of two Epics," Megan snapped. "How long would you and the team have survived in Newcago without Prof's shields and healing abilities? Sparks! You've only been here in Babilar a couple of days and you'd be dead *already* without my help. You can't fight them, David."

"Well," I said, stepping forward despite that gun—which was still pointed right at me. "I should think that your examples only prove that we *can* fight the Epics. So long as we have the help of other Epics."

Her expression shifted, lips tightening, eyes hardening. "You realize Phaedrus will turn on you. You've hired the lion to protect you from the wolves, but either will be happy to eat you once the food runs out."

"I—"

"You don't know what it's like, inside! You shouldn't trust us. *Any* of us. Even the little bit I did just now, protecting you from those two, threatens to destroy me." She hesitated. "You'll receive no further help from me." She turned to walk back into the corridor.

"Megan!" I said, feeling a sudden panic. I'd come all this way to find her. I couldn't let her go now! I scrambled out into the hallway after her.

She strode away from me, a dark silhouette barely visible by the light of a few dangling pieces of fruit.

"I've missed you," I said.

She didn't stop.

This wasn't how I'd imagined our meeting. It wasn't supposed to have been about Prof, or the Epics; it was supposed to have been about her. And about me.

I needed to say something. Something romantic! Something to sweep her off her feet.

"You're like a potato!" I shouted after her. "In a minefield."

She froze in place. Then she spun on me, her face lit by a half-grown fruit. "A potato," she said flatly. "That's the best you can do? Seriously?"

"It makes sense," I said. "Listen. You're strolling through a minefield, worried about getting blown up. And then you step on something, and you think, 'I'm dead.' But it's just a potato. And you're so relieved to find something so wonderful when you expected something so awful. That's what you are. To me."

"A potato."

"Sure. French fries? Mashed potatoes? Who doesn't like potatoes?"

"Plenty of people. Why can't I be something sweet, like a cake?"

"Because cake wouldn't grow in a minefield. Obviously."

She stared down the hallway at me for a few moments, then sat on an overgrown set of roots.

Sparks. She seemed to be crying. *Idiot!* I thought at myself, scrambling through the foliage. *Romantic. You were supposed to be romantic, you slontze!* Potatoes weren't romantic. I should have gone with a carrot.

I reached Megan in the dim hallway and hesitated, uncertain if I dared touch her. She looked up at me, and though there *were* tears in the corners of her eyes, she wasn't weeping.

She was laughing.

"You," she said, "are an utter fool, David Charleston. I wish you weren't also so adorable."

"Uh . . . thanks?" I said.

She sighed and repositioned herself on the large set of

roots, pulling her feet up and sitting with her back in the crook of the tree trunk. That seemed an invitation, so I sat down in front of her, my knees before me and my back to the wall of the corridor. I could see well enough, though this entire place was creepy, with its shadowed vines and strange plants.

"You don't know what this is like, David," she whispered.

"So tell me."

She focused on me. Then she turned her gaze upward. "It's like being a child again. Can you remember how it felt, when you were really young, and everything was about *you*? Nothing else matters but your needs, your wants. Thinking about others is impossible—they just don't enter into your mind. Other people are an annoyance, a frustration. They just get in your way."

"You resisted it before."

"No, I *didn't*. In the Reckoners, I was forced to avoid using my powers. I didn't resist the changes. I never felt them."

"So do it that way again."

She shook her head. "I barely managed it before. By the time I was killed, I was practically going crazy from the need to use my abilities. I'd started to find excuses, and that was changing me."

"You seem okay now."

She toyed with her gun, flicking the weapon's safety on and off, her eyes still upward. "It's easier around you. I don't know why."

Well, that was something. It made me think. "Maybe it has to do with your weakness."

She looked at me sharply.

"Just consider it," I said carefully, not wanting to ruin things at the moment. "It might be relevant."

"You think it's what's making me act like myself," she

snapped. "You think that somehow being around you trig-gers my weakness, and that's making me normal. Things don't work like that, David. If being around you negated my pow-ers, I wouldn't have been able to save you—or hide among the Reckoners. Sparks! If that were the case, every time a weak-ness triggered, the Epic would be like, 'What the hell? Why am I being evil? Let's totally get along, guys, and go bowling together or something.'"

"Well, there's no need to get snarky about it."

She pinched the bridge of her nose with her off hand. "I shouldn't even be here with you. What am I doing?"

"You're talking to a friend," I said. "That's something you probably need these days."

She looked at me, then glanced away.

"We don't have to talk about this in particular," I said. "Or about Newcago, or the Reckoners, or anything like that. Just talk to me, Megan. Is that a 24/7?"

She raised the handgun. "Yeah."

"Generation three?"

"Generation two compact, nine-millimeter," she grumbled. "I like the feel of the G2 better than the G3, but the spark-ing things are hard to find parts for. I have to use something small—can't let the others know I need a gun. They see it as a weakness around here."

"What, really?"

Megan nodded. "Real Epics kill with their powers in some kind of flashy way. We like to show off. I've had to get really good with the gun so I can fake my powers killing people, sometimes."

"Wow," I said. "So when we were fighting Fortuity, way back when, and you shot him out of the air . . ."

"Yeah. No cheating involved. I don't have hyper-reflexes or anything like that. I'm kind of a pitiful excuse for an Epic."

"Uh . . . you came back from the dead. That's rather less than pitiful, if you weren't aware."

She smiled. "Do you have *any* idea how much it sucks to have your High Epic status granted by reincarnation? Dying *hurts*. And it wipes a lot of my memories from right before the event. All I remember is dying, and pain, and a black, icy nothingness. I wake up the next morning with the agony and terror dominating my thoughts." She shivered. "I'd rather have forcefields or something to protect me."

"Yeah, but if your forcefields go all Vincin on you, you're dead for good. Reincarnating is more reliable."

"Vincin?" she said. "Like the gun brand?"

"Yeah, they're—"

"Always jamming," Megan finished, nodding. "And about as accurate as a blind man pissing during an earthquake."

"Wow . . . ," I breathed.

She frowned at me.

"That was a *great* metaphor," I said.

"Oh please."

"I need to write that down," I said, ignoring her complaints, fishing for my new mobile to type it out. I looked up at her as I finished, and she was smiling.

"What?" I asked.

"We're not doing a very good job of not talking about Epics," she said. "I'm sorry."

"I guess it was a lot to expect. I mean, it's kind of who you are. Besides awesome. As awesome as a—"

"Potato?"

"—a blind man pissing during an earthquake," I said, reading from my mobile's screen. "Hum. Doesn't exactly work in this situation, does it?"

"No. Not quite."

"I'll have to find another place to use it then," I said with

177

a grin, tucking away the mobile. I stood up, holding my hand out to her.

Megan hesitated, then took something from her pocket and put it in my hand. A small black object, like a mobile battery.

I frowned. "The hand was to help you to your feet."

"I know," Megan said, standing up. "I don't like being helped."

"What's this?" I asked, holding up the little flat square.

"Ask Phaedrus," she said.

Standing had placed her right in front of me, very close. She was tall, almost exactly my height.

"I've never met anyone like you," I said softly, lowering my hand.

"Is that what you told that bouncing bundle of breasts and booty you were dancing with at the party?"

I winced. "You, uh, saw that?"

"Yeah."

"Stalker."

"The Reckoners came to my town," Megan said. "It is in an Epic's interests to keep tabs on them."

"Then you know that I wasn't exactly enjoying myself while at the party."

"I'll admit," Megan said, stepping forward, "that I had trouble telling if you were trying to smash an angry swarm of bugs at your feet, or if you were just really bad at dancing."

That step put her close to me. Really close. She met my eyes.

Now or never.

Heart thumping crazily, I closed my eyes and leaned in. I immediately felt something cold against my temple.

I opened my eyes to find Megan had leaned in, her lips almost to mine, but then had raised her gun and pressed it against the side of my head. "You're doing it again," she said, almost a growl. "Distorting the truth, making people go along with your craziness. This thing between us isn't going to work."

"We'll make it work."

"Maybe I don't want it to. Maybe I want to be hard. Maybe I don't want to like people. Maybe I've *never* wanted to like people, even before Calamity."

I held her eyes, ignoring the gun to my head. I smiled.

"Bah," she said, pulling the gun away. She stalked off down the corridor, brushing the fronds of a fern. "Don't follow. I need to think."

I stayed put, though I did watch her until she was gone. I fingered the batterylike item she'd given me, feeling a lingering pleasure—for as she'd left, I'd glanced at her gun.

This time, when she'd pointed it at me, she'd flicked the safety on. If that wasn't true love, I don't know what was.

23

EXEL strapped the spyril onto me. It was sleeker than I'd expected it to be; the only bulky parts were two large, canisterlike tubes that attached to my calves. A nozzle extended from the back of my right hand, the opening as large as a common hose; it was secured into a black glove with an attached wrist brace. The setup inhibited my wrist motion a little.

My left hand had a different kind of glove on it, with a few odd devices on the back about the shape of two rolls of coins. I prodded at these.

"I'd avoid playing with those if I were you," Exel said affably. "Unless you want to rush your funeral along. I happen to know of a wonderful place in Babilar that sells lilies year-round."

"You're a strange man," I said, though I lowered my hands to my sides per his warning.

"Mizzy?" Exel asked.

"Looks good," she said, walking around and inspecting me. She knelt down and tugged on the line running from my foot to the back portion and nodded. She seemed to know a lot about things like this, particularly Epic-derived technology. When I'd come back with the motivator that Megan had given me—explaining that I'd followed Newton and that she'd dropped it—Mizzy had been the one to run it through tests and determine that everything was all right.

The three of us were on a rooftop in northern Babilar, away from populated areas in a section where only the rare building peeked from the surface of the water. No bridges led between them. Aside from that it was daytime, when most people would be sleeping.

I wore a wetsuit with the spyril, and I pointedly ignored how nervous that made me. Before agreeing to equip me with the device, Mizzy had insisted on teaching me some basic swimming strokes. Almost a week had passed since my meeting with Megan. I was getting pretty good at swimming—or, well, pretty good at not panicking when I got in the water. That was the majority of the battle, I supposed.

I still hadn't figured out a design for foot spikes to stop potential shark attacks. Hopefully I wouldn't need them.

Prof surveyed from the other side of the rooftop. He wore his black lab coat, goggles stuffed into the pocket. He didn't believe my lie about having found the spyril's motivator in the room after spying on Obliteration and Newton. I'd been tempted to tell him about Megan. I'd find a time soon enough. When Mizzy, Val, or Exel weren't around. I didn't think they'd react well to hearing that I'd had a pleasant conversation with the Epic who had supposedly killed their friend.

She didn't do it, I thought to myself for the thousandth time as Mizzy pulled my arm strap tight. *Even if she did have the spyril's motivator.*

"All right," Mizzy said, finally. "Done!"

"Congratulations," Exel said. "You're now wearing the most dangerous piece of equipment we own."

"Where are the rest of the tubes?" I asked, frowning. The canisters and gloves were each attached with some small wires—which were strapped securely to my arms and legs—to a circular device on my back, where Mizzy had installed the motivator.

"No tubes needed," Mizzy said.

"None? No pumps, hoses . . ."

"Nope."

"I'm pretty sure that doesn't make any sense."

"I'm pretty sure you're wearing a freaky, Epic-derived weapon," Mizzy said. "The tensors vaporize metal. This is a stroll in the park compared to that. Granted, our local park is completely submerged. . . ."

I raised my right hand, making a fist. The wetsuit covering my arm *scrunched* as I moved. Her explanation bothered me. Shouldn't we know how things like this actually worked? Of course, I didn't understand how computers or mobiles worked either, and that didn't bother me. Those didn't have mysterious motivators, though, and weren't built after studying the cells of dead Epics.

And they also didn't, so far as I knew, defy the laws of physics.

Those were probably questions for another day. For now, I needed to focus on the task at hand: learning to use the spyril. "So how does it work?"

"This," Mizzy said, taking my left hand and flipping a

switch, "is the streambeam. You point it at water and make a fist."

"Streambeam?" I asked dryly.

"I named it," Mizzy said happily.

I inspected the glove. One of the coin-roll devices on the back kind of looked like a laser pointer. I stepped to the edge of the roof and pointed my left hand at the water just below, then made a fist.

A bright red laser shot from my left hand. Even in full daylight, even with no smoke or anything dusting the air, I could see the beam easily. The device on my back started to hum.

"The streambeam draws out water," Exel said, clapping me on the shoulder. "Or . . . well, teleports the water to you, or something like that."

"You're kidding."

"Nope."

"Now, you have to be careful," Mizzy said, "as your other hand will control the flow. You need to—"

I made a fist with my right hand. Jets of water *erupted* from my feet, flipping me into the air end over end. I shouted, flailing my arms. The streambeam twisted toward the sky, then turned off as I was no longer making a fist. The jets immediately cut out.

The world spun around me, drops of water spraying everywhere, then the force of the ocean hit me as I crashed into it. It was a huge shock, even with Prof's forcefield to protect me. Brackish water sprayed into my mouth and up my nose. For a brief, terrified moment my mind was *convinced* I was drowning to death.

I thrashed, remembering the time before when I'd been towed down by the weight on my ankle. My panic was accompanied by a deeper, more ancient terror—a primal fear of drowning mixed with a fear of what could be out there, in those depths, watching me.

I struggled to the surface, sputtering, and swam awkwardly to the rooftop. I grabbed hold of a partially submerged windowsill and wiped my face, trying to catch my breath, stilling my nerves. Even with the wetsuit, I felt cold.

A laugh bellowed out from up above. Exel. He reached down, and I took hold, letting him help me from the water. I sat on the side of the roof, pulling my legs up. No reason to give the sharks—which I was sure were down there—anything to chew on.

"Well, it works!" Exel said.

"Let me check the flow rates," Mizzy said, kneeling beside me. Today with her jeans she wore a shirt that had frills cut along the hem. Behind the two of them Prof stood with crossed arms, his expression dark.

"Sir?" I called to him.

"Carry on with the practice," he said, turning away. "I have things to take care of. Exel and Mizzy, you can handle this?"

"Sure can," Exel said. "I coached Sam his first few times. Never did try it myself though."

Made sense. I figured it would take some *serious* jets to lift Exel.

Prof stepped onto our boat tied up alongside the rooftop, then took out a paddle. "Contact Val via mobile when you want to be picked up," he said. Then he rowed away toward where we'd hidden the submarine.

"What's up with him lately?" Exel asked.

"Up?" Mizzy asked from behind me as she fiddled with the device on my back. "He's always like that, so far as I can tell. Brooding. Dark. Mysterious." I sensed a blush to her voice, and she ducked down a little farther.

"True," Exel said. "But lately the mystery comes with extra brood." He shook his head and settled down beside me. "David, when manipulating the spyril you *have* to keep the streambeam pointed at water. The moment it isn't, you'll lose access to your propellant, and that will send you crashing down."

"Well," I said, "at least the landing will be soft, right?" I nodded toward the water.

"You've never belly flopped, have you?" Exel asked.

"Belly what?"

Exel rubbed his forehead with a set of meaty fingers. "Okay. David, water doesn't compress. If you hit it at high speed, particularly with a lot of your body at once, it will feel like hitting something solid. Drop from a hundred feet or so, and you'll break bones. Maybe die."

That sounded bizarre, but it didn't really matter so long as I had one of Prof's forcefields protecting me, disguised as a little electronic box hooked to my wetsuit belt. Since he often split the power among several Reckoners at once, it would wear out over time, and focused points of pressure—such as a bullet strike—could penetrate it. But a fall into the water shouldn't be a problem.

"A hundred feet, you say?" I asked. "This thing can get me that high?"

Exel nodded. "And higher. Sam couldn't reach the tops of the tallest skyscrapers, but he could reach many of the medium-height ones."

Mizzy stopped fiddling with my back. "I dialed down the flows," she said. "So you can practice without quite as much force at first."

"I don't need to be coddled," I said.

Exel looked at me seriously, then rested a hand on my shoulder. "I joke about death, David. It's an occupational hazard—you learn to laugh at it when it's all around you. But we already lost one point man from this team. Wouldn't it be silly to lose another one while practicing? What happened just a few moments ago could easily have ended with you flipping into the air, then driving yourself face-first into the rooftop at high speed."

I took a deep breath, feeling foolish. "Of course. You're right." Prof's protections were good, but not infallible. "I'll take it easy at first."

"Then stand back up, Steelslayer, and let's get to it."

24

IT turned out that the difficulty in using the spyril didn't have to do with its power. After a half hour of working, we had Mizzy up the strength of the water jets, as they provided a better footing that way.

The trouble was with balance. Trying to remain stable with two shifting jets of water coming out from your legs was like trying to balance a pot full of frogs on the tips of two half-cooked pieces of spaghetti. And I had to do it while keeping my left arm always pointed downward at the water, or I'd lose my power. I could use my right hand for stabilizing, fortunately. That one had what Mizzy called a handjet strapped to it. With it I could shoot out streams of water to adjust my balance, but usually I overcompensated.

It was all pretty complicated. Left hand with the streambeam had to stay pointed at water. Right hand opening and closing would adjust the strength of the water coming out my footjets, and the right thumb would control the strength of the handjet. But I couldn't use that to stabilize unless I remembered to point it the direction I was falling, which—when you're trying to juggle all of this in your mind—was easier said than done.

Eventually I managed to accomplish a stable hover about fifteen feet above the water. I wavered there, using the handjet to shoot a stream backward to keep from falling when I began to topple in that direction.

"Nice!" Exel called up from below. "Like walking on flexible stilts, eh? That's how Sam put it."

Well, if you wanted to be *pedestrian* with your metaphors.

I lost my balance and crashed back down into the water, relaxing my right hand and stopping the jets. I came up sputtering but let myself float there for a moment, Exel and Mizzy standing above me and looking down.

Falling again was annoying, but I wouldn't let myself get discouraged. I'd had to practice for weeks with the tensors before getting the hang of those.

Something brushed my leg.

I knew it was probably just a piece of garbage moving in the lazy current, but I jerked my legs up and instinctively made a fist. So, when water jetted from my feet, I shot backward like a fleshy speedboat. I released my hand almost immediately, surprised by how easily I'd moved.

I turned around, face forward and legs back so I was on my stomach, and tried the jets again. I eased into the power until I was moving at a decent clip—about as fast as I'd seen Mizzy swimming the day before when she'd been giving me instructions. I checked my goggles and nose plugs to make sure they were secure.

Then I increased the speed.

For some reason, even though my feet were pointed straight back, this spat me out of the water so that I flew just above the surface. It was quick, lasting only a few seconds before I plunged into the water again face-first.

Wow, I thought, surfacing and then spurting from the water again in a splash.

I relaxed my hand, slowing my momentum, then put myself upright. The small amount of force coming from the jets raised me up out of the water about to my waist, the water churning in a donutlike ring around me.

I'd gotten going pretty quickly back there. Could I go even faster? I let myself sink back into the water, then stuck my feet out behind me again and put the jets on full blast, shooting face-first like a torpedo. Water sprayed off me as I splashed up and down, thrilled by the speed. I got the hang of this power-swimming much more quickly than I had the hovering; I was having so much fun that I almost forgot I was in the water.

Eventually I swam up to the others and stopped the jets. Above, Mizzy was gasping. "That," she said, tears in the corners of her eyes, "was one of the most *ridiculous* things I've ever seen."

"You said 'awesome' wrong," I grumbled. "Did you see how fast I was going?"

"You looked like a porpoise," Mizzy said.

"An *awesome* porpoise?"

"Sure." She laughed.

Beside her, Exel was smiling. He knelt down and reached out to help me from the water, but I engaged the jets and shot up at an angle. I managed to land on the rooftop beside them without falling on my face, though much arm-waving was involved.

Mizzy laughed again and tossed me a towel. I settled down

on one of the chairs, shivering. Spring might be upon us, but the air was still chilly. I accepted a cup of hot tea from Exel as he settled down beside me and put in his earpiece. I followed suit.

"That water," I said, speaking in the soft way of the Babilaran Reckoners, "doesn't seem as cold as it should be." I realized, now that I was in the open air and shivering, that it was warmer in the water than out of it.

"It isn't," Exel said. "And it's even warmer down in the southern parts of Babilar. There are currents that move through the streets bearing a tropical warmth all times of year, even midwinter."

"That sounds . . ." I trailed off.

"Impossible?" Exel volunteered.

"Yeah," I said. "But I realize how stupid that sounds, considering everything else happening in this city."

Exel nodded, and we sat for a while, me chowing down on a sandwich I'd dug out of my pack.

"So," Exel said, "are we done for the day?"

"Nah," I said, munching the last bite of sandwich. "We've only been out here for an hour or two. I want to get this *down*. Just let me rest for a minute and I'll get back to it."

Mizzy took a seat and checked her mobile. "Val reports that Newton is in Eastborough right now. No movement this direction. It doesn't look like we've been spotted."

I nodded and took a pull on the tea as I thought. It was sweeter than I was used to. "We'll need to figure out her weakness, if we can."

"I'd rather find out Obliteration's," Exel said. "He scares me."

"He should."

I'd spent the week thinking about Megan, but I probably should have let Obliteration dominate more of that time. Why had he suddenly decided to vaporize Houston? And then in rapid succession two other towns? What had changed, and why had I been wrong about the cooldown on his teleportation powers?

I pulled out my new mobile and searched through the digitized version of my notes. It wasn't too different from my old one, though a few of Mizzy's improvements—such as a slow-charging solar panel on the back—seemed like they'd be useful.

I stopped at a photo of Obliteration, taken in Houston only a few days before he'd destroyed the place. I'd traded half my rations for two weeks to another kid in the Factory for a copy of the photo, which he'd had forwarded on to him from a friend.

In the picture, Obliteration sat in the middle of a city square, cross-legged, basking in the sun with eyes closed and face turned toward the sky. A few days later, Houston was gone—which had shocked me, as I assumed he would remain emperor of the city for years, like Steelheart in Chicago. Nothing I'd read about him had prepared me for such an event.

My notes had been wrong about him. Consistently, not just regarding his powers, but also his motives and intentions. I thought a moment, then pulled up Val's number and pressed the call button.

"Yo," she said softly.

"Mizzy says you're still on reconnaissance," I said.

"Yeah. What do you need?"

"Has anyone spotted Obliteration sitting out in the sun?" I asked. "Here in the city, I mean?"

"Don't know," Val said. "There are lots of rumors about him, but not much concrete info."

I looked up at Exel sitting in his chair beside me. He shrugged. "I can try to find out more if you'd like," he offered.

"Thanks," I said. "Val, just keep your eyes open, all right? I think Obliteration needs to charge himself that way; it's how he acted in the other cities before he destroyed them. We'll want to know if he starts doing that here."

"Right." Val signed off.

"We're worrying about him too much," Mizzy said. She sat by the edge of the rooftop, idly tossing broken chips of brick into the water.

Exel chuckled softly, then spoke over the line. "Well, he *is* the one who is likely to try to melt the city, Missouri."

"I suppose. But what about *Firefight*?" Mizzy stared out over the waters, her brow furrowed in an uncharacteristic way. Angry. "She's the one who killed Sam. She infiltrated the Reckoners, betrayed us. She's a fire Epic too, like Obliteration. Why aren't we talking about how to kill her?"

Fire Epic. I was pretty sure that she wasn't actually— she was some kind of illusion Epic—though honestly I didn't know the extent of what she could do. There was something odd about the images she created, but I couldn't put my finger on it.

"What did Prof tell you about Firefight?" I asked Mizzy and Exel, curious.

Mizzy shrugged. "I have the Reckoners' files on her, though they thought 'she' was a 'he.' Fire Epic; has an aura of flame about her that melts bullets. Can fly, shoot fire."

None of that was actually true, and Prof knew it. Why hadn't he told the team Megan was really an illusionist, and had no fire manipulation powers? I certainly wasn't going to explain—not when I didn't know why Prof was keeping quiet. Besides, as long as Mizzy was still after Megan, it was safer if this team didn't know Megan's true nature.

"The files don't have anything about her weakness though," Mizzy said, looking at me hopefully.

"I have no idea what it is," I said. "She didn't seem too bad when she was with us. . . ."

"Had you fooled right good," Mizzy said, sounding sympathetic. "Yeaaah, I suppose we should be lucky she didn't try that with us. It would be even harder if she'd made herself our friend first, then started killing us." She still looked angry as she fetched herself a cup of tea.

I stood up, setting aside the towel. I still had the spyril strapped on, jets on the backs of my calves, gloves on my hands. "I'm going to go practice that swimming thing some more."

"Just watch out for people," Exel said. "Don't let them see you—we wouldn't want to ruin the reputation of the Reckoners by acting so silly."

"Eee, eee," Mizzy squealed like a dolphin.

"Great," I said, fighting off a blush. "Thanks. That's very encouraging." I removed my earpiece and tucked it into the waterproof pocket on my wetsuit, then replaced my swimming goggles and nose plugs.

I hopped back into the water and did a few more circuits of the rooftop. It *was* fun, even if it was in the water. Besides, I was moving too quickly for sharks to catch me, I figured.

Eventually, when I felt like I had the hang of it, I turned away from the rooftop and ventured into the open water of what had once been Central Park. It was now a large expanse without anything breaking the surface—which was perfect for me, as it meant I didn't risk shooting down into the water and smashing into a barely submerged roof or spire.

I closed my right hand almost to a fist and picked up speed, then splashed through the water—popping out and then crashing back down, over and over. It was exciting at first, but eventually grew monotonous. I forced myself onward. I had to master this device—we were going to need the edge.

Prof's forcefield energy seemed to protect me; I suspected that without his help, my head and face would be taking more of a battering. As it was, I barely felt it. After crossing the entire park in a matter of minutes, I burst from the surface, shooting straight up, then managed to balance on the streams of water and stay in place some twenty feet above the ocean. As I started to tip, I raised my other hand and used the smaller jet on the back of the right-hand glove—controlled by my thumb—to knock me back into place.

Excited that I'd managed to balance, I grinned—then accidentally overcorrected with the handjet. I crashed back down into the ocean, but I was getting used to this. I knew to ease off the power and angle myself upward in a gradual ascent. I emerged from the water and let myself float for a moment, satisfied at my progress.

Then I remembered where I was. Stupid water, ruining my enjoyment of swimming. I jetted sideways to where a short roof peeked out of the surface, then climbed up on it. There, I sat with my legs over the side—barely minding that they were in the water—to rest for a few minutes.

Regalia appeared before me a moment later.

25

I leaped to my feet as her image coalesced from a rising figure of water. I immediately reached for my gun—which, of course, I didn't have on me anywhere. Not that it would do any good.

We'd known she might be watching—you always had to assume that, in Babilar. We could have gone outside her range to practice, but what would be the point? She knew about the spyril already, and we were confident she didn't want us dead. At least not immediately.

She stepped onto the rooftop, still connected to the sea by a tendril of liquid. She held a dainty cup of tea, and as she sat down a chair formed out of water behind her. Like before, she wore a professional suit and shirt, her white hair pinned up in a bun. Her dark African American skin was furrowed, creased with wrinkles.

"Oh, be still," Regalia said to me over her tea. "I'm not going to harm you. I just want to get a good look at you."

I hesitated. I could imagine this woman as a judge on television—distinguished, but harsh. Her voice had the air of a wise mother who was forced to intervene in the petty antics of immature children.

She was a preacher too, I remembered from my notes. *And didn't Obliteration quote scripture at me?* What was the connection there?

The Reckoner in me wanted to leap into the water and get away as quickly as possible. This was a very dangerous Epic. I'd never interacted this way with Steelheart; we'd stayed far away from him until the moment we sprang our trap.

But Regalia ruled the waters. If I leaped into them, I'd only be *more* in her power.

She doesn't want you dead, I told myself again. *See what you can learn.* It went against my instincts, but it seemed the best thing to do.

"How did Jonathan kill the Epic who had those powers?" Regalia asked, nodding toward my legs. "Normally an Epic has to be murdered in order for such devices to be created, you know. I have always wondered how the Reckoners managed it in the case of those jets."

I remained silent.

"You fight us," Regalia continued. "You claim to hate us. And yet you wear our skins upon your backs. What you really hate is that you cannot tame us, as man tamed the beasts. And so you murder us."

"You dare talk to me about *murder*?" I demanded. "After what you did by inviting Obliteration into this city?"

Regalia studied me with an expressionless face. She set her teacup aside and it melted, no longer part of her projection. Wherever she actually was, she was sitting in that chair, so I tried to remember how it looked. It was just a simple wooden seat, with no ornamentation on the sides or back, but maybe it could give us a clue as to where her base was.

"Has Jonathan told you what he is?" Regalia asked.

"A friend of yours," I said vaguely. "From years ago."

She smiled. "Yes. We were both made Epics at around the same time." She watched me. "No surprise at hearing he is an Epic? So you do know. I had assumed he was still maintaining the act."

"Do you know," I shot back, "that if an Epic stops using their powers, they revert to their old selves? You don't need us to kill you, Regalia. Just stop using your powers."

"Ah," she said, "if only it were so simple . . ." She shook her head as if amused by my innocence, then nodded toward the waters out in Central Park Bay. They rippled and moved, small waves forming on the surface and changing as quickly as the expressions on the face of a child trapped in quicksand made of candy.

"You took well to that device," Regalia said. "I watched the other man practice, and he required far longer to accustom himself to its power. You are a natural with the abilities, it seems."

"Regalia," I said, stepping forward. "Abigail. You don't have to be like this. You—"

"Do not act as if you know me, young man," Regalia said. Her tone was quiet but firm.

I stopped in place.

"You have killed Steelheart," Regalia continued. "For that alone I should destroy you. We have so few pockets of civilization remaining to us, and you bring down one that has not only power but advanced medical care? Hubris of the most high, child. If you were in my court, I'd see you locked away for life. If you were in my congregation, I'd do even worse."

"If you hadn't noticed," I replied, "Newcago is running just fine without Steelheart. Just like Babilar would run fine without you. Isn't that why you've forced Prof to come here? Because you want him to kill you?"

She hesitated at that, and I realized I might have said too much. Did I just give away that Prof knew her plan? But if she really wanted him to stop her, she'd expect him to figure it out, right? I needed to be more careful. Regalia was not only an Epic; she was also an *attorney*. That was like putting curry powder in your hot sauce. She could talk rings around me.

But how could I get information from her without saying anything? I made a snap decision and jumped off the rooftop, engaging the spyril and jetting through the water of Central Park Bay. I burst from the water a few minutes later, landing on another roof far north of the one I'd been on before.

"You *do* realize how ridiculous you look doing that," Regalia said, stretching up from the water, speaking even before her new shape fully formed.

I yelped, pretending to be alarmed. I left this building and splashed farther northward until I was at the very northern edge of the bay. Here, exhausted, I broke from the water again and settled onto a rooftop, water streaming from my brow.

"Are you quite done?" Regalia asked as her chair formed from the water just before me again. She picked up her cup of tea. "I can appear anywhere I want, silly boy. I'm surprised Jonathan didn't explain this to you."

Not anywhere, I thought. *You have a limited range.*

And she'd just given me two more data points that would help Tia pinpoint her true location. I slipped off the roof into the water, intending to take another swim and see if I could get her to follow one more time.

"You *are* good with the device," Regalia noted. "Did you

ever know Waterlog, the Epic in whom those powers originated? I created him, you know."

I stopped in the water beside the building, frozen like a beetle who'd just discovered that his mother had been eaten by a praying mantis.

Regalia sipped her tea.

"What did you say?" I asked.

"Oh, so that interests you, does it? His original name was Georgi, a minor street thug down in Orlando. He showed promise. I made him into an Epic."

"Don't be ridiculous," I said, laughing. Nobody could *make* Epics. Sure, once in a while new ones appeared. Though the vast majority had been here since about a year after Calamity's rise, I knew of a few notable Epics who had only recently manifested powers. But no one knew why or how.

"So certain in your denial," Regalia said, shaking her head. "Do you think you know so much about the world, David Charleston? You know how everything works?"

I stopped laughing, but I didn't believe her for a moment. She was playing me somehow. What was her game?

"Ask Obliteration next time you see him," Regalia said idly, "assuming you live long enough. Ask about what I've done to his powers, how much stronger they are, despite what I have taken from him."

I looked up at her, frowning. "Taken from him?" What did she mean by that? What would she "take" from an Epic? And that aside, was she also implying she'd *enhanced* Obliteration's powers? Was that the reason for the lack of cooldown on his teleporting?

"You can't fight me," she said. "If you do you'll end up dead, alone. Gasping for breath in one of these jungle buildings, one step from freedom. Your last sight a blank wall that someone had spilled coffee on. A pitiful, pathetic end. Think on that."

She vanished.

I climbed up onto the rooftop and wiped some water from my eyes, then sat down. That had been a decidedly surreal experience. As I rested I thought on what she'd told me. There was so much that it only grew more troubling the more I thought it through.

Eventually I jumped back into the water and swam to the others.

26

TWO days later I lingered in the library of our underwater base, alone, looking at Tia's map. The points where I'd seen Regalia were marked with red pins and little exclamation points scribbled right on the paper. I smiled, remembering Tia's excitement as she'd placed those pins. Though the math of what she was doing here wasn't particularly interesting to me, the end result certainly was.

I moved to walk away, then stopped myself. I'd done well enough in my mathematics training at the Factory, even if I hadn't enjoyed the subject. I couldn't afford to be lazy just because someone else had things in hand. I wanted to know for myself. I forced myself to turn back and try to figure out Tia's notations. From what I eventually worked out, my points had helped a lot, but we needed more data from the southeastern side of the city before we could really determine Regalia's center base.

Feeling satisfied, I left the library. With nothing to do.

Which was odd. Back in Newcago, I'd always had something to occupy my time, mostly because of Abraham and Cody. Whenever they'd seen me looking idle, they'd handed me a project. Cleaning guns, carrying crates, practicing with the tensors—something.

Here, that didn't happen. I couldn't practice with the spyril down here—and I could only go up above to practice during certain preplanned excursions. Besides, my body ached from the hours I'd already spent power-swimming around the city. Prof's forcefields kept me from getting battered, but they didn't protect my muscles from strain.

I peeked in on Tia—her door was cracked—and I knew from her look of concentration and the six empty cola pouches by her seat that I shouldn't disturb her. Mizzy was in the workroom with Val helping her, fixing one of our boat motors. When I stepped in to talk to them, I got an immediate cold scowl from Val. I stopped dead in the doorway, chilled by that stare. Val seemed to be in an even worse mood than normal in the last few days.

Mizzy gave me a little shrug, wiggling her hand and making Val pass her a wrench. Sparks. I turned around and left them. Now what? I should be doing *something*. I sighed and headed back toward my room, where I could dig into my notes on Epics yet again. I passed Tia's room and was surprised when she called out.

"David?"

I hesitated by the door, then pushed it open farther. "Yeah?"

"How did you know?" Tia asked, head down over her datapad, typing something furiously. "About Sourcefield."

Sourcefield. The Epic we'd killed just before leaving New-cago. I stepped forward, eager. "You found something more? About her background?"

"I've just recovered the truth about her grandparents," Tia said with a nod. "They tried to kill her."

"That's sad, but . . ."

"They poisoned her drink."

"Kool-Aid?"

"A generic," Tia said, "but close enough. The grandparents were a strange pair, fascinated by cults and old stories. It was a copycat killing, or an attempted one, based on an older tragedy in South America. The important thing is that Sourcefield—rather, Emiline—was old enough at the time to realize that she'd been poisoned. She crawled out into the street when her throat and mouth started burning, and a passerby took her to the hospital. She became an Epic years later, and her weakness—"

"Was the very thing that had almost killed her," I finished, excited. "It's a connection, Tia."

"Maybe a coincidental one."

"You don't believe that," I said. How could she? This was another connection, a *real* one—like Mitosis, but even more promising. Was this where Epic weaknesses came from? Something that nearly killed them?

But how would bad rock music nearly kill a guy? I wondered. Touring, perhaps? An accident. We needed to know more.

"I think a coincidence *is* possible," Tia said, then looked up and finally met my eyes. "But I also think it's worth investigating. Nice work. How did you guess?"

"There's got to be some logic to it, Tia," I said. "The powers, the weaknesses, the Epics . . . who gets chosen."

"I don't know, David," Tia said. "Does there really *have*

to be a rationale behind it? In ancient days, when a disaster struck everyone would try to make sense of it—find a reason. Somebody's sins. Angered gods. But nature doesn't always have a reason for us, not the type we want."

"You're going to look into it, right?" I asked. "This is like Mitosis—similar at least. Maybe we can find a connection with Steelheart and his weakness. He could only be harmed by someone who didn't fear him. Maybe in his past he was nearly killed by someone who—"

"I'll look into it," Tia said, stopping me. "I promise."

"You seem reluctant," I pressed. How could she be so skeptical? This was exciting! Revolutionary!

"I thought we were beyond this. The lorists spent the early years searching for a connection between Epic weaknesses. We decided there wasn't one." She hesitated. "Though I suppose that was a challenging time—when communication was difficult and the government was collapsing. We made other mistakes back then; I suppose I wouldn't be surprised to discover we'd been too hasty in making some of our decisions." She sighed. "I'll look into this further, though Calamity knows I don't have the time these days with the Regalia issue."

"I can help," I said, taking another step forward.

"I know you can. I'll keep you informed of what I discover."

I stayed where I was, stubborn not to leave so easily.

"That was a dismissal, David."

"I—"

"The people I work with are very secretive," Tia interrupted. "I've been implying to them that you should be allowed to join our ranks, but if you do you'll have to give up on fieldwork. Having access to our knowledge necessitates preventing you from taking risks, lest you get captured and interrogated."

I grunted, annoyed. I'd been looking forward to the chance, someday, to meet with Tia's lorists. But I wasn't going to give up on running point, not when there were Epics to kill. Being a lorist sounded like a job for a nerd anyway.

I sighed and retreated from the library. This left me with the same problem as before, unfortunately. What to do with myself? Tia wouldn't let me in on the research, and Val didn't want me nearby.

Who would have thought that living in an awesome undersea base would be so boring?

I walked slowly back toward my room. The hallway was quiet except for some echoing sounds from farther down the dark stretch. Faint, with a rasping quality, they called to me like the ding on a microwave as it finished nuking a pizza pocket. I passed door after door until I eventually reached Exel's room. He had the door wide open, and the inside was plastered wall to wall with posters of interesting buildings. An architecture buff? I wouldn't have guessed—but then again, I was having trouble guessing anything about Exel.

The man himself sat filling up a large chair near a small table set with an antiquated piece of machinery. He nodded to me, then continued to fiddle with the machine in front of him. It made buzzing noises.

Feeling welcome for the first time all day, I walked in and settled into a seat beside him. "A radio?" I guessed as he turned a dial.

"Specifically, a scanner," he said.

"I have no idea what that means."

"It just lets me look for signals, mostly local ones, and see if I can hear them."

"How . . . old-fashioned," I said.

"Well, maybe not as much as you think," he answered. "This isn't *actually* the radio, just a control mechanism. We're buried far enough underwater that I wouldn't get good signals here; the real radio is stashed above."

"Still—radio?" I tapped my new mobile. "We have something better."

"And most people above do not," Exel said, sounding amused. "You think the people partying and lounging in this city have the resources to use *mobiles*? Knighthawk mobiles no less?"

I hesitated. Mobiles had been common in Newcago, where Steelheart had had a deal with the Knighthawk Foundry. While that sounded altruistic of him, there was a simpler truth to it. With everyone carrying mobiles, he could force upon them "obedience programs" and other warnings to keep them in line.

Apparently Regalia didn't have something similar.

"Radios," Exel said, tapping his receiver. "Some things just *work*. There is elegance in simplicity. If I were up there living a relatively normal life, I'd want a radio instead of a mobile. I can fix a radio; I know how it works. Calamity only knows what goes on inside one of those modern devices."

"But how do the radios get power?" I asked.

Exel shook his head. "Radios just work here in Babilar."

"You mean . . ."

"No explanation for it," he said with a shrug of his ample shoulders. "Nothing else works without a power source— blenders, clocks, whatever you try. Won't work. But radios turn on, even if you don't have batteries in them."

That gave me a shiver. Even more than the strange lights in the darkness, this creeped me out. Ghostly powered radios? What was *happening* in this city?

Exel didn't seem bothered. He tuned to another frequency, then took out his pen, leaning in, writing. I scooted my chair closer. From what I could tell, he was just listening to random chatter of townspeople. He made a few notes, then moved on. He listened to this frequency for a while without making notes before going to the next one, where he scribbled things down furiously.

He really seemed to know what he was doing. His notes were neat and efficient, and he seemed to be searching to see if some of the people might be speaking in code. I took one of his sheets off the table; he glanced at me but didn't stop me.

It looked like he was also scanning for mentions of Regalia and stories regarding her direct appearance. Most of what he had was hearsay, but I was impressed with the detail of the notes, and with the conclusions he was drawing. Some of the notes indicated the frequency had been muffled, or static-filled, but he'd managed to re-create entire conversations—the words he actually heard underlined, the rest filled in.

I looked up from the sheet. "You're a mortician," I said, skeptical.

"Third generation," he said proudly. "Was there for my own grandfather's embalming. Stuffed the eyes with cotton myself."

"They teach this in mortician school?" I said, holding up the paper.

"Nope," Exel said with a grin. "Learned that in the CIA."

"You're a *spook*?" I asked, shocked.

"Hey, even the CIA needed morticians."

"Uh, no. I don't think it did."

"More than you think," Exel said, tuning to another frequency. "Back in the old days there were hundreds like me. Not all morticians, of course—but similar. People living normal lives, doing regular jobs, placed in areas where we could do a little good here and there. I spent years teaching mortuary science in Seoul, listening to the radios at night with my team. Everyone imagines spies to be the 'cocktails and bow tie' sort, but there weren't actually many of those. Most of us were regular folks."

"You," I said. "Regular?"

"Within plausible limits of believability," Exel said.

I found myself smiling. "I don't get you, Exel," I said, picking up another sheet from his stack. "The other day you almost seemed to sympathize with the do-nothings who flock to this city."

"I do sympathize with them," Exel said. "I'd love to do nothing. Seems like a grand profession. It's never because of the 'do-nothings' that people go to war."

"Says the former spy."

"Former?" Exel asked, waggling a pencil at me.

"Exel, if nobody changes the world, if nobody works to make it better, then we stagnate."

"I could live with stagnation," Exel said, "if it meant no war. No killing."

I wasn't certain I agreed. Maybe I was naive, as I'd never lived through any human-on-human wars—my life had been dominated by the conflict with the Epics. But I figured the world would be pretty boring if all you did was stay the same.

"Well, it doesn't matter," Exel continued. "That can't be. My job now is about doing what I can to make sure people get to live their lives how they want to. If that means basking in the sun and not worrying, then good for them. At least someone in this sorry world is enjoying themselves."

He continued writing. I could have argued further, but I found my heart wasn't in it. If this was what motivated him to fight the Epics, then so be it. We each had our reasons.

Instead I let my attention be drawn by a page of notes relating to a specific topic: Dawnslight, the mythical Epic who supposedly made the plants grow and the spraypaint shine. Exel's page was filled with references to people discussing him, praying to him, cursing by his name.

I could see why people were so interested in Dawnslight. Babilar could not exist without him, whoever he was. But reports placed him in the city long before Regalia had arrived. Dared I hope it was true, that an Epic existed who was this benevolent? An Epic who didn't kill, or didn't even dominate, but who instead made food grow and light appear? Who was this person who created paradise in the buildings of old Manhattan?

"Exel," I said, looking up from the paper, "you've lived here for a while."

"Ever since Prof ordered us to embed," the large man replied.

"Do you think Dawnslight is a real person?"

He tapped his pencil on his pad for a moment, then set it down and reached beside his seat for a pouch of orange soda. You could get it shipped out of Charlotte, like the cola, if you had connections. There was an Epic there who really loved soda and paid to have the machinery maintained.

"You've seen my notes," Exel said, nodding to the sheet I was looking at. "That page is one of many. I've been keeping an ear out for mentions of Dawnslight since I arrived. He's real. Too many people talk about him for him to not be."

"A lot of people talk about God," I said. "Or they used to."

"Because he's real too. You don't believe, I assume?"

I wasn't certain. I fished under my shirt, bringing out Abraham's gift. The stylized S shape that was the symbol of the Faithful. What did I believe? For years my "religion" had been Steelheart's death. I'd worshipped that goal as fervently as any old-time monk in a monkplace.

"Well, I've never been the missionary type," Exel said, "and I think that God might be a topic for another day. But as for Dawnslight, I'm reasonably certain he's real."

"The people here *worship* him as a god."

"Well, they may be a screwy bunch," Exel said, raising his pouch. "But they're a peaceful lot, right? So good for them."

"And their Epic? Is Dawnslight peaceful?"

"Seems so."

I was dancing around it. I needed to just say what I meant. I leaned forward. "Exel, do you think it's *possible* for Epics to be good?"

"Of course they can be. We all have free will. It's a divine right."

I sat back, thoughtful.

"You don't agree, I see."

"Actually I do," I said. I *had* to believe Epics could be good—for Megan's sake. "I want to find a way to bring some Epics to our side, but Prof thinks I'm a fool." I ran my hand through my hair. "Half the time, I think he's right."

"Well, Jonathan Phaedrus is a great man. A wise man. But I once saw him lose to a bluff in poker, so we have empirical evidence that he doesn't know *everything*."

I smiled.

"I think your goal is a worthy one, Steelslayer." Exel sat up straighter and looked me in the eye. "I don't think we can ever beat the Epics on our own. We'd need a lot more firepower. Perhaps all the world needs is for a few Epics to step up and openly oppose the others. Nothing so dramatic as the Faithful believe, no mystical coming of blessed, angelic Epics. Just one or two who are willing to say, 'Hey, this isn't right.' If everyone including the Epics knew that there was another option, perhaps it would change everything."

I nodded. "Thanks."

"Thanks for what? For blabbing my random opinions at you?"

"Pretty much. I needed someone to talk to. Tia was too busy, and Val seems to hate me."

"Nah, you just remind her of Sam. The spyril was his baby, you know."

Well, I guess that made a kind of sense then. Unfair though it was.

"I—"

"Wait a sec," Exel said, holding up a hand. "Listen."

I turned my attention to the radio, focusing on making out the words. The static had been constant as we were talking, but I hadn't realized there were faint voices in the background.

". . . yeah, I see him," a voice said. "He's just sitting there, on the rooftop in Turtle Bay."

"Is he doing anything?" another voice said, the frequency crackling with static.

"Nah." First voice. "His eyes are closed. His face is turned toward the sky."

"Get out of there, Miles." Second voice. Frightened. "He's dangerous. Murdered a lot of people a couple weeks back."

"Yeah." First voice. "Why's he just sitting there, though?"

Exel looked up and met my eyes. "Obliteration?" he asked.

I nodded, feeling sick.

"You guessed he'd be doing this," Exel said. "Nice call."

"I wish I hadn't been right," I said, throwing back my chair and standing. "I need to go find Prof."

Obliteration had started storing up sunlight, like he had in Houston, Albuquerque, and finally San Diego.

If I was right, the city wouldn't survive his next step.

27

I found Prof in the conference room, the room with the large wall/window looking out into the ocean. The waters were clearer today than they'd been the last time I'd been in there, and I could see distant shadows, dark and square. They were buildings—a phantom skyline under the sea.

Prof stood in his black lab coat, staring out into the depths, hands clasped behind him.

"Prof?" I asked, hurrying into the room. "Exel just intercepted a conversation. Someone spotted Obliteration. He's storing energy."

Prof continued to stare into the depths.

"Like in Houston?" I prompted. "The days before he destroyed the entire place? Sir?"

Prof nodded toward the sunken city. "You never visited this place before it sank, did you?"

"No," I answered, trying to ignore the awful window he stared out of.

"I came into the city regularly. To see plays, go shopping, sometimes to just walk. It seemed that the most humble diners in Manhattan served better food than the nicest restaurants back home. And the finest places . . . Ah, I remember the way it smelled. . . ."

"Um, yeah. Obliteration?"

He nodded curtly and turned from the window. "Let's go have a look, then."

"Have a look?"

"You and me," Prof said, striding away. "We're point men. If there's danger, we check it out."

I ran after him. I wasn't going to argue—any excuse to get out of the base was a good one—but this didn't seem like Prof. He liked to plan. In Newcago we'd rarely moved, even on a scouting mission, without careful deliberation.

We entered the hallway and passed the room where Mizzy and Val were working. "I'm taking the sub," Prof announced to them without even a glance. I hurried to keep up, glancing back and shrugging toward a confused Mizzy, who had poked her head out after us.

I picked up my pace and ran ahead of Prof, fetching my gun from the equipment closet. I hesitated, then grabbed the backpack with the spyril inside as well.

"You shouldn't need that," Prof noted, passing me.

"So you think I should leave it?"

"Of course not."

I slung the pack over my shoulder, then joined Prof as he entered the darkness of the docking room. Here we followed a set of rope guides toward the sub. *Why,* I thought, *do I feel like a dog who just swallowed a hand grenade?* There was nothing to be nervous about; this was Prof. The great Jon Phaedrus. We were going on a scouting mission together. I should be excited.

Prof popped the hatch on the sub and we climbed in. Once we were down below, I locked the hatch, and Prof turned on a pale yellow emergency light. He waved me forward to sit in the copilot seat and started up the machine. A few moments later we were moving through the silent depths, and I had to stare out yet *another* window—the front of the sub—at more water.

"So . . . do you need to know where we're going?" I finally asked.

"Yes." His face was lit eerily by the yellow light.

"Well, we heard them say the words Turtle Bay."

Prof turned the sub in a slow curve. "Missouri tells me you're getting good with the spyril."

"Yeah. Well, I mean, I'm practicing. I don't know that I'd say I'm *good,* but I might get there eventually."

My mobile beeped quietly. I winced, then pulled it out. This new one had a different silencing button, and I always forgot to tap it. It used my old pattern, so anyone who knew that could contact me, but the message on the screen was from a pattern I didn't recognize.

Okay, let's talk, it read.

"That's good," Prof said. "The tensors won't be of much use to you here."

"I don't know," I said, trying to work out who was messaging. "When we were fighting inside the office building, it might have been good to slip through a wall unexpectedly."

"The spyril will be more useful," Prof said. "Focus on that

for now. We don't want to mix the powers. Might cause interference."

Interference? What kind of interference? I'd never heard
of such a thing. Granted, I didn't know much about this technology, but if such interference were a problem, wouldn't it
have affected the forcefields Prof gave me?

My mobile buzzed again. I'd silenced it but hadn't turned
off the vibrations. *You there, Knees?* the message read.

My heart jumped.

Megan? I typed back.

Who else would it be, you slontze?

Prof glanced at me. "What's happening?"

"Exel's messaging me," I lied. "With more information on
how to find Obliteration."

Prof nodded, turning eyes forward again. I quickly sent a
message to Exel, asking if he had more information on Obliteration's location, just in case Prof asked him later on. My mobile lit up almost immediately, saying someone else had seen
Obliteration. Directions to the building followed.

In the middle of that, Megan messaged again.

I really need to talk to you about something.

This isn't exactly a good time, I sent back.

Great. Fine.

The terseness of that reply made me sick inside. I was
turning her away after practically begging her to talk to me
earlier? I glanced at Prof. He seemed absorbed by his driving,
and the sub didn't move quickly. I probably had plenty of
time. How suspicious would it be?

Well, maybe I can spare some time to chat. I pressed SEND.

No reply.

Sparks. Why did everything have to happen at once? I
waited for a response, submarine engines churning, sweat

trickling down the sides of my face. Sitting up front here, you could see the whole underwater world stretching out before you, seemingly into infinity itself. Thinking about all this *nothing* made my hair stand on end.

I bent down over my mobile and sent another message to Megan. *Do you know why Regalia claimed she can make Epics?*

This time I got a response almost immediately. *She said what?*

She told me she'd made someone into an Epic, I wrote back. *She seemed to think it would scare me. I think she wanted me to decide that we can't fight back because she can send an unending string of Epics at us.*

What did you tell her? Megan asked.

Can't remember exactly. I think I laughed at her.

You never were very bright, Knees. That woman is dangerous.

But she literally had us in her grasp at one point! I wrote back. *She let us go. I don't think she wants us dead. Anyway, why do you think she would claim something that ridiculous? Did she really think I'd believe she could* make *someone into an Epic?*

Megan didn't respond for a time.

We really need to meet, she finally wrote to me. *Where are you?*

Heading into the city, I said.

Perfect.

Prof is with me, I added.

Oh.

You could meet with both of us, I wrote to her. *Explain yourself. He'd listen.*

It's more complicated than that, Megan wrote. *I was a spy for Steelheart, and I infiltrated Prof's own team. When it comes to his precious Reckoners, Phaedrus is like a mother bear with her cubs.*

Huh? I wrote back. *No, that's wrong.*

What?

I don't think that metaphor works, Megan. Prof is a dude, so he can't be a mother bear.

David, you are a complete and utter slontze.

I could hear the smile in her tone. Sparks, I missed her.

I'm an adorable one though, right? I wrote to her.

A pause, during which I found myself sweating.

I wish it was so easy, her message finally came. *I really, really wish it.*

It can be, I wrote back. *You still willing to meet?*

And Phaedrus?

I'll find a way to lose him, I wrote as Prof began to take the sub to the surface. *Will message you later.* I then tucked the mobile into my pocket.

"We there?" I asked.

"Almost," Prof replied.

"You've been pretty quiet this trip."

"I've been trying to decide if I should send you back to Newcago or not."

The words hit me like a slug from a .44 Special. I blinked, searching for a response. "But . . . you said when we came here, you said you were bringing me because you needed me."

"Son," Prof said softly, "if you think I can't kill Epics without you, then you must have a low opinion of my skills. If I decide you shouldn't be part of this operation, then you'll be out. Period."

"But why would you decide that?"

Prof piloted in silence for a moment, steering the sub slowly around a large chunk of floating debris—it looked like a hot dog stand. "You're a good point man, David," Prof said. "You think quickly and you solve problems. You have excellent instincts under fire. You're bold and aggressive."

"Thank you?"

"And you're exactly the sort of person I've avoided recruiting over the years."

I frowned.

"You haven't noticed?" Prof asked.

Now that he mentioned it . . . I thought about Cody, and Exel, and Abraham, and Mizzy. Even Val, to an extent. They weren't gun-toting, shoot-'em-up types. They were reserved, careful, slow to act.

"I've noticed," I said. "But I didn't really put it together until now."

"The Reckoners are not an army," Prof said. "We're not even a special forces unit. We're trap-layers. We're patient and conservative. You're none of those things. You're a firecracker, always urging us to action, to change the plan. This is good, in a way. You think big, son. It takes people with big dreams to accomplish big goals."

He turned to me, the sub puttering along slowly, not needing his guidance. "But I can't help thinking," he said, "that you don't intend to stick to the plan. You want to protect Regalia, and you harbor sympathies for a traitor. You have aspirations. So you're going to tell me, right now, the things you've been hiding from me. And then we're going to decide what to do with you."

"Now?" I asked.

"Now." Prof met my eyes. "Out with it."

28

PROF held my gaze, making me sweat. Sparks, that man could be intense. He wanted to pretend that his was a quiet, careful group—and in truth, it mostly was. If you didn't count him. He was like me. He always had been.

And because of that, I knew how deadly serious he was.

I licked my lips. "I'm planning to capture one of Regalia's Epics," I said. "When we hit Newton, I want to try to neutralize her instead of killing her—then I want to capture her. Like we did with Edmund back in Newcago."

Prof regarded me for a moment, then seemed to relax, as if that wasn't nearly as bad as he'd feared. "What would be the point?"

"Well, we know Regalia is devious. She's planning something more than we've been able to figure out."

"Possibly."

"*Probably*. You've said she's wily. You've implied she's very careful, and very clever. Sparks, Prof, you have to be worried that she's playing us all, even now."

He turned away from me. "I will admit that it has crossed my mind. Abigail has a habit of . . . positioning people, myself included, in places where she wants them."

"Well, she knows you. She knows what you'll do." I grew more excited—it seemed that I might have dug myself out of a bad situation. "She won't expect you to try a kidnapping, then. It's too bold, and not at all in line with the Reckoner methodology. But think what it could accomplish! Newton might know what Regalia is up to—at the very least, she'll know how Regalia is recruiting these other Epics."

"I doubt we'd learn much," Prof said. "Abigail wouldn't share that kind of information."

"Well, at the very least, Newton could tell us places that Regalia has appeared to her," I said. "Which will help with our map. And there's the chance she knows more. Right?"

Prof tapped the submarine's steering stick, the bubble-like window before him glowing with filtered light from above. "And how would you plan to make her talk? Torture?"

"Well, actually, I was kind of hoping that by keeping her from using her powers . . . you know . . . we'd make her turn good or something."

He cocked an eyebrow at me.

"It happened with Edmund," I said defensively.

"Edmund wasn't a murderer before his transformation."

Well, that was true.

"Beyond that," Prof said, "Edmund is good because he gifts his powers—like I do. He didn't 'turn good.' He just never went evil in the first place. What you really meant, but

220

didn't want to say it for fear of angering me, is that *Firefight* seemed to be good when she was with us. You're hoping that by preventing Newton from using her powers, you can get proof that doing the same for Firefight will return Megan to you."

"Maybe," I said, shrinking down in my chair.

"This is just the sort of thing I worried you were considering," Prof said. "You could have endangered the entire team by pursuing your own goals, David. Can't you see that?"

"I suppose," I said.

"Is that everything?" Prof asked me. "No other hidden plots?"

I grew cold. Megan. "That's everything," I found myself saying.

"Well, I suppose it isn't too bad." Prof let out a breath.

"So I'm staying in Babilar?"

"For now," Prof said. "Calamity. You're either exactly what the Reckoners need, and have needed for years . . . or you're a representation of the reckless heroism we've been wise to avoid. I still can't decide."

He steered the sub right toward a submerged building with a gaping hole in its side. It looked a lot like the place where we docked, but it was a different building. We passed into the opening like a big piece of buttered popcorn passing into the mouth of some decomposing beast. Inside, Prof popped the lever that released a flood of dish soap into the water, to make the surface tension weaker and inhibit Regalia's powers. He turned off the lights and let us surface.

We felt our way out and found the ropes to lead us across treacherous, half-submerged flooring to a set of steps. I couldn't see much of anything, though that was the point.

"Head up those steps," Prof whispered over the line. "We

scouted this building to use as a potential base before we found the other one. This place is unused, far enough from the neighborhoods that no bridges lead to it. The upstairs is a private office suite, which should have a good view of the rooftop in question."

"Got it," I said—holding my rifle in one hand, backpack over my other shoulder—as I felt at the door.

"I'm going to get back in the sub to be ready to pull out in a hurry," Prof said. "Something about all this feels off to me. Be ready to run; I'll leave the top open for you." He paused, and I felt his hand grip my shoulder. "Don't do anything stupid."

"Don't worry," I whispered over the line, "I'm an expert on stupid."

"You're . . ."

"Like, I can spot stupidity, because I know it so well. The way an exterminator knows bugs really well, and can spot where they've been? I'm like that. A stupidinator."

"Never say that word again," Prof said.

Well, it made sense to me. He let go, and I pulled open the door and stepped inside. After pulling it closed, I strapped my mobile to my shoulder and turned on the light. The stairwell led upward in a dark incline, wet, partially rotting. Like the forgotten steps you might find in some old horror movie.

Except people in those movies hadn't been armed with a fully automatic Gottschalk assault rifle with electron-compressed magazines and a night-vision scope. I smiled, dimming my mobile and raising the rifle, engaging the night vision. Prof said this place was abandoned, but it was best to be certain.

I climbed the steps carefully, rifle at my shoulder. I still wasn't completely satisfied with the Gottschalk. My old rifle had been better. Sure, it had jammed now and then. And it hadn't been automatic, and had needed the sights adjusted at least once a month. And . . . well, it had just been better anyway. So there.

Megan would laugh at that, I thought. Getting sentimental about a clearly inferior gun? Only fools did that. The thing was, we talk that way—but we all seem to get sentimental about our guns anyway. I reached to my side, suddenly realizing that it felt wrong not to have Megan's handgun on me any longer. I'd need to requisition a replacement.

At the top of the long stairwell, I entered what had once been a well-furnished reception room. Now overgrown with the ubiquitous Babilar plant life, it was draped in gloom and vines. No windows gave light to this room, and though fruit drooped from the trees and covered the floor, none of it glowed. That only happened after nightfall.

I inched forward, stepping over old expense reports and other paperwork. The room smelled terrible—of rot and fungus. I found myself oddly annoyed at Prof as I walked. What did he mean by "reckless heroism"? Weren't we supposed to be heroes?

My father had waited for the heroes. He'd believed in them. He'd died because he'd believed in Steelheart.

He'd been a fool in that regard. But somehow, more and more, I found myself wishing I could be the same kind of fool. I wasn't going to feel guilty for trying to help people. Prof could say what he wanted, but deep down he felt the same way. He'd agreed to bring down Steelheart because he'd sensed that the Reckoners weren't making enough of a difference.

He would make the right decisions. He'd save this city. Prof *was* a hero. The Epic who fought for mankind. He just needed to admit it. And—

Something under my foot crunched.

I froze and scanned the small room through my scope again. Nothing. I lowered the gun and turned on my light. What in Calamity's shadow . . . ?

I'd stepped on a cluster of small objects that were growing from vines at the bottom of one of the trees. The bizarre plant tendrils grew out from under the bark like whiskers on a man wearing a mask. I had to take a closer look at what I was seeing because I could swear that at their tips were . . . cookies.

Yes, cookies. I knelt down, fishing among them for a moment. I pulled out a piece of paper. *Fortune cookies,* I thought. *Growing from the tree.*

I flipped the paper over, reading the words.

Help me.

Great. I was back in the horror movie.

Unsettled, I stepped back and snapped my rifle up into position. I looked around the room again, shining my mobile into shadowed corners behind tree trunks. Nothing jumped out at me. When I was convinced I was alone, I bent down to the cookies again and searched among them, reading other slips of paper. They all said either *Help me* or *She has me captive.*

"David?" Tia's voice sounded in my earpiece. "You into position yet?"

I jumped almost to the ceiling.

"Uh, not yet," I said, stuffing some of the pieces of paper and the bits of cookie into my pocket. "I just stumbled onto something. Um . . . has anyone ever reported finding cookies growing from the fruit trees?"

Silence on the line.

"Cookies?" Tia asked. "David, is something wrong with you?"

"Well, I've kind of had some indigestion lately," I noted, moving toward the room's other door, behind a decomposing receptionist's desk. "But I don't think that's causing me to hallucinate cookies. Usually indigestion *strictly* causes cheesecake delusions."

"Ha, ha," Tia said dryly.

"Take a sample," Prof said. "Move on."

"Done and done," I said, listening at the door, then shoving it open and checking each corner of the room on the other side. It was empty, though a pair of broad windows shone light in on me. It was an executive office strewn with fallen books and metallic doodads, like those little ball things where you raise one side, then it clicks annoyingly against the others. Only two trees were growing in here, one on either side of the room, sending vines creeping up the bookcases on each wall.

I continued forward, stepping over the debris and doing my best to stay low, approaching the large windows. This building *was* secluded, off by itself in the middle of the ocean. Waves broke against the base, water churning below. Distantly across some kind of bay, other buildings broke the surface of the ocean. Babilar proper.

I knelt down, set aside my backpack, and poked the front of my gun out a broken section of window. Eye to the scope, I dialed up to ten times magnification. It worked beautifully. I could see five hundred yards easily; in fact, dialing up the zoom, I bet I could get to two thousand yards with reasonable detail.

Sparks. I'd never made shots like *that* before. I was good with a rifle, but I wasn't a trained sniper. I doubted the Gottschalk had the range for that shot anyway, though the scope was excellent for peeking about.

"I'm in position," I said. "Which building is it?"

"You see a peaked one?" Exel said over the line. "Next to the two flatter rooftops?"

"Yup," I said, zooming in. It was quite a distance, but no problem for the gun's excellent magnification.

And there he was.

29

OBLITERATION looked much as he had the other two times I'd seen him, except he'd removed his shirt, black trench coat, and glasses, which were now strewn on the rooftop beside his sword. His bandaged chest was exposed, and he sat cross-legged, goateed face stretched toward the sky, eyes closed. His posture was serene, like a man doing morning yoga.

The major difference between now and when I'd seen him before, however, was that he glowed with a deep inner light, like something was burning just beneath his skin.

I felt a surprising surge of anger. I remembered thrashing in the water, the shackle around my leg pulling me toward the depths. Never again.

I focused on Obliteration, holosights putting a dot right on his head. Then I tapped the side of my gun, flipping a switch and sending a feed from the scope to my mobile. That sent the image to Tia.

"Thanks," Tia said, watching the feed. "Hmm . . . Doesn't look good. You thinking what I am?"

"Yeah," I said. "Can you dig out my photos of Houston?"

"I've got better ones," Tia said. "Asked around once I knew he was here. Sending."

I looked away from the scope and took the mobile off my arm. Tia's message arrived soon after, including a set of photos taken in Houston. This was from the height of Obliteration's reign in the city. It had been a terrible place to live, but—like Newcago—there'd been a certain level of stability. As I'd had proven to me in both Newcago and Babilar, people would rather live with the Epics—and their tyranny—than waste away in the chaos between cities.

This meant there had been a lot of witnesses when Obliteration had settled down right before his palace, an old government building he'd repurposed, and started glowing. Most of those witnesses had died soon after. Some had gotten out, though, and more had sent photos from their mobiles to friends outside the city.

Tia's images—which were indeed better than the ones in my files—showed Obliteration sitting as he did now. Different pants, no bandage on his chest, and less scruff on his face, but same posture and glow.

"Those look like the pictures from the first day of him storing power in the other cities, wouldn't you say?" Tia said over the line.

"Yeah," I replied, moving through the images to look at another sequence of shots. Obliteration in San Diego. Same posture. I compared how much he glowed on the first day in both Houston and San Diego, then compared it to how he looked now. "I agree. He's only just begun the process."

"Would one of you two mind explaining to the old man what we're talking about?" Prof asked over the line.

"His primary ability—his heat manipulation—is exo-dynamic," I said.

"Great," Prof said. "Very helpful."

"I thought you were a genius," I said.

"I taught fifth-grade science," Prof reminded me. "And it's not like we taught Epic power theory back then."

"Obliteration," Tia said in a calm voice, "needs to draw heat out of objects to use for destroying things. Sunlight touching his skin works too—not as efficiently, but since it's persistent, it's an easy source for him."

"Before he destroyed Houston and each of the other cities he's annihilated, he sat in the sunlight for seven days drawing energy," I said. "He then released it in one burst. Comparing how much he's glowing now to the pictures from Houston, we can guess how long he's been doing this."

"And theoretically," Tia added, "we can guess how long we have until something very, very bad happens."

"We're going to have to move up our timetable," Prof said softly. "How soon can we prepare the hit on Newton?"

That was still the plan: attack Newton, draw Regalia out, and use this information to pinpoint Regalia's base. The firm way Prof spoke over the line seemed like he was talking directly to me. The Reckoners were going to kill Newton, not kidnap her—and my plan to do otherwise was foolish.

I didn't reply. It probably *was* foolish to try to kidnap her. For now, I'd go along with the plan as it stood.

"A hit on Newton will be tough," Tia said, "considering that we don't know her weakness."

"She repels attacks on her," Prof said. "So what if we just drown her? Force redirection won't save her if she's sinking into the ocean."

I shivered in horror at the thought.

"That could do it," Tia said. "I'll work on a plan."

"Even if our hit on Newton doesn't actually kill her," Prof said, "we will probably be all right. The point of the attack will be to lure out Regalia, pinpoint her base, then take *her* out. If Newton lives on, so be it."

"And Obliteration?" I asked, finger itching on the trigger of my rifle. I removed my hand. Not only was this a shot I couldn't make with any amount of reliability, but Obliteration's danger sense would engage and he'd teleport away. Better he be somewhere we could keep an eye on him. If we started annoying him without a proper plan in place, he might just set up somewhere hidden and store energy.

"Him we can't leave running around free," Prof agreed, speaking softly. "David's right. We'll need another plan for dealing with him. Soon."

I turned the scope of my rifle to scan the area around Obliteration. It was densely populated, as evidenced by the bridges in good repair and the tents with laundry hanging outside. Most people had wisely fled at the sight of Obliteration, but I could see a few who'd stayed, hidden near the edges of buildings or peeking out of nearby windows.

Even after what this creature had done, curiosity got the better of people. Inspecting windows, I gathered that the majority of the people had fled down into the rooms below, hiding among the trees and vines.

"We're going to need his weakness, Tia," Prof said over the line. "We can't rely on exploiting quirks in his powers."

"I know," she replied. "It's just that ordinary research doesn't work for Obliteration. Most Epics spend time around people and their peers. Secrets leak out. But he is so solitary; he tends to kill even other Epics who get too close to him."

Do not sorrow for this end of days, little one. I remembered the words Obliteration had spoken to me. Most Epics, in their megalomania, presumed some kind of dominance over the world. That Obliteration should quote religious texts and act like some divine agent wasn't surprising.

It didn't make the words any less creepy though.

As I scanned the rooftops nearby, I spotted someone standing on one of them, inspecting Obliteration through binoculars. I increased my zoom one level. Didn't I know that face? I brought up my mobile and searched through it for the pictures of Newton's gang members. Yes, this man was one of them, a thug named Knoxx. Not an Epic.

"I see one of Newton's gang," I said, looking back through the scope. "Focused on him now."

"Hmm," Tia said. "This is a deviation from their daily rounds, but it isn't surprising, considering what Obliteration is doing."

I nodded, watching as the man lowered his binoculars and spoke into his mobile.

"Yes," Prof said, "probably just . . ."

Suddenly the man melted.

I caught my breath, losing the rest of what Prof was saying as I watched the man shift into the shape of a small pigeon. It took to the air and flew across the rooftop faster than I could track with my scope. I searched and finally located the animal landing on a different roof nearby, where he re-formed into a man.

"He's an Epic," I whispered. "Shapeshifter. Val's notes say his name is Knoxx, but she said he didn't have any powers. Do you recognize him, Tia?"

"I'll have to search the records and see if any of the lorists mention him," she said. "Newton's gang often recruits lesser Epics; maybe Val's team simply missed noticing this guy had abilities. Is Newton herself there?"

"I don't . . . ," I said, trailing off as something landed beside Knoxx. "Wait. That's her. She just . . . Sparks! She *jumped* from the next building over. That has to be fifty feet easy."

The two started conversing, and what I wouldn't have given to be able to hear what they were saying. Finally, Newton pointed one direction, then the other. Were they setting up a perimeter? I watched as the man formed into a bird again and flew off.

Then Newton was gone. Sparks! That woman could *move*. I had to zoom back two steps to find her running across the rooftop. Her speed was impressive; by the display above my scope's holosights, she was moving at fifty-three miles per hour. I'd read of Epics who could move faster than that, but this was only one of her secondary powers.

Newton bounded up in a short hop and came down on the edge of a roof, then engaged her energy reflection power—she reflected the force of hitting the rooftop back downward, making her move like she was on a trampoline that perfectly conserved her energy. She shot into the air in a powerful, quick-moving arc and easily cleared the gap between buildings.

"Wow," Tia said softly.

"Not as impressive as flying," Prof grumbled.

"No, it's more impressive in some ways," Tia said. "Think of the precision and mastery that requires. . . ."

I nodded in agreement, though they couldn't see. I followed Newton, moving my scope, as she leaped again. She landed on the roof of a large building right next to the one where Obliteration was, then pulled out her sword and started hacking away ropes on the bridge leading to another rooftop. She repeated this with the other two bridges on the building where she stood.

"This is unusual behavior for her," Tia said, sounding uncomfortable.

My hand tightened on the rifle barrel. She'd completely isolated a building right next to the one Obliteration was on. Now the water surrounding the building was pulling *away,* like . . . like people at a party leaving space around someone with bad gas. The water rushed back some ten feet on all sides, then held there, exposing the bottom half of the building. It was rusted over and encrusted with barnacles.

I glanced at Obliteration, sitting and glowing on the rooftop of the building next to the one the water had pulled away from. He hadn't moved, hadn't even reacted.

"What in Calamity's shadow?" Tia whispered. "That water is Regalia's doing, but why . . . ?"

I looked back at the isolated building where Newton strolled over to the stairwell leading down from the roof into the building proper. She took something off her belt and tossed it down the stairs, then threw two more small objects onto the rooftop nearby. Finally, she bounded away.

"Firebombs," I whispered as they exploded in quick succession. "She's burning the building down. With the people inside."

30

I threw down the gun, scrambled back from the window, and leaped for the backpack. I unzipped it and pulled out the spyril.

"David?" Tia asked urgently. "Leave the scope on the building!"

"So you can watch those people die?" I asked, unpacking the wetsuit. Sparks! I didn't have time for that. I started affixing the spyril over my clothing, pulling off my shoes and doing the legs first.

"I need to observe Newton's behavior," Tia said, ever the academic. We were alike in some ways, but this was what separated us—I couldn't detach myself and just watch. "Newton hasn't killed in years," she continued, "save for a few quiet executions of rivals or those who threatened Regalia's peace. Why do something this atrocious now?"

"Regalia is making an example of those people," Prof said softly over the line. "She's using her power in an obvious way, to make it clear that this is her will—and to keep the people in the building from jumping into the water. This is meant to tell everyone to stay away from Obliteration. Like a corpse hung from the walls of a medieval city."

"Makes sense," Tia said. "He's going to have to sit out there for several days, immobile, and Regalia won't want him interrupted."

"We're witnessing her slide from benevolent but harsh dictator into all-destroying tyrant," Prof said quietly.

"I'm not going to 'witness' it," I said, pulling another strap tight. "I'm going to stop it."

"David—" Prof said over the line.

"Yeah, yeah," I spat. "Reckless heroism. I'm not going to just sit here."

"But *why*," Tia said, voice softer. "Why is Regalia doing this? She could swallow the city in water, couldn't she? Why use Obliteration. Sparks . . . Why destroy the city at all? This isn't like Abigail."

"The Abigail we knew is dead," Prof said. "Only Regalia remains. David, if you save those people, she will only kill others. She will make certain her point gets made."

"*I don't care,*" I said, trying to get the thin backplate of the spyril into place. This was a lot harder without Exel or Mizzy to help. "If we stop helping people because we're afraid, or ambivalent or whatever, then we lose. Let them do evil. I'll stop them."

"You're not omnipotent, David," Prof said. "You're just human."

I faltered for a moment, holding the pieces of the spyril. The powers of a dead Epic. Then I redoubled my efforts, pulling on the gloves, locking the wires in place from hands and legs up to the backplate. I stood up and engaged the streambeam— the laserlike line that would draw water once pointed at it. I looked back out through the window. The blaze had fully started, black smoke billowing up into the air.

I'd forgotten how wide the bay was separating me from the burning building. The scope made things look close, but I had a lot of water to cross before reaching the burning building.

Well, I'd just have to work more quickly. I placed my earpiece and mobile into the waterproof pocket of my pants. Then I took a deep breath and jumped out the window.

Pointing the streambeam downward, I started the water jets on my legs enough to slow my impact and splashed down into the ocean water. The shock of the cold and the taste of the briny salt was immediate. Sparks! It was way colder than it had been during practice.

Fortunately, I had the spyril. I pointed myself toward the smoking building and jetted away. This time, unfortunately, I didn't have one of Prof's forcefields, and each time I came crashing down into the ocean porpoiselike, water hit my face like the slap of a jilted lover.

I dealt with it. Gasping for breath each time I emerged from the ocean. Sparks! The waves were a lot stronger out here than they had been in the Central Park sea, and it was tough to see when surrounded by them.

I slowed the jets to get my bearings and had a moment of severe disorientation. I was in the middle of *nothing*. With the waves surging, I couldn't see the city at all, and it seemed like I was in a vast, endless sea. Infinity all around me, the depths below.

Panic.

What was I doing out here? What was *wrong* with me? I started hyperventilating, twisting myself about. Each wave was a threat trying to pull me underneath the water. I got a mouthful of brine.

Luckily, some gut instinct to survive kicked in and I engaged the spyril, jetting myself up out of the water.

Hanging there, water dripping from my clothing, I gasped for air and squeezed my eyes shut. I wanted to move. I *needed* to move. But in those moments, I could more easily have lifted a semi truck filled with pudding.

That water. All that *water* . . .

I took a deep breath and tried to slow my breathing, then forced my eyes open. From my vantage hovering on the spyril jets, I could see over the waves. I'd gotten turned around, and had to reorient myself. I'd crossed half the distance and needed to continue, but it was sparking difficult to motivate myself to release the streambeam and fall back down.

With effort, I let myself down, splashing back into the sea. I used the black smoke rising into the sky as a guidepost. I thought of the people inside the building. With no water to jump to, they'd likely be fleeing from the flames above, moving down to the lower levels. But that would leave them to drown when the waters returned.

How horrible a death that would be, trapped inside a building as the waters rushed back in, perversely stuck between the heat above and the cold depths below.

Furious, I increased the speed of the spyril.

Something snapped.

Suddenly, I was spinning in a rush of water and bubbles. I cut the thrust. Blast! One of the footjets had stopped working. I struggled to the surface, coughing, cold. It was really hard to stay afloat with the weight of the now-powerless spyril towing me down and with my clothing still on.

237

And why was it so hard to float? I was made of mostly water, right? Shouldn't I float easily?

Fighting the swells, I tried to reach down and fix the spyril jet. But I didn't even know what had caused it to stop working, and I wasn't particularly good at swimming unaided. Eventually the inevitable happened and I started sinking. I had to engage the single working jet of my spyril to get back afloat.

I felt like I'd swallowed half the ocean so far. Coughing, I started to panic again as I realized just how dangerous the open waters could be. I positioned my one leg with a working jet behind me, turned the spyril on half power, and pushed myself toward the distant buildings.

I could focus only on keeping myself afloat and pointed toward civilization. It was slow going. Too slow. Keenly, I felt the shame of having rushed in to be a hero only to end up limping along, having nearly created a new crisis instead of solving the first one. What better example of Prof's warnings could I get?

Fortunately, my terror was manageable, so long as I had that spyril jet to give me some measure of control over the situation. As I got closer to the city, the water warmed around me. Eventually, blessedly, I reached one of the outer buildings, a low one with the roof only two stories or so out of the water. The single jet was enough to propel me upward—if at an unexpected angle—and I grabbed the rooftop's lip and hauled myself over, coughing.

Though the spyril had done all the work, I was exhausted. I flopped over, smelling smoke in the air, and stared at the sky.

Those people. I tried to climb to my feet. Maybe I could . . .

The building blazed nearby, only one street over. Fully alight, the top half had burned completely, an inferno. I could feel the heat even from a distance. This was more than the work of just one or two firebombs. Either Newton had continued throwing more in, or the place had been primed to go up. Around the structure, water coursed in a vortex, revealing a broken, wet street far below.

A few corpses spotted the ground. People had tried to leap free of the flames.

Even as I watched, the water was released. It crashed back in upon the building, and the hissing indicated that the fire had managed to creep down toward those levels that had formerly been submerged. The impact caused the top floors of the building to collapse into the water, blowing steam into the air with a horrible noise.

I stumbled to my feet, feeling utterly defeated. On a nearby roof I saw Regalia's watery projection standing with hands clasped before her. She looked toward me, then melted into the surface of the sea and vanished.

I collapsed onto the rooftop. Why? It was so pointless.

Prof is right, I thought. *They murder indiscriminately. Why did I think that any of them could be good?*

My pants buzzed. I sighed, fishing out my mobile. I got a little water on it, but Mizzy said it was fully waterproof.

Prof was calling. I lifted the mobile beside my head, ready to accept my lecture. I could see now what had caused the spyril to malfunction—I hadn't done the wires correctly leading to the left leg. They'd come undone. A simple problem, one that wouldn't have happened if I'd been more careful putting on the equipment.

"Yeah," I said into the phone.

"Is she gone?" Prof's voice asked.

"Who?"

"Regalia. She was watching, wasn't she?"

"Yeah."

"Probably still is, remotely," Prof said. He sounded winded. "I'll have to sneak these people out in the sub, somehow."

I stood up. *"Prof?"* I said, excited.

"Don't look too eager," he said with a grunt. "She's probably watching you. Act dejected." In the background, over the line, I heard a child crying. "Can you quiet her?" Prof snapped to someone.

"You're in the building," I said. "You . . . you saved them!"

"David," Prof said, voice tense. "This is *not* a good time for me. Do you understand?"

He's keeping the water and the flames back, I realized. *With forcefields.*

"Yes," I whispered.

"I left the sub behind. I had to run across the bottom of the ocean to get here."

I blinked in surprise. "Is that *possible?"*

"With a forcefield bubble extending in front of me?" Prof said. "Yeah. Haven't practiced it in ages." He grunted. "I came into the building from below, by vaporizing a section of ground and crossing over into the basement. I'm going to make a forcefield tunnel through the water for these people and hike back to the building we left. Can you meet me there?"

The thought of going back into the bay nauseated me, but I wasn't about to admit that. "Sure."

"Good."

"Prof . . . ," I said, trying to look morose, though I felt distinctly the opposite. "You're a hero. You really *are."*

"Stop."

"But, you saved—"

"Stop."

I fell silent.

"Get back to the building," he said. "I'll need you to pilot the sub and take the people to a place well outside Regalia's range, then let them go. Do you understand?"

"Sure. But why can't you pilot it?"

"Because," Prof said, voice growing soft. "It's going to take every bit of my willpower over the next few minutes not to murder these people for inconveniencing me."

I swallowed. "Got it," I said, then fixed the wires on my boot. I pocketed the phone and pointed the streambeam at the water, testing to make certain everything was operating— then I double-checked the wires just to be certain.

Finally I started out, more carefully this time. It took a long while, but I eventually arrived. Then I had to wait in a room near where we'd docked the submarine for the better part of an hour before I heard sounds.

I stood up as a door opened, and an ashen group of people began to pile out of a hallway. Prof had led them up into another part of the building. I rushed to help, calmed them, then explained how we'd have to enter the submarine in the darkness with everyone being as quiet as possible. We couldn't risk Regalia discovering what Prof had done.

With some effort, I got the coughing, wet, and exhausted group of people into the submarine. There were about forty of them, but we could all fit. Barely.

I helped the last one down, a mother with a baby, then climbed out and crossed through the building to the room where I'd met the people, shining my mobile to make certain I hadn't left anyone.

Prof stood in the opposite doorway, mostly in shadow. His goggles reflected the light so I couldn't see his eyes. He nodded to me once, then turned around and vanished into the gloom.

I sighed and clicked my mobile off, then walked back to the submarine room and used the ropes to guide me. I climbed in and pulled down the hatch, sealing it, then descended into the crowded sub full of wet people who smelled of smoke. Prof's attitude disturbed me, but it wasn't enough to dispel the warmth I felt inside. He'd done it. Despite his complaints about my recklessness, he'd gone and saved the people himself.

He and I *were* the same. He was just a hell of a lot more competent than I was. I took the sub's front seat and called Val to ask for instructions on how to pilot the thing.

31

I set the box of rations down with a thump, then stood and wiped my brow. Several of the Babilaran refugees Prof had saved picked up the boxes and hurried off with them, making quickly for the nearby wreckage of a warehouse. They'd cleaned off some of the soot in the day since I'd dropped them off here in the rotting remains of a small island off the coast of New York, but they seemed to have gained a healthy sense of self-preservation during that time. It must not have been buried very deep.

"Thank you," a woman named Soomi said, bowing. Though it was evening, their spraypainted clothing didn't glow here, so it just looked dirty. Old.

"Just remember our deal," I said.

"We didn't see anything," she promised. "And we won't return to the city for at least a month."

I nodded. Soomi and her people believed that the Reckoners had saved them using secret forcefield technology. They weren't to tell anyone what they'd seen, but even if it got out, hopefully the stories wouldn't implicate Prof as an Epic.

Soomi picked up one of the last boxes and joined the others, hurrying back toward a group of ramshackle buildings with overgrown grounds. It was best not to be seen with food, in case scavengers saw you. Fortunately, the only way off this island was a bridge just to the north, so hopefully they would be safe here.

My heart wrenched to see them without homes or possessions, cast adrift, but this was all we could do. And it was maybe more than we should have done—we'd needed to have Cody airlift us supplies out of Newcago to provide rations for these people.

I turned and made my way down an empty, broken street, rifle over my shoulder. It was a short walk to the old dock where we'd parked the submarine. Val lounged, seated on top of it. She'd stacked the boxes of food on the dock, while the refugees and I had carried them inside.

I hesitated on the dock, looking out toward Babilar to the southwest. It glowed with surreal colors, like a portal to some other dimension. Though the water extending out before me looked flat, I knew that it sloped upward slightly. Regalia had sculpted this city's look intentionally; she even maintained different water levels in different parts of Babilar, creating handcrafted neighborhoods of rooftops and sunken streets.

She does care, I thought. *She built this city like she intended to stay here, to rule. She made it inviting.*

So why destroy it now?

"Coming?" Val called to me.

I nodded and crossed the dock and scrambled aboard the sub—this area was outside of Regalia's range of sight, theoretically, so we could let it surface in the open.

"Hey," Val said as I passed, "when are you going to tell me how you saved them? For real, I mean."

I hesitated at the hatch, light from down inside rising to bathe me. "I used the spyril," I said.

"Yeah, but how?"

"I put out the fire in a room," I said, using the lie Tia and I had prepared. We'd been expecting Val or Exel to prod eventually. "I was able to crowd everyone into the same room, then keep them safe and quiet until Regalia thought everyone was dead. Then I snuck them out."

It was a good enough lie. Val didn't know that the building had basically collapsed once the water came rushing back in. It was plausible that I'd have been able to get the people out.

Good lie or not, I hated telling it. Couldn't Prof be straight with the members of his own team?

Val regarded me carefully, and though her face was too much in shadows to read, I felt like the only rotten strawberry in a line of strawberries. Finally, she shrugged. "Well, nice work."

I hurriedly slipped down into the submarine. Val followed, then locked the hatch and moved to the front seat. She didn't believe what I'd told her, not completely. I could read it in the stiff way she sat down, the too-controlled sound of her voice as she called Tia and said we were on our way back to the supply dump to get the next set of boxes, which would restock our base.

I fidgeted, and we moved under the waves and traveled for a while in silence. Finally, I forced myself to get into the copilot's seat next to Val at the front. I still knew next to nothing about Val. Maybe some disarming conversation would ease her suspicion about what had happened the day before.

"So," I said, "I notice you prefer a Colt 1911. A good, time-tested gun. Is that a Springfield frame and slide set?"

"Don't know, honestly," she said, glancing at the gun she wore on her hip. "Sam gave it to me."

"But, I mean, surely you need to know. For replacement parts."

Val shrugged. "It's just a gun. If it breaks, I'll get another."

Just a . . .

Just a gun? Had she really *said* that?

I found my mouth working, but no sound coming out, as we puttered beneath the waves. The gun you carried was lit-erally your life—if it malfunctioned, you could be dead. How could she say something like that?

Be disarming, I told myself forcefully. *Chastising her won't make her more comfortable around you.*

"So, uh," I said, coughing into my hand, "you must have enjoyed it here, on this assignment. Sweet undersea base, no Epics to fight, a city full of good-natured people. Must be the best job a Reckoner team could get assigned."

"Sure," Val said. "Until one of my friends got murdered."

And now I was "replacing" that friend in the team. Great. Another reminder why she shouldn't like me.

"You've known Mizzy for a while," I said, trying another tactic. "You didn't grow up in the city, did you?"

"No."

"Where were you stationed before this?"

"Mexico. But you shouldn't ask about our pasts. It's against protocol."

"Just trying to—"

"I know what you're trying to do. It's not necessary. I'll do my job; you do yours."

"Sure," I said. "All right." I settled back in my seat.

Wait. Mexico? I perked up. "You . . . weren't in on the Hermosillo job, were you?"

Val eyed me, but said nothing.

"The hit on Puños de Fuego!" I exclaimed.

"How do you know about that?" Val asked.

"Oh man. Was it true, did he really throw a *tank* at you?"

Val kept her eyes forward, tapping a button on the sub's control panel. "Yeah," she finally said. "An *entire* flippin' tank. Broke open the wall of our base of operations."

"Wow."

"What's more, I was running ops."

"So you—"

"Yeah. I was inside when this tank comes crashing right through the wall. He'd dodged around Sam and managed to double back, so he could hit our operations station. Still not sure how he even knew where we were."

I grinned, imagining it. Puños had been a beastly strength Epic, capable of lifting practically anything—even things that should have broken apart as he did it. Not a High Epic, but hard to kill, with enhanced endurance and skin like an elephant's.

"I never did figure out how you beat him," I said. "Only that the team eventually took him out, despite the job going wrong."

Val kept her gaze trained straight ahead, but I caught a hint of a smile on her lips.

"What?" I asked.

"Well . . . I was there," she said, growing slightly more an-imated, "in the rubble of our operations station—a little brick building in the center of the city. And he was coming for me. I was alone, no support."

"And?"

"And . . . well, there was a *tank* in the room."

"You didn't."

"Yeah," Val said. "At first I climbed into the thing just to hide. But then, it was armed, and he walked right in front of the barrel. The tank was on its side, but it had crashed in through the wall rear-end-first. So I figured, what the hell?"

"You shot him."

"Yeah."

"With a tank."

"Yeah."

"That's *awesome*."

"It was stupid," Val said, though she was still smiling. "If that barrel had been bent, I'd probably have blown myself up instead. But . . . well, it worked. Sam said he found Puños's arm seven streets over." She looked at me, then seemed to realize who she was talking to. Her expression dimmed.

"Sorry," I said.

"For what?"

"For not being Sam."

"That's stupid," Val said, turning away from me. She hesitated. "You're kind of infectious, Steelslayer. You know that?"

"It's my gritty, determined manliness."

"Um. No. It's not. But it might be your enthusiasm." She shook her head and pulled back on the steering column, raising the sub up toward the surface. "Either way, you can go be manly hauling boxes. We've arrived."

I smiled, glad to have finally had a conversation with Val that didn't involve a lot of scowling. I got up and made my way over to the ladder. The door to the bathroom was rattling again. We really needed to get Mizzy to fix the blasted thing. I nudged it closed with my toe, then I climbed up and opened the hatch.

The land up above was pitch-black, darkness fully upon

us. This supply dump wasn't as far up the coast as City Island, but we should be well outside Regalia's range. Still, it seemed a good idea to never leave the sub without someone in it, so I'd fetch the boxes and carry them the short distance to the coast, then set them down for Val. She'd get them from shore to the sub, then carry them down the ladder and stack them.

I shouldered my rifle and climbed out onto a quiet dock, water lapping against the wood, as if to pointedly remind me that it was still there. I hurried across the dock and approached a dark building ahead, an old shed where Cody had unloaded our supplies.

I slipped inside. At least there wouldn't be as many boxes this time around. We probably should have carried them all down before, but our arms had been aching, and a short break had sounded really nice.

I turned on the light on my mobile and checked the room.

Then I pulled open the hidden trapdoor in the floor, and climbed down to check on Prof.

32

BURROWED into the rock beneath the shed was one of the secret Reckoner stopover bases, set up with a cot, some supplies, and a workbench. Prof stood by the bench, holding up a beaker and inspecting it by the light of a lantern. That was an improvement; when I'd come down here before, he'd been lying on the cot looking through some old photos—they lay scattered on the cot now.

Prof didn't look up as I came down. "We're grabbing the rest of the supplies," I said, thumbing over my shoulder. "You need anything?"

Prof shook his head and stirred his beaker.

"You going to be all right?" I asked.

"I'm feeling fine," Prof said. "I'm planning to head back

into the city a little later in the evening. Might return to the base tomorrow; might stay away another day. We'll need to give it enough time that Val's team will believe I went to check in on another Reckoner cell."

That had been Tia's explanation for his absence. I watched curiously as he mixed another beaker with a liquid of a different color.

"We're hitting Newton in two days," I told him. "Tia made the call, since she said you weren't being responsive."

Two days was well before Obliteration's expected deadline, which would give us some wiggle room in case things went poorly.

He grunted. "Two days? I'll be back by then." He mixed the two beakers into a jar and stepped back. A large jet of foam launched from the container, reaching almost to the ceiling, then fell back in a frothy splat. Prof watched, then smiled.

"Hydrogen peroxide mixed with potassium iodide," he said. "The kids used to love that one." He reached over and started mixing some other materials.

"Could you come back sooner?" I asked him. "We still don't have a plan to deal with Obliteration, and he's got a gun to the city's head."

"I'm working on how to deal with that," Prof said. "I think if we bring down Regalia, it might scare him away. If it doesn't, we might find intel on his weakness among her notes."

"And if we don't?"

"We evacuate the city," Prof said.

Tia had theorized the same possibility, but it seemed like a bad option to me. We couldn't start a theoretical evacuation until Regalia was dead—otherwise she'd surely move against the fleeing people. I doubted we'd have enough time to get everyone out before Obliteration wasted the place.

"Tell Tia to call me a little later tonight," Prof said. "We'll talk about it."

"Sure thing," I said, then paused as he worked on another mixture. "What are you doing?"

"Another experiment."

"Why?"

"Because," he said, turning away. His face fell into shadow. "Remembering the old days helps. Remembering the students, and their excitement, their joy. The memories seem to push it back."

I nodded slowly, but he wasn't looking at me. He'd returned to his science experiment. So instead I inched forward to see if I could catch a glimpse of the photos he'd been looking at.

I reached the cot and leaned down and picked one up. The photo showed a younger version of Prof, wearing casual clothing—jeans, a T-shirt—standing with some people in a room filled with monitors and computers. Other people were scattered throughout the room, wearing uniform blue shirts.

Prof glanced at me.

I held up the photo. "Some kind of lab?"

"NASA," he said, sounding reluctant. "The old space program."

"I thought you said you were a schoolteacher!"

"I'm not the one who worked there, genius," Prof said. "Look more closely."

I looked back down, and realized that in the photo Prof looked more like a tourist, grinning and getting his picture taken. It took me a second to spot that one of the many people in the photo wearing a blue NASA shirt had short red hair. Tia.

"Tia's a *rocket scientist*?" I asked.

"Was," Prof said. "That was a long time ago. She let me

visit right after we first started dating. Highlight of my life—bragged about it to my students for months."

I looked down at the picture. The man in this photo, though it was obviously Prof, looked like a different species entirely. Where were the lines of worry on the man's face, the haunted eyes, the imposing stature?

Nearly thirteen years of Calamity had changed this man. And not just because of the powers he'd gained.

Another photo peeked out from underneath the sheet. I pulled it out. And Prof didn't stop me, turning back to his experiment.

In this picture, four people stood in a line. One was Prof, wearing his now-trademark black lab coat, goggles in the pocket. Beside him Regalia stood with hand outstretched, a glob of water hovering above her fingers. She wore an elegant blue gown. Tia was there, and there was another man, one I didn't know. Older, with white-grey hair sticking out from his head in an almost crown shape, he sat in a chair while the others stood.

"Who is this man?" I asked.

"Those are also memories from another time," Prof said, not turning to me. "And ones I'd rather not revisit."

"Because of Regalia?"

"Because I thought the world could be a different place back then," Prof said, stirring a solution. "A place of heroes."

"Maybe it still can be that place. Maybe we're wrong about what is causing the darkness, or maybe there's a way to resist it. Everyone's been wrong about the Epic weaknesses, after all. Maybe we don't understand all of this as well as we think."

Instead of replying, Prof set down his beaker. He turned toward me. "And you're not afraid of what would happen if we fail?"

"I'm willing to risk it, Prof."

He narrowed his eyes at me. "Can I trust you, David Charleston?"

"Yes. Of course." Where had that question come from? It didn't seem to follow our conversation.

He studied me, then nodded. "Good. I've changed my mind. Tell Tia I'll head into the city as soon as you leave; she can tell Val and Exel that the emergency with the other Reckoner team got solved quickly, and I came back early."

"All right." Prof had a motorboat from a hidden Reckoner dock. He could get back to the city on his own easily. "But what was that about trusting—"

"Go finish loading those boxes, son." He turned around and began packing up his things.

I sighed, but put the picture down and climbed up, closing the trapdoor, leaving him in the hidden chamber. I grabbed a box of supplies, then almost ran headfirst into Val as I left.

"David?" she said. "What were you *doing* in there?"

"Sorry," I said. "Had to catch a breather."

"But—"

"You left the sub?" I asked.

"I—"

I hurried past her. Sparks! What if some scavenger found it and decided to take it on a joyride? Fortunately, it was still there, sitting in the calm black waters.

Val and I got the boxes loaded quickly, with minimal conversation. I tried to bring Val out again with some questions, but she didn't say much. Even during our ride back in the sub she was mostly quiet. She knew I was hiding something. Well, I didn't blame her for feeling annoyed at that—I felt the same way about the entire situation, honestly.

At the base, we docked and climbed out into the dark room. The docking mechanism was completely airtight, fitted exactly to the submarine. Quite ingenious. They still left the room dark though, in case of a leak. Even outside of Regalia's range the Reckoners were careful. It was one of the things I liked about them.

I found the guide ropes in the darkness and grabbed two pairs of night-vision goggles off the rack on the wall. I handed one down to Val, then put on the other pair. Together we began unloading the boxes. Eventually I grabbed one and hefted it onto my shoulder, then left the darkened docking room and hauled the box toward the storage room down the hallway.

The bright Reckoner base—with its plush couches and dark woods—was an enormous contrast to the desolate landscapes I'd spent the day visiting. It was almost like being in a different world. I carried the box to the storage room and set it down. Behind me I could hear voices from the radio drifting out of Exel's room. He was pulling extra hours on recon duty, listening to broadcasts, double—and triple—checking Newton's routes.

There were more boxes to unload, but I figured I should pass on Prof's message first. I walked down the hallway and rapped on Tia's door.

"Come in," she said.

On the walls she'd plastered maps of Babilar that showed Newton's routes. In the center of the city, several pins noted where Tia thought Regalia might be hiding. There were still too many buildings to search effectively without giving away what we were doing, but we were close.

A dozen or so empty cola pouches lay in the corner of the room, and Tia looked bad. A few stray strands of hair had escaped her bun and stuck out, like frizzy ginger lightning bolts. She had bags under her eyes and her normally pristine business suit hadn't been pressed in days.

"He was there," I said.

She glanced up at me. "What did he say?"

"He says he'll come back tonight. We'll probably need to send the sub back to the city to pick him up. He seems like he's mostly recovered."

"Thank goodness," she said, leaning back in her chair.

"Val's suspicious," I said. "You should tell her what's really going on."

"I wish I knew what was really going on," Tia grumbled.

"What—"

"I don't mean with Jon," Tia said. "Ignore me. I was just venting. Here, I want to show you something."

Tia stood up and walked to the wall, tapping on a section of it. We'd set up the imager in here to turn the wall into a smart screen, like Prof preferred to use as he worked. Tia's tap brought up an image of Knoxx, the Epic in Newton's crew I'd spotted the other day. The wall played the video of him transforming into a bird and flying away. My jerking of the scope followed, tracking the bird poorly until I found it on the other building. The transformation happened again. Tia stopped the screen on the figure and zoomed in on his face. The close-up was grainy, but he was still recognizable.

"What would you say about what you just saw?"

"At least class C self-transmutation abilities," I said. "He was able to change his mass as well as retain his original thought process after transforming; either alone would elevate the transmutation from class D. I'd have to know if he can take other shapes, and whether there are limits like how often he can change, before I can say more."

"This man," Tia said, "has been part of Newton's gang for years. Exel confirmed it with several points of evidence. There is no evidence before this moment that Knoxx had any powers. This means that somehow, Newton or Regalia convinced him to hide his abilities for years. I'm worried, David. If she can hide Epics in plain sight, and can prevent them from displaying their powers, our intel in this city—despite our long investment of time—might be worthless."

I frowned, stepping up to the image and taking a closer look. "What if he wasn't hiding his powers?" I asked. "What if he only gained them recently."

Tia looked at me. "You seriously think Regalia can make people into Epics?"

"I'm not convinced, but she obviously wants us to believe she can create Epics, or at least enhance their abilities. Perhaps she has access to a gifter, or some kind of Epic we've never seen before, and fakes granting powers. Or . . . maybe she simply *can* create new Epics. Seems to me that as much as we'd like to, we can't judge what is unreasonable when applied to Epics."

"Perhaps," Tia admitted. She sat down in her chair beside the desk and fished out another pouch of cola.

"You don't like being forced to take charge," I realized. "To run the operation, without Prof."

"I'm fully capable of being in command," she said.

"That's an answer in the same way that ketchup can be hair gel."

She raised an eyebrow.

"You see, it's technically true, but—"

"I understood," Tia said.

"You . . . did?"

"Yes. And you're right. Jon is the leader, David. I manage things; I make the pieces fit together. But *he* has the vision; he sees things others don't. Not because of his . . . abilities. Just because of who he is. Without him to look over this plan, I worry I'm going to miss something important."

"He says he'll be back in time to help."

"I hope so," Tia said. "Because honestly, that man sure can mope with the best of them when he wants to."

"Was he like that before?"

She eyed me.

"He told me about NASA," I noted. "I saw a picture of you two there, together. I'm impressed."

She sniffed. "Did he tell you *why* I had to invite him to visit?"

"I assumed it was because you two were together."

"We'd only just started dating," Tia said. "Another teacher in his school won a contest we were holding—come pretend to be an astronaut for a few weeks. Train, go through the tests, that sort of thing. We did it occasionally for PR reasons."

"And Prof didn't win?" I asked.

"He didn't enter," Tia said. "He *hated* contests. Wouldn't even put a quarter into a slot machine. But that didn't stop him from feeling torn apart when he didn't get to go." She stared at her pouch of cola without opening it. "We sometimes forget how human he is, David. He's just a man, despite it all. A man full of feelings that, at times, don't make sense. We're all like that. We want what we can't have, even when we have no right to demand it."

"It *will* be all right, Tia."

She seemed surprised by the tone of my voice, and looked up at me.

"You see, he's *not* just a man, Tia," I said. "He's a hero."

"You sound like one of them."

Them?

And then it hit me—she meant the Faithful. Sparks, it was true. *Where there are villains, there will be heroes. Just wait. They* will *come. . . .* My father's words, on the day he died.

As recently as a few months ago, I'd regarded the optimism

of people like Abraham and Mizzy as foolishness. What had changed?

It was Prof. I couldn't believe in some mythical Epics who may or may not someday arrive to save the world. But him . . . him I could believe in.

I met Tia's gaze.

"Well," she said, "finish unloading supplies, then get your gear together. I want you to go install a camera to watch Obliteration and give us a constant visual. We don't know for certain if his energy storage will progress at the same rate as it did previously. I'd rather not be surprised."

I nodded and left the room, closing the door behind me. I walked down the hallway and passed the storage chamber, where I found that Mizzy had been recruited to start carrying the boxes in. She set one down and gave me a perky smile before heading off for another.

I couldn't help grinning after her. She was the definition of what it meant to have an infectious personality. The world was a better place because Missouri Williams was in it.

"Why is it," a voice said softly from beside me, "that every time I find you these days, you're ogling some girl?"

I turned to look and there, standing just inside the storage room, was Megan.

33

MEGAN.

Megan was inside the Reckoner base.

I let out a sound that was definitely not a whimper. It was something far more manly, no matter what it sounded like.

I glanced after Mizzy in a moment of panic, then stepped into the storage room, taking Megan by the arm. "What are you doing!"

"We need to talk," she said. "And you were ignoring me."

"I wasn't ignoring you. Things have just been very busy."

"Busy looking at women's backsides."

"I wasn't . . . Wait." It hit me and I smiled. "You sound jealous!"

"Don't be a buffoon."

"No," I said. "You were jealous." I found I couldn't stop grinning.

Megan seemed confused. "Normally, that's not something people smile about."

"It means you care," I said.

"Oh please."

Time to say something suave. Something romantic. My brain, which had been working a few steps behind all day, finally came to my rescue. "Don't worry," I said. "I'd rather ogle you any day."

Wait.

Megan sighed, peeking out into the hallway past me. "You are a buffoon," she said under her breath. "Is she likely to come back here?"

Right. Enemy High Epic. Reckoner base. "I'm assuming you're not here to turn yourself in?" I said softly.

"Turn myself in? Sparks, no. I just needed to talk to someone. You were the most convenient."

"This is convenient?" I asked.

Megan looked at me and blushed. A blush looked really good on her. Of course, so would soup, mud, or elephant earwax. Megan on a bad day outshined anyone else I'd ever known.

"Come on," I said, taking her by the arm. I didn't want to encourage her to use her powers to hide, not when she was so obviously acting like the Megan I'd known before. Which meant moving quickly. I towed her after me in a heart-pounding rush down the hallway toward my room.

We got there without being spotted. I pulled her in, then shut the door, pressing my back to it and exhaling like an epileptic pilot who'd just landed a cargo plane full of dynamite.

Megan inspected the room. "You didn't get one with a porthole, I see. Still the new kid on the team, eh?"

"Something like that."

"Nice, anyway," she said, strolling forward. "Better than a metal hole in the ground."

"Megan," I said. "How . . . I mean, does anyone else out there know where our base is?"

She met my gaze, then shook her head. "Not so far as I know. I don't meet with Regalia often—I don't think she trusts me—but from what I've heard of the others, they're searching for you. Regalia thinks your base is somewhere on the northern coast, and seems thoroughly annoyed that she hasn't been able to find it."

"How did you find us, then?" I asked.

"Steelheart had me bug everyone in the team," she said.

"So you . . ."

"I can listen in," Megan said, "on some of your calls. Or I could, for a while. Phaedrus is paranoid, changes both his phone and Tia's regularly. Yours is dead. I can only listen in these days if someone calls Abraham or Cody."

"The supply shipment," I said. "You heard where it was, got there before us, then snuck onto the submarine."

Megan nodded.

"I was there," I said. "I didn't see you at all! Were you using your powers?"

"Nah," Megan said, flopping back onto the bed, lying across it sideways. "I only needed good old-fashioned stealth."

"But . . ."

"I was about to sneak aboard after you'd been out of the sub for a while, and then Val came out following you and nearly gave me a heart attack. But I ducked just in time, then went in and hid in the bathroom."

I grinned, though she couldn't see it—she was staring at the ceiling. "You're amazing," I said.

The corners of her lips tugged up at that, though she remained staring upward. "It's getting really difficult, David."

"Difficult?"

"Not using my powers."

I scrambled up to the side of the bed. "You've been doing what I asked? Avoiding the abilities?"

"Yeah," she said. "I don't know why I listen to you. Just makes life difficult. I mean, I'm basically a divinity, right? So I end up hiding in a bathroom?"

I settled down, sitting on the bed beside her. The tension in her voice, that look in her eyes. "Is it working?" I asked. "Do you feel like murdering people indiscriminately?"

"I always feel like murdering you. If only just a little."

I waited.

"Yes," Megan finally said with a sigh. "It's working. It's driving me insane in other ways, but not using my powers has removed some of the . . . tendencies from my mind. But I honestly don't ever feel like killing people. For me, it manifests more as irritability and selfishness."

"Huh," I said. "Why do you think that is?"

"Probably because I'm not very powerful."

"Megan, you're a High Epic! You're wicked powerful."

"*Wicked?*"

"Heard it in a movie once."

"Whatever. I'm not a very powerful Epic, David. I have to use a gun for Calamity's sake! I can reincarnate, yes, but have you seen how weak my illusions are?"

"I think they're pretty awesome."

"I'm not fishing for compliments, David," she said. "We're trying to get me to not use my powers, remember?"

"Sorry. Uh, wow. Your powers are so lame. They're like, about as useful as an eight-by-eighty mounted on a twelve-gauge firing birdshot."

She looked at me, then started laughing. "Oh sparks. You'd have a real good view of the pheasant dying, though."

"Up close and personal," I said. "The way avian massacres were meant to happen."

This made her laugh more, and I grinned. She seemed to need the laughter. There was a desperation to it; though it did occur to me that we should make sure to keep things quiet.

Megan stretched her arms back, then folded them on her stomach, sighing.

"Feel good?" I asked.

"You don't know what it's like," she said softly. "It's horrible."

"Tell me anyway."

She glanced at me.

"I'd like to know," I said. "I've made a habit of . . . ending people with these powers. I don't know if it will make me feel better or worse to know what they're going through, but I think I should hear it either way."

She looked back at the ceiling and didn't speak at first. I'd left one light on in the room, a small reddish-orange lamp with a glass shade. The room was silent, though I thought sometimes I could hear the ocean outside. Waves surging, water rolling. It was probably just my imagination.

"It's not like a voice," Megan said. "I've read what some of Tia's scholars write, and they treat it like schizophrenia. They claim that Epics have something like an evil conscience telling them what to do, which is a load of crap. It's nothing like that.

"You know how, some mornings, you just feel a little angry at the world?" she continued. "Or you're irritable, so that small things—things that normally wouldn't annoy you—set you off? It's like that. Only mixed with an inability to care about consequences.

"Even that's kind of normal—I've been there, felt like that, long before I got these powers. You know how it is when you're up late, and you know that if you don't go to bed, you're going to hate life the next day? Then you stay up anyway, because you don't care? It's like that. As an Epic, you just don't care. After all, you deserve to be able to do what you want. And if you go too far, you can change later. Always later."

She closed her eyes as she spoke, and I felt a chill. I had felt like she'd described. Who hasn't? Listening to her, it seemed perfectly logical to me that an Epic should do what they do. That horrified me.

"But you've changed," I told Megan. "You've resisted."

"For a few days," she said. "It's hard, David. Really, really hard. Like going without water."

"You said it's easier when you're near me."

She opened her eyes and glanced over at me. "Yeah."

"So there's a secret to beating it."

"Not necessarily. A lot of things relating to Epics don't make any sense."

"Everyone says that," I replied, standing and walking to my desk. "We say it so much, I wonder if we just take it for granted. Here, look at this." I dug out my research on Epic weaknesses.

"What's this?" Megan said, standing up as well. She walked over and leaned down next to me, her head so close to mine. "You going all-out nerd on me again, Knees?"

"I've been finding connections between Epics and their weaknesses," I said, pointing at my notes on Mitosis, then Sourcefield. "We say the weaknesses are random, right? Well, there are some large coincidences related to these two."

Megan read. "His own music?" she asked. "Huh."

"What about Steelheart?" I asked, excited. "His powers

were negated by people who didn't fear him. You knew him—is there something in his past you can connect to his weakness?"

"It's not like we went to dinner parties together," Megan said dryly. "Most people in the city, even the higher-ups, didn't even know about me. All they knew was 'Firefight,' my dimensional double."

"Your . . . what?"

"Long story," Megan said, distracted as she looked over my notes on Sourcefield. "Steelheart wanted to keep everything about me as secret as possible. So he kept his distance from the real me, so as not to draw attention. Sparks, he kept his distance from pretty much everyone."

"There's a connection here," I said, flicking the papers with one hand. "There's a connection to all of it, Megan. Maybe even a reason."

I expected her to object, like both Prof and Tia had. Instead, she nodded.

"You agree?" I asked.

"This was done to me," Megan said. "Against my will. I became an Epic. I'd sure like to know if there was more meaning to it all. So yeah, I'm willing to believe." She still stared at the page. "More than willing, maybe."

It was hard not to notice how near to me she was standing, her cheek almost brushing my own. The urge to reach out and pull her even closer was so powerful that, in that moment, I thought I understood how she must feel being drawn to use her abilities.

"If there is a connection to the weakness," I said, to distract myself, "there might be a secret to overcoming the influence of the powers. We can get you out of this, Megan."

"Maybe," she said, then shook her head. "So help me, if this is related to 'the power of love' or some similar kind of bull, I'm going to strangle somebody. . . ." Her face was right next to mine. So close.

"The power of w-what?" I stammered.

"Don't read too much into that."

"Oh."

She smiled. So, figuring it couldn't hurt—the worst she could do was shoot me—I leaned forward to kiss her. This time, remarkably, she didn't pull away.

It felt fantastic. I didn't have much experience, and I'd heard these things were supposed to be awkward, but this time—for once in my life—nothing went wrong. She pressed her lips against mine, head tilted to the side, and wrapped her arms around me, warm and inviting. It felt like . . . like . . .

Like something fantastic I didn't ever want to end. And wasn't going to try to explain, lest I somehow screw it up.

A little voice in the back of my head did buzz a warning, though. *Dude. You're making out with an Epic.*

I turned that piece of me off. How easy it was to not worry about consequences in that moment, just as Megan had said. I barely heard the knock come at my door.

I did notice, however, when that door started to open.

34

MEGAN broke from me and I spun around. Tia—distractedly looking at the tablet in her hands—pushed the door open. She looked up, then right at me.

I went cold.

"Hey," Tia said. "I want to send Val to plant some supplies for the hit on Newton. We can have her drop you off, and you can go place that camera for me. Would you mind? I'd rather not wait."

"Uh . . . sure." I resisted the urge to look around for Megan. She'd been standing just beside me.

Tia nodded, then hesitated. "Did I startle you?"

I looked down at the stack of papers I'd dropped, without noticing it, during the kiss. "Just feeling clumsy today, I guess," I said.

"Be ready in five," she said, setting a small box on my side table—the remote camera. She glanced at me again, then left.

Sparks! I hurried over and shut the door, then looked back at the room. "Megan?" I asked softly.

"Ow." The voice came from under the bed.

I walked over and looked down. Megan had apparently thrown herself to the ground and rolled expertly under the bed. It was pretty cramped down there.

"Nice," I said to her.

"I feel like a teenager," she complained, "dodging my boy-friend's mother."

"I feel like a teenager too," I said. "Because I am one."

"Don't remind me," she grumbled, climbing out and rubbing her forehead, which she'd scraped on something under the bed. "You're like five years younger than I am."

"Five . . . Megan, how old are you?"

"Twenty."

"I turned nineteen right before we left Newcago," I said. "You've got *one year* on me."

"Like I said. You're practically a baby." She held out her hand and let me pull her to her feet.

"We could go talk to Tia," I said as she stood. "Prof's not here, and Tia's more likely to listen to you. I've been working on them, explaining that you didn't kill Sam. I think she'll give you a chance to speak for yourself."

Megan frowned and looked away. "Not right now."

"But—"

"I don't want to face her, David. It's tough enough dealing with all of this right now without worrying about Tia."

I puffed out a breath. "Fine. But we're going to have to sneak you out somehow."

"Walk down the hallway, distract anyone you run into, and clear me a path. I'll hide in the sub again."

"I guess." I walked to the door slowly.

"David," Megan said.

I raised an eyebrow at her.

"Coming down here was crazy," she said.

"Completely crazy," I agreed.

"Well, thanks for being crazy with me. I kind of need a friend." She grimaced. "Sparks. I hate admitting things like that. Don't tell anyone I said it?"

I smiled. "I'll be quiet as a buttered snail sneaking through a Frenchman's kitchen."

I grabbed my rifle from beside the door, slung it over my shoulder, and struck out into the hallway. It was empty. From the looks of the storage closet, Mizzy and Val had finished unloading the boxes; hopefully they weren't annoyed at me for ditching them. I slipped all the way down the hallway and entered the sitting room, the lavish chamber that connected to the submarine dock.

No signs of anyone in here. I turned around.

Val was standing behind me.

"Gah!" I exclaimed.

"Looks like we're going right out again," she said.

"Uh . . . yeah."

Val passed me wordlessly, moving toward the door to the docking room. I needed to give Megan an opening. If Val went inside, there'd be no chance of Megan sneaking into the sub without her noticing.

"Wait!" I yelled. "I need to grab the spyril."

"Go get it then," she said.

"Right." I waited in place for a moment, shuffling from one foot to the other.

"Well?" Val asked, pausing at the door into the docking room.

"Last time I used the spyril, something went wrong. I ended up losing my propulsion in the middle of the bay."

Val sighed.

Come on, I urged.

"You want me to check it over?" she asked, though it was clear it was the last thing she wanted to do.

I let out a breath. "That would be awesome."

"Well, go grab it then."

I ran to get it, noticing, happily, how Val lingered in the sitting room. When I passed the library, Megan glanced out at me—she'd made it that far. I nodded toward Val, held up one finger, and grabbed the spyril pack from the storage room.

I hurried back to Val, then began setting out the spyril's parts on a couch—positioned so that when Val walked over to look at them, she'd have her back to the door to the docking room. Val went over the spyril's pieces quickly and efficiently, checking each for scratches, then ensuring that the cords were attached correctly and tightly.

As Val worked, Megan slipped into the room behind us, then eased open the door into the docking chamber. She vanished into the darkness beyond.

"If something went wrong," Val said, "it wasn't the equipment's fault."

"You look like you know a lot about the equipment," I said, nodding toward the spyril. "Almost as much as Mizzy does."

"Come on," Val said, placing the last set of wires back into the pack. If I'd made any kind of connection with her earlier in the sub, I couldn't spot a sign of it now. She was back to being cold.

"Val, I really am sorry about Sam," I said. "I'm sure nobody could ever replace him, but someone has to use this equipment, and someone has to run point."

"I don't care that you're using the spyril. Honestly, how unprofessional do you think I am?"

"Then why are you so terse with me?"

"I'm terse with everyone," she said, then tossed me the pack and walked toward the docking room.

I grabbed my rifle and followed. Together we entered the short hallway between rooms and I closed the door behind me, plunging us into darkness. From there we crossed and opened the door into the docking room, where we followed the familiar guide ropes that led us to the submarine.

Had I given Megan enough time? Sweating, I waited as Val undid the hatch down into the vehicle. Megan would have had to make her way through the unfamiliar room, open the hatch, then slip in and redo it.

I was given no clues as to whether she'd managed it or not. I climbed down and resealed the hatch while Val settled into the driver's seat. She turned on the soft emergency-style lights and took us down into the depths.

I glanced back anxiously at the bathroom, but nothing seemed out of place. What followed was a short, tense trip through the darkened waters of Babilar. Val didn't try to strike up any conversation as we traveled, and though I wished I could do something about the strained awkwardness between us, I just couldn't manage it right then. Not with the stress of Megan hiding just feet from us.

Eventually Val let us up in the middle of a still, black bay among glowing buildings, none of them too close. We didn't always use the half-sunken buildings for docking. Regalia couldn't look everywhere, and so long as we were quiet, a quick drop-off in the middle of a deserted bay could be stealthier than using the same docking stations over and over.

I peeked out through the hatch, inspecting the distant lights, which were mirrored in the waters below. This city was so *surreal*. Never mind those glows, the phantom sounds of radios playing music in the distance. I still wasn't used to buildings with so much variety to them—stonework, glass, bricks.

I climbed back down and regarded the wetsuit. Then I reluctantly started pulling off my shirt.

"There's a bathroom in the back, kid," Val said dryly.

I glanced at it and found myself imagining being forced into that small room with Megan, pressed against her, somehow trying to change without alerting Val of what was going on. Blushing at the thought, I reminded myself that Megan would probably end up stabbing me or something if we were confined in such a tight space.

I wanted to try anyway.

Unfortunately, my brain seized upon a better idea. Stupid brain. "It looks really cramped in there," I said. "I don't suppose you'd mind going up above?"

Val sighed loudly, but she got up from her seat and brushed past me, climbing up the ladder. I stripped down to my boxers and grabbed the wetsuit.

"You don't look half bad with your shirt off," Megan noted quietly. "For a nerd."

I about fell over, one leg into the wetsuit. Megan had slipped out of the bathroom without me noticing. I'd assumed she'd stay in there until I'd dressed, but apparently not. I worked more quickly, trying to hide my blush.

"Nice work, by the way," Megan whispered. "I was afraid I'd have to ride off with Val, then sneak out on my own. This will be far more convenient. Think you can distract her up above?"

"Sure," I said.

"For a second," Megan added, "I thought you were going

to be forced into the bathroom there with me. Too bad. It would have been amusing to watch you squirm."

I left the wetsuit unzipped, grabbed my rifle and the box with the spyril, then gave Megan a glare. She didn't seem the least bit concerned.

She's not trapped in our base any longer, I thought. *Here there's only Val to worry about.* Megan seemed confident she could deal with that, should it become a problem. She was probably right.

I hiked up the ladder and undid the latch, then set the spyril on the top of the sub before climbing out. I wore the rifle slung across my back, its straps pulled tight. It wouldn't be easily accessible, but I wouldn't have to worry about losing it in the water.

Val stood, back to the hatch, watching the city. I walked over to her, then pointed to the unzipped back of my suit. "Little help, please?"

I made sure to keep her positioned away from the opening into the sub. Once zipped, I didn't look to see if Megan had escaped, but instead put on the spyril. "I have a lot of work to do," Val said as she passed me and climbed down the hatch. "I'll be at it for a few hours, at least. So if you finish before then, find a way to entertain yourself. I'll let you know when I'm ready for you."

I activated the spyril and jumped out into the water. I didn't need to worry about my rifle; it would work fine after being submerged.

Val climbed back inside and locked the hatch. I treaded water there for a moment until the sub lowered into the ocean, revealing Megan in the water on the other side, looking wet and miserable.

"N-nice night," she said, shivering.

"It's not even that cold," I said.

"Says the guy in the wetsuit." She looked around. "Think there are sharks in here?"

"That's what *I* keep wondering!"

"I've never trusted water in the darkness." She paused. "Well, I don't really care for it at all."

"Didn't you grow up in Portland?" I asked.

"Yeah, so?"

"So . . . it's like a port, right? So didn't you ever go swimming there?"

"In the *Willamette*?"

"Uh . . . yeah?"

"Um, let's just say no. I did not." She glanced toward one of the distant buildings. "Sparks. If I get eaten because of you, Knees, I'm never going to let you hear the end of it."

"At least you'd come back from being eaten," I said.

"Doesn't make me eager to try the experience." She sighed. "So we swim?"

"Not exactly," I said. I swam over to her and held out my arm. "Grab hold of me." She hesitantly wrapped her arms around my chest just under my arms.

With Megan holding on tightly, I pointed the streambeam into the ocean, then engaged the spyril. We rose on jets of water, a good thirty feet in the air. The black, glassy surface of the sea stretched out around us, the towers of submerged Manhattan rising beyond like neon sentries.

Megan breathed out softly, still holding on to me. "Not bad."

"You haven't seen the spyril in action?"

She shook her head.

"Then might I suggest you hang on?" I said.

She complied, pulling herself tight against me, which was a not-unpleasant situation. Next, I attempted something I'd been practicing. I leaned forward, turning the jets on my feet backward at an angle, then pushed my hand downward—not the one with the streambeam, but the one with the smaller handjet for maneuvering.

This kept us from toppling down into the water, the handjet giving thrust upward, the ones on my feet thrusting backward. The result was that we shot across the water, the jet on my hand lending us just enough lift to stay aloft. Twenty-seven and a half times in fifty-four, this stunt ended with me crashing face-first into the water. This time, blessedly, I managed it without such indignity.

Wind whipped at my face, the spray of water cold on my skin. I grinned, flying us toward one of the rooftops. Once there, I gave us a burst from below and used the guiding jet on my hand to slow our momentum forward. We shot high into the air, and another spurt of water from my hand nudged us over the lip of the roof, where we landed.

I stood triumphantly, putting one arm around Megan, looking down to see if she was beaming at me in awe.

Instead her teeth were chattering. "So . . . cold . . ."

"But it was awesome, right?" I said.

She breathed out, letting go of me and stepping onto the roof. A few people gawked at us from beside a tent on the far side of the building. "Not particularly *stealthy*," she noted. "But yes, awesome. And you can stop ogling me now."

I tore my eyes away from the way her damp T-shirt, underneath her jacket, clung to her skin and bra. "Sorry."

"No," she said, pulling her jacket tight and doing the buttons, "it's all right. I mean, I teased you for looking at other women. That implies I want you to look at *me* instead. So I shouldn't get mad when you do."

"Mmm . . . ," I said. "So you're gorgeous *and* logical."

She gave me a flat stare. I just shrugged.

"I'm still not sure this will work," she said.

"You're the one who came to see *me*," I said. "And if you hadn't noticed, back in the base, that moment in my room . . . it seemed to be working pretty well then."

We stood, looking at one another, and I hated how awkward it suddenly felt. As if a fat man at the buffet had suddenly forced his way between us to get at the mac and cheese.

"I should be going," she said. "Thank you. For being willing to talk. For not turning me in. For . . . being you."

"I'm pretty good at being me," I said. "I've had all these years to practice—I hardly ever get it wrong these days."

We stared at each other.

"So, uh," I said, shuffling from one foot to the other, "want to go with me to check up on Obliteration? If you're not doing anything else important, I mean."

She cocked her head. "Did you just invite me on a date . . . to spy on a deadly Epic planning to destroy the city?"

"Well, I don't have a lot of experience with dating, but I've always heard you're supposed to pick something you know the girl will enjoy. . . ."

She smiled. "Well, let's get to it then."

35

I pulled out my mobile for a map of the area and Megan looked over my shoulder and pointed to the south. "That way," she said. "We've got a walk ahead of us."

"You sure you don't want to . . ." I gestured at the spyril on my legs.

"What part of 'spying' involves flying through the city and drawing the attention of everyone nearby?"

"The fun part," I said, sullen. I'd practiced for a reason. I wanted to show off what I knew.

"Well," Megan said, "it might not matter, but I'd rather be quiet about this. Yes, Regalia wanted me to seduce you, but I don't want to be blatant—"

"Wait, what?" I stopped in place.

"Oh, um, yeah." Megan grimaced. "Sorry. I meant my explanation to be way better." She ran her hand through her hair. "Regalia wanted me to seduce you. I'm not sure how much she knows of my background with the Reckoners, and I think she came up with the idea of me and you on her own. But don't worry; I decided before even coming here that I wasn't going to actively work against the Reckoners."

I stared at her. That was kind of a large bomb to drop on me, just like that. I knew it was stupid, but suddenly I found myself questioning the affection she'd shown me earlier.

She wouldn't have just told you if she were really planning on doing it, I told myself pointedly. I'd already decided to trust Megan. I'd just have to do it on this issue too.

"Well," I said, starting off and giving her a smile, "that's good. Even if being seduced kind of sounds like it would be fun."

"Slontze," Megan said, visibly relaxing. She took my arm and steered me across the rooftop. "At least if we're spotted, I think Regalia will assume I'm just trying to do as she said."

"And if something goes wrong," I noted, "we can use your illusions to distract her."

Megan shot me a glance as we reached a narrow rope bridge to the next roof. She started across in front of me, presenting a fine silhouette. "I thought I wasn't supposed to use my powers," she said softly.

"You aren't."

"I sense a very large *but.*"

"Funny, because right in front of me, I see a—"

"Watch it."

"—very attractive, um, set of calves. Look, Megan, I know I told you not to use your powers. But that was just a first step, a way to reset and gain control. It's not going to work long-term."

"I know," she said. "There's no way I'll be able to resist."

"I'm not just talking about that," I said. "I'm talking about something bigger."

She stopped on the bridge and looked back at me. We swung gently above the waters below, some four stories down in this case. I wasn't worried about the drop—I was still wearing the spyril.

"Bigger?" she asked.

"We can't fight the Epics."

"But—"

"Not alone," I continued. "I've accepted it. The Reckoners only survive because of Prof and because of things like the spyril. I spent years convincing myself that regular people could fight, and I still think we can. But we need the same weapons our enemies have."

Megan inspected me in the darkness. The only light came from spraypaint on the ropes of the bridge. Finally, she stepped forward and picked at something around my neck. Abraham's necklace, which I wore under the wetsuit. She pulled it out.

"I thought you said these people were idiots."

"I said they were idealistic," I clarified. "And they are. Heroes aren't magically going to show up and save us. But maybe, with work, we can figure out how to . . . um . . . recruit a few of them."

"Did I tell you why I came to Babilar?" she asked, still holding the necklace by its small *S* pendant.

I shook my head.

"Word is," Megan said, "that Regalia can enhance an Epic's powers. Make them stronger, more versatile."

I nodded slowly. "So what she said to me the other day . . ."

"She didn't just make it up then. This is something she's been claiming, in certain circles, for at least a year now."

"Which explains why so many High Epics have come to Babilar," I said. "Mitosis, Sourcefield, Obliteration. She promised to increase their power in exchange for doing as she demanded."

"And if there's one thing most Epics want," Megan agreed, "it's more power. No matter how strong they already are."

I shifted, feeling the bridge rock beneath us. "So you . . ."

"I came," Megan said softly, "because I figured if she really can increase an Epic's powers, she might be able to take mine away. Make me normal again."

Silence hung between us like a dead wombat on a string.

"Megan . . ."

"A foolish dream," she said, dropping the necklace and turning from me. "As foolish as yours. You're as idealistic as Abraham, David." She continued across the bridge, leaving me.

I hurried to catch up. "Maybe," I said, taking her by the arm as we reached the other side. "But maybe not. Let's work together, Megan. You and me. Maybe what you need is a pressure valve of some sort. You use your powers a little here and there, in a controlled situation, to scratch the itch. That lets you practice restraining the emotions. Or maybe there's another trick, one we can discover together."

She moved to pull away, but I held on tight.

"Megan," I said, stepping around her and meeting her eyes. "Let's at least *try*."

"I . . ." She took a deep breath. "Sparks, you're hard to ignore."

I smiled.

Finally, she turned and pulled me toward an abandoned tent, really just a cloth propped up on one side by a pole mounted in the rooftop. "If we're going to do this, you have to understand," Megan said softly, "that my powers are not what they seem."

"The illusions?"

"Not exactly."

She squatted down in the shadows of the abandoned tent, and I joined her, uncertain what we were hiding from. Likely she just wanted to be sheltered as she talked, not so out in the open. But there was something very hesitant about her.

"I . . ." She bit her lip. "I'm not an illusion Epic."

I frowned but didn't object.

"You haven't figured it out?" Megan asked. "That time back in Newcago in the elevator shaft, when you and I were close to being spotted by guards. They shined a flashlight right on us."

"Yeah. You made an illusion of darkness to hide us."

"And did you *see* any darkness?"

"Well, no." I frowned. "Does this have to do with the dowser?" It was the device—a real piece of technology, so far as I knew—that scanned a person and determined if they were an Epic or not. The Reckoners tested everyone in their team with some regularity. "I never *did* figure out how you fooled it. You could have created an illusion on the screen to cover the real result, but . . ."

"The dowser records its results," Megan finished for me.

"Yeah. If Tia or Prof ever looked back at its logs, they'd have noticed a positive identification of an Epic. I can't believe they never did that." I focused on Megan, her face lit softly by some glowing spraypaint beneath us. "What *are* you?"

Megan hesitated, then spread her hands to her sides, and suddenly her wet clothing was dry. It changed, in an eyeblink, from a jacket and fitted tee to a jacket and green blouse, then a dress, then rugged camouflage military gear. The changes came faster and faster, different outfits flickering over her figure, and then her *hair* started changing. Different styles, different colors. Skin tones soon joined the mix. She was Asian, she was pale with freckles, she had skin darker than Mizzy's.

She was using her powers. That put my hair on end, even though I *had* been the one to encourage her.

"With my powers," she said, a hundred different versions of her face passing in a few moments, "I can reach into, and touch, other realities."

"Other realities?"

"I once read a book," Megan continued, her flickering features and clothing finally returning to her normal self, wet jacket and all, "that claimed there were infinite worlds, infinite possibilities. That every decision made by any person in this world created a new reality."

"That sounds bizarre."

"Says the man who just flew through a city using a device powered by the corpse of a dead Epic."

"Well, *research* derived from a dead Epic," I corrected.

"No," Megan said. "An actual corpse. The 'research' involves using bits of dead Epic and drawing their abilities forth. What did you think the motivator on that machine was?"

"Huh." Mizzy had said the motivators were each individual to the device. So . . . like, individual because they had a piece of a dead Epic in them? *Probably just the mitochondrial DNA,* I thought. The Reckoners harvested it from dead Epics, and used it as currency. . . . That was what made the motivator work. It made some sense. Creepy sense, at least.

"Anyway," Megan said, "we're not talking about motivators right now. We're talking about me."

"That happens to be one of my favorite topics," I said, though I felt jarred. If Megan's powers were what she said, it meant I'd been wrong. All those years, I'd been *certain* I knew what Firefight was, that I'd figured out a secret nobody else knew. So much for that.

"Best I can tell," Megan said, "I pull one of those other realms—those *not*-places of possibility never attained—into our own, and for a time skew this reality toward that one. That night, in the elevator shaft, we weren't there."

"But—"

"And we were," Megan continued. "To those men looking for us, the shaft was empty. In the reality they inspected, you and I had never climbed up there. I presented for them another world."

"And the dowser?"

"I presented to it a world where there was no Epic for it to find." She took a deep breath. "Somewhere, there's a world—or maybe just a possibility of one—where I don't carry this burden. Where I'm just *me* again."

"And what about Firefight?" I asked. "The image you showed the world, the fire Epic?"

Megan hesitated, then raised her hand.

An Epic appeared in front of us. A tall, handsome man with clothing aflame and a face that seemed molten. Eyes that glowed, a fist that dripped trails of fire, like burning oil. I could actually feel the heat, just faintly.

I glanced at Megan. She didn't seem to be losing control despite using her powers. When she spoke, it was her voice—the her I knew.

"If there's a world where I don't have powers," Megan said, looking at the imposing figure, "there is one where I have different powers. It's easier to summon forth some possibilities than it is to summon others. I don't know why. It isn't like this one is *similar* to our world. In it, I have a completely different power set, and beyond that . . ."

"You're a dude," I said, noticing the similarity of features.

"Yeah. Kind of disconcerting, you know?"

I shivered, looking over this burning Epic that could have been Megan's twin. I'd been *way* off about her abilities.

I stood up, meeting Firefight's gaze. "So you don't have

to . . . like, swap places with him or anything? To bring him here, I mean?"

"No," she said. "I pull shadows from another world into this one. That warps reality around the shadow in strange ways, but it's all still just a shadow. I can bring him here, but I've never seen his world."

"Does he . . . know I'm here?" I asked, glancing at Megan.

"I'm not sure," she said. "I can get him to do what I want, mostly, but I think that's because my powers seek out a reality where he was already going to do what it is I want him to do. . . ."

I met those burning eyes, and they seemed to be able to see me. They seemed to know me. Firefight nodded his head to me, then vanished.

"I felt heat," I said, looking at Megan.

"That varies," she said. "Sometimes, when I swap in the other reality—splicing it into our own—it's shadowy and indistinct. Other times, it's *almost* real." She grimaced. "We're supposed to be hiding, aren't we? I shouldn't be going around summoning High Epics that glow in the night."

"I think that was awesome," I said softly.

I immediately regretted my words. These were powers Megan had *just said* she didn't want to have. They corrupted her, sought to destroy her. Complimenting her powers was sort of like complimenting someone with a broken leg on how white their bone was as it stuck from their skin.

But she didn't seem to mind. In fact, I could swear she blushed a little. "It's not much," she said. "Really, it's a lot of work for a simple effect. Surely you've read of Epics who could make illusions of whatever they want without having to pull some alternate reality out of their pocket."

"I suppose."

She crossed her arms, looking me over. "All right. We should do something about that outfit."

"What? You think a guy wandering around in a wetsuit with strange Epic-derived devices strapped to his limbs is suspicious?"

She didn't answer me, instead placing her hand on my shoulder. Jeans and a jacket—both almost exactly like ones I actually owned—faded into existence around me, covering up the wetsuit. The bottoms of the legs flared, wide enough to go around the spyril. I was pretty sure that wasn't fashionable, but what did I know about fashion? In Newcago, the rage was outfits based on old 1920s Chicago.

I poked at the clothes. They weren't real, though I *thought* I could feel them just faintly. Or, like, I felt a memory of them. Does that make any sense? Probably not.

She inspected me, raising a critical eyebrow.

"What?" I asked.

"Trying to decide if I should change your face to make it less likely you'll be spotted sneaking up on Obliteration."

"Uh . . . okay."

"There are side effects, though," she said. "When swapping someone's body, I'm always worried I'll end up swapping them out *completely* with the version from another reality."

"Have you done that before?"

"I don't know," she said, arms crossed. "I'm mostly convinced that every time I die, my 'reincarnation' is really just my powers summoning out of another dimension a version of myself that didn't die." She shivered visibly. "Anyway, let's leave you like you are. I wouldn't want to swap your face and get it stuck that way. I've gotten used to the one you have. Shall we move on?"

"Yeah," I said.

We left the abandoned half tent and continued walking toward where Obliteration had set up. "How are you feeling?" I asked.

"Little hungry," she said.

"That's not what I meant." I glanced over at her.

She sighed as we walked. "I'm irritable. Like I haven't gotten enough sleep. I want to snap at anyone close by, but it should fade soon." She shrugged. "It's better this time than it has been in the past. I don't know why—though, despite what it might seem, I'm not really that powerful."

"You said something like that before."

"Because it's true. But . . . well, that might be an advantage. It's why I can do these things and not turn immediately. It's harder for the really powerful Epics. For me, the only time it gets *really* bad is when I reincarnate."

We started across a bridge. "It feels odd," I noted, "having an Epic to talk to about all this so frankly."

"It feels odd," she said, "having your stupid voice say so much about my secrets." Then she grimaced. "Sorry."

"It's all right. A pleasant stroll with Megan wouldn't feel right if a few wry comments didn't accompany us."

"No, it's *not* all right. That isn't me, Knees. I'm not acerbic like that."

I raised an eyebrow at her.

"Okay," she snapped, "maybe I am. But I'm not downright insulting. Or, at least, I don't want to be. I hate this. It's like I can feel myself slipping away."

"How can I help?"

"Talking is good," she said. She took a deep breath. "Tell me about your research."

"It's kind of nerdy."

"I can handle nerdy."

"Well . . . I found those connections between some Epics and their weaknesses, right? Turns out, there's a step beyond that. But to investigate it I'll need to kidnap some Epics."

"You never think small, do you, Knees?"

"No, listen." I stopped her. "This is a great idea. If I can capture some Epics, then use their weaknesses to prevent them from using their powers, I can find out how long it takes them to turn normal. I can interview them, tease out connections from their past that might indicate what creates weaknesses in the first place."

"Or, you know, you could interview the perfectly willing Epic walking beside you."

I coughed into my hand. "Well, um, this scheme may have started because I was thinking about how to rescue you from your powers. I figured if I knew how long it took, and what was required to hold an Epic . . . You know. It might help you."

"Aw," she said. "That has to be the sweetest way someone has ever told me they were planning to kidnap and imprison me."

"I just—"

"No, it's okay," she said, actually taking my arm. "I understand the sentiment. Thank you."

I nodded, and we walked for a time. There was no urgency. Val would take hours on her mission, and Obliteration wasn't going anywhere. So it was okay to enjoy the night—well, enjoy it as much as was possible, all things considered.

Babilar was beautiful. I was growing to like the strange light of the spraypaint. After the dull, reflective grey of Newcago, so much color was mesmerizing. The Babilarans could paint whatever murals they wanted, from scrawled names along the side of one building we passed, to a beautiful and fanciful depiction of the universe on the top of another.

While I still wasn't comfortable with how relaxed people were here, I did have to admit that there was a certain appealing whimsy about them. Would it really be so bad if this were all there was to life? Tonight, as we passed them swimming or chatting or drumming and singing, I found the people annoyed me far less than they had before.

Perhaps it was the company. I had Megan on my arm, walking close beside me. We didn't say much, but didn't need to. I had her back, for the moment. I didn't know how long it would last, but in this place of vibrant colors I could be with Megan again. For that I was thankful.

We passed up onto a tall building, approaching the eastern side of town, where Obliteration waited. I turned our path toward a bridge leading to an even higher building. That would be a good spot to either place Tia's camera or scope out a better location.

"I'm worried that when I reincarnate, it's not really *me* that comes back," Megan said softly. "It's some other version of me. I worry when it happens that eventually, something will go wrong and that other person will mess things up. Things I don't want messed up." She looked at me.

"It's the real you," I said.

"But—"

"No, Megan. You can't spend your life worrying about that. You said that the powers grab a version of you that didn't die—everything else is the same. Just alive."

"I don't know that for certain."

"You remember everything that happened to you except the time right before the death, right?"

"Yeah."

"It means you're still you. It's true—I can sense that it is. You're my Megan, not some other person."

She grew silent, and I glanced at her, but she was grinning. "You know," she said, "talking to you sometimes—it makes me wonder if *you're* actually the one who can reshape reality."

A thought occurred to me. "Could you swap Obliteration?" I asked. "Pull out a version of him without powers, or with a really obvious weakness, then stuff this one into another dimension somewhere?"

She shook her head. "I'm not powerful enough," she said. "The only times I've done anything *truly* dramatic are right after I die, on the morning when I reincarnate. Those times . . . it's like I can pull bits of that reality with me, since I just arrived from it. But I'm not myself enough then to really control it at those times either, so don't get any ideas."

"It was worth asking," I said, then scratched my head. "Though, I suppose even if you could do it, we probably shouldn't. I mean, what good is it to protect *this* Babilar if we let tons of other people die in *another* Babilar." If the things she could do were even from other worlds that did exist, rather than just possibilities of worlds that could have existed.

Man. Thinking about this was giving me a headache.

"The goal is still to get *rid* of my powers, remember," Megan said. "Regalia claimed to be uncertain she could achieve it, but she told me that if I served her, she would see." Megan walked for a time, thoughtful. "I don't know if she was lying or not, but I think you're right. I think there has to be something behind all this, a purpose."

I stopped on the lip of the rooftop, looking at her standing on the edge of the bridge just behind me. "Megan, do you know your weakness?"

"Yes," she said softly, turning to look out over the city.

"Does it have some kind of connection to your past?"

"Just random coincidences," Megan said. She turned and met my eyes. "But maybe they aren't as random as I thought."

I smiled. Then I turned and continued across the rooftop.

"You're not going to ask what the weakness is?" she said, hurrying up behind me.

"No. It belongs to you, Megan. Asking you for that . . . it'd be like asking someone for the key to their soul. I don't want to put you in that position. It's enough to know that I'm on the right course."

I continued on, but she didn't follow. I glanced back at her and found her staring at me. She hurried up in a sudden motion and placed her hand on my back as she passed, letting her fingers trail around my side. "Thank you," she whispered.

Then she took the lead, hurrying across the top of the roof to where our vantage waited.

⌐6

OBLITERATION was still perched in the same place, though he glowed more powerfully now; in the night, he was so bright that it was getting tough to pick out his features. This particular rooftop was high enough to get a vantage on him but was still quite distant—only the powerful zoom on my scope let me get a good look. I'd have to move closer to plant the camera.

I zoomed out a step and found that one of the readouts on the side of my holosight was a light meter. "You getting this, Tia?" I asked over the mobile. Megan sat beside me silently, now that I had an open line to the Reckoners. The only video being recorded came from my scope, so I figured we should be safe.

"I can see him," Tia said. "That's in line with what I

expected—if he follows the pattern from before, we still have a few more days until detonation."

"All right then," I said. "I'll plant the camera and make my way back to the pickup."

"Be careful," Tia said. "The camera will need to be pretty close to be effective. You want support?"

"Nah," I said. "I'll call in if I need anything."

"Okay then," Tia said, though she sounded hesitant. I hung up, deactivated the wireless link to my scope, and pocketed the mobile. I raised an eyebrow at Megan.

"They have this place under guard," she said softly. "The bridges have all been cut, and Newton frequently runs patrols. Regalia doesn't want anyone wandering close."

"Nothing we can't handle," I said.

"I didn't say we couldn't," Megan said. "I'm just worried about you improvising."

"I'd assumed all your complaints about my improvisation back in Newcago were because you didn't want us to actually kill Steelheart."

"In part," she said. "But I still don't like the way you run crazy all the time."

I grunted.

"We need to talk about Steelheart, by the way," Megan said. "You shouldn't have done what you did."

"He was a tyrant," I said, using the scope to check out buildings near Obliteration, scouting out a good place for the camera. I lingered on the gaping block of water where the building had been burned down. Charred beams and bits of other rubble jutted from the ocean like the broken teeth of a giant submerged boxer with his mouth open and head tipped back.

Megan didn't reply, so I glanced at her.

"I feel sorry for them, David," she said softly. "I know

what it feels like; that could have been me the Reckoners executed. Steelheart was a tyrant, but at least he ran a good city. All things considered, he wasn't so bad, you know?"

"He killed my father," I said. "You don't get a pass on murder because you're not as bad as you could be."

"I suppose."

"Do you have this hang-up regarding Regalia?"

Megan shook her head. "I feel bad for her, but she's planning to let Obliteration vaporize the city. She has to be stopped."

I grunted in agreement. I just wished I could shake the feeling that despite our precautions, Regalia was a step ahead of us. I handed the rifle to Megan. "Spot for me?" I asked.

She nodded, taking it.

"I'm going to go for that building just beyond the one they burned down. It's high enough that if I put the camera on the lip just below the roof, it should have a clear line of sight." I fished out the box Tia had given me, a waterproof housing with the small camera inside. I put in my earpiece, then attuned my mobile to a private frequency matching Megan's so we could talk without using the Reckoners' common frequency.

"David," Megan said. She pulled her P226 out of the holster on her leg and offered it to me. "For luck. Just don't drop the thing in the ocean."

I smiled and took the gun, then jumped off the building.

There was certainly something liberating about the spyril. Jets of water slowed me until I touched down, softly, into the water. From there, not wanting to draw attention, I used the jets under the water to zip me through the streets.

About two streets away I noticed that my dimensional clothing—man, that sounded cool—vanished. I was left in just the wetsuit again. It looked like Megan's powers only worked at very close range. That fit with what I'd discovered years ago, when I'd figured out that a shadowy figure was always nearby when "Firefight" was seen in Newcago. Megan had needed to stay near to maintain the crossover.

When I reached the building I looked upward. I'd need to go up some ten stories to get into a position where the camera could see Obliteration. The spyril might be able to get me there, but I was close enough to Obliteration now that if I hovered up that high, someone was sure to spot me.

I took a breath and let the spyril lift me up one story, then I pulled my way into the building through a broken window. "I'm going to climb up through the building," I said softly to Megan. "Have you spotted any of Regalia's watchers?"

"No," Megan said. "They're probably in the buildings too. I'm searching windows."

I took off the spyril gloves and clipped them to my belt, then stepped into the humid, overgrown innards of the building. Most of the fruit had been harvested but there was still enough of it to see by. I managed to climb out of the orchard over the root systems and find a hallway, then I prowled down it.

I passed an old elevator shaft where the doors had been broken open by tree branches, and I kept going until I located the stairwell. I forced the door open to find a twisting stairwell overgrown with roots and vines. It looked like the plants all sent runners into shafts like this one, seeking the water below.

I turned on my mobile's light, careful to keep it dim. I didn't want anyone spotting a moving light through one of the windows, but with all this foliage blocking the view, I figured I should be okay inside the stairwell. I started to climb the steps, making it up the first flight without difficulty.

"This is a *nice* gun," Megan said in my ear as I started up the second flight. "Light readings, wind projections . . . Both active infrared *and* thermal? A control for remote firing? Ooh, recoil reduction gravatonics! Can I keep this?"

"I thought you liked handguns," I said, reaching a section of broken steps. I looked up, then jumped and grabbed a root, which I scaled with some difficulty.

"A girl has to be flexible," Megan said. "Up close and personal is my style, but sometimes, somebody needs to be shot from a distance." She paused. "I think I just spotted a lookout in the building next to yours. I can't get a straight sight. I'm going to reposition."

"Any birds?" I asked, grunting as I climbed.

"Birds?"

"It's a hunch. Before you move, see if there are any pigeons on rooftops nearby."

"Okay . . ."

I managed to climb the system of roots up to the next landing, then I swung off and landed on the steps. The next flight was easy.

"Huh," Megan said. "Look at that. There *is* a pigeon on that rooftop there, all by itself, in the middle of the night."

"One of Newton's cronies," I said. "Knoxx, an Epic with shapeshifting powers."

"Knoxx? I've met that guy. He's not an Epic."

"We didn't think he was either," I said. "He revealed the abilities for the first time a few days back."

"Sparks! You think . . . ?"

"Maybe," I said. "My notes listed Obliteration's teleportation power needing a cooldown time, but he doesn't seem to have that limitation anymore. Now this Knoxx guy. Something's going on, even if it's just some strange plot where Regalia is pretending to have abilities she doesn't."

"Yeah," Megan said. "You there yet?"

"Working on it," I said, rounding another flight of steps. "This is kind of a lot of work."

"Whine whine," Megan said.

"Says the woman watching comfortably from—"

"Wait! David, Prof is here."

I froze in the stairwell beside a faded number fifteen painted on the concrete wall. *"What?"*

"I've been scanning windows," Megan said. "David, Prof is sitting in one. I'm zoomed in on him now."

"Sparks." Well, he *had* said he'd come back to the city tonight. "What's he doing?"

"Watching Obliteration," Megan said softly, the tension bleeding from her voice. "He's not here for us. He doesn't seem to have spotted me."

"He's checking in on Obliteration," I said. "You know that building that collapsed out here?"

"Yeah." Megan sounded sick. "I couldn't stop it, David. I—"

"You didn't need to. Prof saved the people."

"With his powers?"

"Yeah."

Megan was silent on the line for a while. "He's powerful, isn't he?"

"Very," I said, excited. *"Two* defensive abilities, either of which would categorize him as a High Epic. Do you know how unusual that is? Even Steelheart only had the one defensive power, his impenetrable skin. You should have seen Prof when he saved us back in Newcago."

"In the tunnels?" Megan asked. "When I . . . ?"

"Yeah."

"My fail-safe transmission didn't capture that," she said. "Only you talking."

"It was incredible, believe me," I said, still excited. "I've never read about an Epic like Prof and his ability to vaporize solids. Plus, his forcefields—they're class A for sure. He made an enormous tunnel under the water and—"

"David," Megan said, "the more powerful an Epic, the harder it is for them to resist the . . . changes."

"Which is exactly why this is so exciting," I said. "Don't you see, Megan? If someone like Prof can remain good, it means so much. It's a symbol, maybe even a bigger one than killing Steelheart! It proves that Regalia and the others could fight it off too."

"I suppose," Megan said hesitantly. "I just don't like him being here. If he sees me . . ."

"You didn't betray us," I said as I climbed over a large section of roots. "Not really."

"I . . . kinda did," Megan said. "And even if I didn't, there are other issues."

"You mean Sam?" I said. "I've explained that you didn't kill him. I think I nearly have them convinced. Anyway, I'm almost to the top. Where is that pigeon?"

"Building directly south of you. So long as you're quiet, you should be safe."

"Good," I said, catching my breath as I reached floor number eighteen. I'd started on floor ten, and there were twenty in this building. Two more and I could place the camera and be gone.

"David," Megan said, "you really believe this, don't you? That we can fight it?"

"Yes," I said.

"Fire," Megan said softly.

I stopped on the stairwell. "On what?" I asked.

"It's my weakness."

I grew cold.

"Firefight," she explained, "is my opposite. Male where I

am female. In that universe, everything is reversed. Here, fire affects my powers. There, fire *is* my power. Using him as my cover was perfect; nobody would use fire to try to kill me if they thought my own powers were fire-based, right? But by the light of natural fire, the shadows I summon break apart and vanish. I know, somehow, that if I die in a fire I won't reincarnate."

"We burned your body," I whispered. "Back in Newcago."

"Oh *sparks*, don't tell me things like that." I felt as if I could hear a shiver in her voice. "I was already dead. The body was just a husk. I always had Steelheart's people bury my bodies after I died, but I could never watch it. Seeing your own corpse is kind of a trip, you know?"

I waited on the steps. A few pieces of fruit dangled here, lighting the stairwell in a gentle glow.

"So why doesn't Firefight vanish?" I asked. "He's made of fire, which should negate your powers, and then he would go away."

"He's just a shadow," Megan said. "No real fire. That's what I've been able to figure. Either that or . . ."

"Or?"

"Or when I pull his shadow through, he brings with him some of the rules of his universe. I've had . . . experiences that make me question. I don't know how this works, David. Any of it. It frightens me sometimes. But fire *is* my weakness." She hesitated. "I wanted you to know what it was. In case . . . you know. Something needs to be done about me."

"Don't say things like that."

"I have to," Megan whispered. "David, you *need* to know this. Our house burned down when I was just a kid. I was almost killed. I crawled through the smoke, holding on to my stuffed kitty, everything burning around me. They found me on the lawn, covered in soot. I have nightmares about that day.

Repeatedly. All the time. If you do manage to interrogate other Epics, David . . . ask them what their nightmares are about."

I nodded, then felt foolish because she couldn't see that. I forced myself to start climbing again. "Thank you, Megan," I whispered over the line. What she'd given me just then had taken a lot of guts to say.

She let out a breath. "Yeah, well, you're never willing to just let things alone. You've got to find answers. So . . . well, maybe you'll find this one."

I reached the next flight of stairs, then twisted around the stairwell to keep going up. As I did, my foot trod on something that crunched.

I shivered and looked down. Another fortune cookie. I was tempted to just leave it there—the last ones had been seriously weird. Nobody in the base had been able to make sense of them. But I knew I couldn't just leave it. I knelt down, anxious about making too much noise, and held up the slip of paper to the light of a glowing fruit.

Is this a dream? the paper asked.

I took a deep breath. Yeah. Still creepy. What did I do? Respond?

"No, it's not," I said.

"What?" Megan asked in my ear.

"Nothing." I waited, uncertain what kind of response I expected. None came. I started up the stairwell again, watching my feet. Sure enough, I found another set of cookies growing from a vine on the next flight.

I popped one open.

Gnarly, it read. *I get confused sometimes.*

Was that a reply? "Who are you?"

"David?" Megan asked.

"I'm talking to fortune cookies."

"You're . . . Huh?"

"I'll explain in a minute."

I made my way upward slowly. This time I was able to catch a vine curling down, cookies sprouting from it like seeds. I waited for one to grow to full size in front of me, then pulled out the slip.

They call me Dawnslight. You're trying to stop her, right?

"Yes," I whispered. "Assuming you mean Regalia, I am. Do you know where she is?"

I broke open a few more cookies, but this pod all read the same thing, so I climbed up a little bit until I found another cluster.

Don't know, dude, it read. *I can't see her. I watched that other one, though. On the operating table.*

"Obliteration?" I asked. "On an *operating* table?"

Sure. Yeah. They cut something outta him. You're sure this isn't a dream?

"It's not."

I like dreams, the next cookie read.

I shivered. So Dawnslight was an Epic for certain. And this city was his.

"Where are you?" I asked.

Listen to that music. . . .

That's the only response I got, no matter what questions I asked.

"David," Megan said on the line, worry bleeding into her voice, "you are seriously freaking me out right now."

"What do you know about Dawnslight?" I asked her, continuing upward at a slow pace in case any other cookies appeared.

"Not much," Megan said. "When I asked Regalia, she claimed that he was 'an ally' and implied that was all I needed to know. Is that who you were talking to?"

I looked at the slips of paper in my hand. "Yeah. Using

a kind of bizarre Epic texting plan. I'll show you later." I needed to get this camera placed and move on. Fortunately, floor twenty was the final flight. I pushed on the door out of the stairwell, but it didn't budge. I grunted and shoved a little harder.

I winced as it opened with a loud creak. Beyond was an entryway accented by dark wood trim, with a very nice rug covering a marble floor, though that had been broken up by the plants.

"David, what did you just do?" Megan asked.

"Might have opened a door a little too loudly."

"Well, the bird just looked your direction. Sparks! He's flying toward the building. Hurry."

I cursed softly, making my way through the room as quickly as possible. I passed an overgrown reception desk and pushed into the office beyond. The window here looked out right at Obliteration.

I climbed up on the windowsill.

"The bird just landed on a window on your building, one story down from you, but on the south side," Megan said. "He must have heard you, but he wasn't certain of the location."

"Good," I whispered, reaching out and affixing the camera on the outside of the building. This was the east side, so the bird shouldn't see me. The camera stuck in place easily. "Obliteration?"

"Not looking your way," Megan said. "He hasn't noticed. But if that bird really *is* one of Newton's Epics . . ."

If he is . . .

An idea started to form in my head. "Mmm . . . ," I said, tapping the camera to activate it.

"David?" Megan said. "What does that tone mean?"

"Nothing."

"You're improvising, aren't you?"

"Maybe." I ducked quietly back into the room. "Tell me, Megan. What is one surefire way to know if this Knoxx guy has been hiding his powers all along, or if Regalia—either through trickery or some other means—gave him his abilities?"

She was silent for a moment. "Sparks. You want to kidnap him, don't you?"

"Well, Val isn't going to be back for another hour at least. Might as well do something useful with my time." I paused. "I'm really itching to see if that guy has had any nightmares lately."

"And if Prof or Obliteration notices what you're doing?"

"It won't come to that," I said.

"Slontze," Megan said.

"Guilty as charged. Can you get into position to cover me through some of the windows?"

Megan sighed. "Let me see."

37

THIS, I thought as I crossed back through the swanky overgrown office, *is crazy.*

Moving against an Epic I barely knew? One about which I had no research, no notes, no intel at all? It was like jumping into a swimming pool without first looking to see if your friends had filled it with snakes.

I had to do it anyway.

We were blind; Regalia had us all running. Prof had been unresponsive for a day, during our most difficult stages of planning—but worse, even if he helped, Regalia was probably manipulating us based on her knowledge of him and Tia.

I needed to do something unexpected, and the secrets Knoxx knew could make a huge difference. I consoled myself with the idea that at least I wasn't trying to take on Obliteration or Newton on my own. This was just a minor Epic, after all.

I wasn't certain what Prof's reaction would be. I'd told him my plan about kidnapping an Epic—and he'd said that either I was just what the Reckoners needed, or I was dangerously reckless. Maybe I was both.

But he hadn't *specifically* forbidden me to try it. He just hadn't wanted me endangering the team. This wouldn't do that.

I peeked back into the stairwell. What I needed to do was make more noise so that Knoxx would figure out he'd gotten the wrong location. When he came up to check on me, I could clock him. Easy as pie.

Not that I actually knew how to make pie.

I stamped on the floor and knocked an old desk lamp off a side table, then I cursed as if I'd bumped into it. After that I moved back to the stairwell and held Megan's gun up, two-handed and at high ready, mobile darkened so that the only light was the moonlike glow of the plump fruit drooping from branches.

I waited, tense, and just listened. Indeed, I heard something in the stairwell. It echoed, a scraping that sounded far distant down below. Or was it coming from the floor right below me? With the strange echoing, it was difficult to tell.

"He's moving in." I jumped at Megan's voice. Though I'd turned the receiver way down, it seemed like thunder in my ear. "He entered the window and is on the floor just beneath you."

"Good," I said softly.

"There's movement on the first floor too," she said. "Well, the first floor above the water level, anyway. David, I think someone *else* is in that building."

"Scavengers?"

"I can't get a visual. Sparks. I'm having trouble getting any sort of clear look into your location too. It's too overgrown. I've lost Knoxx. Maybe you should flush him out."

"I'd like to avoid gunfire if possible," I said. "Who knows what kind of attention that will bring?"

"Does this rifle have a built-in suppressor?" Megan asked.

"Uh . . ." Did it?

"Yup, here it is," Megan said. "Electron-compressed muzzle suppressor. Sparks, this gun is *nice*."

I felt a stab of jealousy, which was utterly stupid. It was just a gun. And it wasn't even as good a gun as my last one. I immediately felt ashamed for thinking ill of the gun—which was even *more* stupid.

I listened at the stairwell, trying to pick out sounds of someone sneaking up. I heard something, but it came from *behind* me, inside the room where I'd planted the camera.

I stifled a curse. Knoxx had somehow circled around and come in the window of the executive office. My first instinct was to run toward him, but I pressed that down and instead eased open the door to the stairwell and slipped through.

Not a moment too soon. As I watched through the cracked stairwell door, the door into the executive office inched open and a figure emerged into the light of the hanging fruit in the receptionist's entryway. Knoxx. Slender, with buzzed hair and about forty earrings. He wore a mobile on his shoulder and carried a sleek-looking Beretta compact in two hands. He checked his corners, then inched into the room.

"Whoever it was," he whispered, "they were in here."

I couldn't hear the reply; he had in an earpiece.

"You're such an idiot, Newton," he said, kneeling to inspect the lamp I'd knocked over. "It's probably just some kids looking for food that nobody else has touched."

I frowned, surprised that a High Epic let a man like this

talk to her that way. He must be more powerful than I'd assumed.

Knoxx stood and moved toward the stairwell. Again a noise echoed up from down below, and the man hesitated. "I heard something," he said, moving forward less carefully. "From the stairwell, far below. They're running, it seems. . . . Yes . . ." He reached the door to the stairwell. "Okay, I'll check it out. We——"

I kicked the door open into his face.

Knoxx's voice cut off midsentence. I jumped into the room and buried my fist into his stomach, making him drop his gun. I carried Megan's handgun in my off hand, and brought it down, hoping to smack it against the back of Knoxx's head.

He managed to throw himself to the side and I missed, but I immediately lunged and grabbed him around the neck. Abraham had taught me a few grappling moves. If I could choke him, make him pass out . . .

Knoxx vanished.

Right. Transformation powers.

Idiot, I thought as the pigeon fluttered away from me. Fortunately, they weren't the most agile of birds. While the pigeon tried to get its bearings, I ran for the door that led to the executive office—the one with the window. I slammed that door, trapping the pigeon in our smaller chamber.

It fled down into the stairwell.

"David?" Megan asked in my ear.

"He got away from me," I said. "But he dropped his gun, and I kept him from getting out of the building. He's in the stairwell somewhere."

"Be careful," she said, tense.

"I will be," I said, peeking into the stairwell. I couldn't be certain he was unarmed—lots of men carried two guns, and it seemed any clothing and weapons he had on him vanished when he transformed, reappearing when he became a human again. That was pretty standard for shifters of moderate power.

I thought I heard a flutter of wings, and decided to follow it down the stairs. Unfortunately, this meant I could be running into a trap like the very one I'd just set for him.

"Do you see anything?" I asked.

"Watching . . . ," Megan said. "Yes! The floor below the top floor has shadows moving in the fruit lights. He's making a run for it. Want me to send him ducking?"

"Yes please," I said, pressing my back to the concrete wall.

I heard a few shots over the line. A suppressor, even a modern one, didn't completely eliminate the sound of gunfire—but they worked marvels nonetheless. Any spark from her shots would be hidden, which was important at night like this, and the gunfire didn't sound much like gunfire. More like metallic clicks.

There was a cracking of glass from the room nearby. Megan wasn't trying to hit the Epic; her shots just needed to make him more worried about her than he was about me. I thought I heard a man curse in the next room.

"Going in," I said. I leaped off a tree trunk and pulled open the swinging door, then ducked down in a crouch, searching for my mark. I heard heavy breathing, but could see nothing. It was a big room, a kind of large office space with broken cubicles and old computers. As I crept forward I passed a few of those cubicles that had been capped by canvas, making little dwellings filled with discarded pots and the occasional other refuse of human habitation. All were abandoned.

Megan had fired in through the large series of windows on the wall opposite me. Dust floated in the air, lit by fruit that dangled from the ceiling like snot from the nose of a toddler who had been snorting glowsticks.

How would I find Knoxx in this room? He could hide practically forever if he turned into a bird. I'd never—

Something launched out of the cubicle beside me, a black form with fur and claws. I yelped, firing out of instinct, but my aim was off. The thing hit me hard, knocking me back, and Megan's gun thumped against the floor. I struggled, trying to throw the creature off. It wasn't as big as I was, but those claws! They raked me along the side, which burned something fierce.

I flailed, one hand forcing the beast back, the other reaching for my gun. I didn't find it, but instead gripped something cold and metal from inside the covered cubicle beside us. I raised it and slammed it into the side of the beast's head.

A can of spraypaint?

As the beast turned back at me I sprayed it in the face, covering the thing's snout in glowing blue paint. The light let me pick out that the creature was a dog, though I didn't know my breeds. It was lean, with short hair and a pointed face.

It scrambled back, then the edges of its form fuzzed and the dog became a man. He stood, wiping paint from his eyes.

"Help!" I shouted. "You have a shot?"

"Maybe," Megan said. "I thought you wanted him alive, though!"

"I want *me* alive more," I said. "Take the shot!"

Knoxx reached the gun I'd dropped.

Something shattered one of the windows, and Knoxx lurched to the side as Megan's bullet took him in the shoulder. A spray of dark blood painted the wall behind him.

Knoxx slumped down, looking dazed, his face still glowing with blue paint. He groaned and dropped the handgun, then became a pigeon and fluttered away, crookedly.

"Did I get him?" Megan said in my ear.

"Right in the shoulder," I said, breathing out a tense breath. "Thank you."

"I'm just glad I didn't shoot you," Megan said. "I was aiming through infrared."

I groaned, climbing to my feet, hand to my side where Knoxx's claws had caught me. I was alive, but I'd failed to capture him. Still, I should probably count myself lucky.

A flutter of wings sounded from the other side of the room.

I frowned, picking up Megan's gun and inching forward. By the light of drooping fruit I saw spots of dark liquid on the desk nearby. I followed them to where the pigeon crouched on a windowsill, face glowing blue.

It's wounded, I realized. *It can't fly.*

The pigeon saw me and leaped out the window, fluttering awkwardly, losing feathers as it struggled to stay aloft. It barely made it to the next building over before being forced to land.

So it could fly, but not well. I looked down at my side. The clawing hurt, but didn't seem life-threatening. I looked out the window again, then put away the gun and shoved my hands into the gloves clipped to my belt. I raised them, then checked the legjets as the spyril warmed up.

"I'm going after him," I said.

"You're—"

I lost the rest of Megan's words as I jumped out the window. Twin jets of water lifted me from below before I hit the ocean, and I bobbed back up into the air, one hand down—streambeam pointed into the water. I spun for a moment, orienting myself.

Just ahead, the pigeon—still glowing blue across the face and neck—leaped off its perch and tried to flee. I grinned and sprayed the handjet behind me, tipping myself forward so my legs shot water downward and back at an angle.

I was off, wind blowing against my face as I tailed the weakened bird. It moved in a sudden, desperate burst of speed, keeping ahead of me despite its wound. I jetted after it, turning a corner by twisting and thrusting my legs to the side like a skier, then resetting and pointing the new direction.

Ahead, the bird landed on the windowsill of a building to rest. As soon as I got close, it lurched into the air again, fluttering and flapping, a glowing bob of blue.

I roared after it, and realized I was grinning. Ever since I'd started practicing with the spyril, I'd wanted to try something like this. A real test of my skills, fledgling though they were.

The bird, frantic, ducked into a building through a small gap in a broken window. I jetted up behind and used a spray of water from my handjet to shatter the window further, then I followed with my shoulder, breaking into the room. I managed to land without falling on my face—barely—and charged after the blue animal. It darted out another window, and I broke through, leaping into the air again.

"David?" I could barely hear Megan's voice. "Were those windows? Sparks, what is going *on*?"

I smiled, too focused to give a report. My chase wound through the waterway streets of Babilar, passing people on rooftops who pointed and cried out. The bird tried to fly high at one point, but the strain was too much and it came back down to land on a rooftop. *Yes,* I thought. *This is it.* I jetted up onto the roof and landed near it.

As I got my balance, the bird's form fuzzed and reshaped into a man. Knoxx's face was pale where it wasn't blue, and blood covered his shoulder. He stumbled back from me, clutching one hand to his shoulder, pulling out a knife with the other.

I stopped and stared at him for a moment, waiting. Then, finally, he toppled over, unconscious.

"I've got him," I said, staying back in case he was faking. "At least, I think I do."

"Where are you?" Megan asked.

I looked around, trying to orient myself after my frenzied chase. We'd curved through the streets and come back around to near where we'd begun.

"Two streets over from the building where I placed the camera. Look for a rooftop about four stories above the ocean, sparsely populated, a big mural of some people picking fruit spraypainted on the top."

"Coming," Megan said.

I unstrapped my gloves, then took Megan's gun from my pocket. I didn't want to get any closer to Knoxx without backup, but with that wound, would he bleed out on me if I didn't do something? There was too much to lose, I decided. I needed this man alive. I inched forward and finally decided that either he was a really good faker, or he actually was unconscious. I bound his hands as best I could using his own shoelaces, then tried to bandage his wound with his jacket.

"Megan?" I asked over the line. "ETA?"

"Sorry," she said. "No bridges. I'm having to weave all the way around to get to you. It's going to be another fifteen minutes or so."

"All right."

I settled down to wait, letting my tension melt away. It was replaced by a realization of the full foolishness of what I'd just done. I'd obviously underestimated Knoxx's transformation powers—he could turn into more than just a bird. What if he'd been even more powerful than that? What if he'd been a High Epic, impervious to bullets?

Prof had called me reckless, and he was right. While I should have felt triumphant in what I'd done, I found myself embarrassed. How would I explain this to the other Reckoners? Sparks. I hadn't even called Tia.

Well, at least it had turned out okay.

"Listen carefully," a voice said from behind me. "You're going to drop the gun. Then you're going to put your hands into the air, palms facing forward, and turn around."

A jolt of fear washed through me. But I recognized that voice. "Val?" I said, looking back.

"Drop the gun!" she ordered. She'd come out through the stairwell that connected the top floor of this building to the rooftop. She had a rifle tucked into her shoulder, sights on me.

"Val," I said. "Why are you—"

"*Drop it.*"

I dropped Megan's gun.

"Stand."

I obeyed, my hands out to the sides.

"Now your mobile."

Sparks. I ripped it off my shoulder and laid it on the ground, just as Megan said in my ear, "David? What's happening?"

"Kick it forward," Val instructed. When I hesitated, she focused her sights right on my forehead. So I kicked the mobile toward her.

She knelt, gun still on me, and picked it up with one hand.

"Sparks, David," Megan said in my ear. "I'm hurrying as fast as—"

She cut off as Val ended the signal, then slipped my mobile into her pocket.

"Val?" I asked as calmly as I could. "What's wrong?"

"How long have you been working for Regalia?" she replied. "Since the beginning? Was she the one who sent you to Newcago to infiltrate the Reckoners?"

"Working for . . . What? I'm not a spy!"

Val swung the rifle and actually fired, planting a bullet at my feet. I yelped, jumping back.

"I know you've been meeting with Firefight," Val said.

Sparks.

"You've been suspicious since you got here," Val continued. "You didn't save those people in the burning building, did you? It was a plot by you and Regalia to 'prove' how trustworthy you were. Did you even really kill Steelheart? You really didn't think anyone would notice when you helped Firefight enter our base? Calamity!"

"Val, listen. It's not what you think it is." I stepped forward.

And she shot me.

Right in the thigh. Pain tore through me and I dropped to my knees. I wrapped my hands around the wound, cursing. "Val, you're crazy! I'm not working for them. Look, I just captured an Epic!"

Val glanced at Knoxx lying bound on the ground. Then she swung her rifle toward him and shot him square in the head.

I gasped, growing numb despite the pain. "What . . . ," I sputtered. "After all I just did to—"

"The only good Epic is a dead Epic," Val said, sights back on me. "As a Reckoner, you should know this. But you're not one of us. You never were." She growled that last part, and her hand tightened on her weapon, her eyes narrowing. "You're the reason Sam is dead, aren't you? You gave them intel on us, on all the Reckoner cells."

"No, Val," I said. "I swear it! We've been lying to you, yes, but on Prof's orders." Blood dripped between my fingers as I squeezed my leg. "Let's call Tia, Val. Don't do anything rash."

Anything else *rash.*

Val kept the sights right on me. I met her gaze.

Then she pulled the trigger.

38

I tried to dodge, of course, but there was no chance I could get out of the way quickly enough. Beyond that, I was worn out and had just been shot in the leg.

So, when I came out of my awkward roll, I was surprised to find myself still alive. Val was surprised too, judging by her expression, but that didn't stop her from shooting me again.

The bullet stopped at my chest, implanting itself into my wetsuit but not breaking skin. Little spiderweb cracks of light spread out from it, then quickly faded.

Though I was glad to be alive, dread washed over me. I knew that effect—Prof's forcefields sometimes looked like that when they absorbed a blow. I looked up and found him, a silhouette in the night, standing on the single bridge leading to this rooftop. It swung slowly back and forth in the darkness.

Prof wasn't lit at all. He was a brick of blackness, lab coat fluttering in the lethargic breeze.

"Stand down, Valentine," Prof said softly, drawing her attention.

Val turned to look, then visibly jumped. She obviously hadn't figured out how I'd survived—but of course, she didn't know that Prof was an Epic. To her the forcefields were a product of advanced Epic technology.

Prof stepped onto the rooftop, the glow of the mural beneath lighting his face. "I gave you an order," he said to Val. "Stand down."

"Sir," she said. "He's been—"

"I know," Prof said.

Uh-oh, I thought, sweating. I started to rise, but a glare from Prof made me flop back down. The pain in my leg flared up again, and I pressed my hand back against the wound. Odd how in a moment of panic, I'd completely forgotten that I'd been shot.

I *hate* getting shot.

"His mobile," Prof said, holding out his hand to Val. She produced it, and Prof typed something in. I had the screen set to lock with a passcode the moment it was turned off—so he shouldn't have been able to get it back on. But he did.

"Text the person he's been communicating with," Prof said to Val. "That is Firefight. Say exactly this: 'Everything is all right. Val thought I was one of Regalia's men with Knoxx at first.'"

Val nodded, lowering the gun and sending a message to Megan.

Prof looked at me, crossing his arms.

"I . . . ," I said. "Um . . ."

"I'm disappointed in you," Prof said.

Those words crushed me.

"She's not evil, Prof," I said. "If you'd just listen to me—"

"I *have* been listening," Prof said. "Tia?"

"I've got it, Jon," Tia answered, her voice coming in over my earpiece. "You can listen to the entire thing again here, if you want."

"You bugged my phone," I whispered. "You didn't trust me."

Prof raised an eyebrow at me. "I gave you two chances to come clean, the latest being just earlier this very night. I *wanted* to be wrong about you, boy."

"You *knew*?" Val asked, turning to Prof. "All along, you knew what he was doing?"

"I didn't get where I am without learning to read my men, Val," Prof said. "Has Firefight replied?"

Val looked down at the screen of my mobile. I lay back, sick to my stomach. They'd been listening in. They *knew*. Sparks!

"She says, 'Okay. You're sure everything's all right?' "

"Say yes," Prof told Val. "And say, 'You should stay away for now. Val called Prof over, and we're going to head back to base. I think I can explain things away to them. I'll let you know what we find out from this Epic.' "

As Val tapped on the phone, Prof walked over to me. He placed his hand on my leg and got out a little box, the thing he called the harmsway—his "technology" for healing others.

The pain in my leg went away. I looked at him and realized I was having difficulty holding back tears. I didn't know if they were from shame, pain, or pure rage.

He'd been *spying* on me.

"Don't feel so bad, David," Prof said softly. "This is why you're here."

"What?"

"Firefight did exactly as we expected," Prof said. "If she was so good she could infiltrate my own team, I knew she'd have little difficulty compromising you. You're a good fighter, David. Passionate, determined. But you're inexperienced, and you melt for a pretty face."

"Megan's *not* just a pretty face."

"And yet you let her manipulate you," Prof said. "You let her into our base, and you told her our secrets."

"But I . . ." I *hadn't* let her into the base. She'd done that on her own. Prof didn't know everything, I realized. He'd bugged my mobile, but obviously that only gave him information when I had it on. He didn't know things Megan and I had talked about in person, only what we'd said over the line.

"I know you don't believe me, David," Prof said. "But everything she told you, everything she has done, has been part of a game. She played you. Her mock vulnerability, her supposed affection . . . I've seen it all before, son. All lies. I'm sorry. I'd bet even this 'weakness' she told you about is a fabrication."

Her weakness! Prof knew Megan's weakness. She'd told it to me over the mobile. He didn't believe, but he still knew. I felt a spike of alarm.

"You're wrong about her, Prof," I said, meeting his eyes. "I *know* she's being sincere."

"Oh?" Prof said. "And did she tell you about how she killed Sam?"

"She didn't. I—"

"She did," Prof said quietly, firmly. "David, we have it on film. Val showed it to me when I got to Babilar. Sam's mobile was recording as he died. Firefight shot him."

"You didn't tell me that!"

"I have my reasons," Prof said, standing up.

"You used me as bait," I said. "You said . . . this is why I'm here! You were planning a trap for her from the start!"

Prof turned to walk back to Val, who nodded at him, showing him the screen of my mobile.

"Let's move," Prof said. "Where's the sub?"

"Down below," Val said. "I didn't plant the supplies. I tracked David instead. You should have told me."

"The plan required him to believe that we didn't know what he was doing," Prof said, taking my mobile and putting it into his pocket. "The fewer who knew, the better." He looked back at me. "Come on, son. Let's head back."

"What are you going to do?" I demanded, still sitting where I'd been shot, my blood a stain beneath me. "About Megan."

Prof's expression darkened, and he didn't reply.

From that, I knew. The Reckoners had used ploys like this before, luring an Epic into a trap with a series of false texts they thought were from an ally.

I had to warn Megan.

I turned and threw myself off the rooftop, engaging the spyril. Which didn't work. I had about enough time to let out a shout of surprise before I hit the water four stories down from the roof.

It did not feel pleasant.

Once I sputtered out of the water and grabbed the side of the building, I looked up. Prof stood on the edge of the roof, tossing something up and down in his hand. The spyril's motivator. When had he lifted that? When he was healing me, probably.

"Fish him out," he said to Val, loud enough that I could hear. "And let's get back to the base."

39

I spent the next day in my room.

I wasn't confined there, not explicitly, but when I left, the looks I got from Val, Exel, and Mizzy drove me back into solitude.

Mizzy was the worst. At one point I stepped out to go to the bathroom and passed her working in the supply room. She looked at me and her smile faded. I could see anger and disgust in her eyes. She turned back to packing the supplies and didn't say a word.

And so, I spent the time lying on my bed, alternatingly ashamed and furious. Was I going to get kicked out of the Reckoners? The possibility made me sick. And what of Megan? The things Prof said . . . well, I didn't want to believe them. I *couldn't* believe them. At the very least, I didn't want to think about them.

Unfortunately, thinking about Prof made me furious. I had betrayed the team, but I couldn't help feeling that I'd been betrayed even more by him. I'd been *set up* to fail.

When the next morning came, I woke up to noises. Preparations. The plan moving forward. I stewed in my room for a time, but eventually I couldn't take it any longer. I needed answers. I pushed myself off the bed and went out to the hallway. I braced myself as I passed the storage room, but Mizzy wasn't there. I heard noises from the far end of the hallway behind me, in the room with the sub. That would be Val and her team packing for the mission.

I didn't go that way. I wanted Prof and Tia, and I found them in the meeting room with the glass wall. They looked up at me, then Tia glanced at Prof.

"I'll talk to him," Prof said to Tia. "Go join the others. We'll be a man short on this mission, and I want you running operations from inside the sub. Our base is compromised. We won't be returning here."

Tia nodded, picking up her laptop, and walked out. She gave me a glance but nothing else as she shut the door. That left only me and Prof, lit by the lamp on Tia's desk.

"You're going on the mission," I said. "The hit on Newton, to expose Regalia."

"Yes."

"A man short," I said. "You're not taking me?"

Prof didn't say anything.

"You let me practice with the spyril," I said. "You let me think I was part of the mission here. Was I really just bait *the whole time*?"

"Yes," Prof said quietly.

"Is there more to the plan, then?" I demanded. "Things you haven't told me? What's really going on here, Prof?"

"We haven't kept much from you," he said with a quiet sigh. "Tia's plan to find Regalia is legitimate, and it's working. If we can get Regalia to appear in the region Tia wants, it will leave us with only a few buildings Regalia could be hiding in. I'm going to run point, execute the plan against Newton. Chase her through the city, tempt Abigail to appear. If she does, we'll know her base location. Val, Exel, and Mizzy will move at Tia's word and run an assault to kill her."

"Sounds like you could use another point man," I said.

"Too late for that," Prof said. "I suspect it will take time for us to rebuild trust. On both sides."

"And Obliteration?" I asked, stepping forward. "There's been almost *no* talk about how to deal with him! He's a bomb—he's going to destroy the entire city."

"We don't need to worry about that," Prof said. "Because we already have a way to stop Obliteration."

"We do?"

Prof nodded.

I flogged my brain like a dog who had made a mess on the carpet, but I came up with nothing. How would we stop Obliteration? Was there something they hadn't told me? I looked at Prof.

And then I saw it in his grim expression, his tightly drawn lips.

"A forcefield," I realized. "You enclose him in a bubble of it as he releases the destructive force."

Prof nodded.

"All that heat has to go somewhere," I said. "You'll just be bottling it up."

"I can expand the shield," he said, "projecting the heat away from the city. I've practiced it."

Wow. But, then, was this really anything more than he'd done in saving me from the blast that killed Steelheart? He was right. We'd had the answer to at least delaying Obliteration right here all along. The heat probably wouldn't kill Obliteration himself—he seemed immune to his own powers—but it would slow him. And who knew, maybe a focused and concentrated blast reflected back upon him *would* actually be able to destroy him. It was at least worth trying.

I walked forward, approaching Prof, who still sat at Tia's desk before the wall of dark water. Something brushed against it outside, something wet and slimy, but I lost sight of it in the blackness. I shivered, then looked back at Prof.

"You can do it, right?" I asked. "Hold it in? Not just the explosion, but . . . other things?"

"I'll have to." Prof stood up and walked to the glass wall, looking out at the dark waters. "Tia tells me that many Epics like Obliteration have a moment of weakness after they expend a large blast of energy. He might be vulnerable. If he survives the heat of his own blast, I might be able to bring him down right after while his powers are dampened. And if not, at least I can stop him long enough for it to matter—and for the other team members to deal with Regalia."

"And Megan?" I asked.

He didn't reply.

"Prof," I said. "Before you kill her, at least try out what she said. Light a fire. See if it destroys the images she creates. You'll have proof that she was telling me the truth."

Prof reached up and touched the glass of the window. He'd left his lab coat on the back of the chair and was wearing only a pair of slacks and a button-down shirt, both the same oddly antiquated style that he favored. I could almost imagine him out in the jungle with a machete and a map, exploring ancient ruins.

"You *can* control the darkness inside," I said to him. "And since you can do it, Megan can too. It—"

"Stop," Prof whispered.

"But listen, it—"

"Stop!" Prof yelled, spinning on me. His hand moved so fast I barely saw it before he grabbed me by the throat and hauled me into the air, turning and slamming me back against the large window.

I let out a *gurk*. The only illumination in the room was that lamp on the desk, backlighting Prof, hiding his face in shadows. I scrambled, choking, trying to pry his fingers free from my throat. Prof took me under the arm with his other hand and lifted me up, relieving some pressure on my throat. I was able to wheeze in a short breath.

Prof leaned against me, forcing more air out of my lungs, and spoke slowly. "I've tried to be patient with you. I've tried to tell myself your betrayal isn't personal, that you were seduced by an expert illusionist and con woman. But damn it, son, you're making it *very hard*. Even though I knew what you'd do, I hoped for better. I thought you, of all people, understood. We *can't trust them!*"

I struggled to wheeze something out, and he let me breathe a little more.

"Please . . . put me down . . . ," I said.

He studied me for a moment in the dim light, then stepped back, letting me drop to the floor. I gasped for air, pushing myself up beside the wall, tears rolling from the corners of my eyes.

"You should have come to me," Prof said. "If you'd just come to me instead of hiding everything . . ."

I struggled to my feet. Sparks! Prof had a *grip*. Did his power portfolio include enhanced physical abilities? I might have to change the entire subset of Epic I'd categorized him under.

"Prof," I said, rubbing my neck, "something is very, very *wrong* about this city. And we're blind! Yes, your plan for Obliteration is a good one, but what is Regalia plotting? Who is Dawnslight? I didn't get a chance to tell you. He contacted me again, yesterday. He seems to be on our side, but there's something strange about him. He mentioned . . . surgery on Obliteration? What is Regalia planning? She has to know that we're going to try to kill some of her pet Epics. She seems to be encouraging it. Why?"

"Because of what I've been saying all along!" Prof said, throwing his hands into the air. "She's *hoping* we'll be able to stop her. For all I know, she brought Obliteration here so we could kill him."

"If that's true, it would imply an element of resistance inside of her," I said, stepping forward. "It means she's fighting back. Prof, is it so far a stretch to believe that she might be hoping you'll be able to help her? Not kill her, but restore her to what she once was?"

Prof stood in the darkness, a hulking silhouette. Sparks, he was so *intimidating* when he chose to be. Broad-chested, square-faced—almost inhuman in his proportions. It was easy to forget how big he was; you start thinking of him as the manager, the leader of the team. Not as this figure of lines and muscles, cut of blackness and shadow.

"Do you realize how dangerous this talk of yours is?" he asked softly. "For me?"

"What?"

"Your talk of good Epics. It gets inside my brain, like maggots eating at the flesh, worming their way toward my core. I decided long ago—for my sanity, for the world itself—that I could not use my powers."

I felt cold.

"But now, here you come. Talking about Firefight, and how

she lived among us for months, using her powers only when necessary. It starts me wondering. I could do it too, couldn't I? Aren't I strong? Don't I have a handle on it? When you left me yesterday, in the room by myself, I started creating forcefields again. Little ones, to bottle up chemicals, to glow and give me light. I keep finding excuses to use them, and now I'm planning to use my powers to stop Obliteration—create a shield bigger than any I've created in years."

He stepped forward and grabbed me by the front of my shirt again. He yanked me close.

"It's not working," Prof hissed at me. "It's destroying me, step by step. *You* are destroying me, David."

"I . . ." I licked my lips.

"Yes," Prof whispered, dropping me. "We tried this once. Me. Abigail. Lincoln. Amala. A team, just like in the movies, you know?"

". . . And?"

He met my gaze in the gloom. "Lincoln went bad—you call him Murkwood these days. He always did love those sparking books. I had to kill Amala."

I swallowed.

"It doesn't work, David," Prof said. "It *can't* work. It's destroying me. And . . ." He took a deep breath. "It has already destroyed Megan. She texted this morning. She wants to meet with you again. So at least something good will come out of this."

"No!" I said. "You're not—"

"We'll do what we do, David," Prof said quietly. "There will be a reckoning."

I felt a mounting horror. I had an image of Sourcefield powerless in the deluge of Kool-Aid, struggling with the bathroom door, looking back at me with pleading in her eyes. Only in my mind, she had Megan's face.

A pulled trigger.

Red mixing with red.

"Please," I said, frantic, scrambling for Prof. "Don't. We can think of something else. You heard about the nightmares. Is that what happens to you? Tell me, Prof. Was Megan right? Do they have something to do with weaknesses?"

He took me by the arm and shoved me backward. "I forgive you," he said. Then he walked toward the doorway.

"Prof?" I demanded, following him toward the door. "No! It—"

Prof raised a hand absently and a forcefield sprang into place in the doorway, separating us.

I pressed my palms on it, watching Prof walk down the hallway. "Prof! Jon Phaedrus!" I pounded on the forcefield, for all the good that did.

He stopped, then looked back at me. In that moment, his face in shadows, I didn't see Prof the leader—or even Prof the man.

I saw a High Epic who had been defied.

He turned and continued down the hallway, vanishing from my sight. The forcefield remained. If the jackets were any guide, it could stay in place as long as it was needed, and Prof could travel quite a distance without it vanishing.

A short time later I spotted the sub in the enormous window, passing in the dark water. They left me without my mobile, the spyril, or any way to escape.

I was alone.

Just me and the water.

PART FOUR

40

I spent the next hour or so slumped at Tia's desk in the meeting room, the huge window looming over me like a roommate who just heard you unwrap a bag of toffee-pulls. I stood up and began pacing, but moving only reminded me of what the team would be doing out there. Running, fighting for their lives. Trying to save the city.

And here I was. Benched.

I looked up at Prof's forcefield. I couldn't help feeling that Prof specifically wanted me out of the way for this operation— that catching me with Megan was an excuse, not a reason.

Megan. Sparks! *Megan.* He wouldn't really kill her, would he? My thoughts kept turning back to her over and over, like a penguin who couldn't be convinced that these plastic fish weren't real. She'd trusted me. She'd told me her weakness. Now Prof might kill her because of it.

I hadn't completely sorted out my emotions regarding her. But I *was* sure I didn't want her to get hurt.

I stalked back to the desk and sat, trying to keep my eyes off that dominating view of the dark waters. I started digging through the desk drawers, looking for something to distract myself. I found an emergency sidearm—just a little nine-millimeter, but at least I would be armed if I could ever get out of this stupid room—and ammunition. In another drawer I found a datapad. It had no connectivity to the Knighthawk networks, but it did contain a folder with a copy of Tia's notes about Regalia's location.

The map showed the path that the Reckoners would use for today's trap. They'd follow Newton on her rounds, then hit her in a specific spot in an attempt to make Regalia appear. I found a little *X* on the datapad's battle map with an oblique reference to Prof in position for an emergency—and I now recognized that as an indication of where Prof would be waiting to stop Obliteration if necessary. But what were they planning to do about Megan?

Prof has my mobile, I thought. *He wouldn't even have to work to set a trap for Megan. All he'd have to do is send her a text asking to meet, then attack her.* And if she died by fire, she wouldn't reincarnate.

Feeling even more anxious, I started looking through the datapad, though for what I didn't know. Maybe Tia had recorded something about a plan to hurt Megan.

There. A file named "Firefight." I tapped it.

It turned out to be a video file.

Within seconds I knew what it was. A man, puffing with exertion, moved through one of the jungle-esque rooms of a

Babilar high-rise. The recording was from his viewpoint, likely captured by one of the earpieces that the team often wore.

The man pushed through vines, passing fruit with a deep inner glow. He looked over his shoulder, then scrambled over a fallen tree trunk and peeked into another room.

"Sam." It was Val's voice. "You weren't supposed to engage."

"Yeah, yeah," he said. "But I did. So now what?"

"Get out."

"Working on it."

Sam crossed through this second room in a rush, moving along the wall. He stepped over a coffeemaker that had sprouts growing out of the top, hurried through a small break-room kitchen, and finally found a wall with windows. He glanced out at a drop of four stories, then looked back into the jungle.

"Go," Val said.

"I heard something."

"Go faster, then!"

Sam remained with a hand on the window frame. In the light of a glowing fruit I could make out his gloves. He was wearing the spyril.

"All we're doing is *watching*, Val," he whispered. "This isn't what I signed up for."

"Sam . . ."

"All right," he grumbled, then used his elbow to knock some of the glass out of the frame so he could climb through. He pointed the streambeam down into the water below, but hesitated.

Something rustled in the room. Sam spun, a jarring motion of the camera accompanied by a muffled crunch as a vine brushed his earpiece.

Megan stood behind him, shadowed by draping foliage,

wearing jeans and a tight T-shirt. She seemed surprised to see him, and didn't have her weapon out.

All grew still.

I found myself rising from my seat, words formed in my mouth. I wanted to scream at the screen, even though it was just a recording. "Just go," I said. I *pleaded*.

"Sam, *no*," Val said.

Sam reached for the gun at his side.

Megan drew faster.

It was over in under a second. I heard the shot, and then the camera lurched again. When it settled, Sam's camera faced a nearby wall. I heard Sam's breathing, labored, but he didn't move. A shadow settled over him, and I could hear shuffling and figured that Megan—ever conscious of firearms—was disarming Sam and checking to see if he was feigning injury.

Val started whispering something over and over. Sam's name.

I realized I was sweating.

Megan's shadow retreated and Sam's breathing grew worse and worse. Val tried to talk to him, told him that Exel was on his way, but Sam gave no response.

I didn't see his life end. But I heard it. One breath at a time until . . . nothing.

I sank down into the seat as the video stopped, Val's voice cutting out halfway through a yell for Exel to hurry. I felt like I'd watched something intimate, something I shouldn't have.

She really did kill him, I thought. It had kind of been self-defense, hadn't it? She'd checked on the noise he was making. He'd drawn a gun. . . .

Of course, Megan reincarnated if killed. Sam didn't.

I lowered the datapad, numb. I couldn't blame Megan for defending herself, but at the same time, it tore at me to think of what had happened. This could have been avoided so easily.

How much of what Megan had told me could I trust? After all, Prof had been spying on me. And now it turned out Megan really *had* killed Sam. Unfortunately, I realized that deep down, I wasn't surprised. Megan had seemed uncomfortable when I'd mentioned Sam to her, and she hadn't explained herself or what had happened. I hadn't given her the chance.

I hadn't wanted to know.

Who could I trust? My emotions were a messed-up jumble, a churning stew of confusion, frustration, and nausea. Nothing made sense anymore. Not like it should have.

Gasping for breath . . . , Regalia had said to me.

I latched on to a thought, something different, something to pull me away from the muddle of how I felt about Megan, Prof, and the Reckoners. That day back when I'd first been practicing with the spyril, Regalia had appeared. She'd talked about how I'd die alone someday. *Gasping for breath in one of these jungle buildings, one step from freedom,* she'd said. *Your last sight a blank wall that someone had spilled coffee on. A pitiful, pathetic end.*

Though I hated to see any of this again, I rewound the video to Sam's last sight, his camera pointed at the wall. That wall *was* stained as if something had spilled on it.

Regalia had seen this video.

Oh, *sparks*. How much did she know? My discomfort with this entire mission flooded back. We didn't know half of what we thought we did. Of that I was certain.

I hesitated for a moment, then swiped everything off Tia's desk but the datapad.

I needed to think. About Epics, about Regalia, and about what I actually knew. I bottled up my emotions for the moment, and I set aside everything we assumed we knew. I even set aside my own notes, which I'd gathered before joining the

Reckoners. Obliteration's powers proved that my own knowledge could be distinctly faulty.

So what did I actually *know* about Regalia?

One fact stood out to me. She'd had the Reckoners in hand, and had decided not to kill us. Why? Prof was certain she wanted him to kill her. I wasn't willing to make that leap. What other reasons could there be?

She confronted us that first night expecting to find Prof there, I thought. *Sure, she could have finished off most of us without a thought. But not Jonathan Phaedrus.*

She knew him as an Epic. She was familiar with his powers. She had let us live, ostensibly to deliver the message that Prof was to kill her. Well, I didn't accept that she wanted to die. But why else would she goad Prof into coming to Babilar?

Regalia knew how Sam died, I thought. *In great detail. Detail that Megan was unlikely to have explained.* So either she'd watched that video, or she'd been there on that night.

Could she have pulled the strings from behind the scenes, engineering Sam's death? Or was I simply searching for ways to exonerate Megan?

I focused back on our first night in Babilar, when we had faced Obliteration. That fight had worn us out, and after we'd run, Regalia had appeared in her glory—but had been shocked that Prof wasn't there. What if Regalia had done this all to find a way to kill Prof? Prof knew a lot about Regalia's powers. He knew her limits, her range, the holes in her abilities. Could she have the same intelligence on him?

I suddenly imagined it all as an intricate Reckoner-style trap, one laid by Regalia to bring Prof here and eliminate him. A plot to remove one of the most powerful potential rivals to her dominance. It seemed like a tenuous connection, a stretch. But the more I thought about it, the more convinced I became that Prof was in serious danger.

Could it really be that we had not been the hunters here at all? Were we, instead, the ones being trapped?

I stood. I had to get out. Prof was probably in danger. And even if he wasn't, I couldn't risk him attacking Megan. I needed answers from her. I needed to talk to her about Sam, about what she'd done. I needed to know how much of what she'd told me was a lie.

And . . . the truth was I loved her.

Despite it all—despite the questioning, despite feeling betrayed—I loved her. And I'd be *damned* before I let Prof kill her.

I strode to the door and tried to pry the forcefield out of the way. I tried pushing, thumping—I even grabbed the chair from the desk and beat it against the forcefield. All, of course, had no effect.

Breathing hard from the exertion, next I tried to break the wood of the frame *around* the forcefield. That didn't work either. I had no leverage and the building was too sturdy. Maybe with tools and a day or so, I could break through one of the walls into another room, but that would take way too long. There were no other exits.

Except . . .

I turned and eyed the large window, taller than a man and several times as wide, looking out at the ocean. It was midnight, and therefore dark, but I could see shapes shifting out there in that awful blackness.

Each time I went into the water, I felt that void trying to suck me down. Consume me.

Slowly, I walked to Tia's desk and fished in the bottom drawer, picking up the nine-millimeter. A Walther. Good gun, one that even I'd admit was accurate. I loaded the ammo, then looked up at the window.

I immediately felt an oppressive dread. I'd come to an

uneasy truce with the waters, yet I still felt like I could sense them eager to break through and crush me.

I was there again, in the blackness, with a weight on my leg towing me down into oblivion. How deep were we? I couldn't swim up from down here, could I?

What a stupid idea. I set the gun on the desk.

But . . . if I stay here, there's a good chance they both die. Prof kills Megan. Regalia kills Prof.

In the bank nearly eleven years ago, I'd cowered in fear when my father fought. He'd died.

Better to drown. I gathered up all of the emotions I felt at looking into the depths—the terror, the foreboding, the primal panic—and held them in hand. Then crushed them.

I would *not* be ruled by the waters. Pointedly, deliberately, I picked up Tia's gun again and leveled it at the window.

Then I fired.

41

THE bullet barely harmed the window.

Oh, it made a tiny hole, which sent out a little spiderweb of cracks—like you see in bulletproof glass that takes a slug. Only this was just a nine-millimeter, and the window in front of me had been built to withstand a bombing. Feeling stupid, I shot again. And again. I unloaded the entire magazine into the glass wall, making my ears ring.

The window didn't break. It barely sprung a small leak. Great. Now I was going to drown in this room. Judging by the size of that leak, I only had . . . oh, somewhere around six months before it filled the entire place.

I sighed, slumping down in the chair. Idiot. And here I'd faced the depths, challenged my fears, and prepared myself for a dramatic swim to freedom. Instead I now had to listen to tinkling water dripping onto the wood floor—the ocean making fun of me.

I stared at it pooling on the ground and had another really bad idea.

Well, I've already sold the family name for three oranges, I thought. I dragged one of the room's bookshelves over and obscured the doorway and the forcefield. Then I took out one of the desk drawers and put it under the leak to contain some of the water. A few minutes later, I had a respectable pool in there.

"Hello, Regalia," I said. "This is David Charleston, the one called Steelslayer. I'm inside the Reckoners' secret base."

I repeated this several times, but nothing happened of course. We were all the way out on Long Island, well outside Regalia's range. I'd just hoped that maybe, if she really *was* playing us all, Prof and Tia's information about her range might be—

The water in my drawer started to move and shift.

I yelped, stumbling back as the little hole I'd made in the window expanded, water forcing its way through in a larger stream. It rose up, growing into a shape, then stopped flowing as color flooded the figure.

"You mean to tell me," Regalia said, "that all this time I had my agents searching along the northern coast, when he had a sparking *underwater base*?"

I backed away, heart thumping. She was so calm, so certain, wearing her business suit, a string of pearls around her neck. Regalia was not out of control. She knew exactly what she was doing in this city.

She looked me up and down, as if evaluating me. Tia's information about Regalia's range was wrong. Maybe her powers, like Obliteration's, had been enhanced somehow.

Everything that was happening in this city was wrong.

"So, he locked you away, did he?" Regalia asked.

"Uh . . ." I tried to decide how to game Regalia. If that was even possible. My vague plan of acting like I wanted to defect to her side seemed pitifully obvious now.

"Yes, you *are* an articulate one," Regalia said. "Well, brains don't necessarily accompany passion. In fact, they might often have an inverse relationship. What will Jonathan do to you, I wonder, when he finds out you've revealed his base to me?"

"Megan already found it," I answered. "So far as Prof thinks, this place has been exposed and is no longer a valid base."

"Pity," Regalia said, looking around. "This *is* a fine location. Jonathan always did have a keen sense of style. He might fight against his nature, but aspects of him so blatantly show his heritage. His extravagant bases, the nicknames, the costume he wears."

Costume? *Black lab coat. Goggles in the pocket.* It *was* a little eccentric, actually.

"Well, be quick with your request, boy," Regalia said. "It is a busy day."

"I want to protect Megan," I said. "He's going to kill her."

"And if I help you with this, will you serve me?"

"Yes."

This is one of the most cunning Epics in the world, I thought to myself. *You really think she'll believe you'd swap sides, just like that?*

I was banking on the fact that she'd shown an interest in me earlier. Of course, she had also said that she was mad at me for killing Steelheart. Perhaps, now that her plan to bring down Prof was in full swing, she'd just crush me.

Regalia waved a hand.

Water shattered the wall, ripping apart the hole I'd made and destroying the glass. I didn't even have time to grab the gun off the desk as the water filled the room, plunging me into darkness. I sputtered and thrashed. I may have faced my fear of these depths, but that didn't mean I was *comfortable* in them.

I was completely incapable of thinking or swimming consciously. I'd have died there if Regalia hadn't towed me upward. I had a sense of motion, and when I broke the surface—gasping and cold—my ears hurt for some reason.

The water beneath me grew *solid* somehow. A small pedestal of water raised me up, and Regalia appeared standing beside me. I lay there, shivering and wet, and eventually I realized we were moving. The water pedestal was zipping along the surface of the ocean, carrying me with it, approaching the glowing painted walls and bridges of Babilar.

Regalia could appear wherever she wanted—or, at least, she could appear anyplace that she could see. So this wasn't about transporting her, but about moving me.

"Where are we going?" I asked, getting to my knees.

"Has Jonathan ever told you," Regalia asked, "what we know about the nature of Calamity?"

I could see it up there, that omnipresent glowing dot. Brighter than a star, but far smaller than the moon.

"You can view Calamity through a telescope," Regalia continued, speaking in a conversational way. "The four of us did it quite often, back in the day. Jonathan, myself, Lincoln. Even with a telescope, it's hard to make out details. He glows very brightly, you see."

"He?" I asked.

"But of course," Regalia said. "Calamity is an Epic. What else did you expect?"

I . . . I couldn't respond. I could barely even blink.

"I asked him about you," she said. "Told him you'd make

a wonderful Epic. It would solve all kinds of problems, you see, and I think you'd take to it quite nicely. Ah, here we are."

I struggled to my feet as our water platform stopped moving. We were in the lower section of Babilar, near where the operation to take out Newton would soon begin. It seemed Regalia knew about that too.

"You're lying."

"Do you know of the Rending?" Regalia asked. "That's what we call the time just after an Epic first gains their powers. You'll feel an overwhelming sensation driving you to destroy, to break. It utterly consumes us. Some learn to manage with the feelings, as I have. Others, like dear Obliteration, never quite get beyond them."

"No," I whispered, feeling a growing horror.

"If it's any consolation, you'll probably forget most of what you're about to do. You'll wake up in a day or so with only vague memories of the people you killed." She leaned in, voice growing harsher. "I'm going to *enjoy* watching this, David Charleston. It is poetry for one who has killed so many of us to become the thing he hates. I believe, in the end, that is what convinced Calamity to agree to my request."

She slapped me in the chest with a liquid hand, shoving me off her platform. I fell backward into the waters, and they churned about me, raising me in a pillar toward the night sky. I sputtered, righting myself, and discovered that I was hanging some hundred feet in the air, as if on an enormous jet made by the spyril. I looked upward.

And there was Calamity.

The star burned fiercely, and the land around me seemed to grow red, bathed in a deep light. Like on that first night, so long ago, when Calamity had come and the world had changed. Impossibilities, chaos, followed by Epics.

It dominated my view, that burning redness. I didn't feel as if I—or it—had changed locations, and yet suddenly it was all that I could see. I felt, against reason, that I was so close I could reach out and touch the star. And within that blazing, violent redness, I *swore* I saw a pair of fiery wings.

My skin grew cold, then shocked alive with a tingling, electric sensation—as if recovering from numbness. I screamed, doubling upon myself. Sparks! I could *feel* it coursing through me. A foul energy, a transformation.

It was really happening.

No, no . . . Please . . .

The redness upon the land retreated, and my water pillar slowly lowered. I barely noticed, as the tingling feeling continued, more frantic, like thousands of worms squirming under my skin.

"It is unsettling at first," Regalia said softly as I lowered down to sea level beside her. "I have been assured that you will be given powers that are 'thematically appropriate.' I suggested the same water-manipulation abilities that young Georgi possessed. That, if you have forgotten, is the Epic who was killed to make that abomination you call the spyril. I think you'll find being an Epic to be *far* more liberating than using some device to ape us."

I groaned, rolling over, face toward the sky. Calamity now seemed only a distant prick, but that red glow upon the land remained—faint, but noticeable. Everything around me was bathed in a shade of crimson.

"Well, on with it," Regalia said. "Let's see what you can do. I am *distinctly* interested to see how your former teammates react when you bumble into the middle of their careful planning, manifesting Epic powers, murdering everyone you see. It should be . . . amusing."

A distant part of my brain realized that this was why she'd

been so fast to help me escape the base. She hadn't believed I was defecting; she intended to use me, and my new powers, as a way to disrupt the Reckoners' plans.

I rolled back over, finding my way to my knees, still positioned on a section of water that Regalia had made solid. My face reflected in the waters, lit by spraypaint on a nearby building.

Was I now an Epic?

Yes. I felt it was true. What had just happened between me and Calamity was no trick. But still, I had to test it. I had to know for absolute certain.

And then I would kill myself, quickly, before the desires consumed me.

I reached out to touch the water.

42

I felt something.

Well, I felt the water, of course. I mean something else. Something inside of me. A stirring.

Hand on the surface of the water, I peered into those depths. Just beneath me was an ancient steel bridge cluttered with a line of rusted cars. A window into another world, an old world, a time before.

I imagined what it would have been like to live in this city when the waters swept in. My fears returned, the images of being crushed, drowned, trapped.

Only . . . I found that they didn't control me as they once had. I was able to shove them aside. Nothing would ever again be as bad as standing before the glass wall beneath the ocean and firing a pistol toward it, inviting the sea to come and crush me.

Take it, a voice said in my head. A quiet, distant voice, but a real one. *Take this power. It is yours.*

I . . .

Take it!

"No."

The tingling vanished.

I blinked at the waters. Calamity's light had retreated, and everything looked normal again.

I stumbled to my feet and turned to face Regalia.

She smiled. "Ah, it takes hold!"

"Nah," I said. "I'm a washing machine at a gun show."

She blinked, looking totally befuddled. ". . . What did you just say?"

"Washing machine?" I said. "Gun show? You know. Washing machines don't use guns, right? No fingers. So if they're at a gun show, there's nothing they'd want to buy. Anyway, I'm good here. Not interested."

"Not . . . interested. It doesn't matter if you're interested or not! You don't get a *choice*."

"Made one anyway," I said. "Thanks, though. Nice of you to think of me."

Regalia worked her mouth as if trying to speak, but no sound came out. Her eyes bulged as she regarded me. Gone was her posture of dominance and control.

I smiled and shrugged. Inside, I was working frantically on some way to escape. Would she destroy me, now that I'd failed to become part of her plans? The only place for me to go was into the water—which, considering her abilities, didn't seem wise.

But I wasn't an Epic. I had no doubt that she'd just *tried* to give me powers, as she said she could do. I had no doubt that I'd heard Calamity's voice in my mind.

It just hadn't worked on me.

"Epic powers," I said to Regalia, meeting her gaze, "are tied to your fears, aren't they?"

Regalia's eyes widened even further. A piece of me found it supremely satisfying to see Regalia so flummoxed, and it seemed further proof to me that everything else she'd done had been calculated. Even when she'd seemed out of control, she'd known what she was doing.

All except for this moment.

She glanced away and cursed. Then she vanished. I, of course, immediately dropped into the ocean.

I sputtered a bit but managed to paddle myself to the nearest Babilar building. Mizzy would have laughed to see my silly version of a swimming stroke, but it worked well enough. I hauled myself up out of the water and into the building through a window. It took about five minutes to find the stairwell—there were paths worn through this building, probably made by people gathering fruit—and climb to the roof two stories above.

It was a typical Babilar night, with people sitting out, legs hanging off the edges of their rooftops. Some fished, others lazily gathered fruit. One group sang softly as someone played an old guitar. I shivered, soaked through, and tried to sort out what had just happened to me.

Calamity was an Epic. Some kind of . . . super-powerful gifter, perhaps? Could it be that there had really only been one single Epic all along, and everyone else held an offshoot of his powers?

Well, Regalia was in communication with him, whoever he was. She'd left me alone. Was it because her failure to make me an Epic had spooked her? She'd looked to the side at the end; it was hard to remember sometimes that she was actually in her hidden base, with other things happening around her there. Perhaps something had distracted her.

Well, I was free, for the moment. And I still had work to do. I took a deep breath and tried to orient myself, but I had only a vague idea of where I was. I jogged up to a group of people cooking soup beside some tents; they were listening to the music of a quiet radio—probably a live broadcast by someone else in the city. They looked up at me, and one offered me a water bottle.

"Thanks, uh, but I can't stay," I said. "Um . . ." How could I say this without sounding suspicious? "I'm totally normal and not weird at all. But I need to get to Finkle Crossway. Which direction is that again?"

An aging woman wearing a glowing blue knit shawl pointed with a lazy gesture. "Ten or so bridges that way. Turn left at the really tall building, keep going. That'll take you past Turtle Bay, though. . . ."

"Um. Yeah?"

"Big Epic there," a man filled in. "Glowing."

Oh, right. Obliteration. Well, surprisingly, he was the least of my problems. I took off, running the direction indicated, trying to keep my attention on the task at hand, not on Calamity. I needed to save Megan, get some answers, warn Prof that Regalia's range was wider than he and Tia thought.

What would Prof do when he saw me free from the base? It probably wouldn't be good, but I had to believe that he'd listen to me when I explained that Regalia had appeared at the base.

Ten bridges? That was a long run, and time was short. The Reckoners had likely already started putting their plan into motion. I needed my mobile. Sparks, I needed more than that! I needed a weapon, information, and—preferably—an army or two. Instead I ran, alone and unarmed, across a wooden bridge where each board had been painted a different color.

Think, think! I couldn't reach them in time, even running all the way. So what could I do?

Well, I knew the plan. The Reckoners would follow Newton doing her nightly rounds. That would start midtown, then sweep through the city down toward old Chinatown, where the hit would happen. So, if I could position myself in the middle of that path, they'd theoretically come to *me* instead of me needing to find them.

By asking a few more people for directions, I was able to make my way to Bob's Cathedral, a place I knew would be along Newton's route. The grandly named locale was just a rooftop spraypainted on the top and sides like a series of stained glass windows. The place had a dense population, and Tia suspected that it was on Newton's rounds because it let her show off and remind everyone who ruled the city.

I slowed my pace as I neared, joining a line of people moving up a bridge toward the colorfully painted building. Sparks, the place was busy. As I reached the top, I found that it was a market, full of tents and shacks. The tents displayed wares ranging from things as simple as hats made from Babilar tree fronds to products as exotic as salvage from the old days. I passed one man who had bins of windup toys. He sat behind them with a small screwdriver, fixing a broken one. Another woman sold empty milk jugs, which she claimed were perfect for storing fruit juice. A few full ones sat out glowing brightly to prove her point.

The press of bodies and the chatter was—for once—something I found relieving. It would be easier to hide here, though I had to make certain I was in position to spot Newton when she came. I lingered by one stall that was selling cloth-ing. Simple stuff, really just sheets of cloth cut with armholes.

One was a cloak, though, that glowed bright blue. Perfectly unobtrusive here in Babilar.

"Like what you see?" asked a young girl seated on a stool beneath the awning.

"I could use the cloak," I said, pointing. "But I don't have much to trade."

"You've got nice shoes."

I looked down. My sneakers. Good rubber on those, the type that was getting harder and harder to find. If I was going to be chasing the Reckoners, I suspected I'd need my footwear. I fished in my pockets and only came out with one thing. The chain that Abraham had given me, with the symbol of the Faithful dangling at the end.

The young girl's eyes widened.

I stood for a long moment.

Then I traded my shoes instead. I wasn't certain how much my shoes were worth, but I just kept haggling, adding things until I walked away with the cloak, a pair of worn-out sandals, and a pretty-good-looking knife.

I put on my new gear and found my way to a tavern on the side of the rooftop, a place Newton stopped for a drink most nights before continuing on to harass the various shopkeepers of the cathedral. It sold alcohol that glowed faintly in the night. If there was a universal law regarding mankind, it was that they'd find a way to ferment anything, given time.

I didn't order a drink, but instead settled down outside on the ground next to the tavern's wooden wall, hood drooping over my eyes. Just another idle Babilaran. Then I tried to decide what I'd do if Newton actually appeared.

I had about two minutes to think on it before she strolled right past me. She was dressed in the same retro-punk style from before, a leather jacket with pieces of metal jutting out of it, like it was wrapping paper that had been pulled tight around a death machine. Short hair, cut and dyed various colors.

She was tailed by two of her flunkies, dressed with similar flamboyance, and they didn't stop to get a drink. Heart racing, I stood up and followed them as they prowled through the market. Where was Val? She'd be the one tailing Newton— Exel and Tia would be somewhere nearby in the submarine. Would Mizzy be on sniper duty, then? Bob's Cathedral was a tall building, so there weren't many places nearby to give a proper vantage, and sniping would be tough with all these people. Maybe Mizzy would be stationed somewhere farther south, close to where the trap was supposed to take place.

I was intent on finding Val or Exel, so I saw when a man emerged from the crowd and hurled a piece of fruit at Newton. It soared through the air and made contact in a way— Newton's powers engaged immediately, reflecting the energy. The fruit bounced back and exploded when it hit the ground. The Epic spun around, searching for the source of the attack.

I froze in place, sweating. Did I look suspicious? Newton pointed, and one of her flunkies—a tall, muscular woman wearing a jacket missing the sleeves—took off after the man who'd thrown the fruit. He was doing his best to disappear into the crowd.

Sparks! This wasn't part of the plan; it was just a bystander making a snap decision. Suddenly *another* piece of fruit flew at Newton, coming from another direction, along with a cry of "Building Seventeen!" This one was deflected too, of course, and the crowd immediately began to make itself scarce. I had no choice but to join them, lest I be left standing alone when the roof cleared.

This was exactly the sort of thing the Reckoners hated. I could imagine the chatter over the mobiles now, Val explaining that some locals had gotten it into their heads to get retribution for the building Newton had burned down. As much as I appreciated some people of Babilar finally showing a spine, I couldn't help but be annoyed by their timing.

Tia would want to abort, of course, but I doubted that Prof would let it happen over something as simple as this. I joined a bunch of people crowding into a nearby shop tent, the owner yelling for them not to lay their hands on anything. I pocketed a pair of walkie-talkies, feeling only slightly guilty about it. As I was stuffing them into my cloak, I heard an odd noise. Whispering? Like someone talking under their breath.

Something about it seemed familiar. Cautious, I looked around. Standing not three people from me, pressed in by the hiding crowd, was a woman in a nondescript glowing green cloak. I could just make out her face peeking out underneath her hood.

It was Mizzy.

43

YES, it *was* Mizzy, a pack slung over her shoulder, muttering quietly to herself—no doubt speaking to the other Reckoners. She didn't seem to have noticed me.

Sparks! I'd been so focused on finding Val that I hadn't thought they might finally let Mizzy take point.

A scream came from outside. It seemed that Newton's goons had found one of the malcontents.

Mizzy danced from one foot to the other, anxious; she wouldn't want to let Newton get away from her. Conversely, *I'd* found my target, and was perfectly happy letting Newton go bother someone else.

I needed to get Mizzy alone, only for a few minutes, then explain myself. How to do that without her immediately calling to Prof and the others? I had little doubt that Val would shoot me, no questions asked—she already had—and Prof would probably be in line right after her, if his powers really were starting to get to him. Mizzy, though . . . I might be able to convince Mizzy.

First I had to get the earpiece out of her ear. I wiggled through the tent, riding the shifting press of people as some in front peeked out to see what was happening. I managed to place myself right behind Mizzy.

Then, heart pounding, I took out the knife—leaving it sheathed, since I didn't actually want to hurt her—and pressed it against Mizzy's back. At the same moment, I put my hand over her mouth.

"Don't move," I whispered.

She went stiff. I reached my hand into her hood and grabbed the earpiece, then fiddled with it, flipping the off switch. Perfect. Now I just—

Mizzy twisted, grabbed my arm, and I'm not sure what happened next. Suddenly I was bursting out the back flaps of the tent, the world spinning. I hit the rooftop on my shoulder, the knife skidding from my hand.

Mizzy was on top of me a second later, arm raised to punch, her face framed by glowing green cloth. She saw me and immediately gasped. "Oh!" She patted me on the shoulder. "David! Are you all right?"

"I—"

"Wait!" she exclaimed, clamping her hand over her mouth. "I hate you!"

She raised her fist again and punched me right in the gut. And Calamity, she could *punch*. I growled, twisting—mostly in pain—and threw her off me. I managed to stumble to my feet and went for the knife, but Mizzy grabbed me under the arm and . . .

Well, everything flipped around again, and suddenly I

was on my back, completely out of breath. This wasn't how it was supposed to go. I was way bigger than she was. Wasn't I supposed to win in a fight? True, I didn't have much hand-to-hand training, and she seemed to have . . . well, more than "not much."

She had dropped her pack in the chaos and was reaching into her cloak for a gun. Not good. I managed to get to my feet again, wheezing, and jumped for her. She might get to pound on me some more, but so long as she was doing that, she wouldn't be shooting me. Theoretically.

However, what she pulled out wasn't a gun; it was a mobile. Almost as bad—she was going to call the team. I slammed into her as she was distracted. The mobile bounced away, and Mizzy struggled against my grip, getting her arm up and ramming her thumb right into my eye.

I yelped, throwing myself backward, blinking at the pain. Mizzy rolled for her mobile. So I kicked it.

Kind of too hard. It skidded right off the side of the roof. Mizzy threw herself that direction in a futile attempt to grab it. I took a moment to look around—one eye still squeezed shut. The tent we'd been in was shaking, one of the poles having collapsed as Mizzy threw me out the back. Off to our right, one of Newton's gang members was prowling through the streets between tents, perhaps looking for the people who had attacked her, perhaps just watching the perimeter. I ducked to the side and pulled up my hood again, my back against the wall of a wooden shack.

Nearby, Mizzy looked up from the edge of the rooftop and glared at me. "What's *wrong* with you?" she hissed.

"Someone poked me in the eye!" I snapped back. "That's what's wrong."

"I—"

"Quiet!" I said. "One of Newton's gang is coming this

way." I peeked around the side of the building and immediately cursed, ducking back around. Newton was there too
now. Both were walking in our direction.

Sparks! I thought, searching for shelter. It was impossible to hide in the shadows of this stupid city because there
weren't any. The painted ground glowed under my feet with a
sequence of vibrant, glassy colors.

One of the shacks ahead of me had a door that leaned open.
I scrambled for it. Mizzy cursed and ran after me, pack over
her shoulder. Inside I found a set of steps. What I'd mistaken
for a shack was actually part of the larger skyscraper. A lot of
these buildings had little structures on top, housing stairwells
or storage. This one had steps that led down to the top floor.

I pulled off my cloak and wrapped it up as Mizzy crowded
in behind me. She shut the door, then pressed a gun against
my side.

Great.

"I don't think it was related," a woman's voice said from
outside. "This was just a coincidence."

"They're getting restless." That was Newton's voice.
"A populace needs to be properly cowed to serve. Regalia
shouldn't hold me back."

"Bah," the first voice said. "You think you could do a better job, Newton? You'd lose control of this place in two weeks
flat."

I frowned at that comment, but only then did I realize the
conversation was growing louder. With a start at my own stupidity, I twitched toward the stairs leading down.

Mizzy grabbed my shoulder and pressed the handgun into
me more firmly. By the light of her hood, I could see her lips as
she mouthed, "Don't move."

I pointed outside. "They're coming in here!" I hissed.

Mizzy hesitated and I risked pulling out of her grip, then

scrambled down the steps as quietly as I could. She followed reluctantly. It wasn't happenstance that Newton had been coming this direction; she'd been looking for this very building.

Indeed, I heard the door open above us. I tried to move as quietly as possible down the stairwell, but soon found myself face to face with a wall of plants. Sparks! No way through. The stairwell was completely overgrown.

I spun around and put my back to the plants, heart pounding. Mizzy, still wearing a glowing cloak, joined me.

"I'm out of sight," Newton's voice echoed softly in the stairwell from above. "Yeah, I'm pretty sure they're following. You want to keep on with this?"

Silence.

"Yeah, fine," Newton said. "Then what am I to do?"

More silence. She was talking to Regalia and had wanted to duck out of sight while she did it, so her tail wouldn't overhear her or record her lip movements. Ordinarily that would be smart—except for the fact that she'd chosen a location populated by two Reckoners.

Well, one and a half Reckoners.

"Yeah, I suppose," Newton said.

More silence.

"Fine. But I don't like being bait. Remember that." The broken door above opened, then swung closed. Newton was gone.

"What did you tell her?" Mizzy demanded, stepping away from me and leveling the gun in my direction, pack still over her shoulder. "She knows we're following her? How much have you betrayed?"

"Nothing and everything," I said with a sigh, letting myself slide down into a seated position, my back to the vine-covered wall. Now that the tense moment had passed, I realized just how much I hurt from being thrown around by Mizzy.

I'd started to take for granted that such things wouldn't hurt as much as they should, because they hadn't in a long time. Prof's forcefields had done their job well.

"What do you mean?" Mizzy demanded.

"Regalia knew about all our plans already. She appeared to me in the base."

"What?" Mizzy looked appalled. *"You let water into the base?"*

"Yeah, but that's not the important part. She appeared there. Mizzy, that's supposedly outside of her range. Regalia has been playing us all along, and the plan is in serious danger."

Mizzy's face, shadowed and lit only by the glow of her cloak, was creased in worry. She bit her lip, but when I shifted, she straightened the arm holding the gun—and her grip didn't waver. She was young and inexperienced, but she wasn't incompetent. My aching shoulder and eye were proof of that.

"I need to contact the others," she said.

"Which is why I came to you."

"You put a knife to my back!"

"I wanted to explain myself," I said, "before you brought the Reckoners down on me. Look, I think Regalia is planning to kill Prof. She's been leading us along, setting up a trap for him. She knows he's the only one who can stop her from dominating, so she wants to bring him down."

Mizzy wavered. "You're working with her."

"Regalia?"

"No. Firefight."

Oh. "Yes," I said softly. "I am."

"You admit it?"

I nodded.

"She killed Sam!"

"I've seen the video. Sam pulled a gun on her, Mizzy, and

she's a trained marksman. He tried to shoot her, so she shot back first."

"But she's evil, David," Mizzy pleaded, stepping forward.

"Megan saved my life," I said. "When Obliteration tried to kill me. That's how I got away from him, when you were otherwise occupied."

"Prof said she was toying with you," Mizzy said. "He said you'd been compromised by your . . . affection for her." Mizzy looked at me as if begging for it to not be true. "Even if he's wrong, David, she's an *Epic*. It's our job to kill them."

I sat in that darkened stairwell, eye smarting—I could still see with it, fortunately, but it hurt. Mizzy had gotten me pretty good. I sat there wondering, remembering. Thinking about the kid I'd been, studying every Epic. Hating them all. Making my plans to kill Steelheart.

I knew what Mizzy felt like. I'd been her. It was crazy, but I guess I wasn't that person anymore. The shift had started back on that day I'd defeated Steelheart. I'd flown away in the copter, carrying his skull in my hands, overwhelmed. My father's murderer dead, but only because of the help of another Epic.

What did I really believe? I fished in my pocket and pulled out the pendant Abraham had given me. It caught light from somewhere, a glow reflecting off a metal banister above, and sparkled. The symbol of the Faithful. "No," I said, finally understanding. "We don't kill Epics."

"But—"

"We kill criminals, Mizzy." I reached up and put on the necklace, then I stood. "We bring justice to those who have murdered. We don't kill them because of what they are. We kill them because of the lives they threaten." I'd been thinking about this the wrong way all my life.

Mizzy looked at that small pendant, with its stylized sym-

bol at the end, hanging outside my shirt. "She's still a crimi-
nal. Sam—"

"Will you execute her, Mizzy?" I asked. "Will you pull
the trigger, knowing you've negated her powers and there's
nothing she can do? Will you watch that moment of realization in her eyes? Because I've done it, and I'll tell you: it's not
nearly as easy as it sounds."

I met her eyes in the dim light. Then I started walking up
the steps.

Mizzy held her gun on me for a moment, hand quivering.
Then she looked away and lowered the weapon.

"We need to warn the others," I said. "And, since I was
stupid enough to ruin your mobile, I need to reach the submarine instead. Do you know where it is?"

"No," Mizzy said. "Nearby, I think."

I continued up the steps.

"He's planning to kill her," Mizzy said. "While we're here,
tailing Newton, Prof is going to trap and kill Firefight."

I continued up the steps, a cold sweat chilling my brow.
"I have to get to him. Somehow, I need to stop him from—"

"You won't get there in time," Mizzy said. "Not without
this, at least."

I froze in place. Below, Mizzy unslung the pack from her
shoulder and unzipped it.

She had the spyril inside.

44

I rushed back down the stairs and helped Mizzy get out the spyril. I started strapping it on.

"I'm helping you," Mizzy said, kneeling beside me and working on my leg straps. "Why am I *helping* you?"

"Because I'm right," I said. "Because Regalia is smarter than we are—and because everything about this mission feels off, and you know something awful is going to happen if we go through with it."

She sat up. "Huh. Yeaaah, you should have said that stuff earlier. Maybe I wouldn't have punched you so much."

"I tried," I said. "The punching kind of got in the way."

"Really, somebody needs to teach you some hand-to-hand. Your showing was *pathetic*."

"I don't need hand-to-hand," I said. "I'm a gunman."

"And where's your gun?"

"Ah . . . right."

I shrugged the spyril's main mechanism onto my back and pulled the straps tight while Mizzy handed up the gloves. "You know," she said, "I was really looking forward to using this thing to prove how awesome I was, so Prof would agree I'd make a great point woman."

"And do you have any idea how to use the spyril?"

"I put the thing together and I maintain it. I've got heaps of theoretical knowledge."

I raised an eyebrow at her.

"How hard can it be?" She shrugged. "*You* figured it out, after all. . . ."

I grinned, but there wasn't much emotion behind it. "Do you know where Prof was going to trap Megan?"

"Down by where we're planning to hit Newton. He set up a meeting between you and her, using your phone."

"Down where . . . But that's a long ways from where Obliteration is set up."

Mizzy shrugged. "Prof wanted to do the Firefight hit in the same region as the Newton hit. The point is to get Regalia to manifest there, right? Giving Tia the last data point she needs to pinpoint where Regalia's hiding. Of course, if her range is greater than we think, that's all pointless. . . ."

"Exactly," I said.

Prof's plan made sense, though, at least with the limited information he had. If the point was to draw Regalia, then hitting two of her Epics—instead of one—would be that much more likely to get her attention.

"If Prof is down in Chinatown," I said, "then who's watching Obliteration?"

"Nobody. Prof said it was unlikely he'd be charged enough to release his power today. And we have the camera, so Tia can watch him."

I felt cold. Everything we'd done could have been part of Regalia's plan, camera included. "How quickly do you think you can get there to check on Obliteration?"

"Ten, fifteen minutes, running. Why?"

"Let's just say I have a really, really bad feeling about all of this."

"Okaaaay . . ." She stood back, the spyril strapped into place on me. "You looked far more dashing with the wetsuit, you know. It gave you a kind of crazy-Navy-SEAL-special-ops-dude feel. Without it, you have more of a crazy-homeless-guy-who-strapped-a-toaster-to-his-back vibe."

"Great. Maybe it will make people underestimate me."

"Prof's an Epic, isn't he?" she asked softly.

I glanced at her, then nodded, fitting my hands into the gloves one at a time. "When did you figure it out?"

"I'm not sure. It just kind of makes sense, you know? The way you've all been acting around him, the secrets, the way Tia wouldn't explain how you rescued those people in the building. I probably should have put it together earlier."

"You're smarter than I am. He had to put a forcefield in front of my face before I realized what he was."

"So this isn't about us getting revenge or putting down Epics or even punishing criminals," Mizzy said, sounding exhausted. "It's a power struggle. A turf war."

"No," I said firmly. "It's about making Prof be the man I know he can be . . . the Epic I know he can be."

"I don't get it," Mizzy said. "Why isn't he those things already?"

"Because," I said, pulling the second glove tight, "sometimes you have to help the heroes along."

"All riiight," she said.

"Here," I said, handing her one of the walkie-talkies I'd stolen. "We can keep in contact with these."

She shrugged, taking the hand radio. She fished a plastic baggie out of her pocket and put it in. "In case it falls in the water," she noted, shaking it.

"Good idea," I said, taking one of the baggies.

Mizzy hesitated, then handed over her gun as well. It was dark, but I thought she was blushing. "Here," she said. "Since I'm obviously not cut out for using one of these."

"Thanks," I said. "Ammo?"

She only had one extra magazine. Well, it was better than nothing. I slipped the magazine into my pocket and the handgun into my waistband.

"All right," I said. "Let's go."

45

I burst up out of the stairwell, spyril humming on my back, and emerged to a nauseating scene. Newton's people had found the malcontents who had thrown the fruit, it appeared, for two men hung dead from tent poles near where I emerged. A glowing piece of fruit had been stuffed into each of their mouths; iridescent juice ran down the sides of their faces and dripped from their chins.

I saluted them as I ran past. They'd acted foolishly, but they'd fought back. That was better than most in this city. As I ran, merchants looked up from stalls where they packed away wares. Some people knelt praying to Dawnslight, and they called to me, inviting me to join. I ignored everyone, making my way straight to the edge of the rooftop, then leaped. A moment later I shot into the air on jets of water.

I leaned forward, the buildings blurring past as the spyril powered me down the street. I had to cut the jets to quarter power to drop below a swinging bridge, but I popped back up on the other side, smiling as I caught sight of a dozen or so children lined up, pointing toward me.

My hand radio crackled. "This thing working?" Mizzy asked.

"Yup," I said back.

No reply.

Right. Stupid thing. I pointedly pushed down the broadcast button. "It's working, Mizzy," I said, raising the walkie-talkie to my lips.

"Great." Her voice was staticky. Sparks! These things were only about one step up from two cans with a string between them.

"I might not always be able to reply," I said back to her. "When I'm using the spyril, I need both hands to turn."

"Just try to keep the radio from getting too wet," Mizzy said. "Old technology doesn't mix well with water."

"Understood," I said back. "I'll treat it like a giant, angry, man-eating dragon."

"And . . . what does that have to do with anything?"

"Well, would *you* throw water on a giant, angry, man-eating dragon?" Buildings full of neon light whooshed past me on either side. At this rate, I'd reach Prof's location in minutes.

"No sign of the submarine or the others up here, David," Mizzy said. I had to hold the thing right up to my ear to hear over the sound of the wind. "They should have sent someone to investigate why I went silent. Something must have stopped them."

"Continue on to Obliteration," I said. "We don't have time to waste. Tell me what he's doing."

"Gotcha," Mizzy said.

I just had to—

A spurt of water rose up beside me from below and formed into Regalia. She hung in the air next to me, moving at my same speed, a small line of water connecting her to the ocean's surface.

"You have upset my plans," she noted. "I'm not fond of people who do that. Calamity won't respond to my questions of why you didn't gain powers."

I continued jetting along. Maybe she'd keep talking and give me a chance to get closer to Prof.

"What *did* you do?" she asked. "To reject the boon? I hadn't thought it possible."

I gave no reply.

"Very well then," Regalia said with a sigh. "You realize I can't let you reach Jonathan. Good night, David Charleston, Steelslayer."

The water spraying from my jets below suddenly split, blowing out to the sides instead of striking the ocean surface. But I didn't fall, at least not by much, as the water wasn't holding me aloft—the force of it jetting out did that. Regalia, it appeared, didn't quite understand the physics of the spyril. I wasn't surprised. Epics rarely have to pay attention to physics.

I jetted to the side and ignored her interference, dodging around a building by using the handjet to maneuver. Regalia appeared beside me a moment later, and large columns of water rose from the street below to grab me.

I took a deep breath, tucked my radio in the baggie in my pocket, then threw myself to the side, dodging down another street. Dozens of tendrils from the deep below snaked upward, reaching for me. I had to turn my jets downward and shoot straight up in order to avoid being snared. Unfortunately, Regalia's tendrils followed, twisting and writhing just beneath me. My jets started to lose power as I got too high—the streambeam could only reach so far.

I had no choice but to twist in the air and jet back downward. I crashed through the side of a tendril, a wash of crisp coldness enveloping me, but exited the other side in a spray. The tendril tried to wrap around me, but it was a hair too slow. They relied on Regalia's direction to work, and seemed to only be as fast as she could give them orders.

Feeling a boost of confidence, I wove between the other tendrils of water as I fell, wind buffeting my face, before finally twisting and slowing my fall when I was near to the surface. I shot down another street, weaving from side to side as enormous waves of water formed beneath, seeking to crash down upon me. I managed to get out of the way of each one.

"You," Regalia said, appearing beside me, "are as annoying a rat as Jonathan himself."

I grinned, spraying downward with the handjet and bobbing myself upward over another growing tendril. I twisted to the side and slashed between two others. I was now thoroughly soaked—hopefully that radio's baggie would hold.

This was the most thrilling thing I'd ever done, jetting through this city of dark velvety blacks and vibrant colors, passing amazed locals, open-mouthed, on rocking boats. In Newcago there had been a rule to never let me drive, just because of a few unfortunate incidents with cars and . . . um . . . walls. With the spyril, though, I could move with freedom and power. I didn't need a car. I *was* a car.

As I came to another batch of tendrils, I jetted to the side, leaning into the turn like a surfer, then shot down a side road. I almost smashed right into an enormous wall of water, as tall as the rooftops on either side, rising to tower over me. It immediately began to crash downward.

In a panic I screamed and jetted sideways through a window and into one of the buildings. I hit the floor in a roll, my jets cutting off. Water smashed into the wall outside, washing into the windows and across me. Various office paraphernalia surged upward, banging against tree trunks, but the water quickly rushed out the other direction.

Wet, frantic, I scrambled deeper into the office jungle. Tendrils of water broke in through the windows at my back, snaking after me. Sparks! I instinctively scrambled deeper into the structure, farther from the water outside—and the source of Regalia's power. But that also put me far from the source of the spyril's power. Without it, I was just a wet guy with a handgun facing down one of the most powerful Epics who had ever lived.

I made a snap decision and continued inward, for now, shoving my way past old desks and enormous mountains of overgrown roots. Maybe I could lose her in here. Unfortunately, as I made my way inward, I heard water tendrils breaking through windows on the other side of the building. I scrambled out into a hallway and found water creeping toward me, running across the old carpet.

She was flooding the place.

She's trying to see, I realized. She could send water in through the windows and cover the floor of the entire office. She'd be able to see into any nook. I ran the other direction, trying to find a stairwell or another way out, and burst into another large office space. Here, translucent tentacles of water wove between the trunks of trees like the prehensile stalks of some enormous, many-eyed slug.

Heart beating more quickly, I ducked back into the hallway. Light shone behind me from fruit that had been knocked by the tentacles, sending dancing shadows down the hall. A disco for the damned.

My back to the wall, I realized I was trapped. I looked at the fruit next to me.

Worth a try.

"I could use some help, Dawnslight," I said.

Wait, was I praying now? This wasn't the same thing at all, was it?

Nothing happened.

"Uh . . . ," I said. "This isn't a dream, by the way. Some help. Please?"

The lights went out.

In an instant, the fruit just stopped glowing. I started, heart pounding. Without the glowing fruit, the place was as black as the inside of a can of black paint that had also been painted black. Despite the darkness, though, I heard the tendrils thrashing and coming close.

It looked like turning the lights out was the best Dawnslight could do for me. Desperate, I fumbled my way down the hallway in one last mad dash toward freedom.

The tendrils of water struck.

Right at the place where I'd been standing before.

I couldn't see it, but I could feel them brush past me, converging on that location. I stumbled away, listening to the crash of water hitting wall, and fell back against one of them in the dark—a large, armlike glob of water, cold to the touch. I accidently put my hand into it, and my skin sank right through.

I pulled it out with a start and backed away, hitting another tendril. None of them stopped moving, but they didn't come for me. I wasn't crushed in the darkness.

She . . . can't feel with them, I realized. *They don't convey a sense of touch! So if she can't see, she can't direct them.*

Incredulous, I poked another of the tendrils in the darkness, then slapped it. Perhaps not the smartest thing I'd ever done, but it provoked no reaction. The tendrils continued thrashing about randomly.

I backed away, putting as much room between myself and those tendrils as possible. It wasn't easy, as I kept stumbling over tree trunks. But . . .

Light?

A single fruit glowed up above. I chased it. It hung in front of a stairwell, and the floor here was dry. No water for Regalia to peer through.

"Thanks," I said, stepping forward. My foot crunched something. A fortune cookie. I grabbed it and opened it.

She's going to destroy the city, it read. *You don't have much time left. Stop her!*

"Trying," I muttered, squeezing between vines to climb into the stairwell and starting upward. Fruit glowed to light my way, then winked out behind me.

On the next level was a floor where all of the fruit glowed, but no water tendrils sought to capture me. Regalia didn't know where I'd gone. Excellent. I crept out into another office room. This floor was cultivated, to an extent, with carefully kept pathways and trees that had been trimmed into a garden. It was a striking sight, after the wildness of the other levels.

I started down a path, imagining the people who had decided to take this floor and make it their own personal garden, buried in the middle of a building. I was so captivated by the imagery I nearly missed the blinking fruit. It hung right in front of me and pulsed with a soft light.

A warning of some sort? Cautious, I continued forward, then heard a footstep on the path ahead.

My breath caught, and I ducked off the path and into the foliage. The fruit closest to me went out, making the area around me darker. A few moments later Newton strode down the path and passed right under the fruit that had pulsed.

She had her katana out resting on her shoulder, and she carried a cup of water.

A cup of water?

"This is a distraction," Newton said. "Unimportant."

"You'll do as told." Regalia's voice rose from the cup. "I heard him moving down there, but he's gone silent. He's hiding in the darkness, hoping we'll go away."

"I have to make it to the confrontation with the others," Newton protested. "Steelslayer is meaningless. If I don't fall into their trap, then how are you going to—"

"Obviously you're right," Regalia said.

Newton stopped in place.

"You are a wonderful help," Regalia continued. "So brilliant. And . . . Blast. I need to deal with Jonathan. Find that rat."

Newton cursed under her breath and continued on, leaving me behind. I shivered, waiting until I heard the door to the stairwell shut, then I stepped back out onto the path.

Regalia was worried enough about me to pull Newton away from other plans to hunt me. That seemed a very good sign. It meant she felt that keeping me from warning Prof was extremely important.

So I had to break through and reach him. Unfortunately, the moment I stepped out of this building, I'd be in the bull's-eye again. I'd have to push through it, dodging as I had been before. I walked up to a window and prepared to leap out, but then found that my pocket was buzzing. I dug in it, pulling out the baggie, and removed the radio.

"Are you there? David, please answer!"

"I'm here, Mizzy," I said softly.

"Thank heavens," she said, tense. "David, you were *right*. Obliteration isn't here!"

"Are you sure?" I said, checking out the window.

"Yes! They've set up a kind of white mannequin thing with a floodlight right underneath it, so it glows like Obliteration. They then filled the rooftop with other powerful floodlights; that makes it seem like he's still here, but he isn't."

"That's why she wanted to keep everyone away," I said. Sparks. Obliteration was somewhere in the city, planning to destroy the entire place.

"I'm almost to Prof," I said. "Regalia keeps getting in my way. See if you can turn off the lights. That will warn the other Reckoners, assuming I don't make it."

"Okaaaay," Mizzy said. "I don't like this, David." She sounded scared.

"Good," I said back. "Means you aren't crazy. See what you can do. I'm going to make a final push toward Prof."

"Right."

I tucked the radio away, then glanced at a glowing fruit hanging nearby. "Thanks again for the help," I said. "If you have anything more like that to throw my way in the future, I wouldn't say no."

The fruit blinked.

I nodded grimly, then took a deep breath and jumped out the window.

46

I got about two streets from the building before Regalia found me. She appeared on the surface of the water along my path, standing tall, her eyes wide and alight and her hands to the sides as if to hold up the sky. Waves rose around her like the peaks of a crown emerging from the water.

This time she didn't bother with conversation. Jets of water erupted beneath me. The first one clipped me along the side, slashing through both clothing and skin. I gasped in pain, then started weaving and bobbing, using the hand-jet to dodge to the side as Regalia sent an enormous ripple through the water that crested some fifteen feet high. It chased me around a corner but broke against a building as I landed on the roof and ran across it. I passed tents and screaming people and caught the scent of something odd in the air. Smoke?

I leaped off the other side of the building, and as I did, a blur zipped across the rooftop beside me. I yelped, cutting my jets and dropping just beneath the blur, which launched toward me, trailing an afterimage of neon red.

The blur passed right over my head, then landed on the building across from me, where it pulled to a stop, revealing Newton, katana in hand. She whipped out a handgun and spun in my direction.

Sparks! I should have been expecting her. I dove downward, passing the stories of a nearby building in a flash, and hit water as the popping noises of gunfire sounded above.

The water was an icy shock, jets propelling me face-first under the surface. Diving for the water had been my first instinct in order to avoid that gunfire, and it worked, as I didn't get shot. But it did put me in Regalia's grasp.

The water around me began to constrict, to thicken, like syrup. I twisted, thrusting my feet downward, and engaged the spyril at full force.

It was as if the water had become tar, and each progressive inch of movement was harder than the inch before it. Bubbles grew trapped as I breathed them out, frozen like in Jell-O, and I felt the spyril shake violently on my back. Blackness surrounded me.

I didn't fear that blackness any longer. I'd looked it in the eye. My lungs strained, but I shoved down the panic.

I broke the surface. Once my arms were free, the spyril thrust me out into the air with a triumphant jet, but tendrils of water waited for me. They wrapped around my legs.

I pointed the streambeam of the spyril right at them.

My machine sucked up those tendrils like it did any other water, spraying them out the jets at the bottom and freeing me in a heartbeat. I burst higher into the air, dazed from lack of oxygen. I reached a rooftop and let the jets cut out, rolling across it, breathing deeply.

Okay, I thought, *no more going underwater with Regalia around.*

I'd barely caught my breath when water tendrils climbed up over the roof, like the fingers of an enormous beast. Newton landed near me in a blur, trailing glowing color from her hair. She came right at me, fast as an eyeblink, and all I could do was engage the spyril, my streambeam pointed right at one of Regalia's tendrils.

The sudden jet of power lurched me across the rooftop away from Newton. Just barely. Worse, only one of the foot-jets engaged. I didn't know if it was the constriction down below, the tendrils that had grabbed me after, or the rough landing. But the machine had always been finicky, and it had chosen this moment to finick.

Newton moved past me, her sword striking the ground where I'd just been lying, throwing up sparks. She reached the side of the rooftop, where another building rose up alongside this one, no space between. There she stopped.

And, from what I saw, stopping was pretty dramatic. Best I could tell, she came out of her super-speed run by throwing one hand up against the wall of the building next door. All of her momentum was transferred to the structure and, in the bizarre way of Epics, completely scrambled the laws of physics. The wall exploded into a spray of dust and crumbling bricks.

She turned around, dropping her sword—now jagged and broken—and reached to her side, slipping another one out of a sheath at her waist. She spun the sword, regarding me, and walked forward more casually. Around us, Regalia's tendrils continued surrounding the entire building, creeping up over the sky, making a dome. This small rooftop was abandoned, and its painted graffiti reflected off the water around us. Liquid began to pour in over the lip of the roof, flooding it with an inch or two of water, and Regalia took shape from it beside Newton.

I pulled out my gun and fired. I knew it was pointless, but I had to try something, and the spyril just sputtered when I engaged it—both jets refusing to spit anything out now. The bullets bounced off Newton, reflected out toward the closing dome of water, making little splashes. Newton leaned down, one hand on the ground, preparing to sprint, but Regalia raised a hand and stopped her.

"I want to know," she said to me, "what you did earlier."

My heart thumping, I scrambled to my feet and glanced to the side, looking for a way out. Regalia's dome of water completely encased the rooftop, and new tendrils were rising from the flooded roof to try to snatch me. Desperate, I pointed the streambeam at one and tried to engage the spyril. The jets at my feet wouldn't work.

But, to my relief, the handjet did. I was able to slurp up the tendril and shoot it the other way. I got the next, then the next, then started shooting them at Newton as I hopped backward. My attack just splashed away from her, but she seemed to find it annoying.

More and more tendrils came for me, but I sucked each one up, jetting them outward.

"Stop *doing* that!" Regalia roared, voice booming. A hundred tendrils grew up, far more than I could target.

Then they immediately started to shrink.

I blinked at them, then looked at Regalia, who seemed as baffled as I was. Something else was coming up out of the water around me. Plants?

It was roots. *Tree* roots. They grew wickedly fast around us, sucking in the water, draining it from every source it could find, feeding upon it. Dawnslight was watching. I looked back at Regalia and grinned.

"The child is acting up again," Regalia said with a sigh, crossing her arms and looking at Newton. "End this."

In an instant Newton became a blur.

I couldn't outrun her. I couldn't hurt her.

All I could do was gamble.

"You're beautiful, Newton," I yelled.

The blur became a person again, plants curling up at her feet. Her lips pursed, she looked at me, eyes wide, sword held in limp fingers.

"You're a wonderful Epic," I continued, raising my gun.

She backed away.

"Obviously," I said, "that's why both Obliteration and Regalia are always sure to compliment you. It couldn't, of course, be because compliments are your weakness." That was why Newton let her gang be so rowdy and insubordinate. She hadn't wanted them complimenting her by accident.

Newton turned and ran.

I shot her in the back.

It wrenched my gut as she fell face-first to the overgrown ground. But at my core, I was an assassin. Yes, I killed in the name of justice, bringing down only those who deserved it, but at the end of the day, I *was* an assassin. I'd shoot someone in the back. Whatever it took.

I walked up, then planted two more bullets in her skull, just to be certain.

I looked at Regalia, who stood, arms still crossed, among the growing flora around us—saplings becoming full trees, fruit sprouting, swelling, and sagging from limbs and vines. Her figure started to shrink as Dawnslight drank up the water that formed her current projection, and her dome fell apart, showering down upon me and the rooftop.

"I see that I spoke too freely when punishing Newton," Regalia said. "This is my fault, for giving away her weakness. You really *are* an annoyance, boy."

I raised the handgun and pointed it at Regalia's head.

"Oh please," she said. "You know you can't hurt me with that."

"I'm coming for you," I said softly. "I'm going to kill you before you kill Prof."

"Is that so?" Regalia snapped. "And do you realize that while you've been distracted, the Reckoners have already executed their plan? That your idolized Jonathan Phaedrus has killed the woman you love?"

A shock ran through me.

"He used her as bait, to draw me," Regalia said. "Noble Jonathan murdered her in an attempt to make me appear. And I did, of course. So that he'd have his little data point. His team is storming my supposed sanctuary right now."

"You're lying."

"Oh?" Regalia said. "And what is that you smell?"

I'd smelled it earlier. With an edge of panic, I ran to the side of the building and looked toward something I could barely make out against the darkness. A column of smoke rising from a nearby building—the place where Mizzy said Prof had been waiting.

Fire.

Megan!

47

REGALIA let me go. That probably should have worried me more than it did.

I focused only on reaching that building. I fiddled with the leg wires on the spyril and managed to get one of the jets working. That let me awkwardly cross the gaps between rooftops. I landed on a building next to the one belching the column of smoke, and heat blasted me despite the distance. The fire was burning from the lower floors upward. The roof itself wasn't yet consumed, but the lower floors were engulfed. It seemed like the entire structure was close to collapsing.

Frantic, I looked down at the glove of my handjet. Might it be enough? I jetted across to the rooftop, where the heat was actually less intense than it had been when facing the burning lower floors. Sweating, I sprinted across the roof and found a stairwell access door.

I shoved it open. Smoke billowed out, and I got a lungful. Driven back by the heat, I stumbled away, coughing. I squeezed tears from my eyes at the smoke and looked at the spyril strapped to my arm. Thoughts of using the spyril like a fireman's hose seemed silly now. There was no way I could get close enough, and there wouldn't be water inside the building anyway.

"She's dead," a quiet voice said.

I started, jumping to the side and reaching for Mizzy's handgun. Prof sat on the side of the rooftop, shadowed by the little stairwell shack so that I hadn't seen him at first.

"Prof?" I asked, uncertain.

"She came to save you," he said softly. He was slumped down, a shadowy mountain of a man in the gloom. No neon glowed near here. "I sent her a dozen messages with your phone, made it seem like you were in danger. She came. Even though I'd already started the fire, she broke into the building, thinking you were trapped inside. She ran, coughing and blind, to the room where she thought you lay trapped and pinned under a fallen tree. I caught her, took away her weapons, and left her in there with forcefields on the doorways and the window."

"Please, no . . . ," I whispered. I couldn't think. It wasn't possible.

"Just her alone in the room," Prof continued. He held something in his hand. Megan's handgun, the one I'd given back to her. "Water on the floor. I needed Regalia to see. I was sure she'd come. And she did—but only to laugh at me."

"Megan's still down there!" I said. "In what room?"

"Two floors down, but she's dead, David. She has to be.

Too much fire. I think . . ." He seemed dazed. "I must have been wrong about her all along. And you were right. Her illusions broke apart, you see. . . ."

"Prof," I said, grabbing him. "We have to go for her. *Please.*"

"I can hold it back, can't I?" Prof said. He looked to me, and his face seemed too shadowed; only his eyes glittered, reflecting starlight. He seized me by the arms. "Take some of it. Take it away from me, so I can't use it!"

I felt a tingling sensation wash through me. Prof, gifting me some of his powers.

"Jon!" Tia's voice barked from the mobile on his shoulder, where he'd strapped it, apparently eschewing an earpiece. "Jon, it's Mizzy. . . . Jon, she's got the camera that was watching Obliteration, and she's been writing messages on paper and holding them up for us to see. She says Obliteration isn't there."

Clever, Mizzy, I thought.

"No, that's because he's *here,*" Val's voice said over the line. "Prof, you've got to see this. We've swept Regalia's base at Building C. She's nowhere to be seen, but there's something else. Obliteration, we think. At least, *something* is glowing in here, and glowing powerfully. This looks bad. . . ."

Prof looked to me, then seemed to grow stronger. "I'm coming," he said to them. "Hold that building."

"Yes sir," Val said.

Prof darted away, a forcefield forming to make a bridge for him from this building to the next.

"It's all wrong, Prof," I called after him. "Regalia isn't bound by the limits you thought she was. She knows all about the plan. Whatever Val just found, it's a trap. For you."

He stopped at the edge of the rooftop. Smoke billowed out

of the building around us, so thick it was growing hard for me to breathe. But for some reason, the heat seemed to have lessened.

"That sounds like her," Prof said, his voice trailing back to me in the night.

"So . . ."

"So if Obliteration is really there," he said, "I have to stop him. I will simply need to find a way to survive the trap." Prof charged across his forcefield, leaving me.

I sat down, drained, numb. Megan's handgun lay on the ground before me. I picked it up. Megan . . . I'd been too late. I'd failed. And I still didn't know what Regalia's trap entailed.

So what? a piece of me said. *You give up?*

When had I ever done that?

I shouted, standing up and charging toward the stairwell down. I didn't care about the heat, though I assumed it would drive me back. Only it didn't. It felt practically cold in the stairwell.

Prof's forcefield, I realized, driving myself onward. *He just gifted one to me.* One had protected me against Obliteration's heat. It would work just as well against this fire, it appeared.

I kept my head down, breath held, but eventually had to suck in some air. I muffled my mouth and nose with my T-shirt, which was soaked from the fight with Regalia, and it seemed to work. Either that, or Prof's forcefield kept the smoke away from me. I wasn't one hundred percent sure how they worked, even still.

Two floors down, where Prof said he'd left Megan, I entered a place alight with fire. Violent flames created an alien illumination. It was a place a man like me wasn't supposed to go.

I gritted my teeth and pushed forward, trusting in Prof's forcefield. Part of me, deep inside, panicked at the sight of all this fire—walls burned from floor to ceiling and flames dripped down from above, Dawnslight's trees engulfed in orange. There was no way I could survive this, could I? Prof's forcefields were never a hundred percent effective when given to someone else.

I was too worried about Megan, too desperate and shaken, to stop moving. I shoved my way through a burning door, charred wood breaking around me. I stumbled past a hole in the floor, my arm up warding against the heat I could not feel. Everything was so *bright*. I could barely see in here.

I took in a breath but felt no pain from the heat. The forcefield wouldn't cool the air as I drew it in. Why wasn't I burning my throat with each breath? Sparks! Nothing made sense.

Megan. Where was *Megan*?

I stumbled through another doorway and saw a body on the floor, in the middle of a burned rug.

I cried out and ran to it, kneeling, cradling the half-burned figure, tipping the charred head to see a familiar face. It was her. I screamed, looking at the dead eyes, the burned flesh, and pulled the limp body close.

I knelt in the inferno of hell itself, the world dying around me, and knew I had failed.

My jacket was burning, and my skin was darkening from the flames. Sparks. It was killing me too. Why couldn't I feel it?

Crying, reckless, I grabbed Megan's body and blinked away the horrid light of fire and smoke. I stumbled to my feet and looked toward a window. The glass was melting from the heat, but there was no sign of a forcefield—Prof must have already dismissed the forcefields surrounding the room. With a yell, I ran for the window, holding her, and crashed out into the cold night air.

I fell a short distance before engaging the spyril. The single jet I had fixed still worked, fortunately, and slowed my fall until I was hovering in the air outside the burning building, holding Megan's corpse, water jetting beneath me and smoke breaking around me. Slowly, on a single jet, I raised us to the next building over and landed before setting Megan down.

Charred flakes of blackened skin fell from my arms, revealing pink flesh beneath—which immediately became a healthy tan. I blinked at it, then suddenly realized why I hadn't felt pain, and why I'd been able to breathe in the heated air. Prof hadn't just given me a forcefield, he'd gifted me some of his healing powers as well. I touched my scalp and found that though my hair had burned away, it was growing back— Prof's healing power restoring me to the way I had been before entering the inferno.

So I was safe. But what did it matter? Megan was still dead. I knelt above her, feeling helpless and alone, broken inside. I'd worked so hard, and I'd still failed.

Overwhelmed, I bowed my head. Maybe . . . maybe she'd lied about her weakness. She'd be okay then, right? I touched her face, turning it. Half of it was burned, but when I nudged her head to the side, I could ignore the burned part. The other side looked barely singed. Just a little ash on the cheek. Beautiful, like she was just sleeping.

Tears leaking down the sides of my face, I took her hand. "No," I whispered. "I watched you die once. I don't believe it happened again. Do you hear me? You aren't dead. Or . . . you're coming back. That's it. Do you have that recording going like last time? Because if you do, I want you to know. I believe in you. I don't think . . ."

I trailed off.

If she came back, it meant she'd lied to me about her weakness. I wanted that to be true, desperately, because I wanted her to be alive. But at the same time, if she'd lied about her weakness, what did that mean? I hadn't demanded it, hadn't wanted it, but she'd given it to me—so it seemed something sacred.

If she'd lied to me about her weakness, then I knew I wouldn't be able to trust anything else she said. So, one way or another, Megan was lost to me.

I wiped tears from my chin, then reached out one last time to take her hand in mine. The back of the hand was burned, but not too badly, yet her fingers were stuck together in a fist. It was almost like . . . she was clutching something?

I frowned, prying her fingers apart. Indeed, her palm held a small object that had been melted to her sleeve: a small remote control. *What in Calamity's light?* I held it up. It looked like the little remotes that came with car keys. It had melted at the bottom but looked to be in good shape otherwise. I hit the button.

Something sounded from just beneath me. A faint clicking noise, followed by some odd cracks.

I stared at the control for a long moment, then scrambled to my feet and ran to the side of the building. I pushed the button again. There. Was that . . . gunfire? Suppressed gunfire?

I lowered myself with the spyril to a window two stories down. There, set up in the shadows of a window, was the Gottschalk, sleek and black, with suppressor on the end of the muzzle. I moved to the side and pushed the button. It fired remotely, pelting the wall of the burning building with bullets.

It was firing into the room where Megan had been.

"You sly woman," I said, snatching the gun. I raised myself on a jet of water and ran back to her body and rolled it over. The heat had dried the blood, darkened the skin, but I could make out the bullet holes.

Never had I been so happy to see that someone had been

shot. "You set it up so you could shoot yourself," I whispered, "in case things went bad. So you'd reincarnate, rather than risking death by fire. Sparks, you're *brilliant*!"

Emotion flooded me. Relief, exultation, amazement. Megan was the most awesome, most clever, most *incredible* person ever. If she'd died by bullets, she *was* coming back! In the morning, if what she said about her reincarnation timing was true.

I touched her face, but this . . . this was just a husk now. Megan, *my* Megan, would return. Grinning, I grabbed the Gottschalk and stood up. It felt good to have a solid rifle in my hands once again.

"You," I said to the gun, "are officially *off* probation."

Megan had survived. In the face of that, anything else seemed possible.

I could still save this city.

48

"MIZZY," I said, holding the walkie-talkie to my ear as I ran in the direction Prof had gone. "Does this stupid thing still work?"

"Yup," came the reply.

"Clever move, using the camera to get a message to Tia."

"She saw?" Mizzy said with an exuberant perkiness that seemed a distinct contrast to the agony I'd been through a few moments ago.

"Yeah," I said, charging across a bridge. "I overheard a message from Tia to Prof. That might get him to scrap the mission."

Unlikely. But it was possible.

"You found Prof?" Mizzy asked. "What happened?"

"Too much to explain," I told her. "They say they stormed

Regalia's supposed base—Building C, on Tia's map—and found Obliteration glowing inside. I'm sure it's some kind of trap."

"That's not Obliteration they found."

"What? Val said she'd found him."

"He appeared back here just after I knocked out the lights," Mizzy said. "Nearly gave me a heart attack. Didn't seem to notice me hiding, though. Anyway, he wasn't glowing at all, but I got a gooooood look at him. Whatever Val found, it isn't Obliteration."

"Sparks," I said, trying to push myself faster. "Then what is Prof walking into?"

"You're asking me?" Mizzy said.

"Just thinking out loud. I'm heading uptown. Can you get here? I might need fire support."

"Already on my way," Mizzy said, "but I'm pretty far. Any sign of Newton your direction?"

"Newton's dead," I said. "I managed to guess her weakness."

"Wow," Mizzy said. "Another one? You're *really* making the rest of us look bad. I mean, dude, *I* couldn't even shoot an unarmed, powerless enemy who fell in my lap."

"Call me if you spot Obliteration," I said, then stuffed the radio back in its bag and into my jeans pocket. My jacket was basically ruined—I'd ripped it off and left it behind—and even my jeans were ragged, burned up one side. Worse, the spyril was in shambles. I'd lost the cords on one half entirely. The other half sputtered when I used it, and I didn't know how long I'd trust it to hold me.

I passed a rooftop, noting the number of people crowded into the jungle of a building nearby, who peered out through the windows and hid beneath fronds. My confrontation with Regalia had been pretty blatant. Even the relaxed Babilarans knew to take cover after something like that.

Trusting my memory of Tia's maps, I continued right across a particularly ratty bridge. I had a ways to go before getting to the base, unfortunately. I ran for a short time until my path took me across a strange rooftop that consisted of a large square balcony running around the outside, with a big structure in the middle. Here I had to slow, as people had built awnings above the balcony, and the space underneath the awnings was crowded with junk. The people here hadn't been near enough to my fighting to be afraid, so they just lounged there enjoying the night, reluctantly making room for me.

As I drew near to the other side, one particularly oblivious Babilaran stood right in the pathway. "Excuse me," I said, leaping over a lawn chair. "Coming through."

He didn't move, though he did turn to me. Only then did I see that he was wearing a long trench coat, face bearing a goatee and spectacles.

Uh . . .

"And I looked," Obliteration said, "and beheld a pale horse. On him was Death, and Hell followed with him. Power was given unto them to kill with sword, and with hunger, and with death."

I stumbled to a halt, unslinging my rifle.

"Do you deny," Obliteration whispered, "that this is the end of the world, slayer of angels?"

"I don't know what it is," I said, "but I figure that if God really wanted to end the world, he'd be a little more efficient about it than all of this."

Obliteration actually smiled, as if he appreciated the humor. Frost began to crust the area around him as he drew in heat, but I pulled the trigger before he could release the burst of destruction.

He vanished while my finger was still on the trigger, exploding into a glowing afterimage. I spun around, catching him as he teleported behind me. This time he looked surprised as I shot him.

As his form exploded for the second time, I threw myself off the side of the building and thrust my hand downward. Thankfully, the spyril jet worked, slowing me. I used its stream to push myself into the building through a broken window, where I ducked down and froze.

I didn't have time to deal with Obliteration right now. Getting to Prof and the team was more important. I—

Before I could form my next thought, Obliteration exploded into existence beside me. "I read John the Evangelist's account a dozen times before destroying Houston," he said to me.

I yelped and shot him. He vanished, then appeared on the other side of me.

"I wondered which of his horsemen I was, but the answer was more subtle than that. I read the account too literally. There are not four horsemen; it is a metaphor." He met my gaze. "We have been released, the ones who destroy, the swords of heaven itself. We are the end."

I shot him, but he discharged a burst of heat so powerful that it overwhelmed Prof's forcefield. I gasped and the bullet I'd fired melted away. I threw up my arm as the ground vaporized, then the wall, and then half my body.

For a moment, I was *not*.

Then my skin grew back, the bone re-formed, and my train of thought started again. It was as if I'd skipped a beat in time, just a fraction of a moment. I was left breathing deeply, sitting on the blackened floor of the room.

Obliteration cocked his head at me and frowned. Then he vanished. I rolled and fell out the window before he could return, engaging the broken spyril to stop me from dropping into the water below.

Sparks! The blast had vaporized the handjet, along

with . . . well, half my body. I still had the streambeam, Megan's pistol, and my rifle—and fortunately, the single jet on my foot worked as I engaged it. But my jeans were completely missing one leg, and there was no sign of the broken half of the spyril.

Without the handjet, I couldn't maneuver. I launched myself down the street to another building and made it into a window—this one had mostly been unbroken, and crashing through it left gashes on my skin.

The wounds healed, but not as quickly as before. Things, I realized, were about to get very dangerous. When Prof granted us power via our jackets, it ran out after taking a few hits. He'd given me a big dump of healing ability, but it seemed I was reaching the limits. Not good.

I ran through the building and pulled up in a hallway. Back to a wall, I let out a huge breath.

Obliteration exploded into existence just inside the window I'd broken through. I caught sight of him, but ducked back down the hallway before he spotted me.

"And Abraham took the wood of the burnt offering," Obliteration called, "and laid it upon Isaac his son. He took the fire in his hand, and a knife, and they went both of them together. . . ."

I felt sweat trickle down the sides of my face as Obliteration stepped into the hallway and spotted me. I pulled around the corner, out of his sight.

"Why are you working with Regalia?" I called out, my back to the wall. "You congratulated me for destroying Steelheart. She's just as bad."

"And so I will end her eventually," Obliteration said. "It is part of our arrangement."

"She'll betray you."

"Likely," Obliteration agreed. "But she has given me

knowledge and power. She has taken a piece of my soul, and it lives on without me. And so, I become the seeds of the end of time itself." He paused. "She had not warned me that she had persuaded the archangel to grant you a portion of his glory."

"You can't kill me," I called, glancing down the hallway at him. "There's no reason to try."

He smiled and frost crept forward down the darkened hallway, reaching like fingers toward me, freezing a fruit that hung from a vine like a single lightbulb above. "Oh," Obliteration continued, "I think that you'll find a man can do many things thought impossible, if he tries hard enough."

I had to deal with him. Quickly. I made a snap decision and withdrew the suppressor on the front of my gun. Then I ducked around the corner and shot him, making him vanish. I tossed my gun into a side room and ran the other direction. A moment later I held down the button on the remote, triggering the rifle to fire in the room.

I charged through the building to a window on the other side and ducked out onto a balcony. I turned, pressing my back against the wall, and hit the remote again, firing the gun while digging Megan's handgun out of my pocket with my other hand.

Cursing filtered out from inside the building. Obliteration must have found the gun and not me. Now, if I could just get out of here . . .

Suddenly he was on the balcony beside me, letting out a wave of heat.

Damn it! I aimed and shot him with Megan's gun to make him vanish. It worked, though I was left with charred skin.

I clenched my teeth against the pain. With the healing coming more slowly, I had time to feel the pain.

I checked Megan's gun. Two bullets left.

What I couldn't figure out was how he was finding me. It

had happened before; he seemed to be able to track us somehow. Did he have some kind of visionary power? How did he teleport away, then know exactly where to teleport back to find me?

Then it clicked.

I turned just as Obliteration appeared beside me again. He was shouting scripture and glowing with power. I didn't shoot him.

This time, I grabbed him.

49

IT was something I could never have managed without Prof's powers. The heat was incredible and threatened to set me ablaze. Obliteration's surprise, however, worked to my advantage as I raised the pistol and shot him in the head.

He teleported.

I held tight, and he took me with him.

We appeared in a dark, windowless room, and Obliteration immediately turned off his heat. He did it so quickly, it had to be something he'd trained himself to do by reflex. Wherever we were, he couldn't destroy this place. I let go but grabbed his glasses, ripping them free as I fell backward.

Obliteration cursed, his normally calm demeanor breaking down in his outrage at being tricked. I backed away, throwing myself against the wall of the dark room. I couldn't make out much, though the pain of the burns he'd given me made it difficult to pay attention to anything else. I'd dropped the gun, but gripped the spectacles tightly with my other hand.

He pulled his sword from beneath his trench coat and looked toward me. Sparks! He could obviously see well enough without the glasses to find me.

"All you have done," he said, walking toward me, "is box yourself in with me."

"What nightmares do you have, Obliteration?" I asked, slumped against the wall. Prof's healing powers were working very, very slowly now. Gradually the feeling in my hands was returning, first as a tingling, then as sharp pinpricks. I gasped and blinked against the pain.

Obliteration had stopped advancing on me. He lowered his sword, the tip touching the floor. "And how," he said, "do you know of my nightmares?"

"All Epics have them," I said. I was far from certain about this, but what did I have to lose? "Your fears drive you, Obliteration. And they reveal your weakness."

"I dream of it because it will someday kill me," he said softly.

"Or is it your weakness because you dream of it?" I asked. "Newton probably feared being good enough because of her family's expectations. Sourcefield feared the stories of cults, and the poison her grandmother had tried to give her. Both had nightmares."

"And the angel of God spake unto me in a dream," Obliteration whispered. "And I said, Here am I. . . . So that is the answer." He threw his head back and laughed.

The pain in my hands only seemed to be getting worse. I let out a whimper despite myself. I was basically an invalid.

Obliteration rushed to me, kneeling, taking me by the

shoulders—which were now bare, and burned. Pain flared and I cried out.

"Thank you," Obliteration whispered. "For the secret. Give my . . . regards to Regalia."

He let go, bowed his head to me, and exploded into a flash of light and ceramic.

I blinked, then curled up on the floor and trembled. Sparks! Earlier the healing had happened so quickly that it had felt refreshing, like a cool breeze. Now it happened at the speed of a drop of rain rolling down a cold pane of glass.

It seemed like an eternity that I sat there suffering the pain, but it was probably only three or four minutes. Eventually the agony subsided and, groaning, I climbed to my feet. I flexed my fingers and squeezed them into fists. My hands worked, though my skin stung as if I had a bad sunburn. That didn't seem to be going away. The blessing that Prof had given me was no more.

I stepped forward and kicked something with my foot. Obliteration's sword. I picked it up, but all I found of Megan's gun was a melted piece of slag.

She was going to kill me for that.

Well, Obliteration obviously had enough control over his powers to not melt objects he preferred to keep intact. I clutched the sword as I felt my way through the small dark room to a door. I opened it; beyond was a narrow wooden stairway, framed by banisters on both walls. From what light there was I could see that I'd been in some kind of small supply room. My clothes had basically been vaporized. All I had left was Abraham's pendant, which still hung around my neck, one side of the chain melted. I pulled it off, worried that the melted chain would snap.

I found a length of cloth—it looked like it could have once been curtains—and wrapped it around myself. Then, holding the sword in one hand, pendant in the other, I climbed the stairs slowly, step after step. As I ascended the light grew brighter, and I began to make out odd decorations on the walls.

. . . Posters?

Yes, posters. Old ones, from the decades before Calamity. Bright, vibrant colors, women in ruffled skirts, sweaters that exposed a shoulder. Neon on black. The posters had faded over time, but I could see they'd been hung meticulously back in the day. I stopped beside one in that silent stairwell. It showed a pair of hands holding a glowing fruit, a band's name emblazoned at the bottom.

Where *was* I?

I looked up toward the light at the top of the stairs. Sweating, I continued to climb until I came to the top and to a door with a chair next to it. The door was cracked open, and I pushed it farther, revealing a small, neat bedroom decorated like the stairwell with posters on the walls, proclaiming a glorified urban life.

Two hospital-style beds lay in the room, out of place, with steel frames and sterile white sheets. One held a sleeping man in his thirties or forties hooked up with all kinds of tubes and wires. The other held a small wizened woman with a tub of water next to her.

Another woman wearing medical scrubs stood over this patient. As soon as I entered, the doctor looked at me and gave a little start, then walked out the way I had come in. The only sounds were those of the heart rate monitors. I stepped forward, hesitant, feeling an uncanny, surreal sensation. The aged woman, obviously Regalia, was awake and staring at something on the wall. As I entered, I noted three very large television screens.

On the center one, Prof, Val, and Exel stood just inside a room glowing so brightly I could barely make them out.

"So," Regalia said. "You've found me."

I looked to the side. A figure of her as I knew her had appeared from the tub of water. I looked back at the woman in the bed. She was far, far older than her projected self. And far more sickly. The real Regalia there breathed in and out with the help of a respirator and didn't say anything.

"How did you get here?" the projection asked.

"Obliteration," I said quietly. "He located me too easily each time I hid from him. I realized that he had to teleport somewhere when he vanished. It stood to reason that he was coming to you and getting instructions on where to go. He can't see everything in the city, but *you* can." I looked at the television screens. "At least, everywhere with water." She'd set these up so she could watch other places, obviously.

But why? What was going on in that room with Prof, Val, and Exel? I looked back at Regalia.

The projection glanced at the elderly figure in bed. "It is frustrating that we still age," she said. "What is the point of divine power if your body gives out?" She shook her head as if disgusted at herself.

I slowly moved through the room, trying to figure out what to do next. I had her, right? Of course, she had that tub of water, so she wasn't entirely defenseless.

I stopped next to the other bed, the one with the man I didn't recognize. I glanced down at him and noted the blanket—like a child's blanket—draped around his shoulders. It depicted fanciful trees and glowing fruit. "Dawnslight?" I asked Regalia.

"Why Calamity would choose a man in a coma to grant powers to, I have no idea," Regalia said. "The Destroying Angel's decisions often make so little sense to me."

"He's been like that for a long time, then?"

"Since his childhood," Regalia said. "With his powers, he

seems aware of the world around him at times. The rest of the time, he dreams. Trapped forever in his childhood some thirty years ago . . ."

"And this city becomes his dream," I realized. "A city of bright colors, fanciful paints, of perpetual warmth and gardens inside buildings. A child's wonder." I thought quickly, trying to put the pieces together. Why? What did it mean? And how could I stop Regalia?

Did I need to? I looked at the aged figure, so frail. She barely seemed alive. "You're dying," I guessed.

"Cancer," Regalia's projection said with a nod. "I've got a few weeks left. If I'm lucky."

"Why worry about Prof, then?" I asked, confused. "If you know you're going to die, why go through so much effort to kill him?"

Regalia didn't reply. While her real body rasped in the background, the projection folded her hands in front of herself and regarded the center screen. Prof stepped forward in the blaze of light. He too carried a sword, one of the types he fashioned for himself by using his tensor power. And he'd dared make fun of Obliteration for carrying one.

He strode through the light, holding a hand before himself like he was fighting against the flow of some powerful stream. What should I do? Regalia didn't seem to care that I was here—Sparks, she probably didn't care if I killed her or not. She was practically dead anyway.

Could I threaten her? Somehow force her not to harm Prof? The thought not only nauseated me, but looking at her frail body, I doubted I could so much as touch her without provoking some kind of terminal reaction.

The screen dimmed suddenly; the real Regalia was tapping something on her armrest, a control of some sort. It darkened the screen, adding some kind of filter to cut through the glare.

It allowed me to see what Prof couldn't, because the room he was in was so bright.

The source of the glow wasn't a person as I had suspected. It was a box with wires coming from it.

What in the world? I was so confused I just stared at the screen.

"Did you know," Regalia's projection said, "that Jonathan is not so unique as he assumes? Yes, he can give away his powers. But every Epic can do that, under the right circumstances. All it takes is a bit of their DNA and the right machinery."

They cut something outta him, Dawnslight had said. Obliteration, with bandages . . .

A bit of DNA and the right machinery . . .

A mounting horror grew within me. "You created a machine that replicates Obliteration's powers. Like the spyril, only capable of blowing up cities! You used an Epic . . . to create a *bomb*."

"I've been experimenting with this," Regalia's projection said, arms crossed. "The Angel of the Apocalypse is . . . unreasonable to work with sometimes, and I have needed my own methods for transferring powers."

On the screen, Prof had reached the device. He touched it, then drew back, confused. I could barely make out Val and Exel behind him in the room, their hands thrown up against the light.

"Please," I said, looking to Regalia. I advanced on her with my sword. "Don't hurt him. He was your *friend*, Abigail."

"You keep implying I want to kill Jonathan," Regalia said. "Such a terrible assumption." The real her pushed a button on her armrest.

On the television screen, the bomb exploded. It erupted like an opening flower—a wave of destructive energy so powerful it would annihilate Babilar entirely. I watched it bloom, radiate outward.

Then stop.

Prof stood with hands upraised like a man gripping some enormous beast, a silhouette against the red light. A sun appeared right there in the center of the room, and he *held* it. He contained it with such tension to his body that I felt as if I could feel him straining, working to hold it all in, not let a single bit escape.

Such *power*. This bomb had been charging for quite some time, it seemed. Regalia could have pulled the trigger and vaporized Babilar weeks ago.

Prof roared, a primal and terrible shout, but he held on to that energy. And then he created something enormous, a shield of vibrant blue that ripped open the roof of the room they were in like two hands and created a column of fire into the sky. He let the energy out, siphoning it away harmlessly into the air.

I knew, with rising horror, it wouldn't be enough. Oh, he might save the city, but it still wouldn't be enough. The corruption grew hand in hand with the amount of power expended. Even if I was right, and he'd be able to control it in small amounts, he'd never be able to handle so much at once.

Prof used his powers as I'd never seen him use them, on a level like Steelheart had used when transforming Newcago to metal. This was an act of inhuman preservation, proof that a hero had come. It was also a condemnation. He'd been on the edge before. Now this . . .

"Too much," I whispered. "Far too much. Prof . . ."

"I didn't lure Jonathan here to kill him, child," Regalia whispered from behind me. "I did it because I need a successor."

50

"**WHAT** have you done?" I screamed at Regalia. I spun and rushed to the bedside, ignoring the projection. I seized the aged woman by the front of her gown with one hand, pulling her up toward me. "What *have you done*?"

She breathed in, then spoke with her own voice for the first time, rasping, feeble. "I have made him strong."

I looked back at the screen. Prof dispersed the last of the energy and fell to his knees. The room grew dark, and I realized the filter was still on. I dropped the sword and fiddled with the buttons on the side of Regalia's bed, trying to bring the light back up on the monitor so I could see what was happening.

The screen returned to normal. Prof was kneeling in the room, his back to us. Before him, the floor ended in a perfect circle, vaporized in the release of power. A trembling figure walked up to him from behind. Val. She reached him and hesitantly put a hand on his shoulder.

He raised an open palm to the side, not looking. A forcefield surrounded Val. Prof squeezed his palm shut into a fist. The forcefield collapsed to the size of a basketball, Val still inside. In a heartbeat, she was snuffed out, ended.

"No!" I screamed, scrambling back in horror at the awful sight. "No, Prof . . ."

"He'll kill the Reckoners quickly," Regalia's projection said softly, almost in regret. "A High Epic's first move is usually to remove those who knew him best. They are the ones most likely to be able to find his weakness."

I shook my head, appalled. It couldn't . . . I mean . . .

Prof swung his hand out. I heard Exel shout. His voice cut off mid-phrase.

No . . .

Prof stood up and turned, and finally I could see his face, twisted, shadowed, marred by hatred and anger, teeth pulled together, jaw clenched.

I didn't know this man any longer.

Mizzy. Tia. I had to do something! I—

Regalia was coughing. She managed to do it triumphantly. Growling, I seized the sword and raised it over her. "You monster!"

"It was . . . coming . . . ," she said between coughs. "He . . . would have let it . . . out . . . eventually."

"No!" My arms trembled. I shouted, then brought the blade down.

And killed my second High Epic for the day.

I stumbled back from the bed, blood spreading onto the white sheets, some of it staining my arms. On the screen, Prof walked lethargically past Val's remains. Then he stopped. A piece of the wall in his room had opened up, showing a series of monitors like the ones in this room.

One showed a map of Babilar with a circle on it. A place out in New Jersey—this house? It seemed likely, as the other screen in front of him flickered, then showed a shot of the room I was in. Regalia dead in her bed. Me, standing with bloody arms, wrapped in a cloth at my waist.

I looked up at the corner of my room and saw for the first time a video camera there. Regalia had set all of this up so she would be able to confront him after what he'd done. It seemed . . . it seemed she'd wanted him to come to her.

Prof looked me over in the screen.

"Prof . . . ," I said, and my voice sounded in his room, across the city. "Please . . ."

Prof turned from the monitor and strode from the room. In that moment I knew. It wasn't Tia or Mizzy I needed to worry about protecting. Neither of them had ever killed a High Epic.

I had.

And so he was coming for me.

51

"DAWNSLIGHT?" I said, shaking the slumbering figure in the other bed.

He didn't move. Coma. Right.

"I could use some help again," I said to him, but of course I got no response.

Sparks! Prof was coming. I left the room in a mad scramble, passing the doctor who, without comment, rose from her chair by the door and hurried back in, perhaps to gather her things and make a hasty exit.

Smart.

Prof had . . . *killed* Val and Exel without a second thought. He'd do the same to me. I hurried through the building, looking for the way out onto the street. What was that low, rumbling sound I heard in the distance?

I'd leave the building and find a place to hide. But . . . could I really hide from Jonathan Phaedrus? I had no resources, no contacts. If I hid, he'd find me. If I fled, I'd spend the rest of my life—probably a short life—running.

When he got here, he might very well kill Dawnslight, and in so doing, destroy Babilar. No more food. No more light.

I stopped in the living room, panting. Running did no good. I would need to face Prof eventually.

I'd do it now.

So, despite every instinct screaming at me to hide, I turned and looked for a way up onto the roof. The place was a sub-urban home that was surprisingly well maintained. What had happened to Dawnslight's family? Were they out there some-where, worried over their dreaming son?

I finally found the stairs and climbed up to the third floor. From there I climbed out of a window onto the roof. Unlike most of the buildings in Babilar, this one was peaked, and I carefully walked up to the tip. The sun, not yet risen, had brought a glow to the horizon. By that light I saw the source of the roar I'd heard earlier: the water was retreating from Babilar.

It washed outward like a sudden tide, exposing skyscrapers covered in barnacles. Sparks. The foundations had to be in-credibly weakened from being submerged for so long. The tide might very well destroy the city, killing everyone Prof had given himself to save. One careless swing of my sword might have cost thousands of lives.

Well, no buildings were collapsing at the moment, and there was nothing I could do about them if they did.

So I sat down.

Sitting up there in the night's last darkness gave me some perspective. I thought about my part in all of this, and whether

I'd pushed Prof too hard to become a hero. How much of this was my fault? Did it matter?

Regalia probably would have managed all of this if I hadn't been hounding Prof. The most disturbing part was that she had accomplished it by preying upon Prof's own innate honor.

I was certain of one thing. Whatever had happened to Prof, it wasn't his fault. Any more than it would be a man's fault if, drugged to oblivion by a cruel prank, he thought the people around him were devils and started shooting them. Regalia had killed Exel and Val, not Prof. Of course, maybe she couldn't be blamed either. She was in the power's grip too.

If not her, then who? I looked away from the horizon and toward that glowing red spot. It hung on the opposite side of the sky from the sun.

"You're behind this," I whispered to Calamity. "Who are you, really?"

Calamity gave no answer as it—he?—sank below the horizon. I turned back toward Babilar. I might not be to blame for what had happened to Prof, ultimately, but that didn't mean I was innocent. Ever since coming to Babilar, I'd stumbled from one crisis to another, rarely following the plan.

Reckless heroism. Prof was right.

So what do I do now? I thought. *Prof, the real Prof, would want me to have a plan.*

Nothing came to me. Of course, this wasn't the time to plan. The time to plan was before everything went wrong, before your mentor was betrayed and corrupted, before the girl you loved was shot. Before your friends died.

Something appeared in the distance, moving over the waters, and I sat up straighter to get a better look. A small disc—a forcefield, I realized—with a figure in black standing atop it. It grew larger and larger as it sped through the air.

So Prof could use his fields to fly. His power portfolio was *amazing*. I stood up, balancing on the rooftop, gripping the necklace that Abraham had given me, which dangled from its chain in my fist.

It flashed bright as the sun finally broke over the horizon, bathing me in light. Was it my mind, or was the light stronger than it should have been?

Prof approached on his flying disc, his lab coat fluttering behind him. He landed on the other side of the small peaked roof from me, and regarded me with a strange interest. Again I was struck by how different he seemed. This man was *cold*. It was him, but a him with all of the wrong emotions.

"You don't have to do this, Prof," I told him.

He smiled and raised a hand. Sunlight bathed our rooftop.

"I believe in the heroes!" I shouted, holding up the pendant. "I believe they will come, as my father believed. This is not how it will end! Prof, I have faith. *In you*."

A forcefield globe appeared around me, breaking the roof tiles under my feet, enclosing me perfectly. It was exactly like the one that had killed Val.

"I believe," I whispered.

Prof squeezed his hand closed.

The sphere compressed . . . but suddenly, though I'd been inside it a moment ago, I wasn't in it now. I could see it right in front of me, shrunken to the size of a basketball.

What?

Prof frowned. That sunlight, it was getting brighter, and brighter, and . . .

And a figure of pure white light *exploded* into existence between me and Prof. It blazed like the sun itself, a feminine figure, radiant, powerful, golden hair blown back and shining like a corona.

Megan had arrived.

Prof summoned another forcefield globe around me. The figure of light thrust a hand toward him, and suddenly that globe was around Prof *himself* instead. Megan was changing reality, making possibilities into fact.

Prof looked even more surprised this time. He dismissed the globe and summoned another around the figure of light, but when it started to shrink it was around him again in an eyeblink, closing him in, threatening to crush him.

He dismissed it, and I saw something else in his eyes I'd never seen before. Fear.

They're all afraid, I thought. *Deep down. Newton fled from me. Steelheart killed anyone who might know anything about him. They're driven by fear.*

That wasn't the Prof I knew, but it *was* the High Epic Phaedrus. Confronted by someone who manipulated his powers in ways he didn't understand, he became terrified. He stumbled away, eyes wide.

In the space of a heartbeat, we were somewhere else.

Me and the glowing figure. One building over, inside a room with a window through which I could see Prof standing on the rooftop. Alone.

The glowing figure beside me sighed, then her glow vanished and resolved into Megan, completely naked. She fell, and I managed to catch her. Outside the window, on the next building over Prof cursed, then hopped on his disc. He sped away.

Sparks. How was I going to deal with him?

The answer was in my arms. I looked down at Megan, that perfect face, those beautiful lips. I'd been right to have faith in the Epics. I'd just chosen the wrong one.

Her eyes opened, and she saw me. "I don't feel like killing you," she whispered.

"More wonderful words have never been spoken," I said back.

She stared at me, then groaned, closing her eyes again. "Oh hell. The secret *is* the power of love. I'm going to be sick."

"Actually, I think it's something else," I said.

She looked at me. I was suddenly made conscious that she was very, *very* naked, and I was nearly naked as well. She followed my eyes, then shrugged. I blushed and put her down, then moved to find something for her to wear. As I stood, however, clothing appeared on her—the standard jeans and shirt, shadows of clothing from another dimension. Good enough for now, I supposed.

"What *is* the secret, then?" she asked, sitting up and running her hand through her hair. "Every other time I've reincarnated, I've been *bad* when I first came back. Unable to remember myself, violent, destructive. This time . . . I feel nothing. What changed?"

I looked her in the eyes. "Was that building already on fire when you ran into it?"

She pursed her lips. "Yeah," she admitted. "It was stupid. You don't need to tell me it was. I knew you probably weren't in there, not for real. But I thought—maybe you were, and I couldn't risk that you might be. . . ." She shivered visibly.

"How afraid of the fire were you?"

"More than you can possibly know," she whispered.

I smiled. "And that," I said, gathering her into my arms again, "is the secret."

Epilogue

ABOUT five hours later I sat on top of what had once been a low building in Babilar, warming my hands at a cookfire. The building now rose some twenty stories over the once-submerged street below.

Not a single building had collapsed as the waters left. "It's the roots," Megan said, settling down next to me and handing me a bowl of soup. She wore real clothing now, which was kind of unfortunate, but likely more practical, as it had gotten really cold in the city all of a sudden. "Those roots are tough stuff, tougher than any plant has a right to be. They're literally holding the buildings up." She shook her head as if amazed.

"Dawnslight didn't want his utopia to fall if he did," I said, stirring my soup. "The fruit?"

"Still glowing," Megan said. "The city will survive. He

was warming the water somehow to keep the place from getting too cold, though. He's going to have to find another way to deal with that."

Other people moved about us. The people of Babilar were banding together in what they saw as a crisis, and we were just two more refugees. If any who passed saw something different about me, recognized me from one of the fights, they didn't say anything. At least, nothing more than a few hushed whispers to their companions.

"So," Megan said, "this theory of yours . . ."

"It *has* to be fear," I said, exhausted. How long had it been since I'd had any sleep? "I faced down the waters, and then was immune to Regalia trying to make me an Epic. You rushed into a burning building to save me, despite your terror, and you awoke free from the corruption. Epics are afraid, at their core. It's how we beat them."

"Maybe," Megan said, uncertain. Sparks. How was it that someone could look so good simply stirring soup? And while wearing clothing a size too big, her face red from the chill? I smiled, then noticed she was staring at me too.

That seemed to be a very good sign.

"The theory makes sense," I said, blushing. "It's like oatmeal on pancakes."

She cocked an eyebrow at me, then tried her soup. "You know," she said, "you're not actually bad at metaphors . . ."

"Thanks!"

". . . because most of the things you say are *similes*. Those are really what you're bad at."

I nodded thoughtfully, then pointed my spoon at her. "Nerd."

She smiled and drank her soup.

As good as it was to be with her, I found the taste of my soup bitter. I couldn't laugh. Not after what had happened.

We ate in silence, and as Megan stood she put a hand on my shoulder.

"If either of them had been told," she said softly, "the cost they would have to pay to save the city, do you doubt they'd have agreed to it in a heartbeat?"

I reluctantly shook my head.

"Val and Exel died as part of an important fight," Megan said. "And we'll stop it from consuming others. Somehow."

I nodded. I hadn't confronted her about Sam yet. There would be time for that eventually.

She went looking for a refill. I stared at my bowl. Sadness gnawed at me, but I didn't give it free rein.

I was too busy planning.

A moment later I picked out a voice from those around us. I stood, lowering my bowl, then pushed my way past two chatting Babilarans.

"He's a goofy-looking fellow," Mizzy was saying. "Tallish. Terrible fashion sense . . ." Then she saw me, her eyes opening wide. "Um . . . he has some good attributes too. . . ."

I grabbed her in a hug. "You heard the broadcast."

"Yeaaaah," she said. "I have no idea what you're talking about."

"I asked some people to broadcast a message to you and Tia, hoping you'd pick it up on your radio and . . . You didn't hear it?"

She shook her head, which was annoying. I'd wracked my brain trying to come up with a way to make sure Prof didn't get to her. I'd thought the radio idea would be a good one. After all, we'd been able to use the shortwave to reach Abraham in Newcago.

Missouri held up a small slip of paper and showed it to me. Fortune cookie paper. *Missouri,* it read, *hide. Hide now.*

"When did you find this?" I asked.

"Last night," she said. "Right before dawn. About a hundred of them said that. Creeped me out, I'll tell ya. Figured I should do what it said. Why? You look sad."

I'd have to tell her about the others. Sparks. I opened my mouth to explain, but at that moment Megan returned.

The two of them locked gazes.

"Uh, could we not shoot one another?" I said, nervous. "For now? Pretty please?"

Mizzy looked away from Megan pointedly. "We'll see. Here. I think this one is for you, maybe?" She held up another slip of paper. "It was the only one that was different."

I hesitantly took the paper.

Dream good dreams, Steelslayer, it read.

"Do you know what it means?" Mizzy asked.

"It means," I said, folding the paper in my hand, "that we have a lot of work to do."

THE RECKONERS SERIES
CONTINUES WITH

CALAMITY

SPRING 2016

ACKNOWLEDGMENTS

ANOTHER book has arrived! Once again, my name may be on the cover, but a ton of unseen hands helped with its creation. This book is unusual in that it was the first one I created with the specific help of the Dragonsteel Think Tank, a name I'm giving right now (and will probably never use again) for the brainstorming group who went out to lunch with me and helped me work through problems in the outline.

They include the Insurmountable Peter Ahlstrom—my editorial assistant, and a face you may see popping up on my blog and Facebook page, answering questions and making occasional posts. Seriously, folks, this guy is awesome. As a key member of my first writing group (with Dan Wells and Nathan Goodrich, whose name you may have read at the front of the book), Peter has been a huge help all along. If you see him at a convention, give him a pat on the back.

Also at that lunch were Karen Ahlstrom, keeper of the Dragonsteel internal wiki, and Isaac Stewart—mapmaker extraordinaire and now full-time employee at our company. They gave great help with this novel, as did the other members of my current writing group, not including those listed above: Emily Sanderson, Alan Layton, Darci & Eric James Stone, Benn & Danielle Olsen, Kara Stewart, Kathleen Dorsey Sanderson, and Kaylynn ZoBell.

The talented team at Random House include my editor, Krista Marino, who did a fantastic job with the book (and with giving periodic polite reminders of due dates), and Jodie Hockensmith, who consistently goes above and beyond the call of publicity duty in working with surly authors. Other Random House folks deserving of applause include Rachel Weinick, Beverly Horowitz, Judith Haut, Dominique Cimina, and Barbara Marcus. The copyedit was done by the talented Michael Trudeau.

My agents, Joshua Bilmes and Eddie Schneider, were—as always—a wonderful resource, as were the entire team at JABberwocky. I'm pretty much convinced they're Epics in disguise by this point, considering all they manage to get done. My UK team on this book include Simon Spanton—my editor at Gollancz, who always makes sure my trips to London are welcoming and full of flavor—and John Berlyne of the Zeno Agency, my tireless advocate.

Beta readers on this book were Brian Hill and Mi'chelle & Josh Walker. Montie Guthrie, Dominique Nolan, and Larry Correia helped me out with firearms terminology and practices. Gamma readers and community proofreaders were Aaron Ford, Alice Arneson, Bao Pham, Blue Cole, Bob Kluttz, Dan Swint, Gary Singer, Jakob Remick, Lyndsey Luther, Maren Menke, Matt Hatch, Taylor Hatch, Megan Kanne, Samuel Lund, Steve Godecke, and Trae Cooper. If I ever become an Epic, I'll kill you guys last.

Finally, I'd like to thank my wonderful wife, Emily, and my three rambunctious boys. They make life worth living.

Brandon Sanderson